THE
GENESIS CODE

THE
GENESIS CODE

JOHN CASE

FAWCETT COLUMBINE | NEW YORK

A Fawcett Columbine Book
Published by Ballantine Books

http://www.randomhouse.com

Library of Congress Cataloging-in-Publication Data
Case, John.
    The genesis code / John Case.
        p.   cm.
      ISBN 0-449-91101-2
      I. Title.
    PS3553.A7914U53   1997
813'.54—dc21   96-47717

Manufactured in the United States of America

First Edition: April 1997

10   9   8   7   6   5   4

For Bob LaBrasca
1943–1992
Bodhisattva from Racine

God from God, Light from Light
true God from true God,
begotten not made. . . .

—Nicene Creed
Council of Chalcedon
451 c.e.

THE
GENESIS CODE

PART I
JULY

1

Father Azetti was tempted.

Standing on the steps of the parish church, fingering a rosary, he gazed across the empty piazza in the direction of his favorite trattoria—and looked at his watch. It was 1:39 in the afternoon. And he was starving.

Technically, the church was to remain open from eight until two, and then again from five until eight. That's what the plaque on the door said, and Father Azetti had to admit that the plaque had a certain authority. It had been in place for nearly a hundred years. Still . . .

The trattoria was in the Via della Felice—a grandiose name for what amounted to a medieval alley, a cobbled lane that twisted away from the central square to dead-end at the stone wall that defined the town's outer limits.

One of Italy's most remote and beautiful hill towns, Montecastello di Peglia rested on a dome of rock, a thousand feet above the Umbrian plain. Its crown and glory was the Piazza di San Fortunato, where a small fountain bubbled in the cool shadow of the village's only church. Quiet and pine-scented, the little square was a favorite place for lovers and art students, who came to its ramparts for a panoramic view of the countryside. High above the quilted landscape, they gazed out at Italy's "green heart," and swooned to see the sunflower fields, trembling in the heat.

But not now, not at the moment. At the moment they were *eating*.

And Father Azetti was not. A soft breeze turned the corner and took him prisoner with the smell of baking bread. Grilled meat, and lemon. Hot olive oil.

His stomach growled, but he had to ignore it. Montecastello was, above all else, a village. There was no real hotel, only a small pensione run by a pair of expatriate Brits. Having lived in the town for less than a decade, Father Azetti was an outsider, and would remain so into the next millennium. As such, he was suspect, and, being suspect, he was under constant surveillance, watched by the town's ever vigilant older residents, who pined for his predecessor. (Or, as they called him, "the *good* priest." Azetti? "The *new* priest.") If, during the hours of confession, Father Azetti should close the church a minute too soon, someone would certainly take notice and Montecastello would be scandalized.

With a sigh, the priest turned from the piazza and slipped back into the gloom of the church. Built in an age when glass had been a treasure, the building was condemned from conception to perpetual twilight. Apart from the dim glow of electrified candelabra, and a bank of guttering candles in the nave, the structure's only illumination came from a line of narrow windows, high on the west wall. Though few and small, the windows sometimes had a dramatic effect when, as now, they shaped the afternoon sun into shafts of light that tunneled down to the floor. Passing the mahogany tableaux that marked the stations of the cross, Father Azetti saw with a smile that the confessional waited for him in one of these pools of natural brilliance. Stepping into the light, he relished the effect, even as it blinded him. Hesitating, he imagined the scene as others might see it, and then, embarrassed by his narcissism, stepped into the confessional and pulled the curtain shut. Seating himself in the darkness, he began to wait.

The confessional was a wooden booth, a very old one, partitioned down the middle to separate the priest and the confessor. In the center of the wall between them was a screened grille that could be opened or closed by a sliding panel on the priest's side. Below the grille was a wooden shelf that ran the length of the partition. Father Azetti was in the habit of resting his fingertips on this narrow ledge as he inclined his head to hear the whispered confessions. It was clearly a habit that he shared with many priests before him: the little shelf was worn into faint scallops by centuries of pious hands fingering the wood.

Father Azetti sighed, raised the back of his hand to his eyes and squinted at the luminous dial on his wrist. It was 1:51.

On those days when he had not missed breakfast, the priest enjoyed the hours that he spent in the confessional. Like a musician playing Bach, he listened to himself, and heard his predecessors in every changing chord. The antique booth was resonant with old heartbreaks, whispered secrets, and absolution. Its walls had listened to a million sins—or perhaps, as Father Azetti thought, to a dozen sins, committed a million times.

The priest's musing was interrupted by a familiar noise from the other side of the partition—the sound of a curtain pushed aside, followed by the grunt of an old man sinking to his knees. Father Azetti composed himself and opened the grille with a brush of his hand.

"Bless me, Father, for I have sinned . . ."

The man's face was in shadows, but the voice was familiar. It belonged to Montecastello's most distinguished resident—Dr. Ignazio Baresi. In some ways, Dr. Baresi was like himself—a worldly outsider transplanted to the stifling beauty of the provinces. Inevitably, each man was whispered over, and just as inevitably, they'd become friends. Or, if not friends, then allies, which was as much as the differences in their ages and interests would allow. The truth was, they had little in common beyond too much education. The doctor was a septuagenarian whose walls were crowded with diplomas and certificates, attesting to his achievements in science and medicine. The priest was somewhat less distinguished—a middle-age activist on the back burner of Vatican politics.

And so, they came together over a chessboard on Friday evenings, sitting in the piazza outside the Caffè Centrale, sipping Vin Santo. Their conversations were spare, and absent any intimacies. A remark about the weather, a toast to one another's health, and then: pawn to king's bishop four. Even so, after more than a year of idle remarks and occasional reminiscences, they knew one or two things about each other. It seemed enough.

Lately, however, the doctor's comings and goings had been less regular. The priest knew that the old man had been ill, but now, listening to him, he realized that Baresi had taken a turn for the worse. His voice was so weak that Father Azetti had to press his temple to the grille so he could hear.

Not that the priest was particularly curious. As with most of those who made their way to his confessional, Azetti barely needed to listen. After ten years he knew their weaknesses. At seventy-four, the doctor would have taken the Lord's name in vain, he would have been uncharitable. Before he'd taken ill, he might have lusted after a woman, might even have committed adultery—but all that was over for the poor man, who now seemed weaker by the day.

And, in fact, there was an unsavory air of anticipation in the village about the doctor's coming end, an avid expectation from which even Father Azetti was not entirely free. After all, *il dottore* was a wealthy, pious, and unmarried man. He'd been generous to the town, and to the church, before. Indeed, Father Azetti thought, the doctor—

What?

The priest focused his attention on the doctor's faltering voice. He'd been rambling in the self-justifying way that confessors often did, avoiding the sin while emphasizing his *intentions* (which were, as always, good). He'd said something about pride, about being blinded by pride—and then, there was his illness, of course, and the realization of his own mortality. He'd seen the error of his ways. There was nothing remarkable in that, Azetti thought: the prospect of death had a way of focusing one's sensibilities, and in particular, one's moral sensibilities. Father Azetti had been thinking about this when the doctor finally got to the point and began to describe the sin itself: what he'd actually done.

The priest listened, and the word burst from him in a gasp: "*What!?*"

Dr. Baresi repeated what he'd said, speaking in a hushed and urgent voice. And then he began to elaborate, so that there could be no mistake about what was being said. Listening to the terrible and persuasive details, Father Azetti felt his heart lurch in his chest. What the man had done—what he'd *committed*—was the most spectacular sin imaginable, a sin so deep and terminal that heaven itself might never recover from it. Was it even possible?

The doctor was silent now, breathing hoarsely as he waited in the dark for absolution from his friend, his ally.

But Father Azetti was speechless. He couldn't say a word. He couldn't even think, or breathe. It was as if he'd been plunged, chest-deep, into a mountain stream. It was all he could do to gasp, and even then his mouth was like wood, and dry.

The doctor, too, was suddenly tongue-tied. He tried to speak, and then broke off in a ragged gasp. He cleared his throat with a strangled sound that was, at first, embedded deep within his chest—and then erupted with such ferocity that the booth trembled. The priest feared the man would die on the spot. Instead he heard the door crash open, and instantly the doctor was gone.

Father Azetti remained where he was, rooted to the spot like a witness to a fatal accident. Almost of its own accord, his right hand made the sign of the cross. A second later he was on his feet. Tearing the curtain aside, he stepped from the darkness of the booth into a shaft of sunlight.

For a moment it was as if the world had disappeared. There was nothing but dust, rising to heaven in a column of buttery light. Slowly, his eyes began to adjust. They fumbled in the dazzle until, squinting, he saw the doctor's frail shape, hobbling up the aisle. The ghostly orb of his white-haired head bobbed in the gloom as he poled his way to the door with his cane, pounding the tiled floor. The priest took a step toward him, and another.

"*Dottore!* Please!" Father Azetti's voice boomed in the church, and hearing it, the old man hesitated. Slowly, he turned to the priest, and the priest saw that the look on his face had nothing to do with contrition. The doctor was on a bullet train to hell, and fear radiated from him like a halo around the moon.

And then he was gone.

2

Father Azetti wrote *Chiuso* on a piece of cardboard, so that all would understand the church was closed. Then he pinned the note to the door, locked up, and left for Rome.

The doctor's voice was like a klaxon in his head, now quiet, now louder, now dopplering off into silence. It was as if a state of emergency had been declared in his soul, and the declaration came at him over and over again, from every direction. The hushed and desperate monotone of Baresi's voice was like a low-grade infection that wouldn't go away. The words nagged at him, and all he could summon in his own heart were the empty words: *do something. Something!* And so he was. He was going to Rome. In Rome they would know what to do.

He begged a ride from the husband of the woman who cleaned his rooms, asking for a lift to the nearby (and larger) town of Todi. Once in the car, he felt better, the pressure eased by the salve of action: he had embarked, he was on the way.

The driver was a large and boisterous man given—as Father Azetti was in a position to know—to excessive card-playing and a fondness for *grappa*. He had not worked for years, and perhaps concerned for his wife's income, was excessively solicitous, constantly apologizing for the car's poor suspension, the heat, the state of the roads, and the insane behavior of other drivers. Whenever the car lurched to a stop, he thrust out a protective forearm, as if the priest were a small child who did not know enough of the fundamental laws of physics to brace himself when the brakes were applied.

Finally they arrived at the railroad station and the man jumped from his seat and dashed around to the passenger side. The door of the old Fiat, which had been battered in some ancient collision, opened with a complaining screech. The air outside the car was scarcely cooler than inside, and a thin ribbon of sweat wandered down the priest's back. There was a parting barrage of questions from the driver as he escorted Azetti to the ticket window: Did the father want him to purchase the ticket? Should he wait at the station until the train arrived? Was the father sure that he did not want a ride to the main station in Perugia? The priest refused everything, *No-no-no-no-no-no— grazie, grazie!* Eventually, the man moved off with a courtly bow and an unmistakable expression of relief.

Father Azetti had nearly an hour to wait before the train to Perugia arrived. In Perugia he would take the shuttle to the other station, and wait another hour for the train to Rome. Meanwhile, he sat on a small bench outside the train station in Todi, baking in the heat. The air was heavy with dust and ozone, and the black robes of his order pulled the sunlight toward him.

He was a Jesuit, a member of the Society of Jesus. Despite the heat, he did not relax his shoulders or let his head droop. He sat erect. His posture was perfect.

Had he been an ordinary parish priest in a small town in the Umbrian countryside, the entire matter of Dr. Baresi's confession would probably have gone no further. Indeed, if he'd been a simpler priest, it was unlikely that he'd have *comprehended* the doctor's confession, let alone its implications. And if he had understood, he wouldn't have had the faintest idea what to do with the information or where to go with it.

But Giulio Azetti was no ordinary priest.

There was a term, popular these days in the secular world, for odd twists of fate: synchronicity. But for a religious person, synchronicity was an alien, even a demonic, concept. Father Azetti had to look at the chain of incidents as if they were hinged together by an unseen Hand, a matter of volition and not of chance. Looked at in this way, his presence in that particular confessional, listening to that specific confession, was a matter of ingenious design. He thought of the folk expression for this: *God moves in mysterious ways.*

Seated on the platform, Father Azetti meditated upon the *dimensions* of the sin confessed to him. Simply stated, it was an abomination—a crime not only against the Church, but against the cosmos. It offended the natural order, and contained within itself the end of the Church. And not only the Church.

Prayer was a shield, and he tried to pray, to use it as a screen, as white noise—but it was no use. Dr. Baresi's voice seeped through, and not even the sign of the cross would wave it away.

Father Azetti shook his head ever so slightly and let his eyes rest on the dusty weeds that grew in the cracks of concrete near the train bed. Just as the seeds that had fallen in those cracks contained within themselves the promise of this destructive vegetation, so, too, the sin confessed by the doctor, if unaddressed, contained . . . *what?*

The end of the world?

So intense was the July heat that the very scene in front of him—the railroad tracks, the buildings beyond—seemed to shimmer and melt in the air. Underneath his robes he was coated in a film of sweat.

He wiped his forehead with the back of his sleeve and began to rehearse what he would say when he got to Rome—assuming that Cardinal Orsini would receive him.

It's a matter of great importance, your grace . . .

I have learned something that menaces the faith in a profound way . . .

He'd find the words. The harder part would be to penetrate the Church's bureaucracy. He tried to imagine the circumstances under which the cardinal—a Dominican—would agree to see him. Surely Orsini would recognize his name, would remember him, would know that his request for an audience was not frivolous. Or perhaps familiarity would work against him; perhaps the cardinal would think he'd come to plead his own case, seeking a return to Rome after his long exile in Umbria.

He pressed his eyes shut. He would find a way. He would *have* to find a way.

And then the ground beneath his feet began to tremble, and a tense hum rose through the soles of his shiny black shoes. Nearby, a little girl in pink plastic sandals began to jump up and down. Father Azetti stood up. The train was coming.

3

The train from Perugia to Rome was an old *locale* with upholstered seats and framed pictures of Lake Como. It stank of cheap cigarettes, and stopped at what seemed like every intersection to take on new passengers. Played out by the hunger that he felt (he still hadn't eaten) and by the tedium of the train, Father Azetti slouched in his seat, his eyes fixed on the fading afternoon. Eventually, the countryside became more crowded and less interesting, finally yielding to the bleak industrial suburbs of the Italian capital. Arriving at the Stazione Termini, the train squealed and shuddered to a halt. Its air brakes heaved a sigh of relief, the doors flew open, and passengers flooded the platform.

Father Azetti looked for a telephone, and after some difficulty, reached Monsignor Cardone in Todi. He apologized. He was in Rome on a matter of great urgency.

"*Roma!?*"

He hoped to return in a day or two, but it might take longer—in which case someone else would have to carry out his duties in Montecastello. The monsignor was so shocked, he could manage no more than another outraged squawk (*"Che?!"*) before Azetti apologized yet again and hung up.

Because he had no money for hotels, the priest spent the night slumped on a bench in the train station. In the morning he washed up in the men's lavatory and went looking for a cheap café. Finding one just outside the terminal, he sipped a double espresso and wolfed down a sugary roll that resembled but was not a croissant. His hunger blunted, he plunged back into the terminal and went in search of the big red M that indicated the subway. Azetti's destination was a city-state nestled in the heart of Rome: the Vatican.

This isn't going to be easy, he thought, not easy at all.

—

Like any independent state, the Vatican's affairs are managed by a bureaucracy—in this case, the Curia, whose mission is to guide the immense entity that is still known as the Holy Roman Empire. Besides the Secretariat of State, which handles the Church's diplomatic affairs, the Curia is composed of nine sacred "congregations." Each is comparable to a federal department or ministry—responsible for one or another aspect of the Church's affairs.

The most powerful of these departments is the Sacred Congregation for the Doctrine of the Faith, which until 1965 was known as the Congregation for the Holy Inquisition of Heretical Error. More than 450 years old, "the Inquisition" remains a vital part of the Church's everyday affairs—not that anyone calls it that, not anymore.

In addition to overseeing the curricula of Catholic schools throughout the world, "the CDF"—as it is popularly known—continues to investigate heresy, judge threats to the faith, discipline priests, and excommunicate sinners. In extraordinary cases a part of the congregation may be appointed to perform exorcisms, grapple with Satan, or take action in the case of attacks upon the faith.

It was in connection with these last responsibilities that Father Azetti had traveled to Rome.

The head of the CDF was Stefano Orsini, *Cardinal* Orsini, who thirty-five years earlier had been a student with Azetti at the Vatican's Gregorian University. Orsini was now a prince of the faith, the head of a Vatican inner sanctum that included nine lesser cardinals, twelve bishops, and thirty-five priests—each of whom was an academic of the first order.

The cardinal's offices were in the shadow of St. Peter's Cathedral in the Palace of the Holy Office—a building Azetti knew well. He'd spent his first years as a priest working in a small, brightly lighted room on the second floor, surrounded by books and manuscripts. A great many days had come and gone since then, and as he mounted the stairs to the third floor, he felt his heart begin to pound.

It wasn't exertion, it was *the steps*—the way in which the marble dipped and thinned in the middle of the stairwell, worn down by centuries of feet. Seeing the depressions in the stone, and knowing that he'd last climbed these stairs nearly twenty years before, he realized that his life was wearing away, and that it had been doing so for many years. Like the steps, he, too, was beginning to disappear.

The idea stopped him in his tracks. For a moment he hesitated on the landing, gripping the handrail until his knuckles glowed. A feeling like nostalgia moved through him, but it wasn't nostalgia, it was something . . . heavier, a sense of loss that brought an ache to the back of his throat. Slowly, he resumed his climb, and as he did, he moved deeper and deeper into his own homesickness.

He was an outsider now, a visitor in his Father's mansion, and his intimacy with the building's details—the texture of the paint, the silky brass of the banister, the way the light fell in slanted rectangles on the marble floor—was enough to break his heart.

He had always thought that he would spend the bulk of his life inside the walls of the Vatican. In the library. Teaching in one of the Church's universities. In this very building. He had been ambitious enough to think that one day he might even wear the red hat of a cardinal.

Instead he'd spent the past decade ministering to the faithful in Montecastello, where his "flock" consisted of shopkeepers, field hands, and small businessmen. It was uncharitable, but he couldn't resist the thought: What was a man like himself doing in a place like that?

He held a doctorate in canon law and knew the ways of the Vatican inside out. He'd worked for years in the Sacred Congregation for the Doctrine of the Faith, and later in the Secretariat of State. He'd performed his duties admirably, compassionately, intelligently, *efficiently*—and so had come to be seen as something of a rising star. Sent abroad for the usual "seasoning," he'd received an appointment, first as subsecretary to the Apostolic Nuncio in Mexico, then in Argentina. It was obvious to everyone that someday he, too, would be a *nuncio*—an ambassador of the Pope's.

But that wasn't to be. He ran afoul of the Curia by leading demonstrations against the brutal military regime in Buenos Aires. He'd pushed the government and police for news of citizens who'd disappeared, and given interviews to the foreign press, interviews so incendiary that diplomatic notes had been exchanged—not once, but twice.

With the election of Pope John Paul II, it was suddenly obvious that the Vatican would no longer tolerate the political activism of priests like Azetti. The new pope was a Dominican, a cold war Polish conservative who saw "social justice" as a secular pursuit and not, properly, a religious one.

At most times in history, the Dominicans and the Jesuits pursued quite different agendas. And so it was not surprising that the whole of the Society of Jesus came under criticism. The entire order was admonished for what the new Pope called a "lack of balance," for paying more attention to politics than to serving their Church.

Father Azetti chafed at the admonition. Although the fourth vow of the Jesuits is obedience to the Pope, he chafed at that, too. How could he be a priest and *not* stand up for the poor? In an off-the-record conversation with an American reporter in Buenos Aires, Azetti made the point that it wasn't political activism that John Paul II opposed—it was activism of a particular kind. He might have left the remark at that, and gotten away with making his point, but he'd elaborated. So that there could be no doubt about what he meant, he went on to say: *specifically*, anticommunist activities are encouraged—but speaking out against fascists is not to be tolerated, never mind that thousands are being tortured and killed.

Two days later the remarks were published, more or less verbatim, by the *Christian Science Monitor*, which accompanied the article with a photo of Azetti at the head of a march in the Plaza de Mayo. Beneath the picture was his name and a one-word caption: *Schism?*

Under the circumstances, Azetti was lucky not to be excommunicated. Instead he was recalled to the Vatican and, in effect, stripped of rank. As an exercise in "humility," he was dispatched to a parish so small and remote that no one could tell him exactly where it was. Someone thought that it was near Orvieto. Or maybe Gubbio. Umbria, in any case, but where? Eventually, with the help of an ordnance map, he located the place: a pinprick to the north of Todi. He'd been there ever since, his career withering to the dimensions of a parish priest.

That was then.

Now, Father Azetti entered the spare antechamber that he remembered so well. It was a simple room, with two wooden benches, an antique desk, and a single crucifix on the wall. A ceiling fan turned slowly, stirring the heat.

The receptionist was gone, the desk empty, but not still. A swarm of winged toasters flapped silently across the screen of a portable computer. Azetti looked for a bell to ring, but finding none, resorted to a tentative cough. That done, he muttered "Hello?" Finally, he took a seat on one of the benches. Then he picked up his rosary and began to pray.

He was on the twelfth bead when a priest in white robes emerged from the cardinal's office and, seeing him, paused with a look of surprise. "May I help you, Father?"

"*Grazie*," Azetti said, jumping to his feet.

The priest extended his hand with the words, "Donato Maggio."

"Azetti! *Giulio* Azetti—from Montecastello."

Father Maggio wrinkled his brow.

"It's in Umbria," Azetti added.

"Oh," Maggio said, "of course." The two men stood for a moment, smiling awkwardly at one another. Finally, Maggio sat down at his desk. "How can I help you?"

Azetti cleared his throat. "You're the cardinal's secretary?" he asked.

Maggio shook his head and smiled. "No, I'm just sitting in for a couple of weeks. It's busy here, you know. Lots of changes. Actually, I'm an assistant archivist."

Azetti nodded, twisting his hat in his hands. He might have guessed at Maggio's true position. Twenty years and the phrase jumped instantly into his head: *an archival mouse*. That was the term they'd used for those toiling deep in the archives, dragging out parchments and old illuminated texts for the cardinals, the bishops, the professors at the Vatican universities. Maggio had the red drippy nose and the myopic eyes of the species. After a while—the poor lighting, the centuries of book mold, the close work—they all shared these characteristics.

"So . . ." Maggio said with a frown. "What can I do for you, Father?" He was a little disappointed that the priest had not asked why it was "busy" or the nature of the "changes" he'd mentioned. Then Maggio might have hinted at the Pope's condition, and watched the man's eyes widen at the news. This priest seemed lost in his own head and Maggio had to repeat himself. "Once again—how can I be of assistance?"

"I'm here to see the cardinal."

Maggio shook his head. "I'm sorry."

"It's *urgente*!" Azetti said.

Maggio looked doubtful.

"A threat to the faith," Azetti explained.

The archival mouse smiled thinly. "He's very busy, Father. You must know that."

"I do! It's just—"

"Anyone can tell you: appointments have to be arranged well in advance." The man droned on, detailing the proper approach. Azetti should have consulted the monsignor of his diocese. But since he hadn't . . . and since he was *already* in Rome—an appointment might still be made with one of the more senior staff, to whom Azetti could outline the matter. And if it was then deemed appropriate, a conversation with the cardinal *might* be possible—though this would certainly take weeks. Perhaps longer. Perhaps . . . a letter?

Father Azetti drummed his fingertips on the brim of his hat. He had been accused of arrogance before, of thinking his concerns paramount when the Church had other priorities. But in this case? No. An intermediary would not do, and neither would a letter. His business was with the cardinal. *This* cardinal.

"I'll wait," he said, returning to the bench and sitting down.

"I am afraid you don't understand," Maggio said through an anemic smile. "The cardinal is unable to see everyone who'd like to meet with him. It's simply not possible."

"I understand," Father Azetti said. The secretary made a small, helpless gesture. "But I will wait."

And so he did.

Each morning, Azetti arrived at St. Peter's Cathedral at seven A.M. He said his prayers and sat on a bench near the famous statue of St. Peter, watching the devoted approach and wait to kiss the bronze foot of the great apostle. Centuries of kisses had obliterated the separation of the toes; the entire front of the foot was worn smooth. Even the sole of the sandal had melted into the bronze flesh of the foot.

At eight o'clock Azetti climbed the steps to the third-floor antechamber, where he gave his name to the white-robed Father Maggio. Each day, Maggio nodded coldly and duly wrote Azetti's name, with spiky and hostile precision, in a ledger. The country priest took up his position on the bench—where he remained, uncomfortably, until the end of the day. At five o'clock, when the cardinal's chambers were closed, he retraced his steps down the stairs, walked through the Bernini Colonnade and out the Gate of St. Anna.

While he waited he had plenty of time to reflect on the man he wanted to see. He remembered Orsini from their university days, the man's large and clumsy body so at odds with his sharp, incisive mind. Orsini's brilliance was cold and laserlike, devoid of compassion or even of interest in anyone else's point of view.

His only passion was the Church, and in the pursuit of that passion, he bulldozed all who got in his way. His ascent through the Vatican hierarchy was predictable and swift. No one was surprised by his eventual posting as the head of the CDF. It was a policeman's job, in a way, and Orsini had a policeman's soul. He reminded Father Azetti of the coldhearted policeman in *Les Misérables*—relentless, unforgiving. Virtue turned to stone.

Of course such men are necessary, even indispensable—and Orsini was the ideal man in whom to confide Dr. Baresi's confession. He would know what to do and he would see that it was done.

Azetti didn't want to think about that—about what might be done, or what might have to be done. And so he often lost himself in prayer.

He spent the evenings at the *stazione*, where he discovered after the first night that if he left his round-brimmed hat on the bench next to him while he slept, he might wake to find a few thousand lire in its bowl. Though his sleep was fitful, no one bothered him. And in the morning, after he washed up in the men's room, he went to the little café, where he spent the alms that he received on coffee, *cornettos*, and mineral water.

By the fourth day Father Maggio had ceased to be polite. He ignored Father Azetti's *buongiornos* and acted as if the priest were no longer there. Meanwhile, other intermediaries came and went, asking if they could help. Politely, but firmly, Azetti rejected their offers, saying that he could only discuss the matter with *il cardinale*.

Occasionally someone would stick his head into the room, hoping to get a look at the very crazy priest, and just as quickly the head would disappear. There were whispers, too, and snatches of conversation in the halls. At first the remarks expressed a certain curiosity. There was an amused edge in the voices of the staff, but gradually the voices hardened into annoyance.

"What does he *want?*"

"He *wants* to see the cardinal."

"Impossible."

"Well, of course!"

Clearly, he was becoming not just an irritation but an embarrassment. For one thing—despite his ablutions in the railroad station—he was beginning to stink. The decline in his personal hygiene embarrassed him considerably, because he was by any standard a fastidious man. He endured the decline simply because he had no choice. Despite every effort at cleanliness, grime settled into the cracks and crevices of his skin and embedded itself in his clothing. His hair was filmy with oil, and there was nothing that he could do about it.

His attempts to wash were undertaken at night, when the men's room had an abandoned feel. Even so, it seemed that he was always interrupted. Most seemed to find it entertaining to pause and watch a priest at his public toilette.

Not that it did much good. The sinks were tiny and offered only cold water. The soap was a sort of latherless goo, and *worse,* there were no towels, just machines that blew hot air. No matter how hard Father Azetti tried, or how acrobatically he positioned himself, there were parts of him that simply could not be blown dry without creating a scene. So the grime clung to him. He understood for the first time what it was like to be homeless.

"Can't we have him removed?" a voice asked. By the sixth day they had begun to discuss him quite freely, as if he were a foreigner or an animal who could not understand them. As if he weren't there at all.

"And how would that look? He's a priest!"

Never once did Azetti waver. All he had to do was recall Baresi's words. He would not, he could not, return to Montecastello the sole repository of the doctor's confession. Rather than that, he would wait forever.

On the seventh day, Monsignor Cardone arrived from Todi and took up the seat beside him.

A wizened, birdlike man, the monsignor said nothing for a full minute. He fixed his bright black eyes on the wall in front of him and held his silence, gazing out from under a thatch of gray eyebrows. Finally, he offered a sharp little smile and placed a hand on Father Azetti's knee. "I was told you were here," he said.

"Ah," Father Azetti replied, as if he'd been curious, and as if that curiosity was now satisfied.

"*Giulio.* What *is* it? Perhaps I can help."

Azetti shook his head. "Not unless you can intercede with the cardinal. Otherwise . . ." He shrugged.

The monsignor did his best. He charmed. He spoke to Azetti as one sophisticated cleric to another. Surely Azetti knew—better than most—how these things were done. There were channels and protocols—formalities! Surely he knew—better than most—how precious the cardinal's time must be, and how it was the staff's job to protect him from distraction. Come, let's walk together.

No. Grazie. Molto grazie.

Finally, the monsignor attacked. Really, Azetti, you're in dereliction of duty. You've abandoned your church! There's been a christening, a death—a funeral mass! What could possibly be so important? People are talking!

And then he cajoled. If Azetti would confide in him, the monsignor would intercede on his behalf. As it was, the cardinal in all probability did not even know that Azetti was waiting all these long days.

Azetti shook his head. "I can't tell anyone," he said, "except the cardinal."

Eventually the monsignor bounced angrily to his feet. "If you persist in this, Giulio—"

Azetti tried to think of words that might dilute the monsignor's wrath, but before he could say anything, Donato Maggio stuck his head in the room.

"The cardinal will see you now," he told the priest. Orsini had decided that this was, after all, the easiest way of getting rid of him.

Stefano Orsini sat behind an enormous wooden desk, his black robes trimmed in crimson, a red skullcap perched atop his head. He was a large man with a loose-skinned, fleshy face and enormous brown eyes. They were the eyes of a dog, a large dog, but not a friendly one. His features tightened for a moment as the priest's aroma preceded him into the room, and then he looked up. "Giulio," he said. "How very nice to see you. Sit down. I'm told you've been waiting for a long time."

"Your grace." Father Azetti sat on the edge of a leather wing chair and waited for Father Maggio to leave the room. His mind was teeming with the words that he'd rehearsed. And then he saw that, rather than leaving, Maggio took a seat near the door and crossed his legs.

Azetti coughed.

The cardinal prompted him. "So?"

Azetti glanced in the direction of Father Maggio.

The cardinal's eyes shifted from one priest to the other and back again. Finally he shook his head and said, "He's my *assistant*, Giulio."

Azetti nodded.

"And he stays," the cardinal added.

Azetti nodded again. He could see that the cardinal's patience was wearing thin.

"Is it *parole* you're after?" the cardinal asked in a disdainful voice. "Tired of the country life?"

Azetti heard Father Maggio snicker behind his back. But he didn't mind. For the first time, he realized that he'd lost something in the countryside—and that was his ambition. But as terrible as that sounded, even to him, he knew in his heart that it wasn't at all like losing a leg. It was more liked being cured of a fever. As his eyes moved around Orsini's office he realized that despite his nostalgia on that first day, nothing could induce him to return to the machinations of a life within the Vatican. In Montecastello he'd found something more precious than ambition.

He'd found his faith.

But this was not something that he could tell Orsini. That was so despite the fact that the cardinal was himself a rarity in the Vatican— he, too, was a true believer, an ardent and steadfast soldier of the cross. Still, Father Azetti knew that Orsini would have no interest in his soul. He was interested in power, and Azetti understood that any profession of faith would not be taken at face value but as a feint or ploy, a political maneuver.

"No," he said, "I'm not here on my own behalf." He looked into Orsini's predatory eyes. "There's something the Church needs to know." He hesitated. "Something that can only be—"

The cardinal held up a hand and offered a cold smile. "Giulio . . . *please*. Spare me the introductory remarks."

Father Azetti sighed. With a nervous glance at Father Maggio, he plunged ahead, forgetting the speech that he'd rehearsed throughout the week. There was a blank moment when his head swarmed with words, and then:

"I've heard a confession," he stammered. "I've heard a confession that almost stopped my heart."

4

In the days that followed, Cardinal Orsini worried.

He worried about Man. He worried about God. And he worried about himself. What was he to do? What could *anyone* do? The implications of Dr. Baresi's confession were so profound that for the first time in his life Orsini felt that he'd been asked to shoulder a burden that was too heavy for him. Obviously, the matter should be taken directly to the Pope, but the Pope was barely conscious half the time, his lucidity flickering in and out like a weak radio signal. An issue like this . . . it could kill him.

The problem was compounded by the isolation that it imposed. There was no one in whom Cardinal Orsini felt he could confide. Indeed, other than himself, the only person in the Vatican who knew of the matter was Father Maggio—a circumstance for which he had only himself to blame. Azetti hadn't wanted him there, but he had insisted: *He's my assistant, Giulio.* And then a pause. *And he stays.*

Why had he said that? Because, he told himself, you've spent too much time in the Vatican, and too little in the world. You're an arrogant man who couldn't imagine a parish priest having anything of interest to say—and now Donato Maggio is your only confidant.

Donato Maggio. The thought made him groan out loud. Maggio was a research-archivist and sometime clerk who was not shy about expressing his theological views. A traditionalist who prayed (loudly) for "a more muscular Catholicism," Maggio had referred more than once to "the real mass"—which was, of course, a barely veiled criticism of the reforms enacted at Vatican II.

If the Tridentine rite was "the real mass"—because it was said in Latin with the priest's back to the congregation—then the new mass was a fraud. And, as such, a sacrilege.

Though he'd never discussed any theological issue with Father

Maggio, Cardinal Orsini could guess where the priest stood on an array of issues. Not only would he despise the new mass, in which Latin gave way to English, Spanish, and other living languages, Maggio would also frown on the ability to fulfill the requirement of Sunday worship by attending a service on Saturday night. Like other traditionalists, he would oppose all attempts to modernize the Church in an effort to make it more accessible. With Maggio, however, it wouldn't be a matter of opposing proposed measures, such as the ordination of women, permitting clergy to marry, or the legitimization of birth control—Maggio's conservatism went deeper than that. He wanted to roll back reforms already in place. He was a Neanderthal.

Accordingly, there was no point in asking Maggio's opinion of what Dr. Baresi had done. Priests like Maggio did not have opinions: they had reflexes, and those reflexes were predictable.

In the end it didn't matter. Father Azetti had come to the Vatican with his ticking bomb at a time of unusual activity—which meant that Cardinal Orsini's isolation didn't last long. The Pope's illness was grave enough that the College of Cardinals had begun—discreetly—to caucus its members in search of a suitable successor. Short lists of likely popes—*papabiles*—were being drafted and revised, and cell phones had been banned inside the Holy Office lest journalists, or others, listen in on conversations that weren't meant to be overheard.

It was a busy time in which the ordinary business of the day consisted of secret meetings and whispered confidences. Under the circumstances, with the Pope's health in precipitous decline, Cardinal Orsini found himself in one smoke-filled room after another. It was a superheated atmosphere in which matters of enormous importance were being discussed at the most incidental encounter: the next Pope, the future of the Church.

Tormented as he was by Dr. Baresi's confession, which was more momentous than any of the other matters, it was inevitable that Cardinal Orsini would share the burden that he'd been given with several of his colleagues. And so he did, soliciting the advice of two or three confidants—no more.

The reaction, in each case, was one of shocked contemplation, followed by the observation that there was nothing to be done—or one thing only, and *that* too terrible to contemplate. And yet . . . everyone agreed that to do nothing was an action of another kind. And one, moreover, whose consequences might be equally great.

To do nothing . . . Orsini thought. To do nothing was tantamount to letting the world run down like a windup clock, a clock that had been ticking since the beginning of time.

The matter was so overwhelming that Orsini's colleagues inevitably confided in their own friends, and the news spread. Within a week of Azetti's stammering disclosure in the chambers of Cardinal Orsini, debate began to rage inside the walls of the Vatican. It was a secret debate in which one prelate after another wandered the archives of the Vatican's library in search of guidance that, in the end, was nowhere to be found. There was no wisdom from the past that would settle this matter. It was agreed that the problem raised by Dr. Baresi's sin was unanticipated in the history of the Church—and this for the simple reason that it had never before been possible.

The result was a vacuum of dogma that ultimately yielded a consensus of its own. After weeks of informal argument, the Curia decided that whatever Dr. Baresi had done, *it was God's will.* Accordingly, there was nothing for anyone else to do, unless and until the Pope recovered—or there was a new Pope to whom the matter might be submitted. At which point His Holiness might then address the matter *ex cathedra.* Until then everyone should back off. And so they did.

Except Father Maggio, who, learning of this decision, took the next train to Naples.

The offices of Umbra Domini, or "Shadow of the Lord," were in a four-story villa on the Via Viterbo, a few blocks from the Neapolitan opera house. Founded in 1966, not long after the Second Vatican Council was gaveled to an end, the order's canonical status had remained the same for thirty years: it was a "secular institute," with more than fifty thousand members, and "missions" in thirteen countries. While it had long sought the more elevated status of a "personal prelature," most Vatican watchers were of the opinion that Umbra Domini was fortunate to be in the Church at all.

The order's objections to the reforms of Vatican II had been broad, deep, and loud. Its spokesmen attacked the Council's efforts to "democratize" the faith, seeing in them a surrender to the forces of modernism, Zionism, and socialism. The most galling of the reforms, in Umbra Domini's view, was the abandonment of the Latin mass, which shattered more than a thousand years of tradition and severed the common bond that held Catholics together in every corner of the world. In Umbra's view, the vernacular mass was "a bastard rite, a Catholic-Lite version of a God-given liturgy." According to the organization's founder, the new mass could only be explained in one way: obviously, the Throne of St. Peter had been occupied by the Antichrist throughout the deliberations of Vatican II.

Nor was this all. While the order's beliefs were not encoded in a public document, it was known to condemn the liberal view that other religions have elements of truth, and that—as Vatican II proclaimed—their followers "stand in the love of God." If this was so, the order argued, then the Church was guilty of persecution and mass murder. For how else to explain sixteen hundred years of papally mandated, doctrinal intolerance, culminating in *the Inquisition*? Unless, as Umbra Domini insisted, the doctrine had been correct all along, and followers of other faiths were in fact infidels—and enemies of the true Church.

Critics of the order called for the excommunication of its followers, but the Pope hesitated, unwilling to provoke a schism. For years Vatican emissaries met secretly with Umbra Domini's leaders, until, in the end, a compromise was reached. The order was given official recognition by the Vatican, and permission to conduct the mass in Latin, on condition that it take what amounted to a vow of silence. In future, Umbra would issue no public statements, and all proselytizing would be restricted to word-of-mouth.

Inevitably, Umbra Domini turned inward. Its leaders disappeared from public view and ceased to give interviews. Occasionally a newspaper article appeared in the United States or Europe, warning that the organization was becoming a cult. The *New York Times* accused it of "obsessive secrecy and coercive recruiting practices," while noting the immense wealth that it had somehow managed to accumulate in only a few years. In England the *Guardian* went further. Pointing to "the improbable number of politicians, industrialists, and magistrates" who are members of the group, the newspaper hinted that "a neofascist political organization is emerging in the guise of a religious order."

The allegation was dismissed, charmingly, by the very man Father Maggio had come to Naples to see. This was Umbra Domini's youthful and charismatic "Helmsman," Silvio della Torre.

At the time he addressed the allegations about the order's neofascist nature, della Torre spoke to an audience of new members—which included, way at the back of the crowd, pressed in fact against a wall— Donato Maggio. The address took place in the tiny and ancient, Neapolitan Church of San Eufemio—an edifice that had been given to the order in its early years and one that still served as its "home" pulpit.

It was a building with a history. The Christian church was built in the eighth century, atop the site of an ancient temple to Mithras. Despite its antiquity, the church building had been so far "down on its knees" in 1972—the roof leaking and the walls crumbling—that the only alternative to donating it to Umbra was to permit it to be razed for the sake of public safety.

Umbra had restored the church, as it had promised, although there was little in the primitive building to appeal to the "culture vultures" who swooned at the sights available to them in other churches. Within a half day's drive they might behold the works of Giotto or Michelangelo or Leonardo, or Fra Lippo Lippi. Of Raphael and Bernini. San Eufemio hardly attracted the art lovers.

True, the exterior was graced with a pair of eighth-century cypress doors—quite plain, however enduring. But the interior space was cramped and gloomy. There were virtually no windows, and those few shed little light, because they were made of the mineral selenite, a precursor of glass that was translucent in a strong light but nowhere near transparent.

And the other attractions were somewhat . . . off-putting. The heart of a currently out of favor saint was contained in an ugly reliquary. And pride of place was given to a very old and spooky Annunciation. The painting itself was so darkened with age that only a brilliant day permitted enough light to make it visible. And then: a wooden-faced Virgin contemplated the Holy Spirit, which was not depicted as the traditional dove but as a disembodied eye floating in midair.

From within this gloomy space, della Torre shone like a candle. On the day he responded to press allegations that Umbra was a neofascist organization—which was the day Donato Maggio joined Umbra Domini—the young priest handled the controversy with consummate ease. First he smiled, and then thrust his hands into the air and shook his head ruefully.

"The press," he began, "the press amazes me, because it is at once utterly inconsistent—and absolutely dependable. First, they complain that we talk too much," he said, alluding to the days when Umbra loudly trumpeted its views. "And now," he continued, "they complain that we don't talk at all. Because it suits their purpose, they mistake privacy for secrecy, fraternity for conspiracy—and so prove the point of their . . . dependability." An amused murmur rose from the congregation. "The press *always* gets *everything* wrong," della Torre said in conclusion. "And you can count upon it." The newbies grinned.

For his part, Father Maggio was at once a Dominican and also a member of Umbra. There were many priests in Umbra's ranks; since it was a lay order, there was no contradiction in this dual allegiance. But Donato Maggio was perhaps a bit unusual in that he was not only a member of a religious order, but one who worked inside the Vatican. Therefore, he had a foot in two worlds, and understood the fear that each provoked in the other. To the Vatican, Umbra Domini was a barely tolerable extremist group, a sort of Catholic Hezbollah, waiting to explode. For its part, Umbra Domini saw the Vatican for what it was, or what it seemed to be: an obstacle. Massive, senile, and *there*.

Though Father Maggio had never formally met Silvio della Torre, there was no difficulty in arranging a private meeting. On learning that one of Cardinal Orsini's aides wished to speak with him on a matter of great urgency, della Torre suggested dinner that same evening. It was possible, Maggio thought, that della Torre had leapt to the conclusion that his position as secretary to Cardinal Orsini was a permanent one, but . . . so what? Even if Maggio was a lowly archival mouse, della Torre *would* want to hear what he had to say.

They met in a little trattoria, not far from della Torre's church. The restaurant was called I Matti, and though it was rather ordinary-looking from the outside, it was surprisingly elegant within. Father Maggio was greeted deferentially by the maître d' and escorted up a flight of stairs to a private room above the ground floor. The room held a single table, which rested on a plank floor beneath a tall Palladian window. There was a small fireplace, where a jumble of wood crackled and sparked, and antique sconces that dispensed a golden glow. On the table, a white cloth, candles, and a sprig of baby's breath.

Silvio della Torre was gazing out the window when Father Maggio entered the room. As he turned, acknowledging the maître d's "*Scusi, signore,*" Maggio saw what had been hidden by the darkness of the church: that the head of Umbra Domini was dramatically good-looking. He was a man in his mid-thirties, broad-shouldered and tall. Quietly, but expensively, dressed. His thick, curly hair was so black it seemed almost blue in the light. But what surprised Maggio the most were della Torre's eyes. They were a faded aquamarine, neither blue nor green, and rimmed by thick, luxuriant lashes.

"Jewels in a setting wrought by God," Maggio thought, pleased at the phrase. Of course—he was practically a professional. In his spare time he often wrote poetry. Della Torre got to his feet, and Maggio saw that his features resembled those of every other statue in the Forum. Maggio scribbled in his head: "A classic Roman profile . . ." but then turned his attention to the man himself. His heart beat double-time. He was having dinner with Silvio della Torre!

"*Salve,*" della Torre said, extending his hand. "You must be Brother Maggio."

Maggio stammered that he was, in fact, that person, and the two men took their seats. Della Torre made small talk as he poured them each a glass of Greco de Tufo, then raised a toast. "To our friends in Rome," he said, and they clinked.

The meal was simple and delicious, and the conversation was the same. Over plates of bruschetta they talked about soccer, about Lazio and Sampdoria, and the agonies of Serie A. A waiter opened a bottle of Montepulciano. Moments later a second waiter entered with plates of agnelotti, stuffed with tartufo and leek. Maggio remarked that the agnelotti were like "tender little pillows," and della Torre responded with what, to Maggio, sounded like a dirty joke (but perhaps he misunderstood). As they ate and drank, the conversation shifted to politics, and Maggio was thrilled to learn that he and della Torre agreed on very nearly everything. The Christian Democrats were a mess, the Mafia was resurgent, and the Freemasons were everywhere. And as for the Jews, well . . . They gossiped about the Pope's condition and discussed the chances of each likely successor.

A waiter came with the next course—trout—and expertly boned the two fish. When he left, della Torre remarked that he was happy to find that, in Father Maggio, Umbra Domini had a friend in the Congregation for the Doctrine of the Faith. Maggio was flattered, and in between forkfuls of meltingly succulent trout he displayed his knowledge of the congregation's inner workings and the personalities of the men who had access to *il terzo piano*—the third floor of the Apostolic Palace, where the Pope's apartments could be found.

"It's always helpful," della Torre said, "to know what Cardinal Orsini and the Holy Father are thinking."

The trout gave way to salad, and soon afterward to a thick *bistecca alla fiorentina*, streaked with carbon. Finally, the dinner was over. The waiter came in, cleared the plates, and brushed the crumbs from the table. He put a bottle of Vin Santo before them and a plate of biscotti. Then he stirred the fire and, after asking if there would be anything else, he left the room, pulling the door shut behind him.

Della Torre poured each of them a glass of Vin Santo. Then he leaned toward Father Maggio and, fixing his eyes on the priest, lowered his voice to a silky growl. "Donato," he said.

Father Maggio cleared his throat. "Silvio?"

"Enough of this bullshit—why are we here?"

Father Maggio concealed his surprise with a white linen napkin, dabbing it daintily against his lips. Finally, he put the napkin aside, took a deep breath, and cleared his throat again. "A priest—a country priest—came to the Vatican—this was a few weeks ago—and told a story."

Della Torre nodded his encouragement.

"Well," Maggio said with a shrug, "sometimes . . . I hear what the cardinal hears—unless it's a matter that's considered too momentous for my ears. This didn't seem important at the time and so I remained in the office while the priest talked. And now . . ." Father Maggio chuckled ruefully. "Well, now I'm sure the cardinal is unhappy that I was there."

"It's a sensitive matter, then."

Father Maggio nodded. "Yes," he said.

Della Torre pondered this for a moment. Finally, he said, "And this was 'a few weeks ago'?"

"In between discussions about the new Pope, they've been talking about little else ever since."

"And why is that?"

"Because they had to decide what to do."

"Ah! And what did they decide?"

"They decided nothing. Or to do nothing. It's the same thing. That's why I'm here."

Della Torre looked thoughtful. After a moment he refreshed Father

Maggio's glass and said, "Well, *Donato* . . . perhaps you should tell *me* the story."

Father Maggio furrowed his brow and leaned forward. He rested his elbows on the table and put the tips of his fingers and thumbs together. Slowly, he tapped them against one another and said, "It began with a confession . . ."

When the story was done, della Torre was on the edge of his chair, with a dead cigar in his hand. Embers sizzled and spit in the fireplace, but there was no other sound in the room. "Donato," della Torre said, "thank you for telling me this."

Father Maggio threw back the last of his Vin Santo, and stood. "I have to get back," he said.

Della Torre nodded.

"Thank you for having the courage to bring this to me. *They* couldn't decide what to do," he said, "because there was nothing to decide. There's only one thing that *can* be done."

"I know," Father Maggio replied. "They had a failure of nerve."

Della Torre got to his feet. Maggio offered his hand, and della Torre, rather than shaking it, took it in both of his. Slowly, he brought the back of the priest's hand to his lips and kissed it. For a moment the priest imagined that he felt the man's tongue against his skin, and then it was over.

"*Grazie,*" della Torre said. "*Molto grazie.*"

PART II

NOVEMBER

5

Until the evening of November 7, Keswick Lane was one of those streets about which it is always said that "nothing ever happens." Curling through a real estate development in the town of Burke, a northern Virginia suburb of Washington, D.C., the street was lined with $400,000 homes, BMWs, and the best gas grills money could buy. The houses in Cobb's Crossing, as the development was known, were uniformly Nouveau Colonial in design. Each house was different, if only in color and architectural details, but all were of the same vintage—six years old. Because the developers had taken care to preserve as many trees as possible, and spent heavily on landscaping, the neighborhood bore a superficial resemblance to an old and settled one.

The true tale was told by the unblemished and deep black asphalt of the street itself, which followed a graceful curve to the west, ending in a cul-de-sac. In many ways it would have been an ideal block for young children, who might have played there without fear of traffic. But with a single exception, the children on Keswick Lane were too old to play in the street. Because the houses were expensive, the people who lived in them—lawyers, mostly, some lobbyists and business executives—tended to be of a certain age, and so did their children. For the most part, the kids were everywhere but on the street. They were taking lessons in horseback riding or karate, playing soccer or lacrosse, or blasting demons on their computer monitors.

So the sidewalks on Keswick Lane, and Keswick Lane itself, had a deserted feeling. The sight of a pedestrian—of any age—was rare.

Except, of course, for the dog walkers. Nearly every house on the street had a dog in residence. During the week, their owners tended to be gone all day, which meant that it was in the evenings that the dogs enjoyed their only real outing, a dutiful turn around the tidy blocks of Cobb's Crossing.

On November 2 there were still reminders of Halloween to be seen, saggy pumpkins on front porches, the occasional segmented cardboard skeleton hanging from a front door, fake cobwebs in some of the windows. In the quiet minutes before midnight, a woman who had just returned from a performance of *Tosca* at the Kennedy Center was walking her Labrador retriever, Coffee.

Coffee and his owner stopped across the street from 207 Keswick Lane when the dog paused to sniff intently at the base of a mailbox post.

Suddenly, his muzzle rose and a low growl rolled from his throat. A patch of fur stood up on his back and his ears lifted. Just as he barked, it happened: There was a flash of light followed by a crash of glass as a man exploded through the picture window of the house across the street.

The man was on fire.

He landed, burning, in a hedge of azaleas, staggered to his feet in an aura of flames, collapsed and rolled on the darkened lawn. Across the street the dog strained at his leash and howled, even as his mistress stood in the darkness, stock-still and staring. She couldn't seem to process what she saw; her attention was held, not by the man, but by the window through which he'd burst.

It was actually a single plate of glass fitted with a wooden lattice that gave it the appearance of a window with many small panes. A section of this lattice was caught on the man's body, and the woman was transfixed by the sight of it—a piece of white wooden grid, fringed with fire, crumpling and snapping as the man rolled back and forth across the lawn. It reminded her of a fireworks display that she'd seen in Mexico, on vacation some years before, and the inappropriateness of that memory somehow paralyzed her. For seconds that seemed like minutes she braced herself against the howling dog's protracted lunge— until the man rolled into a clump of river birches, thrashed and lay still.

It was only then that she snapped out of her trance. She released the dog and ran to the man, tearing off her jacket to flail at the flames. His head was on fire, his eyebrows were gone, and he was screaming. Dropping to her knees, she pressed the jacket to his face and rubbed the flames from his hair.

Whuuummmmmmp!

A hollow thump came from behind her. The dog yelped as a wave of heat and light rolled across the lawn. When she looked up, the drapes were in flames. Seconds later the house exploded into fire.

The fleece on her coat was burning, and she tossed it aside. Getting to her feet, she ran to the house next door and banged on the door. A startled man in boxer shorts, a bottle of Red Dog in his hand, answered her pounding. "Nine one one!" she screamed. "Call 911!"

By the time the woman returned to 207—with blankets in her arms—several of her neighbors had congregated on the street in front of the house. Most of them were in their nightclothes, with coats thrown over them. The man on the lawn was no longer on fire. A couple of men, one of them shoeless and dressed only in pajama pants, carried the burned man awkwardly down the driveway, away from the ferocious heat surging from the house. The man was groaning as they set him down on the sidewalk. The woman heard herself talking. "I was walking Coffee," she said. "I was right across the street . . ."

She rattled on in an insistent, irrelevant way that, as a psychologist, she knew was a typical reaction to trauma. It was only when she looked up the driveway and saw the red and yellow Little Tyke car, parked on the walkway next to the garage, that she thought of the people inside—the woman, what was her name? Karen? *Kathy!* And the darling little boy, the only real *child* on the block, the boy who drove that plastic car up and down the driveway on weekends. The boy who came to her door on Halloween, dressed as a rabbit and carrying an orange plastic pumpkin. She remembered it exactly: the boy on the front porch, his mother behind him, smiling.

"And who are *you?*" she'd said, holding back her basket of candy. "Who could you be?"

The child had not quite mastered the pronunciation of the letter R. "Eastuh bunny," he said intently. Behind him, his mother had smiled.

Why didn't she think of them before? The boy's car was beginning to melt, its surface bubbling as it buckled in the heat. Were they home? Were they *in* there?

"Oh my God—oh my *God*," she said, and started running toward the inferno. She was nearly to the front steps when someone grabbed her from behind and pulled her back.

The dog was still barking.

—

In the Fair Oaks Hospital emergency room the nurses were preparing to cut the man's clothing away, when one of them winced. "Polyester," she said, and shook her head. Cotton burned. Polyester melted. When you pulled it away, it took a lot of skin with it.

The victim was wearing a black turtleneck, and the nurse could tell from the charred and viscous mess around the neck that removing the shirt was going to be extremely unpleasant. The burns were third-degree, and infection was almost certain. Even so, he'd recover from that. The real problem was his lungs. He was having trouble breathing, and it was likely that he'd scorched them, breathing super-heated air.

It took a while, but the man's vital signs finally stabilized. With IVs in his arms, he was taken on a gurney to the operating room and prepared for surgery. The first procedure would be to perform a tracheotomy and insert a breathing tube. The lungs were bad enough, but the tissues in the throat were so swollen that he could hardly breathe. The tracheotomy would fix that. And, eventually, they'd begin to debride him, stripping the incinerated flesh and debris from his body, leaving him raw, flayed, and suppurating.

The anesthesiologist was thinking that there's nothing more painful than burns, when the patient began to mumble. It was a horrible sound, a strangled mutter that was just recognizable as a human voice.

"That's funny," one of the nurses said, "he doesn't look Hispanic."

The on-duty resident stood with his gloved hands at shoulder level, in what the nurses jokingly called the "I surrender" stance. "That's not Spanish," he said. "*Dat's* Italian."

"Well, what's he saying?"

The resident shrugged. "I don't know. I never really learned it." He cocked his head and listened again. "I think he's praying."

6

By the time the burned man was on the operating table, the blaze on Keswick Lane had been brought under control and two Fairfax County firefighters were getting ready to go inside in search of victims. The neighbors had already volunteered that two people lived in the house—the woman who owned it, and her three-year-old son. There was no husband. She was a single mother, and her Volvo was in the garage.

Despite the November chill and the late hour, the crowd of onlookers had swollen to more than fifty. It was a chaotic scene, with ambulances and police cars, fire trucks and television crews. Emergency lights strobed through the night—red, yellow, and blue—turning the street on and off. And everywhere, lengths of canvas hose snaked across the lawn, which had become a muddy swamp.

Two camera crews and a radio reporter created their own confusion, trailing a tangle of cables and braces of bright lights. Looking earnest and concerned, they worked both sides of the street, shoving microphones in the faces of firemen and firebugs alike.

"And which house is yours?"

"None, really. I'm a renter? Over in the Hamlets? Anyway, I heard about it on the radio—*police* radio? So I came over."

The fire had been a virulent one, and by all accounts, no one had gotten out alive—with the exception of the burned man.

On their first foray into the house, the firemen searched the charred and sodden wreckage of the ground floor, looking for survivors and finding none. A search of the second floor was delayed by the condition of the staircase, which was structurally unsound.

Outside, a cherry picker, with two young firemen in its basket, was maneuvered into position against an upstairs window, and the window smashed.

Each of the firemen was convinced that his mission was pointless. No one could have survived the conflagration. If anyone had escaped the flames, the smoke would have done him in. Still, there was always the possibility, the very remote possibility, of someone huddled in an interior bathroom, someone with the presence of mind to stuff wet towels against the door. Fires were unpredictable—sometimes they sought you out, and sometimes they left you alone. You could never be sure with fire.

The younger of the firemen leaned in through the window and tested the floor with a crowbar. When the floor showed no signs of giving way, he climbed inside, leaving his partner in the cherry picker, ready to assist.

What the fireman found was just what he'd expected to find: an adult. And a small child. They were still in their beds, or what was left of their beds—the mattresses reduced to box springs and bits of disintegrated cloth. The victims' bedclothes had gone up in flames and left a charred and netted residue embedded in their skin. Next to the child's head were a pair of little glass eyes, the last remains of a stuffed animal. The boy and his mother were still recognizable as human beings, which was "lucky." If the fire trucks had arrived only a few minutes later, or if the hydrant had been farther away, they and the house would be gone. Smoke and bones, and nothing in between.

It was the deputy chief's job to inform the next of kin—which had to be done immediately. When a $400,000 home burned in an expensive suburb like Cobb's Crossing and killed the people inside—that was news, and the news spread quickly. Though the fire hadn't broken out until after the *Post* had put its last edition to bed, there'd be footage of it on the morning news. So the deputy chief made the calls he had to make, and learned that the home belonged to a Kathleen Anne Lassiter, who lived there—or *had* lived there—with her young son. According to insurance records, the next of kin was a brother, Joseph, who resided in McLean.

And who, at that moment, was dreaming.

In his dream, Joe Lassiter was standing on the shore of the Potomac River, just above Great Falls, casting for largemouth bass. He flicked his wrist and the line arced out over the river—a perfect, parabolic dream cast that dipped precisely toward the spot that he'd selected. As soon as it hit the water, the bass struck, and he began to play it, lifting the rod toward the sky.

But, somewhere, a telephone had begun to ring, and it pissed him off. It was bad enough that the goddamn things rang in the middle of concerts at the Kennedy Center, and in the bottom of the ninth at Camden Yards—but this! Some unseen idiot had actually brought his cellular phone fishing. What was the point of *fishing* if you took your fucking *telephone* with you?

He swung the rod smoothly to the right, cranking the reel with his free hand. From a few feet away his own voice floated toward him:

"Hi, it's Joe Lassiter. I can't come to the phone just now, but leave a message and I'll get back to you."

The river, the fish, the rod and the reel . . . evaporated. He lay in bed with his eyes closed, awake in the darkness, waiting to hear the message. But whoever it was hung up. Figures, Joe thought, pushing his head deeper into the pillows.

He wanted back, back in the dream, but it wasn't there anymore. The river was gone, the fish was gone, and the only part that he could recover, the only part that he still felt, was his sour indignation about the phone. The phantom phone. His phone.

And then it rang again. This time, he answered it.

"What?"

The man's voice was professionally calm, reasonable, and official. But what he was saying was far from reasonable and it didn't really sink in until ten minutes later, when Lassiter was in his car, driving through the night toward Fairfax. There had been a fire. Positive identification had not been made, but the bodies—

No, Joe thought. *No.*

—the bodies were consistent with—

Consistent with?

—what we know about the residents. Your sister—

Kathleen—

And her son—

Brandon. Little Brandon.

The road ran along the Potomac, not far from where he'd imagined himself fishing. Across the river, behind the spires of Georgetown University, the sky brightened toward dawn.

They were dead. That's not how the man had put it, of course. "There were two fatalities." Joe Lassiter was clenching his teeth so ferociously that his head throbbed with the pressure. Kathy. For once in her whole, fucked-up life, Kathy had actually been happy. Stable. *Serene!* Against all odds she'd turned out to be a terrific mother, and the kid—

Brandon's face flashed before his eyes, and he looked away, squeezed it out. Rolled down the window and felt the cold air on his face. In Rosslyn, across the river from the Kennedy Center, he swung onto the ramp for 66. There was already a lot of traffic coming the other way.

How could that house burn down? Lassiter wondered. It was practically new, and everything—the stove, the wiring, the three-zone heating system, *everything*—was top of the line. He'd gone along on the home inspection himself. There were smoke alarms everywhere. Carbon monoxide detectors. She even had fire extinguishers! Once she'd become a mother, *safety* had become a very big deal with Kathy.

He knew he shouldn't be thinking about the house. He should be thinking about his sister. He was turning a catastrophe into an abstraction, thinking about it like an investigator, not like a brother. Maybe he was in "denial," but on some level he couldn't believe she was dead. Just being *told* she was dead didn't make it real. He couldn't believe the house had burned down, and if the house couldn't have burned down, how could she be dead? How could Brandon be dead?

How could they not have gotten out?

The man on the telephone hadn't given him enough information. He wanted to know more. He wanted to know everything. He stepped on the accelerator even though he knew it was stupid. *Fatalities.* He wasn't going to save her.

He'd set out for the morgue, which was in the county building, but found himself taking the turns toward Kathy's house, driving like an automaton. A few blocks from Cobb's Crossing the air turned acrid. He could smell the smoke, and it made his heart sink. He'd been holding on to a little spark of hope—somewhere in his mind. It was some kind of mistake: the wrong address, another Kathy Lassiter.

Now it was extinguished. He saw the lights on the fire trucks, pulled the Acura over to the curb, shut off the engine and walked the rest of the way.

He knew that an investigation into the cause of the fire would be under way, as a matter of routine. There is always an attempt to learn a fire's cause. This isn't to satisfy anyone's curiosity, or even to learn from misfortune. The answer to the question—Why did this fire occur?—has important legal and financial implications. Was it a cigarette? A faulty water heater? A defective chimney?

Affixing blame determined who would pay, and how much, and so the question was pursued at once—and vigorously.

There were six cars parked in front of the house, and he noted them with idle and instinctive care: a squad car, two unmarked police cars with bubbles on the dash, two fire department vehicles, and a tan Camry, which might or might not belong to the insurance company's investigator. A uniformed man was playing out a roll of yellow tape from a stake at the corner of the driveway. The tape was imprinted, over and over, with the words:

POLICE LINE—DO NOT CROSS

The smell in the air was intense, a mix of wood smoke and burnt plastic. But the house itself, the sight of the house, hit him like a sucker punch. It was a *dead* house, and for the first time since the telephone call the truth of the words settled into meaning. *Fatalities.* His sister was dead; his nephew was dead. The house smoldered in the middle of a tire-gouged lawn, a mess of charred timbers and blackened metal. The windows of the house were blown out, and without their skin of glass, they had the blank look of a dead man's eyes. Through them he could see the wrecked and gutted interior. He turned and walked over to the policeman, who was tying off a length of the yellow tape.

"What happened?"

The cop was young, red hair, freckles, blue eyes. He looked up at Lassiter with a smart-ass expression and shrugged.

"A *fire* happened."

Lassiter wanted to smack him, but he took a deep breath instead. When he exhaled, his breath was like smoke in the cold morning air.

"How did it start?"

The cop gave him a look, as if he was trying to memorize Lassiter's features. Finally he nodded toward the fire trucks. "They're saying arson."

For the second time in as many minutes, he felt as if he'd been

blindsided. He'd been expecting something else. A cigarette, maybe—
Kathy still smoked, never around the kid, but she still smoked. So,
maybe a cigarette. Or a space heater, or . . . not a space heater, not in
that house, not with *that* heating system. Lightning, then. A cigarette,
some minor appliance shorting out . . .

"What?"

The kid gave him another look. "Who are you?"

Lassiter's mind was working at warp speed. One part of it was
remarking that the kid was on the ball, that he knew that firebugs often
returned to the scene of the crime. And another part was thinking that
of course, he should have known, the cop cars should have tipped him
off. Once arson is suspected, a fire becomes a crime scene. And if victims are involved, it becomes a homicide case.

"Why would anybody want to burn down Kathy's house?" he said
out loud.

7

"Hey, Joe! What are *you* doin' here?"

The voice was mock-accusatory, and hearing it, Lassiter turned. A ruddy face was smiling up at him.

"Jim Riordan," he said.

"I remember."

"So what *are* you doin' here?" The detective's attitude was mostly for the benefit of the people behind him: three men and a woman. They were looking at Lassiter with a mixture of expectation and neutrality.

"It's my sister's house."

The smile faded from Riordan's face. He tugged the lobe of his right ear and shook his head. Finally, he said, "Jesus Christ, Joe. I'm sorry. I didn't know."

He sat across from the detective in a cubicle at police headquarters and waited for Riordan to finish with the telephone. The last time Lassiter had seen him, their positions had been reversed: Riordan had been sitting across from him in Lassiter's own office, looking uncomfortable. The cop had been wearing what Lassiter surmised was his "good suit," an aging pinstripe that seemed about a size too small.

I got a year to go, Riordan had said, leaning toward his desk, *and then I'm out. And what am I gonna do then? Sit on my ass all day? I don't think so. So, I figure, maybe I should start looking now—test the waters, see what I can line up. And I figure I might as well start at the top, y'know? So that's why I'm here, that's why I'm talking to you.*

It was a conversation Lassiter had once or twice a week: if it wasn't a cop, it was someone from the FBI or DEA, the Pentagon or Langley. They all wanted a job, and with their skills, an investigative firm was the logical place to go. But the only thing that made Riordan at all interesting to him as a possible employee was something the detective said on the way out. And that was: *Hey! Things don't work out? I'll work on my screenplay.*

That was interesting. Because cops who could write were as rare as snow leopards, and Lassiter Associates was always looking for investigators who could write reports that could be sent to clients—most of whom were lawyers and stockbrokers. That's why the company had so many journalists working for it. If Riordan could write, there might be a place for him.

"It's your ass," Riordan shouted into the telephone. The outright rancor in his voice wrenched Lassiter back into the present. The detective slammed the receiver down, looked at him and shrugged. "Sorry about that."

Then Riordan tried to find something on his desk. He moved some papers around, found one in particular, and pushed it across the desk toward Joe. "No question, it was arson," he said. "Multiple points of origin, obvious accelerant residues—the whole nine yards."

Lassiter looked at the fire department's preliminary report, which included a rough diagram of each floor of the house. There were X marks in seven places, including both bedrooms. Lassiter knew that natural fires almost always had a different pattern, originating at a single source. He looked at Riordan.

"There's more." The detective drummed his fingers on the desk. "The gas was on—and not just the stove. Down in the basement, too. Water heater had been tampered with. Fire department says the truck's there five minutes later, the house goes up like a rocket. Leaving nothin'. And I do mean *nothin'*."

Lassiter frowned. "So, you're saying . . ."

"I'm saying, whoever it was—this was not a delicate job. It was obviously arson, and whoever set it didn't care who knew it. And it was overkill, you know? It was like . . ." The detective's big features compressed into a puzzled knot. "I don't know what. Like a 'scorched earth' kinda thing. Like they didn't want to leave nothing but ashes." The detective leaned toward him across the desk. He opened his mouth to say something and then thought better of it. He shook his head and a pained expression came over his face. "I shouldn't be telling you all this. I keep forgetting. You're not *investigating* this; you're next of kin."

"Yeah, well," Joe said, as if it didn't matter. "The point is: you were thinking, maybe someone was trying to destroy evidence. And you want to know—evidence of what? What was my sister—"

Riordan interrupted him. "Right now, I'm thinking before this goes any further, I better take you down to the morgue. Drop you off, so you can ID them. I mean, before we start talking about your sister, we better make sure it *is* your sister."

They were on their way out the door when the telephone rang. Riordan hesitated for a second, then pushed past Lassiter and grabbed it.

"*What?*" he demanded, shrugging into his overcoat. The voice on the other end said something, and Riordan shot a look at Lassiter. "Jesus Christ," he said. "Yeah. Yeah. Okay." As they walked through the door to the outside, Riordan extracted a cigarette from a package in his shirt pocket, and lit it.

"What was that all about?" Lassiter asked.

Riordan exhaled. "What?" he asked.

"On the telephone."

Riordan just shook his head, as if to say, Never mind.

Ten minutes later they pulled up in front of the county building. Lassiter unfastened his seat belt and started to get out of the car, but the detective restrained him with the back of his hand.

"Look, Joe," he said in an embarrassed voice, "I have to say something here." He cleared his throat. "Do you agree that a doctor shouldn't operate on his own kid?"

"*What?*"

"A doctor shouldn't operate on his kid, a lawyer shouldn't defend himself, and you . . . you should leave this case to me."

"I'll keep that in mind."

Riordan slapped the steering wheel with the palms of his hands. "I'm talking to a wall, but . . ." He shot a look at his watch. "I've seen it before, you know, ex-cops, spooks, army investigators—guys with *expertise*. They're all over some case where they have a personal involvement—and it's a mess. It's a load of heartache, and on top of that they just fuck it up."

Lassiter didn't say anything, and the detective heaved a sigh. "I got somebody bringing your car over. And then I want you to go home. I'll call you later."

———

Joe Lassiter was in a strange frame of mind, as if he was operating at a remove from himself—as if he was a camera, watching himself. He didn't feel anything, much. It was just: here I am, going to the morgue to identify my sister's body. He saw himself enter the building and make his way to the waiting area, a bland room with generic seascapes on the walls. He spoke to a woman in a white coat with a name tag that read BEASLEY. She entered his name in a large, green ledger and escorted him to the cold room, where bodies were kept in coffinlike drawers set into the walls.

Even as he identified Kathy, and then Brandon, he felt nothing. It was as if he was operating a Joe Lassiter puppet, and the puppet was doing everything while the real Joe Lassiter watched.

His sister's blond hair was now a crusty black skullcap. Her lips were parted, her blue eyes stared up at the fluorescent light. Her eyebrows and eyelashes were burnt off and it gave her face a blank, stupid look. Brandon was even worse, his skin charred and blistered.

He'd seen dead people before, and Kathy and Brandon looked exactly that—dead. They looked as dead as dolls, so dead that they might never have been alive. The woman in the white coat—Beasley—held herself in a stiff, defensive posture, as though waiting for him to go berserk with grief, as though readying herself to let the emotion wash over her. Instead the Joe Lassiter puppet nodded and confirmed the identification in a calm voice. The woman's shoulders relaxed and she wrote something on a form. He heard the sound of her felt-tip pen clearly, squeaking along above the dense whir of the refrigeration units. He signed something without reading it, and they left.

In the corridor, the woman put her hand carefully on his arm. It seemed to him that he couldn't feel the pressure, but only intuited it from the sight of her fingers against his sleeve. "Would you like to sit down for a moment?" she asked. "Can I get you a glass of water?"

"No, it's all right. But I'd like to see the medical examiner."

"Wellll," she said with a worried voice and a frown, "that's not something—"

"Tom's a friend of mine," he said reassuringly.

"Let me just call him," she replied, and picked up the telephone. "He might be in the middle of an au—in the middle of something."

In the waiting room, a pair of Hispanic kids perched, terrified, on one of the orange plastic couches. A police officer waited nearby, and it looked as if, when their names were called, the kids were going to catapult through the ceiling. Lassiter stared at one of the seascapes on the wall—a dull rendition of a stormy shore. Oily waves breaking forever on a jumble of gray rocks.

He heard a singsong voice behind him—"Okay-ay"—and turned as the woman hung up the phone. "If you'll take the corridor down to the end—" she began.

"I know the way."

Tom Truong looked up from his desk, then got to his feet. "Cho!" he said, extending a delicate hand that came with a faint whiff of formaldehyde. He seemed to smile and frown at the same time. "What am I doing for you? You working a case?"

His connection with the medical examiner was an odd one. They'd played soccer together on a thirty-and-over team until a couple of years back, when Lassiter had blown out his knee. Though slightly built, Truong was a vicious defender, with knifelike elbows and a slide tackle that came at you like a scythe. They'd played on the team for a couple of years before the subject of occupations came up—which occurred in a joint called Whitey's, over a pitcher of championship beer. After that, Lassiter occasionally hired Truong as a forensics consultant and expert witness. He was a meticulous and gifted pathologist, and, despite his wobbly English, a brilliant witness. Juries loved him.

"It's not a case," he told Truong. "It's my sister." He raised his chin. "She's back there," he said, "with my nephew."

Truong either thought he was kidding or didn't understand. "What you are saying, Cho?" he asked with a sly look. "You joking me, right?"

"No. The arson case."

Truong's jack-o'-lantern grin faded. "*Las-sit-ter*," he whispered to himself. "Oh, Cho. Very sorry. So very sorry."

"Have you done the autopsy yet?"

He nodded solemnly. "Chimmy ask me special rush. Because the arson." He sighed. "Your sister. And little kid." His eyes tightened into slits. "Well, not the fire killing them."

Lassiter nodded. And then it hit him. "What?!"

Truong's big head bobbed on the thin stalk of his neck. "No smoke particle in lung. No carbon monoxide in blood. These alone tell us victims die *before* fire. And not just that. Additional evidence. You see bodies?"

"Yeah. I identified them. That's why I'm here."

"No. You see *bodies*? Or you see *faces*?"

"Faces."

"You look at body, the both body, you see skin covered with . . . looking like small little cuts. This happen to human being in fire, you know. Standard, because—skin cracking! Flesh liquid, expand in heat—skin not expand, so skin splitting everywhere—release the pressure. But in this case, adult female—you sister—she have little cuts on both her hands and these are different, these are not just skin. Flesh also injured. These are the definite defensive wound, you know. I see these, and I continue my looking and I'm seeing why. You sister—stab in chest. Cause of death, aortal valve. Cut! Young boy . . ." Truong leaned forward across the desk. "His throat cut all the way. Ear to ear." He sank back into his chair, as if the recitation had exhausted him.

His hands came up into the air, then fluttered down like leaves. He pressed them together. "Cho. There no blood left in little boy. They dead, maybe one hour—*then* fire."

Lassiter stared.

"What about guy?" Truong asked. "Husband?"

"What guy?"

"I'm hearing," Truong said, "third person in you sister house. He coming out window, on fire. Since you sister dying like that, I'm thinking maybe he . . ." He shrugged.

"Where is this guy?"

"Burn ward."

"Which hospital?"

Truong shrugged again. "Maybe Fair Oaks. Maybe Fairfax."

8

An hour later, when Lassiter caught up with Riordan, the detective was sitting at a borrowed desk in a doctor's office at Fair Oaks Hospital. A nurse showed him in, and as he entered, Riordan turned around and then stood—a little stiffly, as though trying to hide something behind him. He didn't look happy.

"You don't listen, do you?"

"You didn't tell me you had a suspect."

"He wasn't a suspect until the M.E.'s report came in," Riordan said defensively. "Up to then, he's just another victim."

"Some guy comes flying out the front window of my sister's house—on *fire*—two people dead—and you don't even *mention* it?! And you think he's a *victim*?"

"He *was* a victim! He was burnt to shit."

"Yeah. Well, that just means he's incompetent. Who is he?"

" 'John Doe.' "

"What do you mean, John Doe?"

"Well, he wasn't exactly reciting name-rank-and-serial-number when he came in. And he didn't have any ID on him, either."

Lassiter fell silent for a moment, and then: "Car keys?"

"No. He didn't have any *keys*, he didn't have any ID, he didn't have any *money*. He didn't have shit."

"So, I guess that means—what? That he parachuted in! Is that your theory?"

"Ohhh, come on—"

"Did you check the cars?"

"What cars?"

"Parked cars! The cars in the neighborhood—did you check them?"

Riordan hesitated. "Yeah," he said. "The cars are being checked."

"*Now?* It's—" Suddenly, Lassiter felt exhausted. A seam of fatigue opened in his mind as he tried to do the simple math. The 911 call had come in around midnight. And now it was two o'clock in the afternoon. So fourteen hours had passed, and from Riordan's look, no one had thought to go through the neighborhood, writing down license numbers. Unless "John Doe" was working alone, it was too late now.

"There's no clothes, either," Riordan said. "As I'm sure you were about to ask. They were full of blood, they had to cut them off the guy, and the nurses got rid of them. Biohazard. I tried to chase it down, but they're gone. The only thing we can do is wait till the doctors say I can talk to him. When that happens, I'll ask him the same questions you would, and then I'll take a set of prints. We'll run the prints, and if we're lucky, we'll find out who he is. So why don't you go home and let me do my job?"

"What's *that*?"

"*What*?"

"The thing you're hiding."

Riordan exhaled mightily, glanced at the ceiling, and stepped to the side so Lassiter could see what was on the desk: a nurse's medicine tray. There were two items in it, and one of them was a knife, about seven inches long. It was a big knife, a hunting knife, the kind you'd use to field-dress a deer. Lassiter looked closer. Actually . . . it was a military knife.

"K-Bar."

"What?"

"It's a K-Bar knife," Riordan said. "Ranger stuff. You see 'em at Quantico, Bragg—places like that."

"So maybe he's a soldier."

Riordan shrugged. "Maybe. But the important thing is: he brings this into the house with him. It's not like he breaks in, there's a struggle in the kitchen, someone grabs a knife. . . . This guy comes into the house with a combat knife—it isn't a bread knife, it's a *combat knife*—"

"So what you're saying: the murders were premeditated?"

"Yeah. He knew what he was doin'."

Lassiter looked more closely at the knife. There was a gummy, brownish substance where the blade fit into the haft. It looked like blood. And a few hairs clinging to it. Wispy, blond, very fine. Baby hair. Brandon's hair. And Tom Truong's voice in the back of his mind: *No blood left in little boy.*

The second item in the tray was a bottle, a small one about the size of a miniature liquor bottle. It was very unusual, made of heavy glass, and it looked antique. It closed with a dark metal cap, made in the shape of a crown, with a tiny cross at the very top. Inside the bottle was a half inch of clear liquid.

"The nurses and orderlies had their mitts all over these, of course," Riordan said. "Help me out, would you?" He handed Lassiter a small plastic bag with a printed label stuck to it:

JOHN DOE
MPD–3601
11–02–95

Lassiter held the bag open while Riordan used a pencil to tease the items into the bag without touching them.

"Where is he?"

Riordan didn't answer him. "When I get back, I'll tag these into evidence. We'll get whatever prints we can, cross-check 'em with the nurses' and orderlies', and run 'em through the Bureau. After that, I'll see what I can find out about the bottle. We'll get the liquid tested, and there'll be a full court press on whatever we got on the knife." He paused. "Look—for what it's worth—whoever this guy is, your sister took a swing at him. The examiner found some tissue, tissue and blood, under her nails—right hand. So I'll ask for DNA tests, and we'll do a comparison." He paused again. "Now, maybe you'd please go home."

Lassiter followed Riordan out the door. The detective carried the bag in front of him, pinching the top between his fingers. And then he stopped and put his free hand on Lassiter's arm. "You know—I shouldn't be talking to you like this. Letting you see the evidence. I mean . . ." Riordan looked at his feet. "What I'm saying is—*technically*, you're a suspect."

"Really."

"Really!"

"What are you talking about, Jim?"

Riordan shrugged. "What if your sister left you all her money? What if it turns out you hated her guts? I mean—you know?"

"That's bullshit."

"Sure it's bullshit," Riordan said stolidly. "I'm just saying how it *looks*. We get memos—you know? We have meetings. All the time. And one of the things they pound us about is 'the appearance of impropriety.' "

" 'Impropriety.' "

"No! The *appearance* of impropriety. It's different. No one has to do anything wrong. It just has to look wrong—like showing you this." Riordan nodded at the bag in his hand. "It could be misinterpreted."

Lassiter shook his head, but he didn't say anything. He was feeling too burnt out to be angry. Besides, Riordan didn't mean anything by it. And technically—he was right.

"Anyways," the detective said, starting to walk again, "you got people to call. Arrangements to make. The press is all over this thing, and once they find out it wasn't just a fire . . ." His voice trailed away.

Riordan's common sense was like a splash of cold water. Lassiter realized he'd been in a tunnel, his mind so caught up in trying to make sense of things, that he'd forgotten about the ordinary responsibilities of "calling kin." Suddenly, the practicalities of handling a death in the family flooded his head. Riordan was right. Of *course* he had calls to make. Kathy was his only sibling and their parents were dead, but there was Kathy's ex-husband, her friends, her coworkers down at the radio station. Aunt Lillian. And Brandon. Brandon didn't have a father, but there were *godparents*. There were so *many* people to call, so many people who shouldn't learn about this from television or a newspaper. The list grew in his mind as he stumbled along beside Riordan. *Arrangements.* He would have to put together some kind of service. Pick out caskets. Headstones. Cemetery plots.

There was so much to do, but he couldn't stop thinking about Brandon—the knife and the blood and the hair. Why would—how *could*—anyone cut the throat of a three-year-old kid?

"I'll speak to Tommy Truong," Riordan said. "I'll find out when the bodies can be released and—"

"What's his condition?" Lassiter asked.

"Who?"

Lassiter just looked at him.

"Oh—you mean, John Doe? He's serious, but stable. They say he's gonna live. You glad about that?"

"Yeah."

"Me, too."

Riordan watched Lassiter walk down the corridor until he turned the corner. Lassiter was a big guy, he thought, tall and wide-shouldered, athletic-looking. And *irritating*. Even today, even here, he walked as if he owned the place.

Riordan was thinking that maybe, because of his connection to Lassiter, he ought to take himself off the case. Shift it to someone else. But that was a chickenshit way of looking at things because, all modesty aside, he was the best fucking homicide detective on the force—and he just couldn't live with himself if he passed on a case because it might screw up a job opportunity.

Yeah, Lassiter was going to be a problem. No question about that. But he'd just have to treat Lassiter like anyone else, and if that blew his chances with the guy's company . . . well, that's the way it goes sometimes.

Not that the case was complicated. They had a suspect, and a murder weapon. And they'd get a lot more—Riordan was sure of that. Things tended to fill themselves in. People came forward. And even if they didn't, the Commonwealth's attorney would be filing charges any day. They didn't know the guy's name, and they didn't know his motive—but that didn't matter because they could prove what he'd *done*. The prisons might be filled with John Does who'd killed people for reasons no one could understand.

Besides, they might get lucky. Maybe Mr. Doe was a toon. Maybe a dog told him to do it. Maybe there was life insurance. An ex-husband. A boyfriend.

He hoped it would be something simple or Lassiter would be all over him—despite the little warning back there—urging him to do this, do that, check this out, run that down. No. It was worse than that. The way Riordan saw it, if *he* were Joe Lassiter, and he owned a big investigative agency, and it was *his* sister, and *his* nephew who'd been killed . . . he'd run his own investigation and throw every fucking thing he had at it. And the cop on the case, the selfsame Jimmy Riordan, would be tripping over Lassiter's tracks everywhere he went.

The guy had a dozen people he could put on the case—a couple of dozen! Guys who'd worked for the FBI, DEA, CIA, *Washington Post*—you name it, they had desks at Lassiter Associates. So he could put more people—and, let's face it, *better* people—on the case than the county could, that was for sure. And he had more money to spend, too. Which meant that Jimmy Riordan was going to end up talking to witnesses that Lassiter had already questioned. He'd make connections that Lassiter had made a few days before, and he'd follow leads that Lassiter had already run to ground—but which he would still have to pursue.

It made him tired just to think of it. And in fact he *was* tired. He'd been called in the middle of the night and had been going ever since—most of the time on his feet. And now his feet *hurt*. His adrenaline was spent, and there were cobwebs between his ears. He needed a cup of coffee, but first he should call the station.

Because Lassiter was right about one thing, and that was John Doe's car. He'd have a squad car cruise Keswick Lane and the surrounding streets, checking the license plates. They'd run the numbers through the DMV, and if they found a car that didn't belong in the neighborhood, they'd go door-to-door looking for the owner. If he wasn't around, they'd boot the car and go to the address where the vehicle was registered. If the owner wasn't *there*, they'd find out where he or she worked, check it out. Rentals? They'd boot those right on the spot.

Riordan made the call, then waited at the nurse's station for the supervisor to show up. Finally, he saw her, steaming down the hall, a huge woman with enormous breasts. The breasts made a kind of shelf on her chest, and her glasses, which hung from one of those little chain things, were perched on the shelf. He tried not to stare, but it was hard. (That was another memo. *Excessive visual contact is a form of sexual harassment.*) He wrote down her name, the date, and the time. He told her his own name and said that he was taking possession of John Doe's personal items. She made him sign something. He made her sign something.

He took the bag out to his car, locked it in the trunk, and returned to the hospital. He wanted to speak with the nurse who had removed the items from John Doe's pockets and put them in the bag. He wanted to dot all the *i*'s and cross all the *t*'s because, after O.J., you couldn't be too careful.

The E.R. nurse was on break, but he found her anyway, sitting in the cafeteria by the Bunn-O-Matic, reading a Harlequin romance. He only had a few questions for her, and after she'd answered them, he bought himself a cup of coffee and sat down with his notebook.

It was one of a hundred that he had, a new one for each major case, and each of them was identical. They were black, four by seven, six-ring notebooks with narrow-ruled paper inserts. On the first page of each of the books, Riordan had written the victim's name, the case number, and the number of the statute that had been violated. The handwriting was meticulous—elegant, even. (Say what you want about Jimmy Riordan, Riordan thought, the man's *penmanship* will not quit! Thank you, Sister Theresa!)

There wasn't much in this particular notebook, though Riordan knew that eventually it would be filled. And like the others, once the details were recorded on official department forms, it would take its place on the bookshelf in the little room that he used as an office in his home. Riordan sipped his coffee and thought about the case. John Doe. The only thing he knew about the man, apart from what he'd done, was that one of the residents said he'd been mumbling in Italian.

That could be interesting. Then again, that could be a problem. Riordan stirred a packet of creamer into his coffee, barely changing the color. Maybe John Doe was *Gianni* Doe. Riordan hoped not. He'd had some cases where foreign nationals were involved, and because Fairfax was so close to Washington, the embassies sometimes got in on things. And they weren't helpful.

Besides, Riordan thought, what if this guy's a *real* foreigner? What if he works for an embassy? What if he's got diplomatic immunity?

He took another sip of coffee.

The second sip was never as good as the first.

Joe Lassiter hadn't left the hospital. He was two floors above the cafeteria, following a painted green line that zigzagged down the floor of one corridor and up another. There were arrangements that he had to make, lots of them, but before he did any of that, he wanted to see the man who'd butchered Kathy and Brandon. An orderly said that the green line would take him to the burn ward, and so he was following it.

Unless you were color-blind, colors were a surrogate for literacy. You didn't need to speak English to follow a painted line. You didn't even need to be sane. You could be sick, stoned, flipped-out, or monolingual in Tagalog, and the colors would take you where you wanted to go.

Lassiter had been to the CIA once or twice and they had the same system there, although the purpose was different. Everyone in headquarters had a laminated tag pinned to his suit jacket. The tag read VISITOR, STAFF, or SECURITY, and it came with a colored stripe that didn't tell you where to go, but determined where you couldn't. If you were walking down a corridor with a red line down the middle, and you had a green stripe on your tag, everyone knew you were out of place. *Excuse me! You sure you belong here?*

He went through a pair of double doors, keeping his eye on the floor, following the green line single-mindedly. Like a preschooler. Like *Brandon.* An image of the boy came into Lassiter's mind: the intensity of the kid's concentration when he wrote his name in what were, after all, huge, shaky crayon letters. And another image: Brandon, sleeping, a smile on his face, and his throat slit like a slaughtered animal.

And Kathy. And Tom Truong's voice in his head: . . . *little cuts on both her hands . . . These are the definite defensive wounds, you know . . .*

Kathy. In the dark. Asleep. Hearing something. Not knowing what was happening. A knife slashing down, her hands coming forward in a blind reflex . . .

He walked past a nurse's station, but nobody seemed to notice him. He wasn't sure what he was going to do when he got to the end of the green line. Maybe just look at the guy.

And then—he was there. There wasn't much to see. John Doe was visible through a large rectangular window—at least, he assumed it was Doe: he was the only patient that Lassiter could see, so he figured it must be him. He was hooked up to all kinds of tubes, and the parts of him that were not wrapped in white bandages—and this included most of his head—were smeared with a thick white ointment. Lassiter had burned his hand once, and the name of the white stuff popped into his mind. Silvadene.

As far as Lassiter could tell, nobody had seen the guy before his face went up in flames. So he was really and truly a John Doe. No name. No description. No description *possible.* Who was he? Why did he do it? What was he thinking about right now?

Was he even conscious? Lassiter couldn't tell. But if he was, maybe he could answer a couple of questions. Simple questions. Lassiter was reaching for the doorknob when a man dressed in a paper gown leaned out from behind a privacy screen and, with an angry yelp, charged into the corridor.

The doctor jerked his mask down. He had bright little eyes and an overbite that reminded Lassiter of a chipmunk. "Didn't I make myself clear? I *told* you people! This is a sterile environment." Lassiter didn't say anything, and he didn't back away. He just looked at him, and the look was so devoid of interest that the chipmunk faltered a little before he went on. "*No one* is authorized to enter this ward."

The chipmunk obviously thought he was with the police, and Lassiter saw no reason to set him straight. "Mr. Doe is a suspect in a double homicide," he said. "I'd like to talk to him as soon as possible."

"At the moment," the chipmunk said in a patronizing voice, "my *patient* is heavily sedated and extremely vulnerable to infection. *I* will let *you* know when it's appropriate to interview him."

Lassiter nodded. "Thanks for your help."

"And he won't be doing any talking for a while, in any case."

"Really? And why's that?"

The chipmunk smiled and poked a finger at his own throat. "I told you guys. Trach tube."

"What's that?"

"It means that he can't talk."

Lassiter looked at Doe through the glass, and then back at the doctor. "For how long?"

The chipmunk shrugged. "Look, Detective," he said in an exasperated tone, "all you really have to do is wait, right? He'll have a little scarring, maybe a lot—the left side of his face, the neck, the chest—but he's going to make it. And in the meantime—he's not going anywhere. We'll keep you informed about his status."

"You do that," Lassiter said. He walked away.

That evening, Lassiter stretched out on the couch and flicked on the TV. He must have made forty calls. Half the people he called already knew about it and they pressed him for details. After a while the sheer number of times he recited the facts had the effect of detaching him from what he was saying. His voice rattled on with the neutral composure of a newscaster's, as if he were reporting on crop failures in Idaho.

The other half of the calls were much worse—when they didn't know. They were ambushed by the news, a bombshell in an ordinary day. And however they reacted, he felt battered by their raw emotion.

He bounced from channel to channel but it was impossible to actually watch anything. He was too restless; he couldn't shake the feeling that he'd forgotten to do something important. He got a beer and went up the spiral staircase and out onto the deck on the third floor. The house was perched on the side of a hill, and up here he was in the treetops. He leaned against the railing and looked through the black branches at the pale, occluded sky. There were no stars.

He could hear the phone ringing. At first he decided not to answer it, and then he changed his mind.

"Hello."

Riordan's voice leaped through the telephone. " 'Hello?' Is that what you say? *Hello?* Well, fuck you!"

Lassiter looked at the telephone. "What?"

"What *what*? What the fuck were you doing on the burn ward?"

"Is that what this is all about?"

"I'll tell you what this is all about: John Doe pulled the fucking tube out of his throat."

"He did *what*?"

"He tried to kill himself. The doctors tell me he's so doped up he can't count to fucking one, and yet he pulls out his trach tube. His hand is still curled around the thing when they find him. They have to *pry* his fingers off."

Lassiter felt a sudden rush of fear, a plume of sensation in his chest. He didn't want John Doe to die. He had a lot of questions, and Doe was the guy with all the answers. Also, John Doe was the one who was going to pay, the focus of his vengeance. "Is he all right? Is he going—"

"Yeah, yeah, he'll pull through all right and he didn't short circuit his brain neither. But what I want to get back to is *you*! What the fuck was on your mind? I got this new partner, you know? Junior G-man type. He's always got an idea, and *this* time he's thinking out loud, maybe John Doe didn't try to off himself. Under the circumstances, the guy being so doped up and all—maybe he had some help."

"*What?* Was anybody—"

Riordan interrupted. "And then Dr. Whozee says something about the 'other detective' who stopped by the burn ward. And Junior G-man says, 'What other detective?' And it doesn't sound like any of our guys. In fact, it sounds just like you."

Lassiter admitted it. "I wanted to look at him."

Riordan barked a nasty laugh. "Right. You're window shopping. Well, that wasn't very smart."

"I didn't even get in the door. The doctor kicked me out."

"So I heard."

"Well, you heard right. When did this happen, anyway? The thing with the tube?"

Riordan ignored him. "You tell me. Where'd you go?"

"Wait a minute. You think I was *in there*? You think I put the guy's hands around the tube? You're asking me for an *alibi*?" He nearly hung up. He was innocent of what Riordan was tossing around, and he felt the bruised outrage of the falsely accused. "I came home," he said. "And I've been on the telephone ever since I got here."

"Well, we can check on that," Riordan said.

"Go ahead."

"Thanks to you, I *have* to," Riordan said. "Look, let me tell you something. I don't think you went in there, okay? I think this guy tried to off himself. That's what went down. The doctors are checking him every ten minutes, there's another little kid on the ward, there's a nurse's station tucked back in there, there's people all over the place, there's no *way*. But you—you're a fucking loose cannon. You go down there, you pretend you're a detective—"

"I never said I was a detective. The doctor just—"

Riordan ignored him. "First of all, I get my ass called on the carpet for not posting a guard on Doe—which I already put in the request for, you know, but the uniform just takes his time getting to the hospital. And now I got to waste my time, checking your fucking phone records. And if I *don't* check, it looks funny because everybody knows I know you. And another thing—I don't think you were just window shopping, either. I bet you had some half-assed idea you were going to talk to the guy."

Lassiter took a deep breath and exhaled.

"And that would've been just terrific," Riordan said. "Suppose you get your wish and you have a heart-to-heart with the guy and he spills his guts. What about when this guy comes to trial? You know what a defense attorney would do with that?"

"Why would he try to kill himself?"

Riordan sighed. "Maybe he was overcome with remorse," he said in a played-out voice.

"I wonder—"

"Do me a favor," Riordan interrupted. "Don't wonder. Don't do anything. Help me solve the case: stay the fuck out of it."

Riordan's anger was jump-starting a headache behind Lassiter's eyes. "I'll stay out of it," he said, "as soon as you tell me who killed my sister—"

"John Fucking Doe killed your sister."

"And who he is. And why."

9

It was warm for November, nearly eighty degrees on the day of the funeral. The falling leaves, bright as jewels, spun in the air on a sultry, almost tropical breeze. It was the beginning of winter, but the weather was as balmy as June. This made the brilliant foliage seem out of place, even artificial. Those who came to the funeral from out of town had expected cooler weather, and now they were sweaty and uncomfortable in their cashmeres and tweeds, corduroys and woolens. Even Lassiter was feeling a little woozy. The improbable warmth, the uncomfortable mourners, the twisting leaves—it was as if they were on location, filming a movie, and the movie was being shot out of sequence, and in the wrong season.

He couldn't shake this feeling of unreality. Even the caskets were like stage props, the smaller one pointedly tiny, as if to dramatize the cruelty of what had happened. The minister—from the Unitarian church Kathy had started to attend in the last year—might as well have been cast to play the role. He had precisely the right earnest demeanor, the ability to lock eyes and clasp hands with meaningful emotion.

But it wasn't real emotion, or if it was, it wasn't specific to Kathy: the minister had compassion for everyone—he was steeped in the stuff—which made his grief easy and generic. Not that Lassiter minded, particularly: the church was a large one, and the minister didn't really know his sister. On the telephone, when they arranged the memorial service and the funeral, the clergyman had asked for help in "personalizing the ceremony." He wanted to know how "the deceased was referred to." Was it Kathleen? Or was it Kate, or Kath, or Kathy? He wanted an anecdote or two, something to remind her family and friends of the "living woman."

Now, at the graveside, the minister was saying something dull and predictably uplifting. It was about the boundless terrain Kathy and Brandon inhabited now, about the infinite range of the spirit. At least it sounded dull to Lassiter, the words slotting into the expected space in the ceremony. But his aunt Lillian—the only other relative in attendance—must have been getting something out of it because she leaned toward him and gave his hand a fervent squeeze.

In some ways, he realized, this strangely artificial feeling had been with him ever since he learned of Kathy's death. At first he thought it was a normal reaction to sudden death, a kind of shock. But standing there in the cemetery, he could see that his sense of unreality was so pervasive because, like most people, he'd attended far more cinematic funerals than real ones. And he was waiting for the telltale close-up. Or the slow pan to the grassy knoll, where a mysterious onlooker stood, silhouetted against the sun. A lover paying respects from a safe distance. Or a killer, relishing the calamity that he'd wrought.

Lassiter was waiting for something, music or a camera angle, to put the event in perspective.

But it never happened. That, in the end, was what made it all so unreal. Something was missing—a reason for the deaths that were being mourned. Kathy and Brandon were hardly the victims of random violence—the murders were obviously premeditated—and yet . . . nothing. The police didn't even have a theory. And the man with the answers had taken a turn for the worse. He was unconscious, in critical condition, his damaged lungs infected, his skin suppurating. It might be weeks, Lassiter had been told, before he could be questioned.

The people at the graveside had a subdued and weary look. They'd been flattened by the sudden and brutal death of someone they cared about. For Brandon, there was shocked sadness from the parents of half-a-dozen preschool friends. His teacher, a woman with long brown hair pinned back from her face, wiped her eyes. Her lower lip trembled. Nearby, a little boy stood hand in hand with his mother, a woman in sunglasses and a veiled hat.

To mourn Kathy, there were a few coworkers from National Public Radio, where she worked as a producer. A couple of neighbors. A roommate from Sweet Briar who'd driven four hundred miles in deference to twenty years of Christmas and birthday cards. And Murray—the indefatigable, great-hearted Murray—Kathy's ex-husband. But no close friends, really, because Kathy *had* no close friends.

For the family, there was only himself and Aunt Lillian. The small family showing, however, was not due to Kathy's somewhat reclusive and difficult character. He realized with a start that he and Lillian—his father's seventy-six-year-old sister—were all that remained of two family trees dwindling into deadwood.

Murray was the only one who actually wept. And like the minister, his grief was not really specific to the woman in the casket. Murray was the kind of guy who might get choked up over replacing a favorite couch. Even so, Lassiter was grateful. The uninhibited display of sorrow seemed a tribute to his sister, better than the largest bouquet.

The minister finally stopped talking, finishing with a verbal flourish about beacons in the wilderness. Lassiter threw a handful of dirt on each coffin, and a white rose for Kathy. And then he turned away.

Others followed his example, and he stood ten yards away, up the path, and each of the mourners came up to squeeze his hand or kiss his cheek, and say how sorry they were.

One of the first was the woman with the little boy, who introduced herself as Marie Sanders. "And this is Jesse," she said proudly. Lassiter smiled at the boy and wondered if he was her son; they didn't look anything alike. He had a dark complexion, with bottomless brown eyes and jet-black hair that crowded his forehead with curls. He was beautiful, and so was she, but not in the same way. She was pale, blond, and . . . somehow familiar.

"Do I know you?" he asked.

She didn't seem surprised by the question, but shook her head. "I don't think so," she said.

"It's just that . . . I thought we might have met."

She smiled nervously. "I just wanted to say how sorry I am. Kathy—" She looked down and shook her head. "I saw it on the news."

"I'm sorry. I tried to call her friends—"

"Oh no—please. I didn't know her that well. It was so unlikely, you know, that I would even learn of her death."

"But you said—"

"I don't live here," she said hurriedly. "We were traveling. It was a satellite television and one of the network feeds was from Washington." She stopped talking and bit her lip. "I'm sorry. I'm babbling."

"Not at all."

"I met your sister . . . in Europe, and I liked her *so much*. We had a lot in common. So when I saw her picture and Brandon's on the television . . ." Her voice got shaky, and through the veil he could see that her eyes had filled with tears. "Anyway, something compelled me to come." She took a shaky breath and then recovered her composure. "And I'm sorry," she said. "I'm so sorry for your loss."

"Thank you," Lassiter said. "Thank you for coming."

And then she was gone, and Murray was standing in front of him with tears rolling down his cheeks. "It's so hard," he said, putting his arms around Lassiter. "I'm telling you, Joe, it's so fucking *hard*."

Lassiter himself did not remember how to cry, but his throat ached with the sadness that he felt. He was losing someone who knew him in a way that no one else ever would, someone who shared his childhood. He was losing the "Alliance," the solemn word Kathy had invented for their partnership as children, a kind of mutual protection society against their parents.

Her earnest little face came back to him. In their playroom in Washington, inside a kind of tent that Kathy had built with blankets and bedsheets. He might have been five, Kathy ten. "We have to stick together," she said, "you and me. I've decided we have to form an alliance." It was years before the word was really part of his vocabulary, but he knew what she meant. Kathy had a list of written vows spelling out their responsibilities, which she read to him. *Number 1: Never tell on a member of the Alliance.* They pricked their fingers and dripped blood on the paper and then buried it under the spruce tree. Even as adults they kept the habit of signing letters and cards to each other with Kathy's invented symbol, the sideways A.

Their father, Elias, had been a congressman for more than twenty years. Whenever his name appeared in the papers, which was often, it was followed by a short parenthesis: (R-Ky.). The money that propelled Eli into office belonged to his wife, Josie. Her grandfather had made a fortune in whiskey, and enough of it had trickled down through the generations to make Josie, an only child, quite a catch for the ambitious young man from the wrong part of Louisville.

Neither Eli nor Josie took more than a supervisory interest in their children. Like most people in Congress, they bounced back and forth between Washington and their home state, with the result that Kathy and Joe were raised not so much by Mom and Dad, but by a string of nannies, au pairs, baby-sitters, and later, "assistants."

Joe himself had never given much thought to the gulf that existed between himself and his parents. He was afraid of his father's cruel temper and saw little of his mother. That was just the way it was. He'd attended an expensive private school in Washington, and many of his friends were in much the same boat. But it had bothered Kathy, or it did until she reached the point where she just didn't care anymore.

He knew that because once, when he'd been summoned from the kitchen with a drink for Josie, he walked in on a confrontation between his sister and his mother. Kathy had a fierce look on her face and was saying, "You don't really care about us at all. You just wanted children so you'd have some to put on your Christmas card."

Josie, seated at her vanity, took a sip of her drink. She angled her head and attached an earring. "Why, sweetheart," she said, never actually taking her eyes off her reflection, "that's not *true*. You're very special to me." He could still hear his mother's sugary voice. *Ver*-rah *speh*-shul. Having reassured her daughter, Josie stood, lifted a crystal atomizer, sprayed the air, and then walked through the cloud of scent. "Now give Mummy a kiss," she said. "I'm runnin' late."

Eli handled his parental responsibilities as obligations. He actually penciled his children into his busy days, a fact revealed to Joe by his sister. One night at their house in Washington, she took him into Eli's study and showed him the leather-bound appointment book, where they could find their own place in the congressman's busy schedule.

7:00—Prayer Breakfast with Young Republicans
8:30—RNC Headquarters: Republican Steering Committee
10:15—*Children to Zoo*

Virtually every contact between Eli and his children, at least during the time they were in D.C., was planned in advance.

Take Joe to Camillo's: haircut.

Speak to Kathy re Dreams versus Plans.

They took to scanning the appointment book to see what was in store for them, and feigned illness or made other plans to avoid those functions at which they were to be dragged along as window dressing. They covered for each other; they lied for each other; they presented a united front.

Fund-raiser for Senator Walling. Bring Family. ("Mom! *Mom!*—Kathy's throwing up and . . . I don't feel so good, either.")

—

There was a luncheon after the ceremony. He found himself wanting to talk about his childhood with Kathy. About the Alliance. He looked around for Murray and for the beautiful woman with the little boy. What was her name? Marie. Despite what she'd said, he couldn't shake the feeling that he'd met her before, that he somehow *knew* her. Maybe he was just drawn to her because, apart from Murray, she seemed to be the only other one at the service to take Kathy's death as a personal loss. Eventually he found Murray, or Murray found him. But the woman and the little boy were nowhere to be seen.

When the lunch ended, he drove Aunt Lillian to Dulles. He took the toll road back, and when he arrived at his house, it was almost dark. Normally, he looked forward to the long, curving driveway, the crunch of the pebbles under his wheels, the corduroy rhythm of the car crossing the wooden bridge over the stream. It was the reason he'd built the house, in a way. Most of the time, he thought about work, about plans and meetings and tactical decisions—until he crossed the stream. And then it all fell away.

The lines of the house, rising out of the trees, thrilled him. There wasn't another building like it in the Washington area, in part because the architect was Dutch, and in part because he was a crank. Or a genius. Or a little of both. In any case, an Anthroposophist, and therefore an enemy—on principle—of the right angle. The result was a million-dollar house that amounted to a cluster of sinuous curves, unlikely angles, and large, unexpected volumes.

Those who saw the place had one of two reactions. Some gasped with delight, while others bit their lower lips and nodded wisely, as if to say, "This is what too much money does to people who ought to know better." Lassiter liked to think that he could judge people by their reactions to the house, but the truth was, he couldn't. Some of those whom he liked the most—Kathy, for instance—just shook their heads when they saw it, or smiled politely.

But most people came around when they stepped inside. The house was filled with light that poured through the glass ceiling of a barrel-vaulted atrium running north to south. The rooms were all oversized and flowed, one into another, in an almost seamless way. Black-and-white photos of old New York, and carefully framed drawings of the Yellow Kid, Krazy Kat, and Little Nemo, hung from the walls. There wasn't a lot of furniture: a few big pieces, draped in slip-covers, and a grand piano that Lassiter was using to teach himself to play.

Coming home was the day's reward, but this time the cool white walls and soaring spaces failed to lift his spirits. Instead the house seemed empty and cold, more a fortress than a refuge.

He poured himself a tumbler of Laphroaig and went into his favorite room, the study. Three of the oddly angled walls were lined, floor to ceiling, with bookcases; library ladders rolled on rails. In a corner of the room, a few feet above the floor, was an adobe-style fireplace with logs and kindling stashed underneath. Even though it was warm, he made a fire, and sat there for twenty minutes, drinking scotch and watching the flames snap at the wood.

Finally, he punched the Play button on the answering machine. There were seventeen messages. He turned up the volume on the speaker-phone and wandered outside to listen to them, standing on the deck next to the rail, watching the birch trees thrash in the wind. The air was fresher now, and he could feel the rain behind it, maybe an hour away.

There were a couple of business calls. A hostile takeover was in the works at TriCom, and a lawyer from Lehman Brothers wanted to meet with him. Another call reported "a cock-up" in London. One of his investigators had been "overzealous" (whatever that meant) and the BBC was interested.

Most of the rest were condolence calls from friends and acquaintances who hadn't known Kathy and so hadn't been at the service. There was a call from one of the television stations. Another from the *Post.* And then Monica's throaty voice, telling him how sorry she was, saying that if there was anything, anything *at all* . . .well, her number was the same.

Lassiter thought about it—thought about calling her, thought about the way they'd broken up. Thought: *What is it with me, anyway?*

And the answer came back: *It's the usual thing.*

Or more accurately, it was *becoming* the usual thing. He'd find a woman he really liked, they'd stay together for a year or so—and then it would stall. There'd be an ultimatum, an "extension," *another* extension, and then . . . Monica would give way to Claire—or whomever. In fact, it *was* Claire, although at the moment she happened to be in Singapore for a conference. She'd called two nights earlier, and he told her about Kathy's death. But Claire had never met Kathy, and when she said something about coming back for the funeral, he'd politely refused an offer that was meant to be refused.

He sipped the last of the whiskey in his glass. The truth was, he enjoyed the company of women, one at a time. Monogamy, or at least *serial* monogamy, came naturally to him, and so, also, should marriage. But marriage was something he was determined to get right the first time, and he was romantic enough to think that when the time was right, he'd know it. There wouldn't be any doubt. It would seem the most important thing in the world—whereas with Monica marriage seemed like . . . well, like an option.

The last message was from Riordan, and he listened to it without paying attention. When it was done, he realized that he hadn't heard a word. Rewinding the tape, he pressed Play for the second time.

Riordan was one of those men who was uncomfortable talking to machines. He spoke too fast and much too loud. "Sorry if I was too rough on you," he said, in a voice that didn't sound sorry at all. "Stop by tomorrow, okay? I wanta ask you a coupla questions."

10

Riordan's office was off Route 29, on the third floor of one of those ugly boxes that municipal governments built in the 1950s. The exterior walls were a parade of alternating panels, blue plastic and glass, separated by aluminum strips that had long ago begun to pit. It was at once a modern building, in the sense that it was relatively new, and a dated one, in that it looked far shabbier than the more graceful, nineteenth-century buildings nearby.

It was no better inside. The acoustic tiles on the ceiling were sagging and stained. The linoleum floor was embedded with decades of grime entombed in thousands of layers of floor wax. The stairwells reminded Lassiter of junior high school, and as he mounted their steps, a whiff of sour milk came to him, though he couldn't be sure if it was real or imaginary.

The second floor was reserved for narcotics investigations, and a sign near the stairwell gave a warning:

UNDERCOVER UNITS
ABSOLUTELY NO SUSPECTS
ON THIS FLOOR

Lassiter found the homicide unit on the third floor. There were a couple of self-contained offices, some empty rooms that he assumed were used for interrogation, and a warren of pressed-board cubicles with head-high partitions. It was messy and chaotic and, like a newsroom, everyone seemed to be sitting in front of a computer, typing, or (like Riordan) hunched over a telephone, talking.

Riordan was in his mid-fifties, and had that kind of Irish skin that doesn't so much age as weather. His face and hands were permanently red, but the skin on his body would be milk-white. When he saw Lassiter, his pale blue eyes widened in silent greeting. He looked tired. He bounced his eyebrows, held one finger up and gestured to a chair.

The room was stifling, the heating system geared to the calendar and not the thermometer. All of the detectives were stripped to their shirtsleeves, and Lassiter saw that without exception every one of them was wearing a gun. Shoulder rigs, mainly, and the odd holster in the small of the back. Cops, of course, were used to the constant presence of weaponry, but it was something Lassiter always noticed in a police station: everybody was armed.

It was one of the things that made ex-cops almost unemployable, at least as far as Lassiter Associates was concerned. It wasn't just that they couldn't write. They were conspicuous, even in conversation, driving "vehicles" instead of cars—and they never went anywhere: they "responded to" places. Beyond that, they had a stance, a way of holding themselves that had everything to do with wearing a badge and carrying a gun. Virtually all cops spent some time in uniform and so, like actors and politicians, they expected people to react to them. It didn't matter much if the reaction was negative—so long as it was there. In Lassiter's experience, the syndrome persisted long after they'd left the police force.

Riordan hung up and swiveled toward him. He clapped his big red hands together. "The car," he said. "I thought you'd like to know that we found a rental car on your sister's block and we've traced it."

Lassiter inclined his head but said nothing. He could tell just from the way the detective was talking, so matter-of-factly, that although Riordan had been pissed off about his ill-advised trip to the burn ward, he didn't carry a grudge. That was over.

"Hertz. Right out of Dulles. No question that it's John Doe's car. The trunk stinks. Kerosene, probably. And no one's said squat about the boot we put on it." Riordan paused.

"And?"

The detective shrugged. "Well, the guy used a credit card. Juan Gutierrez. The card is registered to an address in Brookville, Florida. I had the locals take a look. Place is a rooming house, mail gets dumped on a table. There *was* a guy, called himself Juan, had a room there— two, three months ago. Wasn't home much. Wasn't hardly there."

Riordan's phone rang and he picked it up. Lassiter listened for a bit, long enough to tell that the conversation had nothing to do with him, and then he looked at the walls of Riordan's cubicle. They were decorated, if that was the word, with children's drawings. The William Tyler Elementary School. Crudely drawn figures with realistically detailed guns. The bullets came out, evenly spaced, in straight lines — like perforations. Heavy strokes of red crayon marked the sites of the wounds, and in some cases blood flowed in careful, individual drops. Somehow the crayon blood seemed more brutal and visceral than the luxuriant gore of filmed special effects.

Riordan hung up. "Where was I?"

"Juan Gutierrez."

"Oh yeah. From what we got, the place in Brookville was just a mail drop. But we're not done yet. We found a card key in the ashtray of the rental vehicle. Anyway, it takes some footwork. But we run it down and — bibbity-bobbity-boo — it's a Comfort Inn, off 395. Juan Gutierrez — number 214. So we get a warrant. And, in the room, there's an overnight bag, a map of Fairfax County, and a wallet."

"A wallet."

"The wallet holds almost two thousand dollars in cash, a driver's license, a library card, a social security card, and a couple of Visa cards — and all of it's in the name of Juan Gutierrez, Brookville, Florida. So we run some checks, and it comes back that, uh . . . Mr. Gutierrez probably isn't Mr. Gutierrez."

"What do you mean?"

"There's no history on the guy. Everything starts two, three months ago, like he was born at the age of forty-three. He has a library card, issued in August. But he's never taken out a book. He got a driver's license — early September — but he never had a driver's license before. Not so far as we can tell. He never bought a car. He never had a ticket. And his Visa cards are both 'secured' — you know, the kind bankrupts and bad credit risks get."

"Where you give the bank the money up front."

"Right. And he's got a two-thousand-dollar line of credit on each one. He had them since —"

"September."

"You got it. And he used them. There's only been time for one full billing cycle, but on both of 'em he brought the balance back up, pronto. In the return mail, paid by money order, very prompt."

"So he's a ghost." It was a word they used in the investigative business for someone living under a false identity.

"He's a ghost *plus*."

"What do you mean?"

"He didn't rip off this ID, and he didn't just buy it. It looks like he built it up from scratch. And the social security number—it's a *real* number and it belongs to a *real* Juan Gutierrez who lives in Tampa. *That* Juan Gutierrez doesn't drive, he's about the same age as John Doe. If you ran the number, you'd assume they were the same guy."

"So you're saying John Doe went to a lot of trouble."

"Fuckin' A Right. This is damn good ID. Cop stops him, no problem. He wants to rent a car—step right up! He wants to fly somewhere, but he doesn't want to pay cash—because cash is conspicuous?—he's got his Visa cards. He can go to the moon, no one's gonna notice. Now, I'm not saying it's *bulletproof*, because it ain't. But if this guy isn't in custody, if he isn't a suspect in a felony—make that a *major* felony—he's solid. It's good enough that it makes you wonder."

"Wonder what?"

Riordan gave him a look. "If he's a pro. Which brings me to the reason I asked you to come by." Riordan leaned back in his chair. "I think it's time we talked some more about your sister."

Lassiter grimaced. "Why? There's nothing to know."

"I beg to differ."

"You 'beg to differ.' Look—there's nothing in Kathy's life that's going to tell you why someone with the work habits of a professional hit man would cut her throat, burn down the house, kill her kid—"

"Actually," Riordan said, "he didn't cut her throat. He cut Brandon's throat. Your sister was stabbed in the chest."

Lassiter started to say something but gave up.

Riordan cleared his throat, and when he spoke again, his voice had a wounded tone and there was a funny look in his eyes. Lassiter suddenly got a glimpse of what Riordan had looked like as a kid. A kid who'd been unfairly reprimanded. "Look at it my way, Joe. Here I am—I'm pushing this thing for you, I'm busting my ass—"

"Pushing it for *me*? It's a double homicide!"

"For your information, we've got fifty-seven *un*solved homicides on the books. I'm throwing resources at one of them that's all but solved, you understand me? For your information, I talked to Dr. Whozee this morning, and John Doe is not doing so well. His lungs are fucked up. I'm not saying he isn't gonna make it, but the way some people around here see it, I'm blowing time and money on a case that could solve itself any time now."

"You mean if he dies, the case is *solved*?!"

"Yeah, that's exactly what I mean. Once the forensic evidence is conclusive, it's *solved*. If his prints match the prints on the knife—if the DNA tests come back positive—if we can prove that Suspect A committed crime X—" His hands flew up and out to the sides. "—we call that case *solved*. And if Suspect A is also *dead*, that's about as solved as anything ever gets."

Lassiter looked at him. "But we wouldn't know *why*."

Riordan opened and closed his hands a couple of times, making fists and then splaying his fingers. "Why, why—what if there *is* no why? What if a cockroach told him to do it? What if he was stoned and it seemed like a good idea?"

"Except it doesn't look like that, does it?"

"No," Riordan said, "it does not. Not with that ID." He paused, and then went on: "But here's the point: while John Doe is still hanging on, and I'm in a position to look into this thing, I don't expect you to flip every time I ask you a few questions about your sister."

"You're right. And I'm sorry."

Riordan looked mollified. He squeezed off a little smile. "So—tell me about her."

Lassiter shrugged. He felt suddenly tired. "She listened to 'Prairie Home Companion.'"

Riordan scribbled away. "What's that?"

Lassiter sighed. "It's a radio show from Minnesota." Riordan gave him a look. "What I mean by that is—what can I tell you? My sister led an ordinary life. She was a producer at NPR. She worked hard. Her life revolved completely around her work and the kid. Her social life consisted of going to potluck dinners for the nursery school and a Unitarian church group for single parents. Mostly, she kept to herself. She had no enemies."

"Excuse me—you would know?"

He thought about it. He didn't believe Kathy kept much of anything secret from him, but it was impossible to be sure. "We were pretty close. When our parents died, Kathy was twenty, I was fifteen."

"Oh yeah. The congressman. I remember that. Plane crash."

"Helicopter."

"A tragedy," Riordan said in an automatic voice. "So is that where your sister got her money? I wondered how she could afford that fancy house."

"My father managed to run through most of my mother's dough, but we both inherited a couple of hundred grand. Kathy was pretty frugal. Smart investor. When she had Brandon, she sold the town house and moved to the burbs."

"Who'd she leave her money to? I mean, if you don't mind." Riordan rolled his hands through the air. "We didn't get to that yet."

Lassiter was Kathy's executor, as Riordan either knew or guessed. He shook his head. "I could show you the will, but there's nothing there. She left everything to Brandon. If he predeceased her, or they died together, it would all go to charity."

Riordan was scribbling notes. "Which charity?"

"Valley Drive Preschool. Sweet Briar—that was her college. Greenpeace."

"Nothing to you?"

"Just—some personal stuff. Family photos. Like that. Nothing that survived the fire."

Riordan looked disappointed. "What about guys? She got any guys in her life?"

"Not for a couple of years."

"What about the kid? Was she gettin' child support?"

"No."

"Why not?"

"There's no father."

Riordan blinked. "So . . . what? He's dead?"

"No."

Riordan chuckled like a kid. "You tell me how that one worked—and you can go."

"Her 'clock was ticking.' Her words. And since there wasn't a guy in the picture—well, she said she didn't need one."

In fact, Kathy hadn't put it quite so blandly. The day she told him about her intention to pursue motherhood was her birthday. Number thirty-seven. He'd taken her to dinner at the Inn at Little Washington, booked rooms for the night, and there'd been a certain amount of drinking. Kathy didn't drink much, as a rule, but that night, after a glass of sherry, some Dom Pérignon, and an Armagnac, the effects were obvious. She sat across from him with a secret little smile on her face, running the tines of her fork around in the raspberry sauce that was all that remained of her *coeur de crème*. Suddenly, she tossed her head and looked up at him. She took a last sip of liqueur and set it down. "There'll be no more of *that* for a while."

Lassiter was puzzled. Alcohol had never been one of Kathy's problems. "Health kick?"

"In a way." She ran her finger dreamily around the rim of the glass until it produced a sudden loud, ringing tone; she withdrew the finger and giggled. "What if I told you I'm planning to get pregnant?" she said. Her face was flushed rosy.

He hesitated. What he didn't want to say was anything about her past failure to get pregnant, even when she and Murray were "trying." Or her teenage bout with anorexia, when she'd dwindled to seventy pounds and, according to doctors at the time, might have permanently damaged her reproductive system. "I'd say who's the lucky guy? And then I'd ask why half of the Alliance has been kept in the dark about him."

Across from him, Kathy licked the tines of her fork. Her eyes flashed. "What if I told you there is no guy?"

"I'd say the plan was flawed."

Kathy giggled, and careened on. "Not that it's any problem getting fucked, of course—but, 'without protection'? These days? And at the right time? And then if you *do* manage it, maybe the guy comes after you, maybe he sues for joint custody—maybe he wants to move *in*. Trust me, guys can be a big complication. But, luckily, this is the nineties. There are more efficient ways to get knocked up."

"Wait. You're telling me—"

She nodded. "Uh-huh. I have an appointment tomorrow." She smiled. "This one's just to talk—actually, to be 'counseled' about the procedure."

At the time, Lassiter hadn't approved of Kathy's sudden enthusiasm for motherhood, although he tried not to show it. She was so impatient, so antisocial. He couldn't imagine her as a mother. But in the end her instincts had been right. All the trouble—and it took almost four years and a string of expensive and wrenching disappointments—had been worth it. Motherhood transformed her, lifted her free from the guarded and defensive self-involvement that had defined her since childhood. He didn't think it was Brandon's total and unqualified love for his mother that accomplished this. It was more that Kathy fell in love, for the first time—with her son.

—

Across from him, Riordan actually blushed. He was shocked. "Your sister went to . . . one of those places? A clinic? She had, what—artificial insemination?" Disapproval squeezed his features into a knot and he shook his head. Then he took a sneaky look around and leaned closer to Lassiter. "You know, we don't watch out, women are going to take over. No, no, you're smiling, but I'm serious. We'll be like the fucking bees."

Lassiter realized he must have had a surprised look on his face, because Riordan felt compelled to explain.

"Drones." He nodded his head decisively. "Bees can't get along without them, but what do they get? I'll tell ya what they get—winter comes and they get tossed right out of the fucking hive—freeze their asses off." Riordan paused, and nodded sagely to himself. "This seriously could happen to the human race." Another expression came sweeping over his big face, a quick worried look, as if he might have said too much. "Nothing against your sister," he mumbled. And then a big sigh passed through him, a cascade of weariness that ended when his chair scraped back over the floor. He stood up and stuck out his hand. "Thanks for coming in."

"Hey. I appreciate the effort." They shook. "Sorry if I was—"

"Nah—forget it." Riordan looked distracted. "Not that you were a lotta help. I mean your sister—" His big head seesawed sadly. "I got nothing to go on." He patted under his arm and did a strange little shimmying move to settle the gun into a more comfortable position. "It ain't love, it ain't money, it ain't family. I don't know. Maybe the guy *is* a toon."

"Mind if I ask you a question?"

Riordan shrugged into his sport coat and tightened his tie. "What's that?"

"The Comfort Inn. He make any calls from there?"

The detective tapped the edge of a cigarette pack against his wrist, extracted a cigarette with his teeth, and slapped his pockets for matches. The moment they left the building, he lighted up, inhaled, and blew a stream of smoke at the gray sky.

Finally he said, "I don't know. I don't think we checked." He took a prolonged drag from the cigarette and added, "But we will."

11

A few days after the funeral, Lassiter started listening to the car radio again. For a while he'd kept it off because, right after the murders, he was switching from one station to another, trying to find the jazz program on WPFW—and was ambushed by a short news story. It wasn't anything new, really—nothing but a recitation of the facts, and a sound bite from Riordan. Even so, there was something dark, and very disturbing, about listening to the details of your own family's catastrophe, broadcast as a thirty-second news segment between Howard Stern and a traffic update.

I'm tellin' ya, Robin, I was so horny this morning—no, really! / The little boy's throat was cut from ear to ear / There's a fender-bender on the outer loop of the Beltway . . .

Now, as he drove down the parkway, he listened to a piece about a woman whose body had been discovered in the trunk of a car, parked in one of the satellite lots at National Airport. A police spokesman was interviewed. It was the unusually warm weather, he said; it was the smell that drew attention to the vehicle. They'd identified the woman. Lassiter hoped her relatives weren't listening.

Then the news gave way to the traffic. "You're on the brakes southbound on the G.W.," the voice told him, "all the way from Spout Run to Memorial Bridge." No kidding. There were red lights as far as he could see.

Almost two weeks since the murders, and the truth was, he was beginning to get used to it. His mind had made some kind of adjustment. The fact that his sister and nephew had been slaughtered in their beds no longer shocked him. They were dead, just dead, and that was the way things were. It reminded him of the way he felt when his parents were killed. After a while it was hard to remember them. After a while it didn't seem like they'd ever really been alive.

He got off at the Key Bridge and beat his way down the Whitehurst Freeway to E Street.

He'd been at his desk for about an hour when Victoria buzzed and said that there was a reporter from the *Washington Times* on the line, and "it's about your sister's case." It seemed ironic that a reporter should be calling him—after his reflections on the drive into town. And he was surprised. Press interest in cases like Kathy's had a short shelf life, blown off the pages and airwaves by more recent and equally gruesome disasters.

The voice was female, young, and nervous. Southern accent. She had that habit of expressing statements as if they were questions.

"Johnette Daly?" she said. "I'm sorry to bother you, Mr. Lassiter, but I'm on deadline? And I—"

"How can I help?"

"Well, I'd like to get your reaction—I mean if you would have a comment on what happened?"

He was puzzled. His *comment* on what happened? Another button on his phone lit up, so he knew he had a call of some importance—or Victoria would have taken a message. "What is this," he asked Johnette Daly, "some kind of follow-up story?"

There was a pause and then the reporter spoke in a hushed, breathy voice. "Ohmygod. You mean—you don't know?" She didn't wait for an answer, but rushed on. "I was sure they'd call you right away. I don't know if—"

"What's this about?"

"I don't like to be the one to tell you this—but . . . at the Fairhaven cemetery? Someone dug up your nephew—dug up your nephew's *body*, I mean. Some vandal or something. And I—"

"*What?* Is this a joke?"

"The police won't speculate on the incident, sir, and I wondered if you—"

"I'm sorry," he said. "I can't talk to you right now."

He stared at the phone in his hand.

After a minute he called Riordan—who fell all over himself apologizing that a cub reporter, listening to the police radio on a scanner, had been the one to deliver the news.

"I didn't hear about it right away," Riordan said, "because, you know, nobody puts two and two together, that this is the grave of a homicide victim. So it's treated like vandalism. I'm sorry.

Someone should of called you. Someone fucked up." He sighed. "Probably me."

"What the hell *happened?*"

"Far as we can tell," Riordan said, "it was sometime between midnight and seven A.M. There's a guard there at night, but he's in his little building, you know? Watching the tube. Didn't hear anything. Didn't see anything. It's a big place. Anyway, some guy visiting his mother's grave, first thing in the morning, he's the one reports it."

"What'd they do? They dug up Brandon's body. What for? Did they—Jesus Christ! Did they *take* it?" A word crashed into his head: *grave robbers.*

There was a pause and then Riordan cleared his throat. "I guess . . . the reporter—I guess he didn't tell you the whole . . . the whole deal." He spoke slowly, squeezing out the words one by one. "Your nephew's body was . . . *exhumed* . . . and then removed from the casket. And then, according to the lab—I'm reading, now—'the perpetrator used a magnesium fuse—' "

"What?"

"I'm reading the lab report: 'The perpetrator used a magnesium fuse to ignite a mixture of powdered aluminum and iron oxide, commonly known as—' "

"Thermite."

"Exactly. Thermite. And, uh . . . he set fire to the remains. Again. He burned him again." Riordan paused. "Gives me the fucking creeps," he said.

Lassiter was completely nonplussed. "Why would anyone *do* that?"

"You got me." Riordan said something about checking the surrounding jurisdictions for any similar events. "But there's nothing so far. Sometimes we get, you know, desecration of graves. Hate crimes, that kind of thing. Kid stuff, actually. But this?"

"A magnesium fuse? *Thermite?*"

"I know what you're sayin'! There's a lot of weird ideas being tossed around—most of 'em out to lunch."

"Like what?"

"Oh, c'mon—"

"Like *what?*"

"Like someone's after some part of his body, it's Satanists, that kind of stuff. Which is a load of crap. What I want to know is: How does this connect to the murder? Because we don't know that it does." He coughed and then cleared his throat. "Of course: one thing we *do* know."

"What's that?"

"It wasn't John Doe."

Later that afternoon, Lassiter went for a run, hoping to clear his head, but all he could think of was the carbonized mask that had once been Brandon's face. When he finished the run, he got back in the car and, without thinking about it, drove to the cemetery, where he found a small area cordoned off with yellow tape. A uniformed officer leaned against a nearby gravestone, smoking a cigarette. He flicked the butt away and stood straight up when Lassiter approached.

"It's my sister's grave," he said. "And my nephew's."

The officer looked him over, shrugged. "As long as you don't cross the tape."

Lassiter stood there, looking. Kathy's grave was still covered with heaped-up wilted flowers. White ribbons rattled in the breeze. Next to that, Brandon's headstone was lying on its side, marking what was now a raw hole in the ground. There was a big mound of dirt to the side. It looked like more dirt than could fit in the hole. He could see the residue of evidence kits. Powder all over the gravestone, and blotches of white here and there on the ground—where casts had been made of footprints, shovel marks, and the like. And then there was another, shallow excavation to the foot of the original graves—clearly where Brandon's body had lain. The forensic crew had obviously tried to recover all of Brandon's remains. But they had not succeeded. What persisted were just a few black streaks and some small dark chunks of ashes. The sprinkling of ashes reminded him of cinders, of when he was a kid, and the big house in Georgetown and how the help used to throw cinders out on the front steps when it snowed.

The sight of those black streaks and that sprinkling of ashes disturbed him in some deep way. The residues made it real—that someone had actually burned Brandon's little body. Dug it up, removed it from the casket. According to Riordan, the child's body was drenched in gasoline, ignited, and incinerated to the point where nothing was left but what Tommy Truong called "bone litter."

When he got home, the house seemed too big and too silent. He called Claire, and she said she'd come over, and then he called her back. He told her what had happened and added that maybe he'd be better off alone.

He woke up in the middle of the night trying to remember something that he'd thought of in his sleep. It seemed so important. It was something about Brandon's body, and he wanted to call Riordan, he *had* to call Riordan, and tell him. But no matter how hard he tried, he couldn't remember what it was. It was there, in the back of his head, but the more he thought about it, the further it receded, until in the end he didn't even have a feeling for it. Finally, he wondered whether it had really been an insight, or just a dream. Frustrated, he tossed and turned the rest of the night.

In the morning there was a story in the *Washington Post*. He didn't want to read it, didn't even want to see it—but he couldn't help catching the headline.

MURDER VICTIM'S GRAVE VANDALIZED

In the afternoon, he received a strange telephone call from the Evans Funeral Home—which had handled the arrangements for the funerals.

"I was asked to get in touch with you by the police department," a man said, in what seemed to be a perpetually hushed and sympathetic voice. "Once the, ah . . . forensic examination of the remains is completed and the, ah . . . body is released—do you wish us to handle the re-interment?"

He said yes.

"Would you prefer to select a new casket? The police are, ah . . . finished with the original, but it was somewhat *damaged*, you see."

He asked for a new casket.

"Just one more thing, Mr. Lassiter. Ah . . ." And here even the funeral director faltered slightly, as if he were stepping onto untested terrain. "Would you . . . would you like to *be* there when we, ah . . . lay the body to rest?" He coughed. "When we re-inter? I mean—would you want a new *ceremony*?"

Lassiter got that feeling in his chest again, of his heart on the loose. "No ceremony," he managed. "But I do want to be there."

"Very well," the man said. "We'll let you know."

—

Two days later it was another brilliant day and he was at the cemetery again. It was surreal, watching an identical tiny casket being lowered into the identical hole in the ground. But this time there was no minister, no uplifting words, no mourners other than himself and Riordan—who showed up midway through the process. He and Riordan shoveled in the dirt themselves. The physical labor felt good to Lassiter, but it was a small grave and it didn't take long enough. The two of them stood there for a minute, and then Lassiter turned away.

"Hell of a thing," Riordan said, shaking his head. He pulled out a cigarette, but waited until they were well away from the grave before lighting it.

After Brandon's second "funeral," Riordan called him every couple of days. "I got to tell you, Joe—we got *nothing*. I mean, we got a good cast of the shovel blade, we got some great shoe prints—Nikes by the way, Chieftain model, new ones, size ten. And only *one* kind of shoe prints—which suggests only one individual. But other than that? We got squat. No fingerprints on the casket, nothing on the headstone. Whoever it was wore gloves." He paused. "Which in itself is interesting."

Apart from Brandon's grisly exhumation, the homicide investigation plodded along with few interruptions and no important developments. Riordan made a point of making sure that he was kept well informed, hoping in that way to keep him off his back. In these phone calls, they fell into the habit of going over the evidence.

Fingerprints: "Guess whose?"

"I don't have to guess."

It was no surprise that John Doe's prints were all over the knife, the car, and the wallet from the Comfort Inn. It was useful evidence, but it said nothing about his identity: he was still John Doe.

"The guy's not in the system," Riordan said, referring to the FBI computer that held more than a hundred million sets of fingerprints— including those of anybody who'd ever been arrested, for *anything*; anyone who'd ever applied for a security clearance or a weapons permit; anyone in the military; cabdrivers; bus drivers; government workers.

"Everybody's in the system," Lassiter said.

"Just about."

"I know. They got a lot of people. They got me, they got you. What they don't have—they don't have John Doe."

Blood, hair, tissue: "Perfect match. The prints on the knife are his. The blood on the knife is theirs. The hair was like you said: Brandon's. And the skin—"

"What skin?"

"Under your sister's nails—the skin was John Doe's, no question. Even without the DNA test, the doc says our boy was *raked*—four fingers across the cheek, right to left. We couldn't see it because of the bandages."

The knife: "We had an artist sit with him on the burn ward. He did some sketches, and the last one—it's good! It's him: John Doe—no burns, no bandages. But this time with hair and eyebrows—which, of course, he doesn't actually have, not at the moment. Anyway, unless this guy wore a pompadour, we know what he looks like."

"So what?"

"So we took the sketch to twenty gun stores, half a dozen army surplus joints, and—guess what? Clerk in Springfield says he sold the guy a K-Bar knife, three, maybe four weeks ago."

"He *remembers* that?"

"Like it was yesterday."

"And how does he do *that*?"

"Easy. He says the guy stood out like a stork. Says he was wearing one of those droopy foreign suits—"

"Armani."

"Whatever—they don't see a lot of that at Sunny's Surplus. What they see is guys in jumpsuits and cammies, kids with shaved heads and black jeans. . . . This guy was, quote: 'Right out of G.Q.' Unquote. I'm tellin' ya, Joe. The case is a lock."

And so it went. At the hospital, one bored policeman after another stood guard outside the prisoner's room, checking the credentials of everyone who entered and left. But there wasn't much point: all of the visitors were hospital employees, and other than Joe Lassiter and the press, no one called to ask about the man's condition.

It was the Monday before Thanksgiving that Riordan telephoned to say that the doctors were removing the breathing tube from John

Doe's throat. Doe was well enough to answer questions, and an interview was set for Wednesday.

"Then what?" Lassiter wanted to know.

"We'll move him to Fairfax. Then we'll arraign him—in a wheelchair, if we have to."

According to the doctors, the patient's condition was remarkably improved—though he'd never be "as good as new." There was deep scarring to his neck and to the left side of his face, and the tissues of his lungs and larynx had been damaged. "He's not gonna like that," Riordan said.

"Who would?"

"I mean, what I get from the doctors—the guy was a jock. Or *like* a jock. Anyway, they say he's in tremendous shape—or was."

"A runner?"

"No—well, maybe. But this is a big guy. Bulky. A boxer, maybe. Or a linebacker. Bouncer. I dunno. Something *big*. Maybe, I'm thinking—a soldier."

"Why do you say that?"

"Because he's been through the mill. Doctors showed me his X rays, and you can tell—the guy's taken some knocks. Like he's been *tortured* or somethin'."

"What do you mean?"

"He's got some old fractures—and scar tissue. A lotta scar tissue on his back—like he's been whipped."

"What?"

"I'm not kiddin'. You should see it. Plus, he's been shot. He's got what looks like an old rifle wound: front entry, right shoulder. Exited half an inch from the spine. Something else, too."

"What's that?"

"*My* opinion? I think this guy—professionally—I think he lays tile."

"*What?*"

Riordan chuckled, obviously pleased with himself. "That's the other thing. Doc says the guy's got calluses on his knees. Big ones—thick. So I figure—*tile*. I mean—where else you gonna get something like that?"

Lassiter thought about it. Finally, he said, "I don't know."

"Aha," Riordan said. "I rest my case."

12

On the Wednesday morning that Riordan was to interview John Doe, Joe Lassiter drove to his office in Foggy Bottom, where he sat down and pretended to work while waiting for the detective to call.

The office was a large and luxurious one, with a working Georgian fireplace, dove-gray carpeting, and windows that looked out toward Capitol Hill at the far end of the Mall. The walnut-paneled walls were softly lighted, and hung with Hockney lithographs. At one end of the room was a richly carved desk; a pair of wing chairs and a leather couch were at the other. The effect was one of gravity and discretion, and it was meant to put the rich, the cautious, and the troubled at ease.

Lassiter Associates occupied the entire ninth floor of the building, which meant there were three corner offices in addition to the one in which the firm's namesake was resident. One of those offices was a conference room. The other two were assigned to the company's managing directors, Judy Rifkin and Leo Bolton. There were eight other windowed offices, each of which was assigned to a senior investigator or case manager. Field researchers and data-base staff, secretaries, and clerical personnel, occupied a warren of cubicles in the interior of the floor. Besides Joe Lassiter, there were thirty-six people in the firm's headquarters—and about forty others in New York, Chicago, London, and L.A.

Security was tight, and ostentatious—as security is meant to be. It began in the reception area, where a state-of-the-art, video surveillance system recorded the comings and goings of employees and visitors alike. Behind the reception area, access to the windowed offices was controlled by a biometric locking system that scanned thumbprints. Once inside, a visitor would find that all of the windows were hung with rubberized drapes, which absorbed vibration in the unlikely event that someone might try to use a laser device to read conversations off the window glass. The filing cabinets were fitted with heavy combination locks, and there was a shredder next to every desk. Other security features were less obvious. Because Lassiter Associates reported largely to CEOs and lead attorneys, its reports were not meant to be copied. Accordingly, and unless directed otherwise, the company printed its reports on paper impregnated with phosphorus, so that any effort to copy a document—other than by hand—would yield a black page.

The computers in the office were equipped with locks, but from a security standpoint, a more important feature was what they lacked: floppy drives. In effect, this meant that none of the firm's data could be downloaded to disc. There were internal devices that controlled the dissemination of E-mail. And if the data processing system should ever be hacked—and the OpSec people swore that it couldn't be—a 128-bit algorithm made certain that its contents could not be decoded for at least a million years, using contemporary technology.

All of this was expensive and, some thought, excessive—but Lassiter knew the truth. The security paid for itself. This was so because most of the firm's income derived from two sources: litigation involving large corporations and the very rich, and Mergers & Acquisitions, which everybody called M&A's. Whether the matter involved a commodity trader's wife who was seeking a divorce (and half her husband's assets), or a hostile takeover (and the prospect of greenmail), the stakes could be very high. Often, hundreds of millions of dollars were involved, and so secrecy, absolute secrecy, was an imperative. Ideally, to Lassiter's way of thinking, the opposition (and there was always opposition) shouldn't even know that his firm was involved in a matter—unless, as sometimes happened, it was felt that news of the firm's involvement would have a favorable impact in its own right. Then the investigation would be a "noisy" one, with leaks to the press, aggressive surveillance, and adversarial interviews.

Even more to the point, Lassiter thought, *his clients liked it*. The lawyers liked it, the bond sellers liked it, and the CEOs liked it. The cameras, codes, and locking systems gave them a feeling of confidence and, also, of money well spent. Not least of all, Lassiter knew, it made them feel as if they were *players*. Or, as Leo put it: "What the hell? For two hundred bucks an hour, we should put the men's room on springs."

Even so, with all the high-tech in the world at his disposal, Joe Lassiter couldn't get Jimmy Riordan to telephone him. That morning, he'd told his secretary to hold all calls but Riordan's, and the result was an uncharacteristic silence in the southwest corner of the ninth floor. The morning sun dragged quietly into the afternoon, and still the phone didn't ring. Lassiter ordered sandwiches from a takeout called Le Bon Appetit—or, as the GWU kids called it, "the Bone"—and ate alone in front of the fire, leafing through a copy of *Information Warfare*. Slowly, the afternoon dwindled toward evening, and Lassiter thought about going home.

There must have been a problem, he told himself. Maybe Doe wanted a lawyer present, and they were having trouble finding one. Maybe it was the language—though he didn't see how that could be a problem: Riordan had said he was taking a translator along, "someone who speaks Italian *and* Spanish." Maybe Doe had taken a turn for the worse. Maybe—

The telephone rang at five-fifteen, just as the sun was sinking into Arlington Cemetery.

"I just got back," Riordan said.

"And?"

There was a pause. "What I found out? What I found out was absolutely nothing," Riordan said.

"What?"

"Hang on," Riordan said, and yelled away from the receiver: "Yeah, yeah, yeah, give me five minutes, all right?" And then his voice came back. "He stonewalled me. I didn't get word one. *Nada.*"

"What about a lawyer? Did you ask him—"

"You don't get it. I'm telling you: he didn't say jack-shit. Nothing. We read him his rights in three languages and—"

"You sure he understood?"

"Yeah, he understood. You could see it in his eyes. He understood every word we were saying."

"He's got to have a lawyer."

"Of course! And after a couple of hours I got one appointed for him. I figure, what the fuck, maybe *he* can get something out of him. A name. Something. So we wait a couple hours for the lawyer. And then we cool our heels for, I don't know what—*half* an hour—while *he's* in there, talkin' to him. And guess what? The lawyer's doin' all the talkin'. Doe doesn't say fuck-all. So I go back in the room and I *explain* it to him. I tell him what a great country this is, how everybody's equal and how it doesn't matter who you are—it's what you've *done* that counts. Good deeds or bad. I tell him we don't need his name to try him—or even to execute him. For all I care, he can go on trial as John Doe—and when it's over, the sentence will still be the same. He doesn't cooperate—he's a dead man. A generic dead man, but still dead."

"You said that?"

"Yeah, and I told him he's charged with first-degree murder and arson, and that we have the evidence to convict. I listed the evidence and I showed him the knife—"

"You took the knife to the hospital?"

"I took a *couple* of things to the hospital. Don't worry, I signed it out."

"How'd he react?"

"He didn't react. You seen the Sphinx?" Riordan let go one of his sharp chuckles. "The only rise I got out of this guy was when he saw the bottle."

"What bottle?"

"The perfume bottle, or whatever the fuck it is. The little bottle from his pocket."

"What'd he do?"

"I don't know, he sort of . . . you could see it meant something to him. It was like his eyes got . . . wider, or . . . like that."

"His *eyes* got wider."

"Yeah."

"Huh."

Riordan ignored the sarcasm. "I'm serious. The bottle surprised him. So I'm gonna have the lab run another test on the water. Maybe there's something in it they missed. Drugs, or something."

"Then what?"

"Anyway, I'm sitting there with him and his lawyer, and I mention the fact that I'm in a position to make a recommendation to the Commonwealth's attorney. Whether he seeks the death penalty or life—it's a fine line, y'know? I tell him we have evidence of premeditation, we got a chain of evidence solid as a rock, and we got a heinous crime. I tell him the way I see it, he's on a downward spiral: in a couple of days we're gonna move him to the strong room at Fairfax General. And then—"

"What's a 'strong room'?" Lassiter asked.

"Just what it sounds like: it's a hospital room, but the windows are bulletproof. You know how many suspects get injured, committing crime? You wouldn't believe it. So every jurisdiction's got a strong room. In Washington it's at D.C. General. Out here it's Fairfax. Costs a hell of a lot of money, you know, posting a twenty-four-hour guard. So as soon as someone's in halfway decent shape, they get moved to the strong room. There's bars, a steel door—the lock's on the *outside* . . .

"Anyway . . . I explain that after he's well enough to leave the hospital, the strong room, things start getting worse because then we arraign him, and then he goes to county jail. Maybe to the infirmary if he's still iffy, but definitely to the jail. It's a real downward spiral, like I said. Meanwhile, what I know is: the doctors are cutting back on his medication—just for the day—so we can talk and he's not too dopey. And I can see it's getting to him, he's wantin' his little shot. Now, obviously, his lawyer's right there, and I can't actually threaten him, but I did let him know that the medical personnel at the county jail are about as busy as a dog with two dicks—"

"Jesus, Riordan."

"Hey, I'm just telling him the truth. They're busy and he probably won't have the same level of comfort there as he does where he is now. And I'm not lying. I told him: a year ago—and you can look it up in the *Post*—there was a scandal. Terrible thing. Turns out, none of the prisoners in the infirmary were getting *anything* for their pain because the nurse was giving 'em placebos and selling the real stuff on the cell block."

"Jim—"

"So I said *maybe*, if he's a little more helpful, *maybe* he could stay in the hospital—in the strong room—a little longer. A week, maybe. Two. Give him some time to get on his feet."

"And . . . ?"

"Nothin'."

"You're sure he understood you?"

"Yeah."

"If he doesn't say anything, how can you be sure?"

"Because he speaks *English*—he talks to the nurses. He's thirsty. He's hungry. He hurts. He's been speaking to them, all right. Besides . . . this is something I know about. I've probably questioned a couple thousand people. And this guy? *My* opinion? This guy is a very hard case. I can promise you this was not the first time he's been questioned by a cop."

Lassiter believed him. This was, indeed, the kind of thing that Riordan knew. "So . . . that's it?"

"More or less. The doctor kicked us out." Riordan spoke in an irritated singsong: " 'The patient needs his reh-est.' So he sends the nurse for a shot of Demerol, and we're getting up, and John Doe—John Doe looks bad. I mean, he's in considerable pain. You can see it. He's sweating and every once in a while—he moves or something?—there's this sound. Quiet, like: *uhnhhh*. Like he's having a hard time keeping control. So, I put on my hard look and I tell him I'll be back—and he looks up at me with his shit-eating grin, and you know what he says to me?"

"No, what?"

"He says: 'Ciao.' "

"*Ciao?*"

"Like it's 'Baywatch' or something. I swear to God, if he wasn't already in the hospital, I would of put him there."

Lassiter was silent for a moment, and then asked, "So what are you going to do?"

"Everything I told him I was gonna do," Riordan said grimly. "Starting with the move to the strong room. Doc says, if he comes along the way they expect, we can move him next week."

Thanksgiving Day, Lassiter rolled out of bed at eight A.M. to see that the weather was beginning to turn—with a vengeance. Snowflakes drifted past the atrium windows, huge and perfectly defined. It was the kind of snow that fell a flake at a time, the kind of snow that came at the beginning of a Christmas movie.

He dressed quickly, grabbed a couple of cans of tuna fish from the kitchen, and went out to the car. The food was his entrance fee to the Turkey Trot in Alexandria, a flat five-miler that drew about two thousand runners each year. As the car nosed through a vortex of swirling flakes, he leaned over the steering wheel. The visibility was so poor that the cars in front of him were little more than glimmers of red, winking off and on through a wall of falling snow. It was the kind of snow that evokes the remark that "it won't last," or "it won't stick," but by the time he reached Alexandria and found a place to park, the world was draped in white.

Many people claim to do valuable thinking while running, finding that the repetitive motion of the body allows the mind to float free. Lassiter was not one of them. He never thought when running, except in the crudest and most narrowly focused terms: Where to put his foot, whether he should take his gloves off, when he should turn around, and was the pain in his knee serious or just a trick of his mind?

In today's race his thoughts were of the same kind. He thought about his pace and how far the next mile marker was. He plotted vectors that would take him past the runners in front of him. He blinked the snow from his eyes, listened to the stertorous breathing of the people around him, and marveled at how warm he felt—and how cold the air was. His mind drifted with the snow, taking him toward the finish. What he liked about running was the way it stopped the mind. When he ran, it was as if he'd vanished from himself and the only thing left was motion.

Approaching the finish line, he became aware of the welcoming crowd that lined both sides of the road for the last quarter mile of the race. They whooped encouragement, exhorting the runners with shouts of "Looking good!" and "Almost there." When he crossed the line, the digital display was crusted with snow, but he could see his time: 31:02. Not bad, he thought. He heard the race coordinator yelling, "Men to the left, women to the right," and ran into the chute behind a short guy in red tights. He was aware of the people around him, breathing hard, their faces pink, steam rising from their shoulders and the tops of their heads. The snow continued to fall in big weightless clumps.

He would have sworn he hadn't been thinking during the race. His mind had been a blank. And so, as he tore off the Tyvek strip that bore his number and handed it to an official, he was surprised to realize that somewhere on the run he'd come to a decision. As he walked between the tables of orange juice and power bars, cooling down, he turned the decision over in his mind. He was going to take time off. A leave of absence—for as long as it took, a week, a month, whatever. As long as it took to find out why Kathy and Brandon had been murdered, and who was behind it. That was the decision, and it was a done deal. He was already gone. The company just didn't know it yet.

He walked into the school building and found his sweat clothes on the windowsill where he'd stashed them. By the time he had them on and began to stretch out his legs, he was shaking his head over how long it had taken him to reach the decision—even if he couldn't remember thinking about it. What was the point of owning an investigative agency if you didn't use it? If Wall Street wanted to find something out, they came to him. And so did half the lawyers on K Street. So why should Joe Lassiter leave something as important as Kathy and Brandon to *the cops*?

When he got to his car, it was covered in snow. He used the side of his arm to brush what he could from the windshield and then got in. His body was hot from the run, and by the time he found the keys and started the car, the windows were gray with steam. It took a minute for the heater to clear the glass, and then he was on his way.

The wind was beginning to roar now. Stoplights rocked on their cables, and the traffic signs rattled wildly. Snow flew at his headlights in a steady, horizontal stream. Across the slate-gray river, the city was invisible. Only the red light atop the Washington Monument showed itself, blinking on and off, like an evil eye.

He drove directly to his office in Foggy Bottom, taking the Fourteenth Street Bridge to Independence Avenue and then heading west. The power had failed, leaving what little traffic there was to crawl hesitantly through one blind intersection after another.

Fortunately, there was a generator in his building and everything was working. He parked his car in the cavernous space of the underground garage and walked quickly to the elevators. Even belowground he could hear the wind howling, and a chill passed through him. The sweat on his back was beginning to freeze as the elevator carried him to the ninth floor.

There was a shower in his office suite, and he made good use of it. Though his muscles were tight from the run, they softened under the hot water's pounding, and after a while he could feel the lactic acid draining away. Because he ran on the Mall four or five days a week, he kept a selection of clothes in his office closet. Rubbing his hair with a towel, he pulled on a pair of jeans and a sweater, and went to his desk.

For the first time that he could remember, his office annoyed him. The bookcases, the wainscoting, the lithographs—who was he trying to impress? There were a dozen exquisitely framed photographs in the room, but not one of them was of Kathy or Brandon. They were all pictures of himself with famous people: Lassiter conferring with

Prince Bandar; Lassiter shaking hands with the President's National Security Adviser; Lassiter in a helicopter with a clutch of JCS generals; Lassiter in *Forbes*—as if he were a restaurant review.

Pride of place went to a joke, a posed photograph of Lassiter and the Senate Minority Leader teeing off at the Army-Navy Country Club. The senator—chin raised, club high, ankle pronated—was archetypal: a poster boy for old money and American values. Whereas Lassiter appeared to be insane. He stood a few feet away, lips curled and eyes wild, swinging a nine-iron as if it were a Louisville Slugger.

Next to the infamous "PGA shot" was a gift from Judy: a *Washingtonian* piece about the town's most eligible bachelors, mounted in a heart-shaped frame. (Lassiter was number 26—which was flattering, when you thought about it. Or maybe not.)

All of this had been important to him once, or at least amusing, but now—what was the point? To open more offices, make more money, build an even bigger house? What for? The truth was, he didn't even like Bandar—so what was the guy's picture doing on his wall?

He took down the photos and stacked them in the corner. Then he went back to his desk and took out a piece of paper. Drawing a vertical line down the center of the page, he wrote *Company* on the left side and, on the right, *Investigation*.

He sat for a moment, thinking about what he should do. The hard part about replacing himself, even temporarily, was that his responsibilities were broad, deep, and not very well defined. In effect he did whatever he had to do to make things work, which meant that he was a rainmaker *and* a fireman, a supervisor *and* a case manager. You could say that he did a little of everything, or you could put it differently and say that he did whatever he liked. And how, he wondered, do you delegate *that*?

Under *Company*, he wrote *Bolton—all M&A's*, and beneath that he wrote, *Rifkin—All Other Cases*. Leo and Judy were ambitious people, with equal stature in the firm. If he gave either of them precedence over the other, one of them would walk. Even so, it wouldn't be enough to divide the cases between them: there were administrative matters involving cash flow, new business, and client relations. Lassiter decided to parcel out those responsibilities to Bill Bohacker. He was in the New York office, but he could do the job from there. Nearly half of the company's billings were sent to Wall Street, anyway.

Bohacker—Admin.

He thought about it for a moment, and made a note to have Bill come to Washington on Monday. He could take the shuttle and be there by nine. The four of them would meet in the conference room, and they'd sort out the details.

Turning on the computer, he entered the day's password and scrolled through the cases that were being worked on in the Washington office. He was directly and substantively involved in only two of them—but each was for a major client. He'd have to call them and explain about the leave of absence. He didn't think there'd be a problem, but if there was, he'd refer them to Kroll—no hard feelings.

Lassiter made another notation on the left side of the paper— *AFL-CIO (call Uehlein)* and *AmEx (call Reynolds)*. He thought awhile longer and wrote a little more. Then he got up and walked to the windows, where the snow had turned to sleet. He watched a Lincoln Town Car fishtail across Pennsylvania Avenue, and listened to the sleet ticking against the glass.

Returning to his desk, he sat down and looked at the right side of the page, where *Investigation* was headlined. There was nothing under it. With his eyes closed, he leaned back in the chair and thought. What was there? Was there anything Riordan hadn't chased down, anything he could do that the police hadn't already done? He sat in the chair for half an hour before he wrote a word, and the word he wrote was *bottle*.

Only two things had been found on John Doe's person—a big knife and a little bottle. The police knew everything there was to know about the knife, but the bottle meant nothing to them. Riordan was retesting the contents, so there wasn't anything for him to do about that—but maybe the bottle itself was worth pursuing. It looked expensive, or at least unusual. Maybe he could get some pictures and have one of the field people chase it down.

The next words he wrote were *Comfort Inn*. He remembered asking Riordan if John Doe had made any telephone calls from his motel room, but he didn't remember getting an answer. In all likelihood this meant that there weren't any calls, but he ought to check. After all, he thought, looking at the list, it wasn't as if he had too much to do.

13 Lassiter woke to a ringing noise and a cloud of blinding sunlight, a wall of brilliance so bright that he reeled from it, slamming his eyes shut even as he climbed out of bed. The telephone was trilling, and like a vampire trapped by the sun, he staggered across the room with his eyes closed. Finding the phone, he fumbled with the receiver, cleared his throat, and mumbled, "Yeah?"

The person on the other end didn't say anything for a moment, and then: "You asleep?" It was Riordan.

"No," he lied. It was automatic. He didn't know why, but whenever he was awakened by a telephone call, he always denied that he'd been asleep. Even if it was three in the morning, he felt guilty, as if the world expected him to be constantly on alert. If the caller was up, why wasn't he?

"You sure?" Riordan said.

"Yeah—wide-awake—what time is it?"

"Oh seven hundred."

"Hang on for a minute."

The electricity had gone out the day before, and Lassiter had forgotten to reprogram the timer that controlled the shades and shutters on the clerestory windows and skylights. Through the windows he could see the trees, their trunks and branches, twigs and leaves, encased in ice. They dripped and sparkled, the light ricocheting off them with painful brilliance. All in all there was a tidal wave of sunshine pouring into the room. Lassiter reached for a switch on the wall, touched it, and heard a low hum overhead. Slowly, the room dimmed, and he returned to the phone. "What's up?"

"I'm off the case."

"*What? Why?*"

"Well, there's two reasons. First— You sure I didn't wake you up? Sometimes I call people—"

"I'm positive."

"You must be an early riser. Like me."

"Crack-a-dawn."

"Anyway, the way they see it downstairs, the case is solved. If it was up to me—"

"It isn't *solved*."

"I know what you're gonna say, but the other thing is: we got a double homicide in Annandale, and one of the victims is a cop."

"I'm sorry—"

"Twenty-four-year-old kid—*nice* kid—new to the force, stops at a convenience store for a cup of coffee." Riordan paused. "Guy's got a two-month-old daughter, he's on his way home, wife's keeping dinner for him and—*wham!*—he gets whacked buyin' a cup of coffee."

"That's terrible—"

"You ain't heard the half of it. The other victim's Thai. Got her citizenship two days ago. She's working the register on Thanksgiving, five eighty-seven an hour, and—bim bam boom!—she takes three in the face. Welcome to America! Happy Thanksgiving! Rest in Peace."

"Look, Jim—I know what you're saying, but—"

"The other thing is: I got invited to a conference—so I gotta prepare."

"A 'conference'?"

"Yeah. It's, like, one of those hands-across-the-sea deals. Interpol's running it. In Prague. You ever been to Prague?"

"Not for a while. What kind of conference?"

"They got me on a panel with a couple of frogs, a Russky. I'm your typical American detective or something. Talkin' about 'Policework in a Democratic Society'—on account of the Czechs haven't had one, y'know? Not for a long time."

"Think of that."

"Anyway, Andy Pisarcik's gonna take over your sister and nephew's case for a while. He's a smart kid. He'll handle the mop-up and—here, I'll give you his number."

Lassiter wanted to argue. Riordan was one of the best homicide detectives in northern Virginia, but it was pointless to go back and forth with him about it. For one thing, decisions about case assignment were not up to Riordan.

"Can I ask you about a couple of things—while I've still got the chance?"

"Okay," Riordan said in a noncommittal tone.

"Our boy—you ever check to see if he made any calls from the motel he was staying at?"

Riordan hesitated. "I don't know . . . let me see. The Comfort Inn. I know I *requested* it. I'm just getting the file together for Pisarcik. Hang on." Lassiter heard the rustle of papers. "Yeah. Here it is. One call. He made *one* call to Chicago. Less than a minute. It was nothing."

"So who'd he call?"

Riordan hesitated. "Well . . ." The detective was obviously uncomfortable. "What the hell—he called a hotel. Embassy Suites."

"And?"

"What do you think? He got the switchboard. If they connected him to anyone else, it doesn't show—which it wouldn't." Riordan's voice had a defensive edge. "I didn't take it any further. I mean, there's—what?—two hundred rooms in the place. And one minute? For all I know, it's a wrong number."

"What about the bottle?"

"We got some partial prints off it. They're all Doe's. The lab took a second shot at the contents, and it came back water again. Trace impurities. So the bottle adds up to a big 'so what'?"

"You took photographs of it, right? Any chance you could get me some copies—"

A big explosive sigh. "Look, I'll see what I can do. But that's it, Joe—I'm off the case. From now on you talk to Pisarcik."

"Absolutely. But what about the rooming house in Florida? Where 'Gutierrez' got his mail. You got an address?"

Riordan laughed. "Get outta here," he said, and hung up.

As it happened, there were four Embassy Suites in Chicago, and Lassiter didn't have the heart to pester Riordan for the right one. So he called the office and sent one of his investigators, a former FBI agent named Tony Harper, down to the Comfort Inn. Lassiter was pretty sure that Tony could get a copy of the motel bill from the desk clerk— though it would probably cost a bit. And he was right. Two hours later Tony faxed him a copy of the bill and a receipt for a hundred dollars. The receipt was for "Services Rendered."

Besides a single call to the 312 area code, the bill included the number of the Visa card that "Juan Gutierrez" had used to guarantee the room. For twenty-five dollars, Lassiter knew he could buy a credit history on Gutierrez; but for a couple of hundred, he could get something even more useful—an itemized list of every charge that Gutierrez had made on the card. And his other card, too—if he remembered right, Riordan said Gutierrez had two cards, each of which he'd had for only a couple of months. The Agency—they'd find the second card through the first card, and any others, too—no problem.

This wasn't entirely legal, but then neither was speeding. In the Information Age, violations of privacy were the moral equivalent of jaywalking: if you got caught, you paid the ticket and walked away. Lassiter flipped through his Rolodex until he found the number for a data retrieval firm in Florida, a bucket shop called Mutual General Services.

Mutual was an information broker specializing in black data. If you wanted bank records, unlisted telephone numbers, copies of credit card charges or telephone toll records, they could get it for you— quickly and cheaply. According to Leo, they did this "the old-fashioned way—they bribe people." By all accounts, they had someone on the payroll of every major credit card company and long-distance carrier in the U.S. "It's a nice niche," Leo had said. "They only do one thing, but they do it well."

Lassiter dialed Mutual General, volunteered his account number, and told the woman on the other end what he wanted: copies of Gutierrez's credit card receipts for each of the past three months. He gave her the card number, and paid extra to have it expedited.

This done, he turned his attention to the telephone call on the Comfort Inn's receipt. The charge was $1.25: a single long-distance call that was billed for a minute—which meant that the call had lasted something less than that.

He thought about the possibilities. One minute, probably less. It took longer than that to make a reservation. And if it was a guest he'd been calling, he probably hadn't gotten through: the hotel operator would have taken a while to connect him, the phone would have had to ring in the room. . . . So it looked like whoever he was calling had been out. Unless . . . unless John Doe had come to Washington from somewhere else. In which case maybe he was calling "home." Most suite hotels have voice mail—so maybe Doe was checking his calls.

Lassiter had a voice-mail system at the office. He dialed his own line, pressed in the various codes to work through the system, and timed it on his watch to see how long it took. He had two short messages and it took ninety-two seconds. He wrote down the messages, pressed "D" to discard them from his voice mail, and called back. Fifty-one seconds.

Then he dialed the hotel.

"Embassy Suites, how may I direct your call?"

"I'm trying to reach a guest. Juan Gutierrez." He spelled it.

"One moment, please." There was a long wait, filled with bad music. Then: "Sorry about that. I'm afraid we don't have anyone by that name."

One of the things that made him a good investigator was thoroughness. If something seemed to be a dead end, he always tried to make sure that it didn't have a back way out. So, instead of hanging up, he pushed it. "This is the last number we have for him. Could you check again? I know he was there a few weeks ago, and my understanding was that he'd be in Chicago for a while. Maybe he left a forwarding number. Could you check?"

"Are you a friend, or—"

"No. I'm an attorney for Mrs. Gutierrez. She's very worried."

More bad music. He wasn't sure what he expected to learn, even if he found out that Doe *had* been staying there. But maybe there'd be another bill, more phone calls.

The music stopped and the desk clerk came back on the line. "You're right. We did have a guest by that name—but he didn't check out. I mean, not really."

Lassiter pretended not to understand. "I'm sorry, I don't—"

"Well, he left without checking out."

"You mean, he *skipped*? That doesn't sound like—"

"No no—that's not what I mean. We took a credit card impression when he checked in. The problem is—do you mind if I get your name?"

"Of course not. I'm Michael Armitage. Hillman, Armitage, and McLean. New York."

"And you're Mrs. Gutierrez's lawyer?"

"I'm her attorney, yes."

"Well, the problem is that Mr. Gutierrez exceeded the limit on his Visa card. We wanted to discuss this with him, but—we haven't seen him."

"I see."

"So there's an outstanding balance."

"I think we can help with that. But what I wanted to ask was: How long was Mr. Gutierrez there?" The long silence at the other end told him that he'd crossed the line, that he'd asked one too many questions.

"I think it might be best if you spoke with the manager. I can have him call you—"

"That's okay," Lassiter said. "I've got to run, anyway. Thanks very much." And he hung up.

It took him less than five minutes to pack an overnight bag with his running gear and a change of clothes. Leaving the house, he crunched across the snow toward his car, the suitcase in one hand and a cup of coffee in another.

There was a Kinko's Copies in Georgetown, just across the Key Bridge, and he headed for it. He took the parkway down to Rosslyn, looped around, and crossed the Potomac to M Street. He left his car in the parking lot at Eagle Liquors and crossed the alley to Kinko's. Ten minutes later he came out with a sheet of micro-perforated business cards printed on fairly heavy, charcoal-flecked gray stock. The cards read:

> Victor Oliver, V.P.
> Muebles Gutierrez
> 2113 52nd Pl., SW
> Miami, FL 33134
> 305-234-2421

He had no idea if there *was* a 2113 52nd Place, but the zip code was right and the telephone number would be fine. It was a hello phone at the DEA, which meant that someone at the other end would take messages *for* anyone *from* anyone. Of course if anybody did call for Victor Oliver, someone at DEA was going to waste quite a bit of time trying to figure out who he was.

It was a bad weekend to be traveling without reservations. One of the runways was closed at National, and even the flights out of Dulles were backed up for de-icing. Still, by three o'clock Lassiter sat in seat 2B, in the First Class section of a Northwest flight to O'Hare. He considered First Class a waste of money, except on very long flights, but it was all he could get. The seat next to him was occupied by a brown-eyed blonde who was showing more cleavage than seemed comfortable on such a chilly day. Her perfume was powerful, and every time she spoke to him, she leaned into his body and clasped his sleeve. Her fingernails were an inch long and bright red.

Her name was Amanda, and her husband was a real estate developer who traveled a lot. ("In fact, he's traveling right now.") She raised shelties and was on her way back to Chicago from a show in Maryland. Lassiter listened to all this, nodding politely as he turned the pages of the in-flight magazine. Despite this lack of encouragement, she talked all the way to O'Hare, discoursing on the inside politics of competitive dog shows and the "tricks of the trade"—which, as it happened, had a lot to do with hair spray, clear nail polish, and vitamin E. ("A little dab of the oil, right on the nose, and it will *shine*! Now, that's a small thing, but in the shows I go to, it's the small things that count.")

They touched down and the reverse thrust of the engines drowned her out, but not for long. As they taxied toward the terminal she leaned against him, pressing her breast against his shoulder and clasping his hand.

"If you feel like company," she said, handing him her card, "I'm just north of town."

The card was pink, the calligraphic printing elaborate and curlicued. A tiny drawing of a dog was in one corner. There was something vulnerable about the woman, and he found that he didn't want to hurt her feelings. So he slipped the card in the breast pocket of his jacket. "I'm going to be busy as hell," he said, "but we'll see what happens. You never know."

He telephoned the hotel from the TWA Ambassadors Club.

"Embassy Suites. How may I direct your call?" It was a man's voice this time.

"Well, I am not sure," Lassiter said. He was a natural mimic and affected a slight Spanish accent, remembering to avoid contractions—which always makes a voice seem "foreign," even if a listener can't place the accent. "I was a guest at your hotel a few weeks ago, and I am afraid I left prematurely. A family emergency."

"I'm sorry."

"Yes, well, she was a very old woman."

"Ahhh . . ."

"*But*—this is life! And now I would like to settle my bill."

"Oh! I see—so you didn't check out?"

"Exactly."

"Well, of *course*. Emergencies occur. May I have your name? I'll just pull up the records—"

"Juan Gutierrez." He spelled it.

"One moment, please." Lassiter heard the ghostly clatter of a keyboard, and was grateful to be spared the Muzak. "Here it is. You'd reserved the room until the twelfth, is that right?"

"I think so, yes."

"Well, it looks as if we held it for as long as we could, but . . . oh, I see what happened: you reached the limit on your Visa Card!"

"Inevitably."

The clerk chuckled sympathetically. "I'm afraid there's an outstanding balance of $637.18. If you'd like to speak with the manager . . . ? I don't know, he might knock a couple of days off."

"No, no. I have no time at all. In any case, this is not the hotel's fault."

"We could send you the bill—"

"Actually . . . one of my assistants, a Señor—excuse me, a *Mister* Victor Oliver, will be in Chicago tomorrow. I can have him stop by the hotel to settle with you. Would that be all right?"

"Well, of course, Mr. Gutierrez. I'll have the bill waiting for him at the front desk."

Lassiter took a breath. "There is one other thing. I left a few things behind. Would you—would you have *kept* them somewhere?" He managed a wistful tone.

"Ordinarily, we send items that are left in the hotel to the address on the credit card, but when the bill is unpaid—I'm sure your things are in the storage room. I'll see that your assistant gets them."

"Thank you. You have been very helpful. I will instruct Victor to see you personally."

"Well, I don't come on until five, so—"

"Perfect. He has meetings all day. I doubt that he will be able to get there until six at the earliest."

"Anybody at the desk could help him."

"I would prefer if he sees you. You are very sympathetic."

"Well, thanks," the man said. "Tell him to ask for Willis—Willis Whitestone."

Lassiter liked Chicago. The high-rises beside the lake, the glitter and sophistication, always surprised him. He took a taxi from O'Hare to the Near North Side, where he checked into one of his favorite hotels, the Nikko. It was a crisply efficient place, elegant and very Japanese. The ikebana displays were as beautiful as they were simple, and there was an excellent restaurant on the ground floor. He took advantage of it, that same evening, washing down his sushi with two large bottles of Kirin. When he returned to his room he expected to find a chocolate on his pillow—but, of course, it was the Nikko, and what he found was an origami figure instead. A wolf, howling, or maybe it was a dog. Whatever it was, it reminded him of *Blade Runner.*

He spent most of the following morning wandering through the rooms of the Art Institute, then stopped by his company's office to shake hands with the staff. The Chicago office was less than half the size of the one in Washington, but the people were just as good and their billings were up. He congratulated them. Afterward, he had a heavy but delicious lunch at Berghof's—which he then walked off on the way back to his hotel. The streets were alive with Salvation Army bell ringers, Christmas lights, and shoppers.

He changed into a pair of sweats and running shoes at the hotel and set out for the waterfront. A stiff wind was blowing off the lake, but he lowered his head and kept at it, covering about three miles up to the Yacht Club and then turning around. By the time he got back to his hotel, it was dark and he was tired.

The shower rejuvenated him, and he dressed quickly. A slate-blue oxford cloth shirt that Monica used to like ("It's *exactly* the color of your eyes!"); a dark blue suit with nearly invisible pinstripes; a burgundy and black rep tie; wing tips and leather gloves. Everything came from Burberry's except the shoes, which were Johnston & Murphy's, and the overcoat—a single-breasted and somewhat worn black cashmere job he'd picked up in Zurich about eight years ago. Most of the time, he dressed casually, but not now. This was for Willis Whitestone.

The hotel was in the 600 block of State Street. He walked, had a drink in a nearby bar—and timed his arrival for six o'clock. He was a little apprehensive—because after all, he was working blind. What if John Doe had left a gun behind, or a kilo of coke? He took a deep breath and strode into the lobby, looking confident.

Willis Whitestone couldn't have been nicer. Lassiter gave him one of the Victor Oliver business cards, glanced at the invoice, and counted out seven hundred-dollar bills. He waved off the change with the remark that "Mr. Gutierrez said you'd been very helpful." Willis thanked him profusely, stamped the bill paid, and handed him a leather bag. Lassiter slung the strap of the bag over his shoulder, waved good-bye, and stepped back out into the cold Chicago night.

When he got back to the Nikko, he took off his coat, but not the gloves. The bag was a scarred and battered carry-on, but very well made, its leather soft and expensive. It was an elegant but casual piece, stiff on the bottom, soft-sided, and with a thick leather shoulder strap. The label inside said Trussardi. It had a central compartment, accessed by a zipper, and large zippered pockets on either side. He opened all the zippers and spilled out the contents on the bed.

There were a couple of retro-looking shirts that were either very expensive or very cheap, a belt, socks, underwear, and a pair of tropical-weight slacks. More promising was a calfskin case that measured about five by nine inches. Looking inside, he found a canceled airline ticket, Miami-Chicago, a pamphlet from Alamo rent-a-car, and three twenty-dollar traveler's checks countersigned by Juan Gutierrez.

His disappointment was visceral.

There must be something else, he told himself. He lifted the bag and hefted it. He went through each of the pockets with his hands, and felt the sides. He felt around inside the bag. He examined the bottom, inside and out. He did it all again. And again. He thought there might be a false bottom, but the floor of the bag didn't move.

The third time around he found what he was looking for: a flat pocket that ran the length of the bag's base. The leather piping that joined the bottom to the sides came free if you pulled it. Lassiter thought, in fact, that he was ripping a seam, but the piping adhered through the magic of Velcro. What he withdrew was a thick, rectangular piece of stiffened fiberboard—the actual floor of the suitcase itself. It opened like a book, revealing shallow compartments incised into foam. One of the compartments held a sheaf of currency, the other a passport. It was all so carefully done that neither protruded.

Lassiter removed the passport and turned it over in his hands. It was Italian, and he could feel his heart accelerate as he opened the stiff, red, pebbled cover. Inside was a photo of the man who'd killed Kathy and Brandon. *Franco Grimaldi.* The picture was a younger version of the computer-generated image that the police had created. He felt a jolt of delight and trepidation, like a hunter whose prey had just walked into the crosshairs of his scope. Which was strange, considering that the man was already in a hospital bed under armed guard. Still, Lassiter couldn't repress his excitement.

John Doe had a name now, an identity—and Lassiter felt certain that whether or not the man ever spoke another word, he would be able to excavate the mystery of why Kathy and Brandon had been killed.

He'd never before understood this pressing need to know how and why someone you loved had died. He'd read about the families of MIAs, the friends and lovers of Lockerbie victims—and he'd been baffled by their passionate quest for knowledge, for justice, punishment, and *details*. Why couldn't they let it go? Why couldn't they get on with their lives and put it behind them?

Now he knew.

He took a miniature from the minibar, twisted its cap off and dumped a couple of ounces of scotch into a water glass. He sat down at the desk with the passport in front of him and stared at it. On the page opposite the photo were the particulars: Grimaldi, Franco. Born 17–3–55. There was a pasted-on square of white paper bearing an official-looking stamp, and what seemed to be a change of address: 114 Via Genova, *Roma*. Lassiter lifted the piece of paper and saw that there was, indeed, another address under it: something-or-other, Via Barberini. There was a passport number, and personal details. Height in centimeters, weight in kilograms. Lassiter did the conversion in his head. Six-one, 220. Hair: *nero*. Eyes: *marrone*. He flipped through the back pages, where the visas and border stamps were to be found, and a piece of paper fluttered to the floor. Lassiter picked it up.

It was a wire-transfer slip, recording a deposit of U.S.50,000 to Grimaldi's account at the Bahnhofstrasse branch of the Crédit Suisse in Zurich. The transfer had taken place about four months ago.

Lassiter set the slip aside and returned his attention to the passport. He was thinking that he'd be able to follow Grimaldi's travels by looking at the stamps in the back, but the pages were so crowded that he had to make a list. Turning the pages one by one, he deciphered as many of the stamps as he could, writing down each entry and exit on a yellow legal pad. When this was done, he tore out the page and made a second list from the first, this time in chronological order.

The passport covered a ten-year period, with the oldest stamps dating to 1986. These showed that Grimaldi traveled back and forth between Beirut and Rome. Lassiter thought about that: in '86, Beirut was the closest thing on earth to the seventh circle of Hell. The only Europeans living in the city were chained to radiators, car bombs were going off in the streets, and assassinations were commonplace on both sides of the Green Line. What the fuck was Grimaldi doing in Beirut?

After Beirut, he cruised between Italy and Spain, entering the latter through San Sebastian and Bilbao. Basque country. There was a visit to

Mozambique in 1989, with an entry at Maputo—and after that *nothing* for nearly three years. Finally, in June of '92, Grimaldi started to travel again, this time to the Balkans. There was a series of trips to the Serbian capital of Belgrade, followed, a year later, by visits to its Croatian counterpart, Zagreb. And then nothing until 1995, when Grimaldi traveled to Prague, São Paulo, and New York. The last entry, at John F. Kennedy International Airport, was dated September 18, 1995.

Lassiter shook his head, uncertain what it meant. Grimaldi might have a second or even a third passport, perhaps in a different name—and not only that. Italy was a part of the European Union, which meant that his passport would not be stamped when he passed through Customs in most European countries. Grimaldi undoubtedly had taken any number of trips within Europe that no official had bothered to record.

Even so ... *still* ... the three-year travel gap, from 1990 to 1992, was suggestive. A stay in prison? Maybe. Or maybe he'd been traveling under another name. The time spent in Belgrade, Zagreb, and Beirut was also of interest: those were not the destinations of a tourist. And what about Grimaldi's visits to Spain and Mozambique? Were they holidays, and if so, from what? What, exactly, did Grimaldi do when he wasn't killing people? How did he make his living?

With a sense of frustration, Lassiter set the passport aside and fanned out the money on the desk. There was more than one currency, and though he didn't count it, Lassiter could see that it was quite a lot—twenty grand or more. Maybe thirty.

Replacing the floor to the overnight bag, he stuffed the cash and the passport into one of its compartments and tossed the clothes in another. Then he zipped it up. He'd send the bag to Riordan in the morning— anonymously.

Meanwhile, the sooner he got back to Washington, the better. He got on the phone and finally found a seat on the red-eye to BWI. The flight was hardly ideal: it didn't get in until one A.M., and Baltimore was eighty miles from Dulles, where his car was parked. But that didn't matter. There was someone in Washington he wanted to talk to as soon as possible, a very old pal in a very dark corner of the government. Nick Woodburn. Woody.

14

He sat in the backseat of the taxi, on the way from BWI to his office, and thought about Nick Woodburn. As schoolboys, Joe and "Woody" had been the best of friends. Growing up in Georgetown, not far from Dumbarton Oaks, they'd gone to the same camps as children and attended the same private schools. As freshmen, sophomores, and juniors, they'd run track for St. Alban's — and if Woody had not lived up to his nickname, they'd have done so as seniors as well. The Incident (as it was later called) occurred some two weeks before the Penn Relays, when a parents' tour stumbled (in one dad's case, quite literally) upon Woody and a girl from the National Cathedral School, screwing in the herb garden of the cathedral proper. There were gasps, giggles, and bellows of outrage — a general tumult that, in the end, sent Nick Woodburn north to spend his senior year at the Hyde School in Bath, Maine.

It was generally agreed that Woody would not end well; or, as one chum put it, "He'll never get in *anywhere* — he's got pecker tracks all over his permanent record." And, in fact, his applications to Harvard and Yale were rejected, as were those to Princeton, Dartmouth, Columbia, and Cornell. (Brown might have taken him, but he didn't apply to Brown, remarking that "Howard Hunt went there.")

In the end Woody enrolled at the University of Wisconsin, where he lettered in track, majored in Arabic, and racked up a four-point on the way to a Rhodes scholarship.

After Oxford, he found his way to the State Department. For two years he worked as a special assistant in the Office of Political and Military Affairs, a liaison job that kept him shuttling between Foggy Bottom and the Pentagon. After eight years abroad — Damascus, Karachi, and Khartoum — he was brought back to Washington to work in the Intelligence Research Bureau (for inexplicable reasons, this was known as INR, not IRB). He'd been there four years, and was now the bureau's chief.

With fewer than a hundred full-time staffers, the INR is at once the smallest and most discreet component of the U.S. intelligence community. As such, it is incapable of the sins for which the larger agencies have become notorious. It does not, for example, mount paramilitary operations, crack codes, or engage in electronic eavesdropping—though it *will* peruse the take of those who do. It does not put LSD in its employees' drinks, nor does it send assassins into the bush or to the palace. What it does, and does brilliantly, is analyze HUMINT—intelligence generated by diplomats and attachés in 157 American embassies around the world.

Inevitably, then, when Joe Lassiter needed the impossible—which is to say, information from Italy on a holiday weekend—he called his friend.

"Woody. Guess who?"

The voice on the other end exploded with delight. "Heyyy, Joe! Where—" And then a change of tone. "Ohh, Jeez, I'm so sorry about Kath. I was in Lisbon when it happened. You get the flowers?"

"Yeah. I got 'em. Thanks."

"The papers said they found the guy—the one who did it."

"Yeah. In fact, that's sort of why I'm calling. I need a favor."

"Say it."

"The guy's Italian. I was hoping you might be able to ask around. I'm gonna do what I can, using my people, and the police will do their bit. But I thought—"

"No problem. Fax me what you have, and I'll get back to you on Monday."

They talked awhile longer and then hung up, promising to have lunch together, soon. Lassiter put on a pair of gloves and went into the study to copy the pages of Grimaldi's passport. It was a clumsy business. When he was done, he faxed the front page to Woody's office at State. Then he tossed the passport into Grimaldi's bag and took a taxi to Dulles to pick up his car.

On the way back he stopped at Parcels Plus in Tyson's Corner, bought a large box, put Grimaldi's bag into it, and addressed the box to Detective James Riordan at Fairfax County Police headquarters. He invented a return address for Juan Gutierrez, paid cash, and kept his gloves on. He considered sending the box to what's his name—Pisarcik—but decided against it. Pisarcik's name hadn't been in the papers; it wasn't public knowledge that the case had been reassigned.

Riordan would probably guess who'd sent the box, but he wouldn't say anything—unless he could prove it, and then he'd go ballistic. As it was, Lassiter thought Riordan would pass Grimaldi's bag on to Pisarcik without much comment.

When he got back to the office, he went to Judy's door and knocked. It was Saturday, but he guessed that she'd be there. As workaholics went, Judy was even worse than he was.

"Come in!" she shouted, and then, on seeing it was him, contorted her face in a look of comic-book surprise and mock chagrin. She was talking on the phone, the receiver clamped between her shoulder and her ear, and typing furiously into her computer.

Lassiter liked her a lot. She had a narrow, fine-featured face, an aquiline nose, and a nimbus of jet-black hair. This last was curly, and given to a certain amount of shedding because she was always tugging at one lock or another, twisting the strands nervously around her forefinger. She was from Brooklyn, and sounded like it.

"Hey, Joe!" she said, slamming the phone down. "Sorry about that. How ya *doin'*?" Then she modified her voice, suddenly remembering. "I mean—you doin' okay?"

"Yeah, I'm hangin' in. Listen, I stopped by because there's a couple of things—I'm going to take a leave of absence for a while—" Judy started to say something, but he waved her off. "We can talk about it on Monday. Bill Bohacker's coming down and, the bottom line is, he'll be running Admin while I'm gone. Leo's going to handle Mergers and Aquisitions—all except one—and I want you to take charge of the rest. All investigations."

"Wow. I . . . thanks!"

"One other thing."

"Shoot."

"There's an *AmEx* acquisition that I want you to handle."

Judy looked puzzled. "American Express? I don't even know about that one."

"No one does. It's top secret."

"Okay," she said, taking up a pen and notebook. "So, who are they going after?"

"Lassiter Associates."

Judy stared, and then she chuckled. Nervously. "That's a joke, right?"

Lassiter shook his head. "No. They want to make us their in-house intelligence unit."

Judy thought about it for a moment. Finally, she asked, "And this appeals to you?"

Lassiter shrugged. "Not particularly. But then, I'm not part of the deal. They get the company—not me."

"So you're selling out . . ."

"I wouldn't put it that way. But, yeah, there's an offer on the table."

"And you want me to take it?"

"No. I want you to negotiate the best deal we can get. If it's anything like the raise you wangled in September, we'll make out like bandits."

Judy grinned. "That *was* good, wasn't it?"

Lassiter made a face. "It was good for you."

Judy looked at him. "Seriously, Joe, don't you think a lawyer would be more appropriate?"

"No."

"Okay."

"Before I take off, I'll give you a memo on the key points. I don't want the lawyers involved until we have a deal—and then, only after you and I have talked."

Judy nodded. And then she frowned. "Why are you doing this? Because of Kathy? Maybe you should hold off awhile."

Lassiter shook his head. "No, I want to do it. I guess Kathy's a part of it, but . . . the truth is, I'm not having all that much fun anymore. It's like I spend all my time holding clients' hands, arguing with lawyers, and—you know what it's like. It's all due diligence and opposition research. And when you look at it—objectively—most of the time—we're on the wrong side."

Judy laughed. "So you noticed that, too, huh? Why *is* that?"

"Well, it's not exactly a mystery, is it? It's because we charge so much—the only people who can pay our rates are the bad guys."

"So you're serious about this?"

"Yeah. I'm what they call 'a motivated seller.' "

"Okay—I'll look for your memo . . . and I'll get on it."

"Or I could take you to lunch. Bring you up to speed."

"Do I get to pick the restaurant?"

"Yeah. As long as it's Ethiopian or Vietnamese. One o'clock okay?"

"Great." She scribbled something on the pad on her desk and then looked up at him. "You said there were a couple of things. What else do you have?"

Judy liked to affect a disorganized and harried mien, but the truth was, she was all business. Lassiter took out the copy of Grimaldi's passport page and slid it toward her. "This one's for me," he said. "I want you to get in touch with whoever we use in Rome and see what they can find out about this guy."

"Oh . . . my . . . God," she said dramatically. "Is this *the guy?*"

"Yes."

"I'll get it right out, but . . ." A worried look came over her.

"I know: it's the weekend."

"Worse—it's Italy. *Our* guy works, but the bureaucracy? Not in your lifetime."

Lassiter shrugged. "Well . . . as soon as possible." He paused. "And tell him—or her—not to kick over too many cans."

Sunday came and went, and so did Monday. There was an hour-long meeting in the conference room, where the firm's managing directors accepted their increased responsibilities with the peculiar demeanor that's reserved for such occasions—a look of "grave enthusiasm."

When the meeting broke up, Lassiter returned to his office, ostensibly to "clear the decks," in fact to await a telephone call from Nick Woodburn.

But the call didn't come, and the morning ground slowly into afternoon. At two-thirty a geriatric courier in spandex and bicycling shoes delivered an envelope from Riordan. Inside were a handful of eight-by-ten glossies, pictures of the strange little bottle that the police had found in Franco Grimaldi's pocket. The bottle seemed almost irrelevant now that the killer's identity was known, but Lassiter touched the intercom and asked his secretary to "See if Freddy Dexter's around."

There were investigators that worked for the firm who were particularly good at interviewing, and others who excelled in the paper chase, relishing, rather than tolerating, the search for pay dirt amid stacks of pleadings, depositions, and archival material. Freddy, who was very young—just three years out of Boston College—was good at both.

When he came in, Lassiter gave him the photographs and a few suggestions. "Get some copies made, and then take whatever time you need. I want to know who made this thing, what it's for—anything you can find out. There's probably a glass museum somewhere—Corning, Steuben, Waterford. Someone'll know."

"I'll hit the Library of Congress," Freddy said, "and the Smithsonian. If they can't tell me, they'll know who can."

"Also, you might check one of the auction houses—Sotheby's—they'll have a glass specialist, or know where to find one."

"What kind of budget do I have?"

"You can go to New York. You can't go to Paris."

At five o'clock Judy leaned in waving a fax. "This just in," she said. "It's from Rome."

Lassiter gestured to a chair, and held his hand out for the fax.

"You aren't gonna be happy," she said, handing him the page and taking a seat.

"Why not?"

"Because he's billing us a ton, and what he's found out is—"

"Fuck all," Lassiter said, glancing at the fax.

"Exactly. According to our guy, Franco Grimaldi has never been arrested. He's a registered voter. Votes *Motore*—"

"What's that?"

"They want to raise the speed limit."

Lassiter gave her a look. "That's it?" he asked. "That's a political *platform*?"

"Bepi says they have a hundred parties over there. Anyway, Grimaldi's not married—correction! He's 'never *been* married.' No outstanding loans, no litigation, no nothing."

"What about credit?"

"He's got a three-hundred-dollar balance at Rinascente."

"What's that?"

"A department store."

"Terrific." Lassiter looked at the fax. "How about military service?"

"Never went in." So much for Riordan's guess that Grimaldi was a soldier.

"Employment?"

"None."

"*Un*-employment?"

Judy started to say something, but stopped herself. "I see what you mean," she said.

"According to this, he doesn't have a source of income. No welfare—nothing! So how does he live?"

"I don't know."

"Well, I want to find out." Lassiter thought for a moment and said, "Another thing: it says here, he doesn't own a car."

"Right."

"And he votes for these motor guys?"

"*Motore.*"

"Exactly. Which would make him the first pedestrian in history who wants to raise the speed limit."

Judy laughed and reached for the fax. "I'll get back to you," she said, and turned toward the door.

"Wait a second," Lassiter said. "I have another question."

"And the answer," she said, turning back to him, "is nine hundred bucks. He says he worked sixteen hours."

"You believe that?"

"Yeah. He's a good investigator, and he knows it's for you. He wouldn't pad it. He got nowhere and he knows you'll be disappointed. He probably worked longer than he said."

Lassiter picked up the paper. "So what do you think?"

Judy pursed her lips and thought for a moment. "Offhand? I think your guy's spooked-up."

Lassiter nodded. "Yeah," he said. "That's what I think, too."

Tuesday afternoon, Lassiter sat at his desk feeling like a fool. He'd delegated everything to Leo, Judy, and Bill, so the company was effectively running itself—or, at least, he hoped it was. He'd given the only lead he had to Freddy Dexter, and now he was on hold, with nothing to do.

He went to the window and looked out. He built a fire and watched it die. He read the *Wall Street Journal*, and thought about going for a run—and then thought of reasons not to. It occurred to him that he ought to call Claire, see if she was free for dinner, something. Then the phone rang, and the voice on the other end was flat and quiet.

"Joe."

"Woody!"

"I ran your guy," he said.

These were just the words Lassiter wanted to hear, but there was something wrong with Woody's voice.

"Thanks," he said. "I appreciate it."

"Don't thank me yet. I'll tell you what, Joe." A pause. "This guy? This guy fucking scares me to death."

Lassiter was taken aback by the intensity in his friend's voice. "What do you mean?"

"I mean, he scares me enough that I'm sorry I put my name on the cable."

Lassiter didn't know what to say.

"Let me ask you a question," Woody said.

"What?"

"You make any other inquiries about him?"

"Yeah. We have a sub in Rome who handles things for us. Is that a problem?"

"Not for me. But you might want to send your subcontractor on a trip."

"You're kidding."

"I'm not kidding."

Lassiter couldn't believe it. "He got bupkis. He didn't find out *anything*."

"Of course he didn't. That's what I'm telling you: this is a very serious man. You probably got his voting record or something, right?"

Lassiter's silence answered the question as clearly as anything he might have said. And, together, they sat on the phone as only two good friends can do, thinking to themselves.

Finally, Woody said, "Let me ask you something else."

"What?"

"What was your sister *into*?"

"Into? She wasn't 'into' anything, Woody! She had a kid. She had a job. She watched 'Friends.' She liked ice cream. You *knew* her!"

Woody thought about it and sighed. "Well, maybe he got the wrong lady."

"Maybe. But he didn't just get a lady, did he? From what I saw, he pretty much cut my nephew's head off." They lapsed into silence again, and then Lassiter came back to the point. "So what about him? What did you find out?"

"Franco Grimaldi is what we call a heavy hitter. In fact, he bats cleanup. He kills people—which, come to think of it, you already know. You ever hear of SISMI?"

"No. What's a Sismi?"

Woody sighed. "I'm going to send you a package."

"You want a FedEx number?"

"No. A foreign service officer will come by tomorrow afternoon with an attaché case handcuffed to his wrist. He'll take out an envelope with a report inside. He'll give the envelope to you, and then he'll leave. Open it. Read it. Shred it. Burn it. And when you're done? Stir the ashes."

Lassiter was standing at the window, thinking about the edge in Woody's voice, when his secretary leaned in to say, "There's an Officer Pisarcik on the line."

"I'll take it," he said, and then, "Hello?"

"Mr. Lassiter?"

"Yeah!"

"This is Officer Pisarcik with the Fairfax Police—how you doing this afternoon?"

"Fine."

"I'm calling because we have some good news."

"Really."

"Yes, sir! We've identified the suspect in your sister's case—John Doe? He's an Italian citizen: a Mr. Frank Grimaldi. Detective Riordan said you ought to be the first to know."

"Great."

"The other reason I'm calling—I think you already heard: Detective Riordan is no longer assigned to the case."

"So I understand."

"I'll be handling it from here on in, so—well, I thought it might be a good idea for you and me to meet."

"Okay. Why don't you just come by? You know where my office is?"

"Sure do! But, uh . . . I'm afraid today's out. Confidentially?"

"Yeah?"

"We're moving the prisoner at four-thirty—"

"Oh?"

"Yes, sir. We're taking him to the strong room at Fairfax General. After that there's a meeting at the precinct. 'Gender, Race, and Law.'"

"Maybe later this week, then."

"Yes, sir."

Lassiter replaced the phone and glanced at his watch. It was four o'clock, and a light snow was starting to fall. Even so, he figured he could just make it.

Normally, he was a relaxed driver, but this time he pushed it. The Acura wove through the traffic, windshield wipers slapping at the sleet as he headed west on 66 toward the hospital.

What he was doing didn't make sense. He knew that, but didn't care. He wanted to see his sister's killer close up—and not just see him. He wanted to confront him. More than that: he wanted to drag the sonofabitch out of his wheelchair and break his face on the floor.

That's what he *wanted* to do. But he'd settle for less. He'd settle for some kind of response. He wasn't sure what he was going to say. Maybe just, "Hey, *Franco*," so he could see the look on the guy's face when he heard a stranger say his name. *"Franco Grimaldi."*

While Lassiter fought the traffic, Officer Dwayne Tompkins was preparing to assist in the transfer of the suspect, John Doe, from Fair Oaks Hospital. Officer Tompkins was known simply as "Dubbayuh" on the force, because he always said, when asked his name, "That's Dwayne—with a W."

He looked at his watch. He was waiting for the orderly to bring up the wheelchair. It wasn't that the prisoner couldn't walk. Therapists had been making him walk along the corridors for ten days now, and Dwayne had been with him every step of the way. Even so, the hospital's regulations required that patients leave in a wheelchair, no matter how well they could walk.

When the chair came, they still had to wait for Pisarcik to call, saying that the wagon was waiting.

Dwayne's part in the transfer would be to escort the prisoner to the main floor, where Pisarcik would meet them. There, the release papers would be signed, and the Fairfax County Police Department would take official custody of the prisoner.

Dwayne would ride with the prisoner in the wagon, providing an armed presence; Pisarcik would follow in a squad car. That was the procedure. At Fairfax they'd put Doe in another wheelchair, after which Dwayne and Pisarcik would escort him to the strong room.

Then and only then would the prisoner be allowed to get to his feet. They'd put him in the strong room, and that would be that: the last he'd ever see of John fucking Doe.

Dwayne was heartily glad that this prisoner was finally being moved. It meant an end to his stint at what had to be the most boring assignment he'd ever had in his short career. For more than three weeks now he'd been sitting—just sitting!—for eight hours a day outside the guy's door. His biggest excitement consisted of checking the credentials of every nurse and doctor who walked in. Checking them in. Checking them out. If he needed to relieve himself, he had to beep the floor nurse—which was embarrassing. He found himself cutting back on liquids. To top it all off, he didn't even get lunch! They brought it to him. Hospital food, and he had to eat it sitting right there in his chair. Balancing the tray on his knees.

Of course, there was that one little nurse. Juliette. He was going to miss her.

The doctor did some kind of final check, Dwayne had to sign a floor release form, and there she was—little Juliette—helping John Doe into the wheelchair.

"So how do you do this, exactly?" the doctor asked him. "You take him in a paddy wagon?"

"Actually, Doc, we don't call 'em 'paddy wagons' anymore," Dwayne said. "That's, uh . . . racist to the Irish."

The doctor laughed. "So what *do* you call them? What's the politically correct term?"

Dwayne shrugged. "We just call it . . . *you* know, 'the wagon.'"

The doctor laughed again. "Well, in that case, do you take him in the *wagon*?"

"Depends. This guy? Yes. But sometimes—they go in the am-bu-lance."

"Looks like he's ready."

"Rock and roll," Dwayne said, and pulling out his walkie-talkie, called Pisarcik to tell him they were on their way. Then he followed Juliette as she pushed the wheelchair toward the elevator. She was real sexy-looking from the back, Dwayne thought, but one of the other nurses said she was some kinda religious nut—so he could just forget about that.

Even so, when they reached the elevator, he pushed the Down button, turned, and gave her a little wink. You never knew. He just might get lucky.

—

The traffic was worse than Lassiter thought, and when the Acura pulled into the hospital parking lot, it was already a quarter of five. Lassiter left the car in a space reserved for "Hospital Administrator," and walked around to the side of the building. Outside the entrance to the emergency room, a tall policeman stood next to a large van with barred windows, smoking a cigarette.

"Excuse me," Lassiter said. "You know an Officer Pisarcik?"

"Inside," the cop said.

He hurried in through the automatic doors. The E.R. was busy and crowded, as it always was in the evening, and it took a while for Lassiter to get the nurse's attention. "I'm looking for a police officer? Pisarcik?"

The nurse rolled her head toward the east corridor. "All the way down," she said.

He went the way she'd indicated, and found Pisarcik—who couldn't have been more than twenty-five years old—standing near the elevator with a walkie-talkie in his hands.

"You can't be here," Pisarcik said, "we're moving a prisoner."

"I know."

"There's another elevator on the south side."

"I'm Joe Lassiter."

"Oh," Pisarcik said. "How do you do?" He hesitated a moment, and added, "You aren't gonna . . ."

"Do anything stupid? No. I just want to get a look at the guy."

"Gee, I don't know, Mr. Lassiter. This area's supposed to be cleared."

"Well, what if I—"

A burst of static crackled through the walkie-talkie, and Pisarcik turned his attention to it. "Pisarcik," he said.

"I got the subject, ready to move. You clear down there?"

Pisarcik threw a wary glance at Lassiter, and said, "Yeah, we're clear."

"Okay, we're on our way."

Pisarcik turned to Lassiter. "Would you mind standing over there?"

"No," he said, moving away from the elevator. "I don't mind." For what seemed a long while, the elevator light remained on 9. Lassiter leaned against the wall as Pisarcik paced back and forth with the walkie-talkie.

"I got a meeting," the policeman said.

"You mentioned that."

"I think I'm gonna be late."

"It's not your fault. You're working."

Pisarcik spoke into the walkie-talkie. "Yo, Dubbayuh—what's goin' on?"

"They had an emergency. Dude going down to radiology."

"We got a meeting."

"Here it comes back. We're on our way down."

Pisarcik turned to Lassiter. "They're on their way down," he said. Lassiter nodded, his eyes on the elevator lights that indicated the floors.

8

7 "Dubbayuh says this is the most boring assignment he's ever had," Pisarcik remarked.

6 "Really."

5 "Yeah, he's been sitting outside that room for almost a month. If he wanted to take a leak, he had to beep the floor nurse."

4 "Huh," Lassiter said.

3 "I hope I don't get an assignment like that. I'd be embarrassed— even if it *was* a nurse."

3 Lassiter nodded, but the hairs were rising on the back of his neck. "Why's the elevator stopped?"

Pisarcik glanced at the indicator lights. "I don't know," he said. "It's not supposed to, but—"

The light blinked off, the elevator lurched into motion, and they waited for the 2 to light up.

4

5 "What the fuck," Lassiter said, coming away from the wall. Pisarcik's eyes were bigger now, and he almost shouted into the walkie-talkie.

"Hey! Dubbayuh! What's going on? *Dwayne!* Where are you, man?" A burst of static was the only reply, and then the elevator reversed field for the second time.

4 - 3 - 2 - 1. The two men breathed a sigh of relief as the elevator shuddered to a halt in front of them. Then the doors parted.

A policeman was sitting on the floor with his back to the wall. His mouth was open in surprise, and gouts of blood rolled down the right side of his face. The wall was spattered. His gun was gone. And a ball-point pen was buried to the hilt in his right eye.

Pisarcik took a step toward the body, hesitated for a moment, and, ever so slowly, sank toward the floor in what Lassiter realized, too late, was a dead faint. In his peripheral vision he saw the cop's forehead smack into the tiles, but even then he couldn't take his eyes off the dead man and the pen. With a *ping!* the elevator doors rattled toward one another, and Lassiter reached out, reflexively, to block them. Down the corridor, and from what seemed like a long way off, people began to shout. The elevator doors shuddered dramatically, retracted into the walls, and then shot forward a second time; and for the second time Lassiter shoved them back. Again. And again.

Somewhere, a woman screamed, Pisarcik moaned, and people started to run.

15

Muzak.

Lassiter paced back and forth in front of the window in his office, trying to ignore the treacly sound that came at him through the cell phone at his ear. Riordan had him on hold, and—

Suddenly, the Muzak cut out. "We found her," Riordan said.

"Who?"

"The nurse. Juliette-whatshername."

"She's *dead?*"

"No, she isn't dead. She's shaken up. Shakin' like a leaf—"

"So what happened?"

"She says he whispered something—like he couldn't talk? And the cop on guard, he comes closer, 'cause he can't hear. Well, he wasn't *meant* to hear, was he? The next thing, Grimaldi's got him by the tie. Jerks him forward, and . . . suddenly there's a lot of blood. Dwayne's on the floor with a pen in his head and Grimaldi's takin' his gun. So says Juliette."

"Where'd he get the pen?"

"Who knows? It's a hospital. There's pens all over the place."

"Then what?"

"She takes him out in the wheelchair."

"Why the fuck—"

"He's holding a Glock! He's got a blanket over his legs and a semi-automatic in his lap! You want her to argue with him? I don't think so. She does what he says. She hits the override button, and they go to the third floor. Next thing, she's wheeling him down the corridor to a second elevator. No big deal: they look like . . . what they are—a nurse with a patient. So they get in the elevator and go to the basement. Right about then the first elevator opens on the first floor and Pisarcik hits the deck. Next thing: Grimaldi's in the parking lot."

"Just like that."

"Yeah. We even found the wheelchair."

Lassiter dropped onto the couch in front of the fireplace. "Then what?" he asked.

"Then? Then she drove him where he told her to go. Which makes it federal. Armed carjacking. So now the Bureau's involved."

"The more the merrier. Where'd they go?"

"Toward Baltimore. Back roads. Only they never got there. He dumped her on a country road, five miles from Olney. Sheriff found her, walkin' on the shoulder. We're still lookin' for the car."

"He can drive?"

"I guess. From what *she* says, he can walk pretty good, too."

"Then why the wheelchair?"

"Hospital policy. You roll in, you roll out."

Lassiter fell silent.

"You notice," Riordan said, "I'm not even *askin'* what *you* were doin' there."

Lassiter grunted. "What about your partner? Pizarro?"

"Pisarcik. Hey! He's embarrassed! He's got a concussion, everyone thinks he's a pussy. But y'know what? He's a good kid. He'll be okay." Riordan paused and, even over the phone, Lassiter could hear the gears shift in the back of his head. "Lemme ask you something," Riordan said.

"What?"

"You sure you don't have something for me? I mean, maybe you said something—to somebody else—*inadvertently* . . . about the prisoner being moved?"

" . . ."

"*Hello?*"

"I'm not even going to answer that."

"Look, it's not like movin' him was a state secret," Riordan said. "We got people on the force, people in the hospital, people at Fairfax. A lotta people knew. Maybe one of them said somethin'. Maybe *you* did."

"Right," Lassiter said, his voice coagulating with sarcasm.

"Anyway . . . the doctors say this guy's gonna need help."

"What kind of help?"

"He needs treatment. And antibiotics. Some kinda special ointment they use for burns—lots of that. We'll get the word out. Maybe we'll get lucky."

"He could be anywhere by now. He could be in New York—"

"Doesn't matter where he is. With an officer murdered, you're gonna get a whole different level of cooperation. Plus, you got the feds involved. And it's not like this sonofabitch is going to blend in."

"Why not?"

"Because he's Italian—*really* Italian—and his face is a mess. And it's always gonna *be* a mess. People look at him? They look away. But they *look.* Y'know?"

"Yeah. Like an accident." The two men lapsed into silence for a moment. There was something nagging at Lassiter, in the back of his mind, and finally it became a thought. *"How come she had the keys to her car?"*

"What? *Who?* What are you talkin' about?"

"The nurse. Why'd she have the keys to her car? The women I know don't keep keys in their pockets. I mean—she's on duty, right? Women keep keys in their purse, a desk, whatever they have in a hospital—a locker."

"Maybe her shift's over, maybe she's on her way out to the car to get something. Probably, she just *had* them."

"You'll ask?"

"Yeah, sure."

"I just don't think a nurse, on duty, would carry around a bunch of keys all day."

Riordan was silent for a moment, and then: "I don't know. It's an interesting question. So we'll ask her, but—she probably just *had* them, y'know?"

"Yeah. I know. I'm sure it's just . . . one of those things. But don't forget to ask her. Because, what happened is: your case just unsolved itself."

Lassiter stayed in the office until late that night, eating Thai takeout straight from the carton, sitting at his desk. A button beside his knee controlled a panel in the wall that concealed a bank of three television monitors—an architectural modification of the previous tenants, who'd made campaign ads for Dan Quayle. Lassiter touched the button with his knee, and the panel slid to the side.

The news at eleven began with a burst-transmission of frenetic music. Grimaldi's mug shot flashed onto the screen and the anchorman declared that "a daring escape leaves a police officer's family in mourning—and a killer among us." The pronouncement was followed by an ad for the *Washington Post* ("If you don't get it, you don't *get* it!"), and finally "the lead story."

This consisted of a series of stand-ups. A perky blonde (one "Ripsy") did her bit from the vantage point of the hospital parking lot, looking terrific next to an overturned wheelchair. Then it was "Over to you, Bill," and the camera segued to a middle-aged white guy with bloodshot eyes and too much hair; he was standing on a darkened road "not far from Olney." He talked about the nurse's "harrowing ordeal," after which the lens moved to Michelle, a soft-spoken black woman, who sat in a Reston town house with the barely composed mother of Dwayne Tompkins—a woman who regarded the camera with a terrible blank stare and seemed unable to speak.

Lassiter watched the segment with chopsticks in one hand and a beer in the other. He found it hard to pay attention to what was being said. There was something about television that drained just enough reality from catastrophe to make it palatable at dinnertime. His sister's death, his nephew's serial cremation, Grimaldi's escape—somehow, television processed these calamities and turned them into a kind of entertainment. Or, if not entertainment, then "grist for the mill," *background noise*, something other than what it really was, which was . . . personal.

He was thinking about this in a distracted way when he noticed that each of the reporters was wearing the same scarf, or the same kind of scarf—a black and tan plaid that had a peculiar, homogenizing effect on their dissimilarities. It occurred to him that, however different the reporters looked, they were all a part of the same tribe: the Burberry Nation. The Wa-Burberrys.

He smiled at the thought, but the smile quickly faded when he realized that this was exactly the kind of smart-ass observation that Kathy used to make. Irritated, he switched off the television, turned out the lights, and drove home, thinking, At least Riordan's back on the case. And that depressed him even further: Jesus, he thought, talk about a search for silver linings . . .

He found it hard to get to sleep. He couldn't shake the sound of Pisarcik's head hitting the floor, or the image of the pen in the dead cop's eye.

Worse, he tossed and turned with the knowledge that Grimaldi might not be caught a second time—which meant not only that the killer would go unpunished, but that he would never know why his sister and his nephew had been slaughtered.

Ciao.

Eventually he fell into a fitful sleep, and when he did, he dreamed about Kathy and, in particular, about something that had happened when they'd been kids.

Kathy was maybe twelve, and he was seven. They were in Kentucky, out on the lake in the rowboat, more to stay away from Josie than anything else. Kathy was sunk down in the bow of the boat, reading a magazine. She had new prescription sunglasses, white frames picked out two weeks before her birthday, the finished product delivered on that date. She'd loved those sunglasses, wore them all the time, even inside, and even at night.

In the boat the glasses were pushed up on top of her head while she read; she stood up and somehow knocked them overboard. He could still hear her scream; he could still see the glasses swaying down through the water. It seemed the easiest thing in the world to retrieve them. But despite the fact that Kathy jumped right in after them, and both of them returned with snorkels and masks—and spent hours searching—the glasses were gone.

In the dream, he was swimming underwater, and he spotted the sunglasses, sitting on the bottom of the lake, stems crossed, as if Kathy had put them down on a table. He dove and dove, but the gleam always turned out to be a chunk of quartz, a can of Bud, a trick of the light. In the end he always came up to the surface with nothing. And when he woke up, he had the feeling, now as then, that he'd let his sister down.

When he came into work the next morning, Freddy Dexter was hanging Christmas decorations on a tree in the lobby. Seeing Lassiter, he shoved a box of ornaments into the receptionist's hands and chased after him.

"What's up?" Lassiter asked.

"Glass," Freddy said, looking pleased with himself.

"What?" Lassiter looked at him.

"The little bottle," Freddy said, reminding him.

"Oh, yeah. We can talk in my office." They went through the door, one after another, and Lassiter gestured to a chair. Sitting down at his desk, he picked up the phone. "You want some coffee?"

Freddy shook his head. Lassiter hung up the phone, leaned back in his chair and waited. Finally, Freddy cleared his throat. "Turns out," he said, "glass is more interesting than you'd think."

"Really."

"Yeah. I mean, you look through it, you drink out of it—but that's only the beginning. There's more."

"Good. I was sort of hoping there was."

"If you want, I could tell you about all kinds of things: 'ductile qualities,' the blowing iron—"

"The what?"

"The blowing iron. Which was first developed in Mesopotamia. Seriously: you have no idea how difficult it was to produce transparent glass."

"You're right. I don't."

Freddy grinned. "Well, as a matter of fact, no one could do it until about 1400, 1450. Not with any regularity. And we can be grateful for that," he said, "because that's why we have stained-glass windows. Instead of clear glass. Your bottle—"

"Aha!" Lassiter said.

Freddy ignored the sarcasm. "Your bottle would have been state of the art." He paused, and added, "In its day."

Lassiter was silent for a moment. And then: "You mean it's *that* old?"

Freddy shifted from side to side. "Maybe. We're workin' from pictures. And without the bottle itself, you can't tell if it's a fake—a *good* fake—or if it's genuine. Or what. Because what happened was, around the turn of the century, the Italians were counterfeiting everything they could lay their hands on—statues, relics, clothes, glass—you name it. There was, like, this huge burst of tourism. People from the States, and all over. And all of a sudden there was this market for antiques."

"So the bottle . . ."

"Is an antique, or maybe it's a copy of the kind priests used in the Middle Ages—"

"*What?*"

"For holy water. I talked to half a dozen experts—a woman at Christie's, the Smithsonian. They all agreed. The kinda bottle we're talking about, the kind of bottle found on your man—they were all made at the Murano glassworks. In Venice. Because of the markings, and the little metal crown on top—this particular kind of bottle is identified with the Knights Templar. Who carried them in the Crusades." Freddy sat back, obviously pleased with himself.

Lassiter stared at him. "The Crusades," he said.

"Yeah. Against Islam."

"And they held holy water."

"Uh-huh. In terms of old bottles," Freddy said, "holy water was a very important substance. For baser substances, they used pottery. I could tell you a lot more about holy-water bottles than you'd ever want to know. For instance, Marco Polo took some all the way to China. Providing, of course, that he went to China—which is a whole other subject. Anyway, I was told—"

"Did you write any of this down?"

Freddy patted a reporter's notebook in his shirt pocket. "Of course. I'll give you a memo. But I thought you'd want to know right away. Bottom line: it's an old holy-water bottle."

"Thanks," Lassiter said, feeling more perplexed than ever. "That was good work, I think."

"Yeah, well—you're welcome. I think."

That afternoon, a courier arrived from the State Department with an attaché case handcuffed to his wrist, just as Woody had said. He asked Lassiter for a picture ID, and after comparing the photo on the driver's license with the face in front of him, he took a key from his pocket and unlocked the briefcase.

Removing a manila envelope, he asked for Lassiter's signature in a small, black book. That done, the courier handed him the manila envelope, snapped the locks on the attaché case, and left without another word. When the door closed behind him, Lassiter tore open the envelope and extracted a thin dossier, to which a yellow Post-it had been affixed. The Post-it read:

> Run with me tomorrow at Great
> Falls—0600 at the
> Overlook—I'll fill in the blanks.
> Woody

The dossier was headed GRIMALDI, FRANCO. It was dated 1–29–89 and contained various classification and routing stamps, as well as the designation NOFORN—which, as Lassiter recalled from his military days, meant "No Foreign Dissemination." The first page of the dossier was a collection of names and dates.

Aliases: Franco Grigio, Frank Guttman
FNU Gutierrez

Well, he could help them with the FNU, Lassiter thought. The acronym meant First Name Unknown. He made a mental note to tell Woody: *Juan* Gutierrez.

DOB: 3–17–55—Rosarno, Calabria
Mother: Vittorina Patuzzi
Father: Giovanni Grimaldi (Deceased)
Siblings:
    Giovanni 2–12–53 (Deceased)
    Ernesto 1–27–54 (Deceased)
    Giampolo 3–31–57
    Luca 2–10–61
    Angela (Buccio) 2–7–62
    Dante 5–17–64
Addresses:
    114 Via Genova, Roma
    237 Via Barberini, Roma
    Heilestrasse 49, Zuoz (Switzerland)
Military service:
    Carabinieri: 1–20–73
    SISMI: 11–15–73 (ret. 4–12–86)
X-ref.:
    L'Onda
    89MAPUTO 008041—FLASH

The accompanying narrative was less cryptic. It explained that Grimaldi had come to the State Department's attention on January 5, 1989, when a flash cable was received from the CIA station in Maputo, the capital of Mozambique. The cable reported the assassination of "a unilaterally controlled asset in the Secretariat of the African National Congress." Local police were searching for an Italian national, "a mercenary" who'd arrived in Maputo from Johannesburg the night before. Because of the deceased agent's importance to "American equities" in the region, the CIA was taking an interest in the matter.

That said, the dossier's author began at the beginning. He explained that Rosarno is a small port "in the toe of the Boot." A fisherman's son,

Grimaldi was one of seven children, and estranged from his family. The only sibling with whom he was known to be in contact was a sister, Angela, a resident of Rome.

According to the dossier, the subject began his nine months' compulsory military service in 1973, after which he was immediately taken on by the Italian military intelligence service, SISMI. Besides counterespionage and antiterrorist operations, the report noted that until it was reorganized in 1993, SISMI's brief included all foreign intelligence activities, anti-Mafia operations, and electronic surveillances.

Grimaldi had been assigned to L'Onda—"the Wave." This was an elite paramilitary unit, modeled after the British SAS, headquartered in Milan. Its principal responsibilities revolved around domestic terrorism, but as the report noted, its record in this area was "checkered." According to the dossier, L'Onda's reputation as an urban antiterrorist unit was severely tarnished in 1986 by revelations of its own role in a string of assassinations and bombings. These incidents, which included attacks on train stations and supermarkets, killed as many as 102 civilians over a period of eight years. Attributed at first to the ultraleft, the bombings were subsequently found to have been instigated by *agents provocateur* within L'Onda. The incidents were said to be a part of SISMI's "strategy of tension"—which, if successful, would have brought a military government to power. The scheme was exposed in 1986 and, soon afterward, L'Onda was disbanded (or renamed, depending on your point of view). Subsequent exposés involving massive corruption and covert alliances with groups such as the Sicilian Mafia led to SISMI's reorganization. By then, however, Grimaldi was gone.

Several photographs of the subject were attached to the report. One had been taken for a military identification card, and showed a handsome young man with dark and sparkling eyes. The second and third photos were surveillance shots, saturated with grain. Taken with a long lens, they showed Grimaldi emerging from a Land Rover at an unidentified airport in what seemed to be a tropical country. There were palm trees in the background, and Grimaldi—no longer young—had the hard look that Lassiter had seen in the hospital and mug shots.

Ciao.

Lassiter thought back to Jimmy Riordan's comments about Grimaldi's physical condition, about how he'd taken a lot of knocks but was still in tremendous shape. "A soldier," Riordan guessed. And he'd been right. In a way.

Attached to the dossier was a sheet of paper with a handwritten notation at the top: *Assets*. Below the heading were a list of properties:

* A penthouse apartment on the Via Barberini in Rome's swank Parioli district.
* A second apartment at the same address (a footnote indicated that the apartment was leased to Grimaldi's sister, Angela).
* A chalet in Zuoz, Switzerland (which the report noted was a village near St. Moritz).

Apart from the real estate, Grimaldi had an account in the Banco Lavoro with an average balance of $26,000. The report noted that he was believed to have additional accounts in Switzerland, specifically at the Crédit Suisse—but details were "unavailable."

Under *Automobiles*, two were listed: a Jeep Cherokee (in Rome); and a Range Rover (in Zuoz). With the exception of a department store account, Grimaldi had no credit record whatsoever. Obviously where meals and entertainment, clothes and incidentals were concerned, "the Subject" preferred to pay cash.

Lassiter thought about that—because, of course, as "Juan Gutierrez," Grimaldi had taken the trouble to obtain a Visa card. Which was good tradecraft. While cash might still be king in Europe, it had long been suspect in the U.S.: counting out a thousand dollars to buy an airline ticket, or to settle a hotel bill, would be uncommon enough to make the transaction at least mildly memorable.

Lassiter leaned back in his chair and reflected. The dossier had given Grimaldi a personality, an *identity*, but it was the identity of a mystery man, and worse than that, it was out of date. With the exception of the reference to Mozambique, there was nothing in the dossier more recent than 1986. Where, other than Maputo, had Grimaldi been during the past ten years? What had he been doing? Were the addresses in the dossier current, or had he moved on?

Lassiter fingered the Post-it. He hadn't intended to go running in the morning. Not at six A.M. But he would.

Great Falls.

Though it was still dark, the night was lifting as Lassiter drove past the closed booth at the entrance to the park. It was two miles from his house in McLean, and he went there two or three times a week, but never so early in the morning. Woody, on the other hand, was a marathoner who liked to be at work by eight, which meant that his days almost always started before dawn. Most of the time, he ran along the C&O Canal, which began a few blocks from his house in Georgetown. Occasionally, though, he drove up to Great Falls, which offered a softer running surface, spectacular scenery, and heartbreaking hills.

Even from the parking lot, Lassiter could hear the water, roaring in the distance. It was just above freezing, but he was dressed for the cold in an old pair of sweats, the collar and sleeves frayed with age. As he walked toward the Overlook, the sky began to glow in the east, a soft pink that backlit the trees and rocks on the Maryland shore. He passed a post that was etched with the high-water marks of all the century's floods—marks that amazed him because the post stood on a bluff, more than sixty feet above the riverbed. There was an informational plaque and a picture of the '32 flood, which had reached a level several feet above his head. He realized that in the back of his mind this was one of a grab bag full of things that he'd planned to show Brandon someday. When the kid was old enough. Which—now— he'd never be.

Arriving at the Overlook, he leaned against the metal rail and looked down at the boiling water. The sound was tremendous, the view spectacular. It was as if the rocks, pounded and polished for millennia, had softened almost to the point of melting. And then he saw a light, bobbing toward him out of the trees. Woody, running with a headlamp strapped to his forehead. Like a miner, out for a jog.

"Hey," Woody said, "my man." They shook hands as the State Department spook leaned forward, stretching out his calf muscles.

"Thanks for the file."

"Did you burn it?"

"Yeah. Just like you said."

"Good," he said, straightening up. "Let's go."

The two of them started jogging across the picnic area, heading toward an equestrian trail that wove through the woods.

"The only problem," Lassiter began, "is—"

"I know. It's dated."

They ran easily, side by side, avoiding the occasional rocks that cropped up along the path. As they went, Woody began to talk.

"Your guy's a thug."

"No kidding."

"After he left SISMI, he went into business for himself."

"Doing what?"

"Some of this, some of that. Mostly, hunting Basques on a contract with Madrid."

"*What?*"

"Basque separatists. He was hunting them. In Spain. France. Wherever. They paid him by the head."

"How the fuck did *that* work?"

"Like a bounty hunter. Except . . . some of these people were what you call 'soft targets' . . . people with asylum in places like Stockholm. Lawyers, academics . . . and then . . . in eighty-nine? He goes to Mozambique . . . different contract. Same kind of work. Blows away a guy named Mtetwa. Senior official in the ANC. Guy's like a hundred years old or something. Which is provocative. One thing Grimaldi didn't know: Mtetwa's one of ours. And the Agency's pissed."

"Don't go so fast."

"I'm *jogging*."

"You're *running*."

"So now there's a little dossier."

Lassiter was breathing hard as they crossed a footbridge near the bottom of a hill that rose, precipitously, for what looked like a very long way. It took two full minutes to get to the top, and when they did, Lassiter's T-shirt was black with sweat, despite the cold temperature. Pausing, he put his hands on his hips, lowered his head and took a deep breath. The steam rose from his back.

"Why'd he leave SISMI?"

"Who knows? A lot of people left SISMI."

"How come?"

"Sinking ship . . . SISMI was so hopelessly compromised, so completely corrupt . . . you couldn't tell the players without a scorecard. C'mon," Woody said, "I'm getting cold." They continued jogging, and as they did, Woody elaborated. "They'd infiltrated the Mafia, the Masons, the Communists, the Red Brigades—but maybe not. Maybe it was the other way around. I mean, who knew? *We* couldn't tell, and I don't think they could, either. Not really. Everyone had a secret agenda—politics, money, religion . . . whatever."

They lapsed into silence for a second time as the morning grew brighter. Coming to a bluff overlooking the river, they jogged in place, watching a kayaker as he picked his way down the rocks, his bright yellow craft flashing in and out of view.

Woody turned to Lassiter. "Problem is, none of this has anything to do with your sister."

Lassiter nodded. "I know," he said.

"So maybe it's you."

"What do you mean?"

Woody spread his hands, and turned his palms toward the sky. "All those years in Brussels. And even here: your company. You don't think you have enemies?"

"*Enemies?*" Lassiter snorted. "Maybe. But not like that."

"You sure?"

"Yeah. And besides, if someone *did* want to take a shot at me . . . you'd think they'd want me to know about it. Otherwise . . . what's the point?" They watched the kayaker launch his boat. Finally, they began to run again. "So that's it?" Lassiter asked.

"More or less," Woody puffed. "After Mozambique, the guy sorta fades away. Like an old soldier. He's quiet for a few years—and then he kills your sister and her son."

They kept running, moving along a ridge above the Potomac. The ground was washboarded with the roots of trees, and it took all of their concentration not to stumble. Finally, Woody said, "Now what?"

Before Lassiter could answer, a fallen tree loomed in front of him on the path and he vaulted it, landing in stride on the other side. Woody was right beside him.

"I don't know," Lassiter said. "Maybe I should see a travel agent. Go somewhere. Take my mind off things."

"Good idea," Woody said. "Let the cops handle it."

"Exactly."

They ran a little farther and before long burst from the woods into a parking lot, running side by side. "So, where do you think you'll go?" Woody asked.

"I don't know," Lassiter said with a shrug. "I was thinking . . . maybe Italy."

Woody didn't bother to argue; they knew each other too well. "Watch your ass," he said.

16

Rome. Leonardo da Vinci Airport.

Lassiter sat in Business Class, leafing through a battered copy of *Time* as he waited for the 737 to empty out. The aisle next to him was a river of jet-lagged travelers, bloodshot and desperate to get to the terminal—where, of course, they would stand together in yet another line. When, some five minutes after they'd gotten to their feet, the last of the passengers staggered out beneath the weight of an immense backpack, Lassiter dropped the magazine on the seat beside him, got up, and walked into the terminal.

There was a coffee stand near the baggage carousel, and he ordered a latte, paying for it with three one-dollar bills. His fellow passengers were four and five deep at the carousel, waiting for their luggage to lurch down the ramp. They had the look of tired predators, scrutinizing every suitcase as it rolled past, waiting to pounce. Eventually they snatched their bags and raced toward Passport Control, where they waited in line yet again.

Lassiter traveled too much to share their eager excitement. When his own bag rolled into view, he remained at the coffee cart, sipping his latte. He watched the bag circle the carousel, again and again, until he was done. Finally, he collected his suitcase, and was waved through Passport Control.

He always forgot how ugly the Rome airport was. As an engineer, Leonardo might have admired the flying machines, but as an artist he'd have winced at the grim terminal, with its sticky floors and bored carabinieri. Even at the best of times, it was dirty, cramped, and chaotic.

Today it was thronged with holiday travelers from everywhere in the world. The coach of a Finnish bowling team, his players massed behind him, argued with a stern Italian woman who sat behind a plastic counter under a large red question mark. A diminutive Indian couple wove through the crowd, tugging the largest suitcase that Lassiter had ever seen, a sky-blue plastic crate lashed together with bungee cords. Wearing chadors, a squadron of Arab women sat in their robes on the tiled floor, surrounded by children, while Italian businessmen and tourists surged this way and that, pushing and dragging their belongings through an incredible din. Passenger agents darted from line to line, clipboards in hand, asking the same questions over and over again as they affixed tiny stickers to hand luggage. Security guards lounged in pairs, or sauntered this way and that, automatic weapons slung from their shoulders. Lassiter ignored it all as he made his way out of the terminal in search of a cab.

The day was gray, cold, and heavy with a mist that almost, but never quite, coalesced into rain. Lassiter found a cab, negotiated a rate, and sat back in his seat, resting his eyes on the bleak housing projects and light industrial slums that fanned out from the airport on the way into town. Italy can do better than this, he thought.

Italy did. His hotel, the Hassler Medici, hunkered above the newly restored Spanish Steps, its windows gazing out over the Via Condotti, Babington's Tea Room, and the local McDonald's. A long-haired boy and girl were standing in the street outside the hotel, handing out flyers to passersby. Lassiter took a flyer, and got a *grazie* in return.

When he registered at the front desk, the tuxedoed clerk apologized to him for the petitioners, and explained their presence. After centuries of abuse, the steps had decayed to the point where they must be repaired, at enormous expense, or declared ruins. After many delays, the renovation had been undertaken, and when the repairs had been made, a ribbon-cutting ceremony was held. But once the tape had been snipped and publicity photos snapped, the steps were declared closed. Lest they fall into disrepair yet again.

The idea made the desk clerk apoplectic. "They fix them, and then they make sure they never have to fix them again! They want to make the steps a *museo*." A cynical laugh. "But of course they forget! They are *steps*, they are there for a reason." He shook his head. "Today—they are open. Tomorrow?" His hands flew up. "I cannot promise." He smiled and extended a key. "Welcome to the Eternal City, Mr. Lassiter."

His room was big, quiet, and expensively furnished. When the door closed behind the bellboy, he sat down upon the bed and, woozy from the long flight, fell backward with a sigh of relief. He didn't mean to fall asleep, but he was exhausted from the flight, and the rainy gray light made the afternoon seem like evening.

When he woke, it was dark and, for a moment, he couldn't be sure if it was six in the morning or six at night. Laying there in the dark, he forced his mind to focus on where (and when) he was. He'd gotten to the hotel at noon. Which meant that it had to be night.

Leaving the bed, he unpacked his bag as a way of waking up. He laid out his toothbrush and razor in the marbled bath, and undressed. Stepping into the shower, he shut his eyes and let the hot water pound on his shoulders, washing the grogginess away. After five minutes, he left the shower for the comfort of a thick white terry-cloth robe that hung from a hook on the bathroom door. Then he went to the minibar for a bottle of Pellegrino water.

Refreshed and alert, he unzipped the nylon carrying case with the portable Compaq nestled inside, and plugged in its adapter. When the computer had gone through its memory routine, Lassiter went to the travel directory and pulled the trip file for Rome. Then he dialed the number for Judy's guy, the private eye who'd come up empty on Grimaldi.

"*Pronto?*"

"Hi . . . uh—you speak English?"

"*Si-iii.*" He made it two syllables, with the second one ending on a high note. In the background a child was laughing crazily.

"I'm looking for a Mister . . . Bepi . . ." The name was impossible.

"Bepi*straversi!* That's me. Is this Joe?"

"Yeah."

"Judy said you'd call."

"You have some time?"

"Absolutely. And everybody calls me Bepi."

"So! Bepi. Where do you want to meet? I could come to your office—"

"*Un momento . . .*" Bepi clapped his hand over the mouthpiece, and Lassiter heard an explosive entreaty at the other end of the line. "*Per! Favore! Ragazzo!*" Silence. Laughter. And then Bepi's mellifluous voice again: "I think . . . maybe . . . La Rosetta is better. We can have dinner." He gave Joe directions to a trattoria in Trastevere. "I'll make a reservation."

Lassiter dressed quickly and left the hotel a few minutes later. He bought a copy of the *Herald Tribune*. Not far from the news agent's, he stopped at a pasticceria for a cup of coffee. The news was bad, but the coffee was so good that he had another. Nearby, a fountain rained on itself, and a boom box throbbed beside an African street vendor who specialized in writing people's names on grains of rice.

La Rosetta was a tiny trattoria in what had once been a working-class neighborhood but had long since become a fashionable venue for tourists and Romans alike. Lassiter had been there the summer before, when the city was baking and breezes had been at a premium. He and Monica had eaten at an osteria, seated at a small table set out in the narrow street, buzzed by files of sputtering mopeds and Vespas. As he recalled, the experience had been semisweet, a romantic mix of candlelight and diesel fumes.

But it was winter now. The tables and chairs had moved inside, and so had the tourists, businessmen, and lovers. La Rosetta turned out to be a friendly cave, with ropes of garlic hanging from the beams, and a fire in the fireplace. As soon as Lassiter stepped in from the cold, a stylishly dressed young man materialized beside him. He had black hair down to his shoulders, green eyes, and a hopeful smile. Except for the smile, he looked as if he'd stepped from an Armani ad.

"You're Joe, right?"

"Yes."

"Tony Bepi."

They shook hands, and found a table at the back of the room, near the doors to the kitchen. The conversation proceeded stiffly around such bland topics as Rome's pollution and the lira-dollar exchange rate. Finally, the waiter slapped down a carafe of house wine and a bottle of San Gimignano, and took their order.

When he left, Bepi leaned over to Lassiter and, in a low voice, asked: "You are angry?"

"What?"

"Such a big bill—for such a little information!"

"What bill?"

"Grimaldi." He sat back in his seat and nodded understandingly.

Lassiter shook his head. "No. I'm not angry."

"I don't blame you."

Lassiter laughed. "Really—"

"Then. . . ?" Bepi frowned, obviously puzzled about why they were there.

"I spoke with someone," Lassiter said, "someone in the government. He says our friend is a very serious guy."

Bepi repeated the word to himself, mulling its meaning. " 'Serious'?" he asked.

"Dangerous. The man I spoke with said that asking about Grimaldi could create problems for you. So, that's the first order of business. If you weren't careful—"

Bepi waved the thought away, shaking his head. He offered a pack of Marlboros to Lassiter, and when Lassiter declined, asked if the American found smoking "offensive." Lassiter shook his head and Bepi sighed with relief. He lighted a cigarette, sucked the smoke into his lungs, and blew a long stream of gray air toward the next table. "I was," he began, "I was . . . how do you say this? *Vigile.* Vigilant. Judy tells me to be careful. I use a service, you know—and when they do a . . ." He looked puzzled as he struggled for the word. "When they do a . . . *wide* search, and there's nothing there, I already know this man is—what did you say? 'Serious.' "

"Why is that?"

An expansive gesture, another plume of smoke. "We're Italians! We have the most famous bureaucracy in the world! There are half a million people in Italy whose only purpose in life is to stamp things! And then they write your name on a little list. Lots of little lists! So when you run a search and nothing comes back?!" He shrugged and leaned forward once again. "Tell me something: You know Sherlock Holmes?"

"What about him?"

"Well," Bepi said, with a knowing and contented smile, "this is the dog—*she does not bark.*"

Lassiter laughed, and they made small talk until the waiter arrived with half a dozen plates on his arm. He dealt them out, one by one, like cards. When he was gone, Bepi looked directly into Lassiter's eyes and said, "Tell me something else."

"What?"

"Is it SISMI? Or the Mafia? Or both?"

Lassiter looked at him for a moment, thinking that he hadn't given Bepi enough credit. Finally he said, "It's SISMI."

Bepi nodded.

"So it's good you were careful."

The Italian shrugged. "And now you're here about this man? Grimaldi?" He shook his head. "Unless it's very important, maybe this isn't such a good idea. It might not be worth your fees."

"Don't worry about the fees."

Bepi thought about that. Made a little moue. "Can I ask? Who's the client?"

"*I'm* the client. Judy didn't tell you?"

"You know what Judy's like. She said you'd call. Wait by the phone. She didn't say anything else."

"Well . . . the thing about Grimaldi is . . . he stabbed my sister in the heart. And then he cut her son's throat. And they died."

"Unnh!" Bepi winced, and looked away for a moment. "I—I'm very sorry." After a suitable silence, he looked up and said, "So. . . ?" Then his index finger fluttered back and forth, like a gate opening and closing between them.

"I need some help."

"*Si-iii?*" As it had on the telephone, the Italian's voice rose an octave, conveying a sense of cautious or tentative availability.

Lassiter poured each of them a glass of wine, sipped, and shrugged. "I'm going to visit a couple of Grimaldi's addresses, see what I can find out. Maybe look up his sister. I'll need an interpreter—and a guide."

Bepi sipped his wine, thought about it for a moment, and leaned forward. "I will help you."

"You're sure?"

Bepi made a gesture, dismissing the dangers. "If it is as you say," he said, "it's personal, between you and Grimaldi—I'm not worried. This is a civilized country. Even the Mafia . . . they're not sociopaths. If I'm translating for you—I'm like the wallpaper, you know?"

Lassiter nodded, a little uncertainly, and then the two of them dug into their plates of calamari rings and roasted vegetables.

They set out early the next morning in Bepi's car, a Volkswagen Golf. Though the car was an old one, it was spotlessly clean and almost professionally maintained. Even so, a plastic Lenin stood on the dashboard where a plastic Jesus might have been, and a small soccer ball dangled from the rearview mirror. Bepi snapped a cassette into the tape deck, and Verdi poured forth.

A series of near-death encounters followed almost immediately as the Italian wove in and out of traffic, barking invectives at other drivers and leaning on his horn—which tootled inanely through the din of the Roman rush hour. Lassiter showed him the three addresses that he had: the one from Grimaldi's passport and the two that Woody had supplied. Bepi frowned at the addresses. "These are two different worlds," he said. "Which one do you want to see first?"

"The current one. The one from his passport."

The apartment was in Testaccio, a working-class neighborhood just down the hill from the Aventine. It was a six-story walkup, a moldering tenement whose flaking gray exterior was livened only a little by the laundry that seemed to hang from every window. An emaciated old woman was sweeping the sidewalk with a twig broom and talking to herself.

"This can't be it," Lassiter said.

"Why not?" Bepi replied, double-checking the address.

"Because he drives a Range Rover. Because he's got a place in Switzerland."

"This is it, 114."

Lassiter didn't believe it. "It's a mistake."

"Let me talk to the old woman." Bepi climbed out of the car and went up to her with his hands together and his head lowered, supplicating. "*Scuzi, bella . . .*"

It only took a minute, and Bepi was back. "He hasn't been here for a couple of months, but the rent's paid. Let's go upstairs. Maybe we can look at it."

Grimaldi's apartment turned out to be on the top floor, next to a darkened stairwell that smelled of cabbage soup. They stood in front of the door for a moment, gearing up.

"I hate this," Lassiter said.

"What?" Bepi asked.

Lassiter made a gesture. "This kinda thing. I did it once before, in Brussels, and it didn't turn out that well."

"Really?"

"Yeah. It makes me wish I had a gun."

"No problem," Bepi said, conjuring a Beretta from a holster at the small of his back. "Here. Take mine."

Lassiter gaped. "Jesus Christ!" he said. "Put that away! What are you—Sam Spade?"

Bepi shrugged, the gun vanished, and Lassiter knocked on the door—tentatively, uncertain who or what might be inside. When no one answered, he knocked a second time, somewhat louder, and then a third. Finally, he stepped aside to let Bepi open the door, using his Visa card to spring the cheap lock. "I still think it's the wrong place," Lassiter said as the lock slid back and the door swung open.

The room they entered was meticulously clean and as bare as a monk's cell. The old pine floors were smooth and glowing, as if they'd been sanded with steel wool. The walls were empty, except for an old wooden crucifix, its arms entwined with a desiccated palm frond. There were no other ornaments or pictures, and very little furniture. A narrow metal cot; a battered armoire; a gunmetal desk and straight-backed chair; a sink with a cracked mirror above it. A single window looked out on a trash-strewn courtyard, and the only light in the room was an overhead fixture with a forty-watt bulb.

"Look," Bepi said, gesturing to the desk. "The man reads." He picked up one of the books, and looked at another. "Or maybe he just prays."

There were three books. The first was a Bible, its pages so thickened with use that it no longer lay closed, but fanned open to a page of Revelations. Under the Bible was a Latin primer, and beneath that, a religious pamphlet. The pamphlet was entitled, "Crociata Diecima."

"What's that?" Lassiter asked.

Bepi handed him the pamphlet. Beneath the title was a large oval, and inside the oval a line suggesting a hill, with a stark cross at the top. The cross cast a long shadow. Written in the shadow, in bright gold letters, were the words: *Umbra Domini*. Lassiter pointed to the title: "Crociata Diecima."

"What does that mean?"

"Tenth Crusade," Bepi said.

"Which is what?"

"I don't know. I'm not superstitious."

"You mean religious."

"*Ehhh!*" The sound exploded from the doorway at their back, and the two of them spun around, expecting the police, or worse. Instead an old man barged into the room, shaking his finger at them as if they were children, and shouting, "*Vietato! Vietato! Vergogna!*" He grabbed the pamphlet from Lassiter's hands, tossed it back on the desk, and shoved them out the door, his finger wagging like a metronome from side to side.

"What's he talking about?" Lassiter asked, heading for the stairs.

"He says we're bad. He says we should be ashamed."

It was an unnerving display, but by the time they reached the street, they were both smiling. "He *kicked* our ass," Lassiter said, getting into the car. "What was that thing with the finger?"

"*Vergogna!*" Bepi replied, putting the Golf into gear and pulling away from the curb. "Look, he's still there! I think he's getting our license plate number."

Lassiter turned and saw the old man standing on the curb, peering after them. "So what's *vergogna?*" he asked.

"It means 'Shame on you!' " Bepi shrugged. He stuck his hand out the window and waved at the old man. "So? Where to?"

Lassiter took a piece of paper from his pocket and showed it to Bepi. "Via Barberini."

The apartment building was a luxurious one, just north of the Villa Borghese, in one of Rome's most fashionable neighborhoods. The building's facade was faced with creamy marble, and everything else seemed to be glass or brass. They found the superintendent in the lobby, misting a bank of ferns at the edge of a small fountain. Even without looking, Lassiter knew the fountain was filled with Japanese carp.

At first the super didn't remember Grimaldi at all, but a fistful of lire changed all that. Pocketing the money, the old man smiled. Speaking to Bepi in Italian, he said it was a long time ago, but he remembered Signor Grimaldi very well—*and* his sister. With a wink and a nod, he conveyed the idea that Grimaldi was a man of affairs.

"What kind of 'affairs'?" Lassiter asked.

Bepi put the question to the superintendent, then translated. "Both kinds. Business *and* women. He got around."

The superintendent laughed. "Si, si! Giacomo Bondi!"

Bepi began to translate: "He says he was like—"

"James Bond. I get it."

The superintendent went on to describe a man whose life was *larger* than life until—*powww!* He made an explosive gesture, his arms rising into the air like parentheses. Suddenly Signor Grimaldi is *assolutamente diverso.* No women, no parties, no tips! He sells his car, he sells the apartment! He sells the other apartment! He gives away furniture, paintings—*tutto tutto tutto.* Everything must go—until he has nothing. And, in fact, the superintendent said, he himself benefited from the man's philanthropy. Grimaldi gave him a fine leather jacket—*si si si*—*fino, suave.* The old man stroked his sleeve for a moment. Finally, he blew a breath of air through his lips and looked to heaven with an expression of bafflement.

"When did this happen?" Lassiter asked, and Bepi translated.

"Five years ago."

"And after that?"

The superintendent shrugged. *"Niente."*

"Ask him if he knows where the sister went."

Bepi did, and the superintendent muttered a string of si-si-si's. Gesturing for them to follow, he led the way to his office. He took a ledger from the bookshelf, paged through it until he found the names he was looking for, and turned it around for Lassiter and Bepi to see:

Grimaldi #601–03 — 114 Via Genova, Roma
Buccio #314 — 1062 Ave. Cristoforo Colombo, Roma

Thumping the addresses with his forefinger, the superintendent shook his head disapprovingly and made a face. "No good," he said in English.

Their car was parked, Italian-style, where Bepi had left it—on the sidewalk, just up the street from the apartment house. A pretty girl was watching it for them, standing in the doorway of a produce shop, ready to intervene with the traffic police. "Eh, Cinzia," Bepi said, displaying his gap-toothed smile. *"Grazie, eh?"*

An older woman, stern, the proprietess of the florist shop next door, surged out onto the sidewalk and began haranguing them. Bepi said something in a high voice and ran forward, his butt tucked in, as if she was whipping him. The girl laughed gaily, and even the old woman smiled. Bepi held up a finger, went into the shop with the old woman and emerged with a small poinsettia plant, the pot wrapped in red foil.

"I thought—for the sister," he said. "Flowers almost always get me in the door."

Bepi took his time arranging the plant on the floor in front of the backseat, getting newspapers and plastic bags from the trunk to make sure no dirt escaped into the car's interior.

It was at least a forty-five-minute drive, and when Bepi stopped the car, they were in front of a shabby high-rise on the outskirts of Rome. The building was a gray monster, totally without ornamentation. There was graffiti everywhere, and litter—and no attempt at landscaping. Not even grass grew around the building; there was only the sunbaked dirt and asphalt.

Bepi pushed a button and spoke animatedly into a battered grille. A moment later the door gave off a harsh buzz and Bepi yanked it open.

"What did you tell her?"

Bepi shrugged. "The truth. We have some questions about her brother Franco. She was excited, in fact. Did we have news of him? I said yes, in a way." He lifted his eyebrows and held the poinsettia in front of him. The elevator smelled of urine.

Grimaldi's sister, Angela, was thirtyish. She wore a pink track suit and a heavy gold chain around her neck and had a haggard look about her. Bepi presented the poinsettia, which was accepted with a lot of fuss. There was a spate of discussion between the two—which seemed to resolve itself when Bepi acceded to her insistence that glasses of *limonata* were in order.

This took quite a long time, and while they waited Bepi bounced his eyes around the room and back to Lassiter. The place was a mess, the disorder so profound that it spoke of despair. There was a small plastic Christmas tree in the corner, and huge, elaborately framed photographs of children on the wall. Everywhere else there were toys and piles of clothing, newspapers, dirty dishes. From an unseen room came the inane melody of a Nintendo game.

When at last the drinks were brought out on a gilded wooden tray, and they were all seated in the wrecked dining alcove, Angela inclined her head, arranged her body in the chair to its best advantage, and fingered the gold chain at her neck.

Bepi said something by way of introduction, and she tossed him a brittle smile. She twirled a lock of black hair around her finger. Bepi gestured and talked with great earnestness. Lassiter caught the word *fratello*.

Angela became animated and spoke passionately, her hands accompanying her words in broad, slashing gestures. She sounded bitter, but all Bepi said by way of translation was, "She wants to know, what is it now, what has her big brother done now? He has taken away her beautiful apartment. Does he want this one, too?"

"I don't get it," Lassiter said. "What's she talking about?"

The woman spit out a phrase. Then she sighed and her face took on a resentful expression. She jammed a thumb at her heart.

"Her brother destroyed her life," Bepi said.

More rapid-fire discussion.

"Franco *was* very generous," Bepi said. "He bought her the apartment in Parioli—where we were before. And then, about five years ago, he has a . . . uh, religious experience."

"A *what?*"

"He becomes very devout. He takes Angela's apartment back. He sells it and gives the money to charity. The same with her car. And *his* car. And *his* apartment. He gives *everything* to one of those religious groups—and says everyone should live like a monk. Then . . . nothing. He rents a room in the slums. She fights with her husband. Her husband walks out. She's homeless. Then she's here. With the *bambini*. She says"—and here Angela's voice began to rise—"she says the pious shithead ruined her life. He might as well have shot her." Bepi took a deep breath and offered Angela a handkerchief.

Lassiter shook his head. Grimaldi's sister was obviously telling the truth, or the truth as she knew it, but she was just as obviously mistaken. Monks didn't slaughter children in their beds, and once they'd taken a vow of poverty, they sure as hell didn't walk around with $20,000 in cash hidden in the false bottom of an overnight bag. That's what Lassiter thought. But what he said was, "Tell her I'm trying to find out if her brother had some connection to my sister. Tell her my sister's name is—was—Kathy Lassiter."

More discussion. Lassiter caught the words "Stati Uniti," but the woman looked baffled and shook her head decisively.

Bepi shrugged. "No."

"Tell her the 'pious shithead' murdered my sister and her little boy," Lassiter said. "Tell her he's wanted for murder."

The discussion that followed was punctuated by one explosion of skepticism after another. Angela's eyes flew back and forth to the ceiling as she shook her head dismissively. *Non e possibile. Fantastico.* The woman finished with an odd little praying gesture with her hands, rolling her eyes like a Goya.

"She says it's true, Franco was a very hard man in the past—*very* hard—but what you are saying? This is impossible."

"Why?"

"Because he's—practically a priest, she says. He took vows of chastity, of *poverty*. He . . . em"—Bepi made quotations marks in the air—" 'polishes his soul.' He lives in another world. He no longer cares about his poor sister. He no longer cares about his nephews or his nieces. He says *God* will provide for them." Bepi shrugged expressively. "She doesn't mean to speak ill of the Church, of course." He finished with a shrug. "She says you have the wrong person."

The woman had still more to say, and it was equally emphatic and emotional.

"He cannot have murdered anyone," Bepi translated when she finished. "This is not possible because it would send him to Hell. She says her brother is a fucking saint—that's a quote—and that he—I don't know this word—*hits* himself for impure thoughts."

"Whips himself."

"Yes! He whips himself for very small sins—so a great sin—a mortal sin—naturally, this is not possible."

There was nothing else to say. Angela glanced at her watch and got to her feet, signaling that the interview was over. There was an exchange of effusive thank-yous—for the poinsettia plant and the *limonatas*—and then Lassiter and Bepi were back on the grubby street.

"So what are you thinking?" Bepi asked as they walked back to the car.

In fact, Lassiter was thinking of the wire-transfer slip that had fallen from Grimaldi's passport. "I was wondering," he said, "why someone like Grimaldi, who's taken a vow of poverty, would have a Swiss bank account."

17

He and Bepi shook hands outside the Hassler.

In the car they'd agreed that Bepi—continuing to be *discreto*—would chase down a few loose ends on Lassiter's behalf. For one thing, the Italian would call the "estranged" members of Grimaldi's family that were listed on the State Department's dossier. Maybe they were back in touch.

As for Lassiter, he planned to fly to Switzerland in the morning, if he could book it.

"Not to check out Grimaldi's Swiss bank account!?" Bepi said, shocked. "Because, you know—it's . . ." He wagged his head hopelessly.

Lassiter said, "Of course not," although he wasn't being entirely candid. "Grimaldi owned a house there, too."

"Oh, that's right," Bepi said, distracted by the pretty girl collecting signatures for the Spanish Steps petition. "I remember—near St. Moritz. And then?"

Lassiter said he didn't know.

The girl was tugging on Bepi's arm, cajoling him, flirting, and Bepi allowed himself to be dragged toward the young man holding a clipboard. He turned and looked back at Lassiter with a shrug and a grin.

The flight to Zurich was only an hour, and it took Lassiter almost that long to find a hotel. The major hotels were booked. In the end he took a room at the Florida, a pleasant if slightly seedy older hotel, just up the street from Limmat Quai. He'd stayed there once before, when Lassiter Associates had worked a case involving the Steelworkers Union and a West Virginia aluminum foundry owned by a reclusive Swiss billionaire.

The room was much like the one he remembered from that trip:

unexpectedly large, with a single plate-glass window that looked out toward the Zurichsee, a few blocks away. It might have been a beautiful view of the lake, but the glass was fogged with moisture, and the air with snow.

Zurich was one of Lassiter's favorite cities, though he couldn't say exactly why. Gray and stony, ancient and aloof, it crouched at the edge of a dark lake, its icy waters fed by the Alps. It was a city in love with high culture, more German than Swiss, and made for walking. Lassiter tossed his overnight bag into the armoire and left the hotel to wander along the quai. A light snow sifted out of the colorless sky, settling on his shoulders. Heading in the general direction of the Old Town, he watched a pair of swans gliding on the cold, black river. Maybe it was the neighborhood he was in, but it seemed as if Zurich's biggest industries were lithographs, books, and antique musical instruments, with herbal remedies close behind.

Before long he crossed the Münster Bridge into the narrow and cobblestoned streets of the Old Town, with its supernaturally expensive shops. He was hoping the walk would raise his mood, and it did—for a while—but in the end he just felt colder. The shops were beautiful, but under the circumstances, pointless: he needed nothing, and there was no one to give anything to.

He took a turn onto the Bahnhofstrasse and walked for blocks past a series of brilliantly illuminated Christmas windows, until he found himself standing in front of a building that he hadn't realized he'd been looking for: the Crédit Suisse branch where, four months earlier, Franco Grimaldi had received a wire transfer.

He wasn't sure why he'd wanted to see it: it was just a bank. But standing there on the dark Zurich street, knowing that it was a part of Grimaldi's world, that he'd come and gone through those very doors, gave Lassiter hope. Like the bare room on Via Genova, this was one of the killer's places—and Lassiter felt close to him here.

He ate an uninspired dinner in the hotel's dining room, and asked the concierge about the best way to Zuoz. The concierge recommended against driving all the way. "You'll be quicker on the train, at least to Chur, and perhaps drive from there." He would arrange the journey, arrange for the return of Lassiter's rental car. The Swiss were famously incurious, but the concierge, perhaps buoyed by Lassiter's generous tip, made small talk. "Zuoz is beautiful. You go for the skiing? Yes?"

"Yes." What else was he to say?

"It's not so good this year—for the snow—but there is always the glacier at Pontresina."

They talked like this for a few minutes, after which Lassiter returned to his room. Reaching into the minibar, he came up with a miniature of scotch, and tumbled its contents into a water glass. Then he sat back, and dialed Max Lang.

Max was president of the International Brotherhood of Bank Clerks and Financial Services Workers—a Geneva-based trade secretariat with more than 2.3 million workers in countries as far apart as Norway, India, and the U.S.—which meant that Max spent most of his time, as he put it, "flying through the night from one speech to another, one airport to the next."

The steelworkers' case had been different. Max hadn't been asked to give a speech, but to end a war in which fifteen hundred workers had been locked out of their jobs in Emporia, West Virginia. Lassiter Associates had been hired by the union to investigate management. From West Virginia, where the plant was located, the paper trail led to Switzerland. This was surprising in itself; further investigations showed that the plant was secretly owned by a Dutch industrialist—a right-wing playboy who liked nothing better than busting unions.

Lang's secretariat—which, after all, represented bank tellers, clerks, cashiers, actuaries, and insurance workers, among others—had nothing to do with the steelworkers. But as "a fraternal courtesy," its president had gone out on a limb to intervene with the billionaire's bankers—now *there*, Max had a lot of clout. Those bankers were persuaded that union-busting was really not in their best, long-term interests.

The bankers had listened, and in the end they came around. The deadlock was broken. The workers got their jobs back. And Max Lang looked like a hero.

"Max—it's Joe Lassiter."

"Joe . . . heyyyy!"

"How you been?"

"Excellent. You have another case? Like Ravenswood?"

"No."

"Too bad. We really fucked him, didn't we?"

"Yes."

"I mean, we *focked* him."

"In fact, Max, that's what we did."

"Because he deserved it!"

"Right."

"Okay! So *fock* him."

Lassiter laughed: he'd forgotten about Max's penchant for imitating Al Pacino in *Scarface*.

"Oh, Joe," Max said, chortling at the memory. "That was a good time. The best time! Happy endings."

"Indeed."

"So . . ."

"I need a favor, Max."

"Whatever—"

"It's kinda big. You can say no."

Max grunted. "Ask."

"It isn't something we can talk about on the phone."

"Okay."

"Lemme ask you something: you still use PGP?"

"Until something better comes along," Max replied.

"Same key as before?"

"Absolutely."

"I'm going to send you some E-mail—still got the same address?"

"Yeah, sure."

"Great. And then . . . maybe we can get together in Geneva."

"*Wunderbar!*"

"Maybe in a couple of days. I'll call ahead."

"Good."

"And like I said, if this is something you don't feel right about—I mean, it's important, but—"

"Will you send me the *fockin'* file?"

"I'll send it!"

"So send it!"

When they'd hung up, Lassiter took out his portable computer, created a file—*grimaldi*—and typed a short letter:

—

max—

it's a heavy-lift, but . . . i need a history on an account at the bahnhofstrasse branch of the credit suisse in zurich. i thought one of your members might be able to pull it up. (!) anyway . . . the account belongs to an italian. his name is franco grimaldi. the account number is Q6784–319. and what i'm particularly interested in is a wire transfer that was made in july. the amount was $50,000, and i need to know who sent it.

joe

Lassiter saved *grimaldi* to his hard disc and changed directories, switching into */n-cipher, pgp* This was a proprietary version of Pretty Good Privacy, a powerful, public-key encryption program that was all but unbreakable. And it had better be. What he was asking Max Lang to do wasn't just a crime. It amounted to an act of war—an attack on Switzerland's very raison d'être: bank secrecy. For Max to even discuss the possibility could cost him his job, and so Lassiter encrypted the message on his hard disc. It was a simple matter: he called up the Main Window, clicked on Encrypt, and selected *grimaldi* as the file to be encoded. A dialogue box flashed onto the screen, and he scrolled through a long list until he came to *maxlang@ibbcfsw.org.ch.* With Lang's E-mail address highlighted, he hit the carriage return, and *Working* appeared in the center of the screen, blinking on and off. When the word disappeared and the file had been encrypted, he returned to the first menu and clicked on Settings. What he was about to do was more for Max's protection than his own: to make sure that Max didn't decrypt the file and save the plain-text copy to his hard disc, Lassiter selected Advanced Options and flagged the file "Eyes Only." This meant that, once decrypted, the plain text could be displayed and read on the computer screen, but it could not be saved as a file.

With these precautions in place, he sent the file on its way. When he got to Geneva, the answer would be waiting for him. Or maybe not. It was, after all, a heavy lift.

The next morning, Lassiter had breakfast in his room and telephoned Riordan.

"You shouldn't of bothered," Riordan said. "*Update?* How we *doin'?*" He snorted. "I got nothin'. I got zero. The only thing I can tell you is, they found the nurse's car in a ditch, somewhere north of Hagerstown."

"And Grimaldi?"

"*Vanished.* That's the word the papers are using, and that's what I'm using. The guy *vanished*, okay? And it's a fucking disaster. We got an officer murdered in the line of duty—second one in a week. It's Christmas, and there's two funerals. Two! Think about it: we got brave mother No. 1 over here, brave mother No. 2 over there, a sobbing young widow, a fatherless baby all over the place—and what are we lookin' for? A perp with a face like a pork rind!" He snorted. "Not that anyone's seen him—'cause they haven't." Riordan paused to catch his breath. "So, how 'bout you? You gonna brighten my day with a lead? Where the hell are you, anyway?"

"Switzerland."

"Hah."

"I just got here—from Rome."

"No kiddin'. So what'd you find out in Rome?"

"I found out . . . that Grimaldi went through some kind of religious conversion. Liquidated his assets. Gave his money to charity."

"You're shittin' me."

"I'm not."

There was silence at the other end of the line, and then Riordan said, "Religious conversion, my ass."

Zuoz was beautiful, an exquisite town tucked hard against a mountain. Substantial, sixteenth-century houses lined the narrow streets. The houses were painted cream or ocher or gray and had massive and beautiful wooden doors. The sidewalks were full of extremely well-dressed people hurrying through a soft rain.

Even with a detailed map it took him some time to find the address he was looking for, which should have been only a ten-minute walk from the center of town. But despite the map and the town's small size, he got lost and twice had to ask his way, stumbling through the German. "*Isch das der richtig wag to Ramistrasse?*"

"Yes."

He passed a tiny square with an austere and perfectly square fountain—so different from the fountains in Rome. The only ornament was a statue of a standing bear with one of its paws cut off, the emblem of some ancient Swiss family.

Finally, he found the house, a three-story chalet with a brass plaque beside a wooden door that might easily have been older than America. The plaque read:

Gunther Egloff, Direktor
Salve Caelo
Services des Catholiques Nord
Gemeinde Pius VI

Lassiter knocked and waited. Finally, a voice came through a speaker next to the plaque. "*Was ist?*" Lassiter identified himself, and moments later a middle-aged man opened the door, looking prosperous in every detail. A modest paunch, a cashmere sweater, sheepskin slippers on his feet. A pair of reading glasses were in his hand, and a stemmed glass of red wine. There was operatic music from the interior and a smell of wood smoke.

"*Bitte?*"

Lassiter hesitated. His story seemed outlandish and impossible in the face of this bourgeois comfort. Murder. Arson. Terror in the night.

"Do you speak English?"

"A little."

"Because my German—"

"Yes, yes—how may I help you?"

"It's about the owner of the house. Mr. Grimaldi."

A look of surprise crossed the man's face, and then he smiled, holding open the door.

"Come inside, please. You must be cold."

Lassiter thanked the man, and introduced himself on his way through the doorway.

"And I am Egloff," the man replied, ushering him into an enormous room dominated by a massive, fieldstone fireplace. "Will you join me in a glass of wine?"

"That's very kind," Lassiter said as his host turned down the Puccini, took a firetool in hand and poked at the burning logs. "But I'm afraid you're mistaken about the house. Mr. Grimaldi hasn't owned it for several years."

"Really."

"Yes. May I ask? You are American? Canadian?"

"American."

"And tell me: you are interested in the house—or in Mr. Grimaldi?"

"In Grimaldi."

"I see." Egloff poured a glass of wine and handed it to him.

"I'm an investigator," Lassiter said.

Egloff's eyebrows bounced, and he looked amused. "An investigator!"

Lassiter's eyes were drawn to the far wall, where a topographical map depicted a mountainous region in a country without borders. Egloff followed his gaze.

"Can you guess where it is?" he asked.

Lassiter shrugged. "Somewhere in Russia . . . Georgia, maybe."

"Bosnia. We were quite active there. With the refugees."

" 'We'?"

"Salve Caelo."

Lassiter shook his head. "I'm sorry—"

"It's a charity. We do a lot of work in the Balkans."

"Huh," Lassiter said, recalling Grimaldi's passport, and the multiple entries at Zagreb and Belgrade.

"Do you know much about Bosnia, Mr. Lassiter?"

Lassiter made a helpless gesture with his hands. "Enough to know it's complicated."

"But it's not complicated. It's very simple. And I can explain it in two words."

Lassiter smiled. "Really?"

Egloff nodded. "*Islamic imperialism.* What we have in Bosnia is a political melanoma, the beginning of something terrible. *Hmmm?* What do you think?"

"I think that's more than two words," he said.

Egloff laughed. "So it is! I am corrected! But now you must tell me: What is it that you are investigating—in *Zuoz* of all places?!"

"A murder. Murders."

"Oh!? Really, Mr. Lassiter, you are one surprise after another!"

"A woman and her son were killed," Lassiter replied.

"I see. And Herr Grimaldi?"

"He is the murderer."

"Ah." Egloff sat down, crossed his legs, and took a sip of wine. "I don't think so."

Lassiter shrugged. "Then you're mistaken."

"Well . . . if you're certain. But what do you hope to learn?"

"I hope to learn *why*—why he did it."

Egloff made a clucking sound and sighed. "And you came all the way from America? To look at his old house?"

"I was in Rome. And I knew he had a house here, so . . ."

"Yes. Well. The house. As I said, it was his at one time. But that was years ago."

"So you've met him?"

"Oh, yes." Another sip of wine.

"And what was your impression?"

There was a dim rasp from a speaker, an object Lassiter had not noticed that sat on the table next to them. It was an intercom of sorts, the kind of monitor Kathy used to carry around her house, setting it nearby when Brandon was asleep—so that she could hear him if he cried.

"My wife," Egloff said. "She's quite ill."

"I'm sorry."

"I won't be a minute. If you'll help yourself . . . ?" He gestured toward the decanter and got to his feet.

When Egloff left the room, Lassiter studied the watercolors that lined the walls. They were quite extraordinary depictions of religious themes executed in modern dress. An Annunciation showed a girl in a reindeer print nightgown kneeling by her bed, as a muscular angel surged from the television set. There was a Last Supper at a large table in what looked to be a cafeteria. Saul on the road to Damascus was a man with a rucksack, the road full of cars, a shimmering light breaking over his head like a waterfall. After a few minutes Egloff padded back in his sheepskin slippers.

"These are amazing," Lassiter remarked.

"Thank you. My wife did them," he said, settling into a chair and changing the subject. "But as for your Mr. Grimaldi . . . When I saw the house, I thought: Eurotrash. Everything was leather and chrome. Black leather! Can you imagine—in a chalet like this? But then I met the man, and . . . he is not what I expect. He is modestly dressed. He is quiet. He is a gentleman."

"And . . . did you get a good price?"

Egloff hesitated for a moment, and replied, "Yes. A good price—but fair."

"Did he say why he wanted to sell?"

Egloff shrugged. "I had the impression he was having financial difficulties."

"Really?" Lassiter asked. "Because I was told he'd given all his money to charity."

"Oh? And who told you that?"

"His sister."

"I see," Egloff said, seeming for the first time a bit off balance. "Perhaps your organization—you did say it was a charity . . . ?"

Suddenly, Egloff clapped his hands and got to his feet. A regretful smile. "Well, as interesting as this has been, I'm afraid . . . I must get back to work." Taking Lassiter by the arm, he escorted his visitor to the front door, where they shook hands.

"Perhaps," Egloff said, "if you left your business card . . . I may think of something. . . ."

"Fine," Lassiter replied, producing one from inside his jacket.

Egloff glanced at the card. "And while you're in Switzerland, Mr. Lassiter?"

"I'll be at the Beau Rivage in Geneva."

"Very good. And then?"

"Back to Washington," Lassiter said, realizing as he said it that the words were a lie.

Egloff beamed. The door swung open, and they shook hands a second time. Lassiter stepped into the cold, pulling the collar of his coat tightly around his neck.

Egloff gave a little wave. "Ciao!" And then the door swung shut and Lassiter was alone on the front steps. He stood there for a moment, looking at the brass plaque, memorizing the unfamiliar names. *Salve Caelo. Services des Catholiques Nord. Gemeinde Pius VI.* As he turned to leave, his eyes swept past the door, and as they did, the peephole seemed to blink. As if it were the nictitating membrane of a hawk. Or an owl.

But that, he knew, was only his imagination. The door was a door, and if there was a bird of prey watching, it was Egloff.

In fact, he'd planned to go on to Geneva that night, just as he'd said. He even had the ticket—arranged by the concierge in Zurich, on a train leaving from Chur.

While he stood on the chilly platform, checking the timetable to make sure of the schedule, he took a look at some of the tidy, clear maps the Swiss provided for their travelers. And he changed his mind. He was in no hurry to get to Geneva, and there was some business to be done, right here in Chur. He took a room for the night in a small hotel right across the street from the railroad station.

The interview with Egloff had been a disquieting one. Apart from that weird stuff about "Islamic imperialism," the man hadn't asked him a single question about his sister's murder. Which was strange. In his experience, people were seldom so incurious when the subject was murder. What Egloff *had* asked about were his travel plans and the hotel where he'd be staying.

But it wasn't just that, Lassiter thought, looking out his hotel room window at the train station across the street. His meeting with Egloff had been embroidered with coincidences, and coincidences made him nervous.

Still, he had to admit that these particular coincidences were less than huge. Egloff was involved in religious charities—and so was Grimaldi, if only as a benefactor. One of Egloff's organizations had been active in the Balkans—and so, according to his passport records, had Grimaldi. As coincidences went, these were next to nothing. Lots of people gave money to charity; and lots of charities were active in Bosnia. That Egloff and Grimaldi should have so much in common was less than strange. More interesting, Lassiter thought, was the discrepancy about the transfer of the house: Had the house been sold, as Egloff said, or had it been given away, as Angela claimed? To put the matter differently: Had Egloff lied? The question seemed important and, whatever else might be in doubt, this was an issue that Lassiter could resolve . . . and nowhere more easily than in the cantonal capital of Chur.

In the morning he asked the desk clerk for directions to the *handelsregister*, where property records were kept. The office was only a few blocks away, and once there, he explained to the clerk that he was interested in a property in Zuoz. With an efficient nod, the clerk went into another room and returned a minute later with an ancient ledger, an atlas-like tome bound in moroccan leather. Inside, Lassiter found a chronological list of every property transaction that had taken place in Zuoz since 1917. The list was handwritten in a dozen careful, legible hands, all of which had used the same color ink: blue. He turned the pages one by one until he found an entry for Heilestrasse 49.

The ledger recorded the sale of the house to Salve Caelo in 1991. The purchase price was one Swiss franc, or a little less than a dollar. Immediately below the entry were the signatures of Franco Grimaldi (Ital.) and Gunther Egloff. Standing in the *handelsregister* with the property book in front of him, Lassiter traced Grimaldi's signature with his forefinger, and wondered why Egloff had lied.

The Glacier Express hurtled past one postcard view after another until, with a great *shwoooooosh* of its brakes, it came to a rest in Geneva. Lassiter had half an hour to spare, and used it to find a hotel—any hotel but the Beau Rivage. Then he walked to La Perle, where he found Max sitting alone at a table overlooking the lake.

It was Max's fate that he resembled one of those little toy trolls that Kathy had collected as a child. He had the same dimply, wide-cheeked face, the same stubby body, and even the cottony orange hair that the dolls had. He looked like an elf, or maybe one of Santa's helpers. Bouncing to his feet with a huge grin, he shook Lassiter's hand with both of his own. When they sat down, the American couldn't help but wonder if Max's feet actually touched the floor. Probably not.

For a small man, he had an enormous appetite, and soon Lassiter was watching his friend tuck into a double order of carpaccio.

"They say I have the metabolism of a hummingbird," Max said.

"You spent a lot of time hovering?"

Max chewed and twinkled.

"This *is* in fact what I do. *Hovering.*" He giggled, greatly amused. "These are banner years, as you know, for capitalism. Business is booming. There should be more and more clerks, more and more tellers—but no. There are focking automatic tellers in places where two years ago there was not even a telephone. There are automatic tellers in the *Celebes*—in *Phnom Penh!*—where two years ago there was not even a bank! Used to be—banks charged for ATM transactions; now they want to charge extra for doing business with a human being! Soon, all the tellers will be out of work. I'll be out of work! And then, I ask, who will have money to make deposits? So the banks will be out of work. And then it's the end of the world. I'm telling you, Joe, it isn't the meek that's inheriting the world. It's the bean counters! Nothing could be more tragic."

The waiter cleared the plates, and while he went through an elaborate ballet of flaming Max's Steak Diane, Max made a show of fumbling through his briefcase. Then he slid a thin commercial envelope across the table. It was bright red, with white letters taking the rough shape of a cross to mimic the Swiss flag. It read:

> Safety
> PRIVACY
> And Confidence With Your
> Own
> Swiss
> Account

Across from him, Max's face got brick red with amusement at his own joke.

The account history was printed out on a continuous sheet of old-style computer paper, and Lassiter unraveled it in the privacy of his hotel room. Here and there Max had hand-printed an asterisk and made a notation.

Grimaldi had held the account for a dozen years, and during that time, the withdrawals were relatively few and unremarkable. Looking at the entries, Lassiter could guess when Grimaldi had purchased his apartments in Rome, the house in Zuoz, and the cars. In the spring of 1991, however, the pattern changed. On successive days in April, wire transfers were made to Grimaldi's account from the Banco di Lazio in Rome. An asterisk from Max indicated that these reflected real estate transactions—obviously from the sale of Grimaldi's apartments. At this point Grimaldi's balance amounted to nearly two million Swiss francs. Two days later, however, the account was drained by a series of cashier's checks that reduced the balance to exactly a thousand Swiss francs. Three of the checks were for small amounts: SF10,000 to the Roofing Fund of Capella Cecilia, SF5,000 to the African National Congress, and SF5,000 to Euzkadi Educational Fund.

But the fourth check, made out to Umbra Domini, S.A. (Napoli), was for everything else: 1,842,300 Swiss francs.

Lassiter stared at the printout, trying to make sense of it. Two of the smaller checks suggested blood money, gestures to the ANC and the Basque liberation front, whose leaders Grimaldi had hunted. The Roofing Fund was probably . . . just a roofing fund, in the way that "Sometimes a cigar is just a cigar." And then: the 800-pound gorilla. A check for almost $2 million.

Lassiter frowned. His Latin had been confined to a single year of deeply boring lectures at St. Alban's. Ninth grade. Even so, he knew what *umbra domini* meant: Shadow. Lord. Shadow of the Lord. And he knew where he'd seen the words before: on the pamphlet in Grimaldi's slum cell on Via Genova.

18

Lassiter got to his feet, stretched, and looked out the window toward Lac Léman. All the lights were haloed with mist; in the distance a boat glided across the water, moving ever so slowly in an envelope of light. A foghorn lowed from the French side of the lake, and it occurred to him that *this is beautiful.* But the truth was, he didn't feel it in his heart.

What he did find exciting and beautiful was the paper record of Grimaldi's account. Following the money was almost always revealing, and it was in the minutiae of spreadsheets and corporate shell games that he spent much of his time as an investigator, prising the secrets from the numbers.

Returning to the printout, he saw that in '92 and '93 monthly deposits of about a thousand dollars had been made to Grimaldi's account by Salve Caelo—Egloff's "charity." The deposits had continued for about a year, and then they'd stopped. By late 1993 the account was once again drawn down to exactly a thousand Swiss francs. Next to the amount was a notation in Max's hand: *Maintenance minimum.*

After that the account remained inactive until August 4, 1995—the date on the wire transfer slip that had fluttered to the floor in Chicago. On that day, Lassiter saw, $50,000 had been deposited in Grimaldi's favor from an account at the Naples branch of the Banco di Parma. Again there was an asterisk and Max's careful printing:

Account of Umbra Domini!

A week later, on August 11, Grimaldi withdrew all of the money in cash.

So what Lassiter had found in Chicago, the twenty to thirty grand hidden in the bottom of Grimaldi's overnight bag, was almost certainly what remained of the money from Umbra Domini. He thought about this for a while. The only conclusion was that Grimaldi had been hired to do a job. But what job?

And what about the payments in 1992–93? Lassiter looked at the passport pages, and confirmed what he'd remembered: the monthly payments coincided with Grimaldi's time in Serbia, Croatia, and Bosnia. It was almost as if he'd been working for Salve Caelo, and per-haps he had—but doing what? Grimaldi's background was hardly a humanitarian one, though now that Lassiter thought about it, Egloff's view of the region wasn't exactly sympathetic. What had he called it? A *political melanoma*.

Reaching for the phone, he dialed Bepi in Rome, his eyes on the soft lights that ringed the lake. The phone rang and rang, and he was about to hang up when he heard a distant crash, a fumbling noise and the word:

"*Pronto?*" A woman giggled in the background.

"Bepi? Joe Lassiter."

"Joe!" He cleared his throat. "How are you?"

Lassiter apologized for the hour, but said that he needed something right away. Could Bepi find out about a religious organization called Umbra Domini—and a charity, Salve Caelo?

"No problem."

"But *quietly*, okay? I don't want to make a lot of waves."

"*Si, si—discreto,*" Bepi replied.

"Great. Can you do it right away?"

"Ah . . . you need a written report?"

"No."

"Okay. We'll fix a lunch with Gianni. He knows everything about religion! Everything. Whatever you want to know. No problem."

"Great. I'll be in Rome tomorrow. We can meet for lunch."

"Solid."

"What!?"

"*Solid,*" Bepi said. "This is an American jazz expression." He hesi-tated a moment and asked, "Isn't it?"

"Yowzah."

He met Bepi at an outdoor café on the Via Veneto, not far from the American embassy. The air was crisp and cold, but the tables were comfortable, warmed by heat lamps whose orange coils pulsed with

BTUs. A journalist named Gianni Massina, who covered religion for the newsmagazine *Attenzione*, was sitting with Bepi when Lassiter arrived.

Shaking hands with the journalist, Lassiter was startled by Massina's close resemblance to Johnny Carson. But instead of the talk-show host's claustrophobic midwestern gestures, the Italian's body language was expansive. He laughed robustly when Lassiter explained his surprise.

"Ah, yes," Massina said, "the other 'Gianni.' This I have been told many, many times. I only wish I had a fraction of the man's fortune."

"Don't we all."

"Although it is apparently diminished by his obsession with marriage." He shook his head ruefully. "The problem with America," he sighed, "the *whole* problem is that you've never mastered the art of the love affair. Not you personally, of course. I have no idea—I mean, we've just met—but *America*! Well, it's the Puritan heritage. You have laws and divorce. We have sins and affairs." Massina chuckled at his own observations, and then grew serious. "I'm sorry. Here I am, joking, and . . . well, it's a serious business."

A waiter came and they ordered espressos.

"So," Massina said after they'd talked for a few minutes. "My friend says you're interested in Umbra Domini."

"Very."

Massina leaned toward him confidentially. "Then you should be careful." Massina frowned, collecting his thoughts. "They're one of the renaissance religions. You have them in the States, I think."

Lassiter looked puzzled, and seeing this, Massina turned to Bepi. The two men spoke briefly in Italian, and Bepi smiled. "He means 'born again.'"

"Exactly," Massina agreed. "They are born all over again. It's similar to what you have in America. With Pat Robertson. They say the only faith that matters is the old faith. But, of course, in America these groups are mostly Protestant. And they almost always make new churches. Here, they stay inside the Church and form—what do you say? *Associazioni*." Then he found the word: "*Lay* orders."

"You mean, like the Dominicans."

"No. Not like the Dominicans. In groups like Umbra the priests are only a small part. These are more like—I don't know . . ." For the second time, Massina and Bepi spoke rapidly in Italian.

"Like Hamas!" Massina said, looking up. "This is precisely it! You should think of them as a rejectionist front—but Catholic! Very strict. Highly motivated. But, of course, we are talking of religion—not politics."

"So what do they believe in?"

"The old ways. The Tridentine mass—"

"The mass in Latin," Bepi explained.

"Where the priest has his back to the congregation," Massina added. "Since Vatican Two, the priest faces the congregation and speaks the local language."

"This is important?" Lassiter asked.

"It's a matter of life or death," Massina said.

"Actually," Bepi interjected, "it's a matter of life *after* death." Massina acknowledged the witticism with a scowl.

"So if they're a 'rejectionist front'—what are they rejecting?" Lassiter asked.

The Italians answered in unison: "Vatican Two."

Lassiter knocked back his espresso and leaned forward. "Look," he said, "in the belief that there's no such thing as a stupid question: What *was* Vatican Two, anyway? I mean, it's like 'general relativity.' Everybody's heard of it, but no one—"

"It was a turning point," Bepi said.

"A bombshell," Massina corrected. "It almost tore the Church apart. But I'm being melodramatic. It was actually a council, a meeting of Catholic leaders from all around the world to modernize—some would say to liberalize—the Church. The traditionalists were against many of the reforms, and so they formed their own associations, groups like Umbra Domini and the Legion of Christ. In France there was Archbishop Lefebvre."

Bepi looked at Lassiter. "You look confused."

"Maybe you have to be a Catholic to understand."

"Maybe," Massina said. "But perhaps not. Some of these people are . . . unstable. They say the Pope is the Antichrist. They say the devil sits on the Throne of St. Peter. They call the vernacular mass . . . a Black Mass."

Lassiter smiled.

"But they're serious! And, thinking that way . . . anything is possible."

"And Umbra?"

"Umbra is the worst. In the beginning, they are noisy, and we think there will be a schism. We think they will be excommunicated, but . . . no, they become quiet. Accommodations are made. There are compromises. Now they say the mass in Latin, the men and women worship separately, they have their own schools."

"The Vatican doesn't want a schism," Bepi said.

"And it is better for them to stay within the church. Even so, the press calls them 'the Catholic Hezbollah.' "

Bepi laughed out loud. " 'The press'?"

Massina made a moue, and grinned. "Okay! Me! What's the difference? I *am* the press. And what are they? 'Hezbollah' means 'the party of God.' And what is Umbra Domini? The same thing: a radical religious group with political goals. So, I call them 'the Catholic Hezbollah.' And look!" Massina reached into his schoolboy's briefcase and extracted a pamphlet. "Look at this! I brought it for you. *Crociata Diecima!*"

Lassiter glanced at the pamphlet. It was the same one he'd seen in Grimaldi's room on the Via Genova.

"Umbra put these out by the thousands, four or five years ago," Massina said. "It's a recruitment—for the Tenth Crusade."

"Which one is that?"

"The first crusade in five hundred years," Massina said, gesturing to the pamphlet. "Against Islam, of course. They say Bosnia is 'an Islamic beachhead.' And so it's a call to arms. Which is where your other group comes in. *Salve Caelo.* They're run by Umbra."

"The charity," Lassiter said.

With a dismissive puff Massina waved away the description. "What they do isn't very charitable. Near Bihac, they ran a 'refugee camp.' Only this is a big joke, as if Auschwitz was a 'refugee camp.' This camp was a concentration camp, and a staging area for commando raids—against the Muslims, of course. You see the irony? They created the refugees, and then they put them in refugee camps! And they did this, first for the Serbs, then for the Croats. Always against the Muslims."

"So now we know what Grimaldi was doing in Bosnia," Lassiter said. "Charity work." And now he knew the connection between Egloff and Grimaldi.

"They call it 'a more muscular Catholicism,' " Bepi said.

"This is significant," Massina went on, tapping the pamphlet, "because Vatican Two declared that all faiths 'stand in the light of God.' You're not a Catholic, so you can't understand this, but . . . Before Vatican Two, to set foot in a church or temple—well, it was a mortal sin. So this idea—that Muslims, Protestants, *whatever*—can *stand in the light of God*—can share in His grace—well, this was a huge change for a religion that not so long ago was burning heretics at the stake."

Lassiter nodded. "What else do they do?"

"They publish. Books, pamphlets, videos, tapes. About birth control, the Masons, abortion, homosexuality—they say homosexuals should be branded."

"Tattooed," Bepi corrected.

Lassiter thought about it. "How many people are we talking about?"

Massina shrugged. "I think maybe they are fifty thousand now. Maybe more. There are many in Italy, Spain, Argentina—but some in the U.S. Even Japan, I think. Blues and Whites."

Lassiter looked puzzled.

"These are two groups in Umbra Domini," Massina explained. "The Whites are very strict. Each day begins with church. Each day, they give money. The women cover their hair, they hide their bodies. Strict. But the Blues! These are different. The Blues 'leave the world.' "

"What does that mean?"

"They are like monks. Only men can be Blues. They take vows of poverty, chastity—"

"Personally, I am not religious," Bepi said.

"—and they scourge themselves."

"You mean with *whips*?"

Massina shrugged. "It's an old tradition. He's a traditionalist."

"Tell him about the walk," Bepi said.

"What walk?" Lassiter asked.

"It's the same kind of thing," Massina replied. "Another kind of penance. On Sunday the Blues go to communion on their knees. They must walk a certain distance in this way, Christ's walk, carrying the cross to Calvary. And . . . it must be very painful. Because of the stones in the square, the granite steps—"

Lassiter looked away, and heard Riordan's voice in his ear. "A *tile setter*," he said out loud.

"What?" Bepi asked.

"One of the cops thought Grimaldi laid tile for a living—because nobody could figure out the calluses on his knees."

"Well, if he's a Blue . . ."

"Who runs this thing, anyway? A bishop, or what?"

Massina leaned toward Lassiter and smiled. "You're not a religious man, are you?"

"No."

"I thought not. The head of the organization is what is always called—" He made quotation marks in the air. "—'a simple priest.' A man named della Torre," Massina said.

" 'Simple priest,' my ass!" Bepi laughed. "This is like calling—"

"I was about to say, he's quite charismatic."

"—like calling the Beatles 'a garage band.' "

"As I said," Massina continued, "he's quite charismatic. And still young. In his thirties. Dominican, of course. Like the founder."

"Why 'of course'?"

"Well, the Dominicans—they're the great champions of orthodoxy. The Black Friars. The Inquisition was theirs. Anyway, this della Torre—he's a compelling speaker. His church is always packed. Overflow crowds in the streets. He walks through the people and they kiss the hem of his cassock. It's something."

"Where is it?"

"In Napoli. The Church of San Eufemio. It's a tiny little place—very old. Seventh century, I think. It's like a stage set. They've spent a fortune on lighting. I heard they called in a professional from London—who lights stage shows and rock concerts. Anyway, the result is . . . Gothic. When della Torre takes the pulpit, he emerges out of the darkness, and there's a trick to the light, so that it almost seems as if he's lit from within. And when he talks—quietly, passionately—you're pulled forward. And you *will* want to be saved."

"So you've been there?" Lassiter asked.

"Once," Massina replied. "It scared me. I was this close—" He pinched a little air between his fingers. "—to kissing his hand."

"Do you think he'd see me?"

Massina hesitated. "If you went as a journalist . . . yes. He's there to spread the Word."

"So, if I were writing an article—"

Bepi held his hand up and spoke in a pompous voice: " 'New Directions in Catholicism.' "

Massina shrugged. "Who knows? He might see you."

"Does he speak English?"

"He speaks everything. He's studied in Heidelberg, Tokyo, and Boston. Very well educated for a simple priest."

Bepi leaned forward. "Will this be dangerous for Joe?"

Massina laughed. "I don't think so. He *is* a priest, after all. But watch out," he said, turning back to Lassiter. "He might try to convert you."

Naples. Lassiter took a taxi to an address a few blocks from Umbra Domini's headquarters, and walked the rest of the way. Slowly.

Now that he was there, the pretext didn't seem like such a good idea. Though he'd had a set of business cards printed, identifying himself as John C. Delaney, a Washington-based producer for CNN, there was at least a remote possibility that della Torre would be expecting him. After all, he'd banged on Grimaldi's doors in Rome, met with his sister, invaded his bank account, and more or less told all to Gunther Egloff. While it was possible that the Swiss man had forgotten about him the moment the door swung shut at the chalet, Lassiter didn't think so. However idly the questions may have seemed to have been put, Egloff had asked for (and received) his business card, hotel, and destination, about which he'd lied. And then Egloff had watched him leave, standing behind the peephole in the door.

And for good reason. Because there was a chain. A chain of links. Grimaldi to Umbra Domini. Umbra Domini to Salve Caelo. Salve Caelo to Egloff. Grimaldi to Egloff.

This could be embarrassing, Lassiter told himself, and the other side of his brain replied, *Or worse.*

He was standing before a moldering, neoclassical villa whose towering wooden doors were flung open upon a small courtyard. In the center of the yard, a fountain burbled, its waters fed by a cluster-fuck of dribbling gargoyles.

The interior of the villa was as modern as its exterior was antique. The air pulsed with fluorescent light and buzzed with the slow rasp of fax machines, the warble of cellular phones, and the hum of computers. A bilingual woman in a long-sleeve dress looked at his card, without taking it, and directed him to the public affairs office, where press inquiries were handled.

There, he sat for ten minutes, surrounded by a lavish display of books and pamphlets imprinted with Umbra's logo. The gold oval, and within it, against a purple background, a painterly line suggesting a hillside. A cross driven into the hill. And a long shadow with the words UMBRA DOMINI in bright gilt letters. The pamphlets were in several languages, including English, but before Lassiter could look at them more carefully, an urbane young man with a fashionable haircut emerged from an inner office.

"Dante Villa," he said, extending his hand.

"Jack Delaney. I'm with CNN."

"Do you have a card?"

"Of course," Lassiter said, and taking one from his jacket, gave it to him.

"And how can I help you, Mr. Delaney?"

"Well . . . we're thinking of doing a segment on new directions in Christianity."

The young man lifted his eyebrows and tossed his glossy hair. "Yes?"

"Absolutely. And from what we're told, Umbra Domini is one of the fastest-growing lay orders in Catholicism. So, it could be an important part of the larger piece . . . depending."

"Oh? On what?"

"Well, you know what television's like. A lot depends on who we can put on camera. Which, I guess, is the main reason I'm here. I'm told Father della Torre would be good . . . outstanding, in fact. And so . . . I was hoping that I might be able to pre-interview him—just to get an idea what he might say, what he sounds like. It wouldn't take long. And I could tell him a little about what we hope to do."

The young man frowned.

"I'm told he's quite remarkable," Lassiter enthused.

The frown didn't really budge, but the young man asked how long he would be in Naples.

Lassiter winced. "I know I should have made arrangements ahead of time, but it just wasn't possible. We've been working on a totally unrelated piece and I thought, what the hell? Excuse me. I mean, I was in Rome. . . . I figured I might as well drive down. See if I got lucky."

"I see." The young man made a little sucking sound between his teeth. "Father della Torre is of course extremely busy. On the other hand, I am sure he would like to reach out. . . . He does see a great future for the order on"—a smile—"the other side of the pond."

"Oh?"

"Oh, yes. We have a number of centers in the States."

"Really." Lassiter pulled out a steno notebook.

"And they are growing by leaps and bounds. I can show you the data."

"Where are they?"

"Where the people are: New York, Los Angeles, Dallas."

"So it's pretty much an urban phenomenon."

"As a practical matter—yes. We organize around our schools. But we do have some houses of retreat—in the countryside. Simple places, as you can imagine."

"And if we wanted to film—"

"You wouldn't even have to leave the U.S." The young man went to a Rolodex on his desk, spun the wheel and smiled. "In fact, you could do a lot in Washington. Beginning with St. Bartholomew's High School—"

"St. Bart's?!"

"You know it?"

"I used to play against them. In high school. They were in the IAC."

"Excuse me?"

"It's a sport's league."

"Ah—"

"I didn't know St. Bart's was . . ."

"One of ours?" Villa chuckled. "Most people think all Catholic schools are alike. But, of course, they're not." He turned back to the Rolodex. "Maryland's near Washington, isn't it?" He pronounced the word *Mary*land.

"Yeah," Lassiter said, "right next door."

"Well, there's a retreat there. And I see we have an outreach program in something called 'Anacostia.' "

"It's part of Washington."

"Well, then! I'll give you a list."

"Great."

"In fact, I have a press information kit, if you'd like."

"Terrific. That's fabulous. And—as to Father della Torre?"

The young man held out a hand and offered a generous smile.

"How would it be if I get you the printed information that I have available, and check with his secretary. If you'll just have a seat?"

While he waited, Lassiter studied a foldout world map. Naples was in the center, stamped with the Umbra logo—from which rays extended to the different parts of the world where the order had centers. He saw that there were outposts in at least twenty countries: Slovenia, Canada, Chile—they were literally all over the map.

The reverse side had a bar chart of membership by country, and as he began to look at it, the young man returned. He held a loose-leaf notebook, the front bearing the purple and gold Umbra logo and a small sticker that identified the language as English.

"There's a lot of information in here," Dante said, "including an article from the *New York Times* and another one in a Catholic publication, *Changing Times*." A smile. "In case you missed them."

"Terrific."

"As to Father della Torre ..." he said with a beaming smile. He took a quick peek at the fake card Lassiter had given him, which was cupped in his palm. "You have great luck, Mr. Delaney."

"That sounds like my father," Lassiter joked. "I usually go by 'Jack.'"

Dante smiled. "Well, there's a reception for new members at nine, and an ordination at ten. So he has a window around ... let's see ... eleven-thirty should be safe."

"I appreciate this."

"He asks if you'll be bringing a photographer?"

"No. I don't—"

"It doesn't matter. There are a number of glossies in the press kit." Dante tossed his hair back from his face and extended his hand.

Lassiter was beginning to feel guilty about all this goodwill, and not a little disturbed by the slickness of the operation. "What time was that again?" he said, pulling out his notebook as if he had dozens of commitments.

"Eleven-thirty in the morning. And not here—he'll be at the church. You'll find him in the office. Here, let me make you a little map."

19

Returning to his hotel, Lassiter was tired enough to fall asleep, and might have done so if the taxicab had been equipped with working shock absorbers. But it wasn't, and so he sat in the backseat, holding on to a frayed leather strap as the cab rattled and bounced past the Teatro San Carlo in the direction of the port. The exhaustion he felt was owing in part to the strain of pretense—lying drained him and always had. But what really got to him was the impossibility of being in two places at once. Grimaldi was in America, but the answers were in Europe, buried in the medieval muck of Umbra Domini's politics and Grimaldi's background.

Then, too, the realization was just beginning to dawn that Kathy hadn't been Grimaldi's target—Brandon had. Kathy had been killed fighting for her son's life, but Brandon had been *slaughtered*. His throat had been slit from ear to ear, almost ritually—and then, after Grimaldi had made a mess of the fire, it was Brandon who had been disinterred. And cremated for a second time. *Brandon*. Not Kathy.

And not by Grimaldi, who'd been in the hospital.

Someone else had gone to the trouble of exhuming the child and setting the remains ablaze. Which meant that Grimaldi was almost certainly part of a conspiracy. *That* all but ruled out Riordan's theory that Grimaldi might be—what was the word that he'd used? A "toon"—someone whose actions were impossible to explain because reason played no part in them. In Lassiter's experience, madmen did not conspire with one another. They acted. And when they acted, they acted alone.

It gave him a headache to think about it. To think of the murders as a conspiracy cast them in an even stranger light than before, and made their solution seem even less likely. And what could it have to do with Umbra Domini? Because they definitely were the ones paying Grimaldi. He *did* have a headache.

His room was in a small hotel overlooking the port of Santa Lucia. Standing on the balcony with the telephone in one hand and the receiver in the other, he called Bepi to see if they could have dinner together the following night. As he waited, listening to the phone ring in Rome, he watched the sun slide into the Mediterranean like a woman entering her bath, gently breaking the surface of the water and, ever so slowly, disappearing beneath it.

No answer. He dialed Bepi's pager, punched in the hotel's telephone number so Bepi would call him back when he got the message—and that was it. There wasn't anything else for him to do. And then he remembered the press kit.

The notebook amounted to a slick presentation of what seemed to be a well-scrubbed and benign organization, a kind of 4-H Club for the soul. There was a list of Umbra's sister organizations, including its charities, and Lassiter noted that Salve Caelo was among them. But controversy was downplayed, and there was little or no hint of the organization's extremist views.

Instead, the press releases concentrated on Umbra's good deeds and growing membership: There were lots of photos of wide-eyed children playing outside or sitting attentively at their desks in parochial schools that Umbra Domini sponsored. Pictures of youths collecting trash from a littered park, helping the elderly and serving as altar boys. Before and after photos of renovated church buildings vied for space with images of missionaries in the bush. Finally, there was a photo of smiling Muslims working in a vegetable garden at a Salve Caelo "refugee camp" in Bosnia.

The man behind the good deeds was represented by several eight-by-ten glossies. And if the pictures were accurate, Lassiter thought, Silvio della Torre ought to be in the movies. He was Everywoman's boyish leading man, with high cheekbones, eyes of a striking sea-blue color, and a broad, sardonic smile under a halo of jet-black curls.

In addition to the photographs and press releases, the kit contained a handful of newspaper articles about the organization's good works, and two different puff pieces about della Torre himself. Both articles remarked on the priest's facility with languages—he spoke six or nine, depending upon which story you read—and his achievements as a kick boxer. As one of the features put it, "Father della Torre can compete with the best of 'em. So, watch out, Jean-Claude! *Powwww!*"

Finally, there was a "mission statement" of surpassing blandness. Nothing was said of ritual scourging, "Islamic imperialism," or homosexuals.

Instead, the statement emphasized the importance of "family values," the "culture of Christianity," and the "basic tenets of Catholicism."

All in all, the press kit was as effective as a sleeping pill, and Lassiter succumbed to it in his chair.

He woke up feeling better, but his mood took a turn for the worse when he stopped for a morning cappuccino in the café next to the hotel's lobby. A tinny loudspeaker hummed with the annoying and relentlessly cheerful cadences of Europop. He'd never understood what people liked about this crappy music. At least the coffee was good.

The Church of San Eufemio was small and old; the settling earth beneath it had thrown it askew, so that none of the architectural angles were plumb. It was sandwiched between two much larger and newer buildings, and the crooked set of the church made it look as if its neighbors were trying to shoulder it out of the way for good.

A short walkway led to a pair of enormous arched doors, studded with metal, doors so old that the surface of the wood was a series of ridges, the softer pith between the cambial layers having long since eroded away. He'd seen the doors in a photograph amid the publicity material—thrown open, a bride and groom emerging from the dark interior—and remembered that they were said to date from the eighth century. He touched the ridged wood; it felt as hard as stone.

But the doors were not open now, and there was no obvious knocker or even a handle—just a large, old-fashioned keyhole. He walked around, looking for another entrance, and soon found it, off to the side. He paused, quickly rehearsing his spiel: "Jack Delaney . . . CNN . . . 'New Directions in Catholicism.' "

He rapped on the door, and della Torre surprised him by answering the knock himself. The Umbran leader was dressed in a charcoal turtleneck, brown slacks, and loafers. Lassiter saw that Silvio della Torre was, if possible, even better looking than his publicity photos suggested. But unlike the actors Lassiter had met, men who were somehow smaller in the flesh, della Torre was bigger than he'd imagined. The priest was at least as tall as he, broad-shouldered and athletic-looking. He didn't look like Lassiter's idea of a priest, the Platonic ideal which was at least sixty years old, gray-haired, and outfitted in a cassock.

"You must be Jack Delaney," the priest said with a smile. "Dante told me to expect you. Please come in." His English was flawless and unaccented.

"Thank you."

They went through another door and into a sparsely but elegantly furnished office. Lassiter sat on a red leather Barcelona chair and faced della Torre across an old wooden library table. Remembering what Massina had said about della Torre's skill with lighting himself during church services, Lassiter couldn't help but notice the sophisticated array of recessed lighting set into the old plaster ceiling, or the way the light fell on the priest's chiseled features.

"I understand you're doing a piece for CNN. . . ."

"We're thinking about it."

"Well . . . *great!* I sometimes think the major media go out of their way to ignore us."

Lassiter chuckled, as he was meant to do. "I'm sure that's not true," he said.

Della Torre shrugged. "I think so. But," he said, leaning forward, "it's no matter. You're here." Della Torre knit his fingers together, put his elbows on the desk, and rested his chin on the backs of his hands. "How should we begin?"

"Well," Lassiter said, "the idea is to get a feeling for how you'd come across on the air, and also to get a bit of background. If you could tell me a little about the origins of Umbra Domini . . ."

"Of course," della Torre replied, settling back in his chair. "As I'm sure you know, we're a product—some would say, a *by-product*—of Vatican Two." For the next ten minutes, Umbra Domini's capo fielded Lassiter's softballs with a smile.

"How has the organization changed in recent years?"

"Well, Jack, it's no secret that we've become a lot bigger. . . ."

"If you had to name one program that you're most proud of, what would it be?"

"Community Outreach—without a doubt. I'm so proud of it. . . ."

"In your view, what's the biggest challenge currently facing the Church?"

"There are so many challenges. It's such a difficult time! But it seems to me the *biggest* challenge Catholics face is what I like to call 'the temptation of modernity.'. . ."

Lassiter nodded thoughtfully at each of the answers, and dutifully scribbled in his notebook. He was getting a feel for his adversary, and what he felt was something like Teflon, but heavier. Teflon and steel. He decided to switch tactics.

"It's said that Umbra has political ambitions."

"Oh?" Della Torre sensed the change, and cocked his head. "And who says that?"

Lassiter shrugged. "I've got a file full of clips at the hotel. Stories that I downloaded from Nexis. A couple are pretty critical. They say Umbra Domini is tied to right-wing groups like the National Front—"

"That's ridiculous. It's true that some of our members are concerned about immigration issues—but that's a political matter, not a theological one. We're a diverse organization; our members hold many different views."

"They say that Umbra's homophobic."

"Well . . ."

"And that you've called for gays to be tattooed."

"Good! I'm glad you raised that question because it gives me an opportunity to clarify this. It's true, we consider homosexuality a sin—and we've said so in—let's face it—no uncertain terms. In that sense, I suppose there are some who consider us—" Della Torre made quotation marks in the air—" 'homophobic.' But it's also true that Umbra Domini has a pedagogic function. We're teachers, and as teachers, we sometimes use hyperbole to make a point. That's what this is all about. Whatever anyone may have said, no one in Umbra Domini seriously believes that homosexuals should be tattooed. Though I do think it's reasonable that they should register with the police."

"Interesting," Lassiter said, making a note. "Another thing I wanted to ask you about: one of the clips mentions a charity—Salve . . ." He pretended to search for the word.

"Caelo."

"Exactly. Salve Caelo! And the work they've done in Bosnia. They say—"

"I know what they say. They say we ran a concentration camp. And that we did this under the pretext of a relief effort."

"Mmmm."

"I'm familiar with the charge. It's been thoroughly investigated. Nothing's ever been proved."

"Is it true?"

Della Torre looked at the ceiling, as if appealing to a higher authority. Then he turned his gaze on Lassiter. "Let me ask you something, Jack."

"Shoot."

"Isn't it amazing that faith and devotion inspire attack almost as often as they inspire admiration? These stories you're referring to, they're nothing more than envy dressed as gossip."

"*Envy?* What do you mean?"

Della Torre sighed, and when he spoke again, his voice commanded the room, low and passionate. His words were perfectly modulated, his timing masterful, the timbre of his voice deep and rich. "Think of Umbra Domini as a beautiful and virginal woman," he began, leaning forward and fixing Lassiter with his startling blue eyes. What followed was a speech unlike any that Lassiter had ever heard, a patterned voice-roll or wave of words whose meaning was somehow independent of what was actually being *said*. Listening, Lassiter felt almost as if he were entering a trance. Indeed, it seemed he was being sung to. And then an extraordinary thing happened in a very ordinary way: The sun moved behind a cloud; a flat, odd light gripped the priest's face for a moment, and Lassiter saw through the man's vanity. It was in his eyes. They were the kind of eyes that pulled you into them, not blue really, but an underwater shade of aquamarine that seemed to have been taken from the Great Barrier Reef. They were beautiful eyes, but they weren't real. In the strange light, Lassiter could see the too-wet gleam of contact lenses. And not just contacts, colorized contacts. He recognized the shade:

They were Monica's eyes.

He wondered if della Torre had agonized over the choice, as Monica had—vacillating between cerulean-aquamarine and blue-sapphire. Whether he had or hadn't, they'd obviously agreed on the same color—and probably for the same reason. It was a very seductive blue.

Della Torre smiled and shook his head. It was clear that he hadn't noticed the change in the quality of Lassiter's attention. "And so, when I hear attacks on Umbra Domini, when I hear rumors, murmurs of doubt about the order's intentions—it doesn't make me angry. I feel sorrow. And pity. The people who speak in this way, who make up these stories, are stranded in the darkness of their own souls."

Della Torre ended his speech in the way he'd begun—with his elbows on the table and his chin resting on the backs of his interknit hands.

Lassiter was silent for a moment. And then the sun came out and the room pulsed with light. He cleared his throat and, without thinking about it, popped the question: "And Franco Grimaldi?"

Della Torre sat back in his chair and regarded Lassiter with a bemused look. "Grimaldi?"

"One of your people . . ."

"Yes . . . ?"

"He's wanted for murder."

Della Torre nodded thoughtfully. "I see."

"In the States."

"Hmmmm." Della Torre rocked back and forth in his chair. Finally he said, "This is the question you came to ask, isn't it?"

Lassiter nodded. "Yeah."

"Well . . ." The priest shrugged.

"I want to know why he did what he did," Lassiter said.

"And you think I might know?"

"I thought that you might."

"I see. And why would you think that?"

Give him a push, Lassiter thought. "Because you paid him a lot of money."

"I did? And when did I do that?"

"In August."

"I see." Della Torre swiveled in his chair and looked out the window. His brows were knitted together in thought. "When you say *I* paid him—"

"Umbra Domini paid him. There was a check from your bank to his. The Crédit Suisse."

Della Torre grunted, his back to Lassiter, eyes fixed on the window-pane. Finally, he spun the chair around and faced Lassiter. "I'll look into it," he said. And then, almost tenderly, he asked, "You're not a reporter, are you . . . *Jack*?"

"No."

"And the people this man killed—they were close to you?"

"Yeah. They were close." Even as he answered, he wondered about della Torre's choice of words. How did he know that more than one person had been killed?

Della Torre was silent for a while, and then he said, "You know, Joe . . ." He paused again, and let Lassiter absorb the fact that the "Jack Delaney" story was behind them. "You know," della Torre said again, "there's nothing you can do to bring them back."

"I realize that," Lassiter said, "but—"

"Let's not lie to each other anymore. I know about your visit to

Zuoz—Gunther called. And, before that, your travels in Rome. I know what's in your heart, and I certainly don't blame you."

Suddenly, Lassiter's blood was swimming in adrenaline. "So?" he said.

"So let me ask you a question."

Lassiter nodded.

"Do you believe in God?"

He thought about it for a moment. "I suppose so. Yeah, I guess I do."

"And do you believe that the good in the world emanates from God?"

Lassiter thought about it. "I suppose."

"And the devil?"

"What about him?"

"Do you believe in the devil?"

"No," Lassiter said.

"In evil, then. Do you believe in evil?"

"Absolutely. I've *seen* it."

"Well . . . where does evil come from, if not from the devil?"

"I don't know," Lassiter said, suddenly impatient. "I never thought about it. But I know it when I see it. And I've seen it."

"We all have. But that isn't enough. You need to think about it."

"Why?"

"Because it's the reason your sister and nephew were killed."

The room swelled with silence as Lassiter tried to make sense of what the priest was saying. Finally, he said, "What's that supposed to mean?"

"Just what I said. You should think about the origins of evil."

Lassiter shook his head, as if to clear it. "If you mean . . . Grimaldi is evil—I know that. I've seen what he did."

"That's *not* what I mean."

"Then what? That Kathy was? Or Brandon?"

Della Torre looked at him in silence for what seemed a very long while, and then he changed the subject. "Let me show you the church," he said, and got to his feet.

Lassiter followed the priest down a narrow corridor and into a darkened room. Della Torre paused to flick a couple of switches, and the room grew larger with the light, though its dimensions were still unclear. A row of tiny windows, high on the walls, admitted a strange, bluish light that engulfed della Torre. For a moment he seemed a phantasm, more wood smoke than flesh.

"Pray with me, Joe." The priest crossed the room to the pulpit, a heavily carved antique podium that, lighted from below, seemed almost to be floating in the air. Lassiter seated himself in one of the pews, feeling uncomfortable. He hadn't prayed in a very long time, and he didn't much want to now—and especially not in front of della Torre. Somehow, he knew it would be dangerous to get down on his knees in front of this man.

And yet . . . he was feeling so alone, and sitting in the little church reminded him of better days, when he and Kathy had sat together as children in the National Cathedral—"the seventh largest in the world." How many times had they been told that? Hundreds, maybe more. They loved the place, with all its stained glass and soaring music, the spooky crypts down below, the towering, Gothic spaces, fearsome and silly gargoyles. That was lost now.

He'd never go there again.

Della Torre hovered before him in the pulpit, shimmering in the light, and yet somehow solid—like a statue with its hands pressed together in an attitude of prayer, head bowed. The light ricocheted off his cheekbones, and hung like a nimbus around his thick, curly hair. He was perfect.

"No more pain," della Torre whispered, his voice plaintive, a lament that resonated so magically that it seemed to Lassiter the priest was speaking inside his own head. "No more pain." He pressed his palms to his chest and lifted his head toward the ceiling. Lassiter was transfixed. "We come before you in your own house so you may see that one of your children, Lord, is in pain. Take the vengeance from his heart, Lord, and make it your own again—for vengeance is yours. *Fold* him into your heart, Lord. Deliver him of hatred! Deliver him from evil."

The words resonated so that they seemed to come from all around him, and from above as well.

"We come into your house, O Lord—"

"*Scusi!*"

Della Torre froze in the pulpit, his mouth open, like a fish out of water.

"*Scusi, Papa . . .*" An old drunk stood in the aisle, rooted and swaying. For a moment it seemed as if he'd fall, but he did not. With a beatific smile he sank to his knees, looked up at the pulpit—and pitched forward in a swoon, smacking his forehead on the stone floor.

Della Torre seemed paralyzed, and then ... berserk. He was waving his arms and shouting at the fallen man — "*Vaffanculo! Vaffan-culo!*" — and while Lassiter didn't speak Italian, he knew from the tone exactly what the priest was saying. It was more than "Leave." It was "Get the fuck out of here!" Della Torre's face was transformed, the once handsome and compassionate veneer peeled back to reveal the violence underneath. And then, as suddenly as the mask had vanished, it reappeared. Once again della Torre seemed filled with compassion as he stepped down from the pulpit to help the man.

Lassiter joined him in the aisle.

"Let's try to get him to the office," della Torre said. "I know who he is. I can call his wife."

Together, they held the man between them and stiff-marched him along the corridor and into the office. But once in the room, the comatose drunk flailed out with his hands. "*Papa!*" he shouted, and struck the priest with his arm. Della Torre staggered backward, and something fell from his pocket to the floor.

A small bottle. Lassiter watched it bounce on the tiles, first on one facet, then on another. Finally it came to rest; miraculously enough, it was unbroken. Lassiter reached down and picked it up. And stared.

It was the same bottle, or a replica of the bottle, that the police had taken from Grimaldi. He remembered the first time he saw it: sitting with Riordan in the doctor's office at Fairfax Hospital. And on the hospital tray: the little bottle. And the knife. The knife with the blood gummed on the blade and a delicate blond hair stuck to the blood. Brandon's hair. A police photo flashed at the back of his eyes: the crude, molded glass, a cross embossed in each side, the metal cap in the shape of a crown.

"Thank you," della Torre said, holding out a hand. "It's amazing that it didn't break."

Lassiter put his head down. "I think I'd better go," he said. "I have a plane to catch."

And before the priest could reply, he was on his way out the door. Della Torre came after him, following him down the path.

"Joe," he said. "What's wrong? Please—come back! I feel we have unfinished business."

Lassiter didn't turn around. He just kept walking. But his lips moved. And what he said, he said to himself. "You're goddamn right we do."

20

Lassiter remembered nothing of the ride from the church back to his hotel. His mind was on della Torre, and in particular on the priest's peculiar willingness to play along with his pretext of being a journalist. Why had della Torre done that? They might have talked in circles for an hour or two, Lassiter thought, if he hadn't blurted out the question about Grimaldi. And, in fact, the mystery went even deeper. Della Torre knew who he was and what he was up to, so why had he even agreed to meet him? There was no point to the whole charade.

In the end Lassiter decided that della Torre had wanted to meet him, if only to size him up. And by playing him along in such a way that he would *know* he was being played along, the priest had been delivering a message, and flaunting his power. In effect he'd used his knowledge like a thug, letting his coat fall open to reveal the psychological equivalent of a .45 jammed into his waistband.

Either that, or he'd wanted to keep Lassiter busy for a while, and didn't really care what the American knew or didn't know.

This last possibility occurred to Lassiter as the cab pulled up in front of his hotel. He shoved a fistful of lire into the driver's hands, turned, and walked into the lobby. The desk clerk looked up from the small reception desk. "*Signore!*" he blurted.

Lassiter turned, but continued walking, stepping toward the elevator. "What?"

The clerk opened his mouth, closed it, and opened it again. Finally, he threw his hands in the air and said, "*B-B-Benvenuti!*"

"*Grazie*," Lassiter said. "Would you get my bill ready? I'll be right back down."

"But *signore* . . ."

Lassiter pressed the call button on the elevator. "Yeah?" he asked.

"Perhaps," the clerk said, stepping from behind the desk, "if you'd do me the honor . . ." He gestured toward the bar, and screwed up his face in a conspiratorial grin.

Lassiter shook his head. "Too early for me," he said.

"Ah, but—"

"Sorry. Gotta run."

Lassiter's room was on the third floor, at the end of the corridor. As he walked along the hallway he could hear a telephone chirping, and realized that the sound was coming from his own room. Bepi, he thought, and hurried toward the door, searching his pockets for the white plastic card that served as a key. He slipped it into the lock, and waited for the little green light to flash. Talk about good timing. The light flickered, the phone stopped ringing, the door swung open, and someone inside said, "*Pronto?*"

What?

An enormous, squarely built man was seated at the desk in front of Lassiter's computer, telephone in hand. He looked far too big for the chair. Seeing Lassiter, he replaced the phone in its cradle, took a deep breath, exhaled, and got to his feet. Almost casually, he walked toward the doorway.

Lassiter didn't know what to say—Miss Manners didn't cover this one. What came out was: "Who the fuck are you?" As he said it, it occurred to him that the man was built like a mattress. A mattress that needed a shave.

"*Scusi,*" the man said softly, smiling a grim little grin as he turned sideways to edge past Lassiter through the open door.

It was all very quiet and slow. Almost polite. Lassiter touched the man's sleeve. "Wait a second," he said.

And then everything speeded up, all at once. A bowling bowl, or something like it, hit him in the face—his *whole* face, all at once—sending a shower of lights sparking through his head like a swarm of fireflies. He could taste the blood in his mouth as his feet took him backward into the wall, slamming him into the plaster. The breath burst from his lungs as he raised his hands to block whatever was coming next—an optimistic gesture that did nothing to prevent what seemed like a pile driver slamming into his chest. Once, twice—again!

Now his body was lighting up in all the wrong places. His nerve ends were snapping at each other, and the room was flickering like a spent lightbulb—or maybe the flicker was in his head, he couldn't be sure.

Something heavy came down on his neck, hard and fast, and drove him to his hands and knees—where he saw an expensive-looking shoe draw back, as if to kick a field goal. He saw the shoe with amazing clarity—the tassels, the creases in the leather, the stitching . . .

And then he heard a scream. For a moment he thought the scream was coming from himself, but looking up, he saw a chambermaid standing in the doorway, her eyes wide and her mouth open. He started to say something when, suddenly, the shoe changed direction, rushing toward him in a blur that ended deep inside his ribs. He could feel the bones crack, like pieces of kindling and old bamboo. The maid screamed for the second time, or maybe not—maybe this time it was him. But, no. It had to be her because there wasn't enough air in his lungs to push the scream out of his throat. Indeed, he couldn't talk, and now that he thought about it, he couldn't breathe. The whole world was out of air, and he felt like he was dying.

And then as suddenly as it began, it was over. The mattress was gone, and the maid was running up and down the hall, hitting all the high notes. She'd probably saved his life, and he knew that he ought to thank her, but he hurt too much to be polite. And so he got painfully to his feet, shut the door without a word, and staggered toward the bathroom.

Every breath was a knife in his side, and so he took small ones, holding his hands against what felt like a mass of splintered ribs. He made it to the sink. He didn't know why, but the first thing he did was turn on the water. And that seemed to help. The *sound* helped.

Leaning forward against the vanity, he looked up into the mirror. And what he saw wasn't so bad. He was a mess, but not like a train wreck. This was more like a fender bender. He had a bloody nose and a split lip, where one of his eyeteeth had been driven into the soft flesh. He touched the tooth with his tongue and gasped with surprise when it fell over in his mouth. He spat it out—it was a small tooth, and the water washed it away.

With glacial deliberateness he lifted his shirt to reveal a purplish cloud blooming over the ribs on his right side. Tentatively, he touched the hematoma with his fingertips, and almost fainted. The pain rose inside him like a wave, and like a wave, it broke, sending streamers of pain in every direction. The color drained from his face and he made a noise that sounded like all the vowels spoken at once, a strangled gasp that ended only when he ground his teeth together. You need an

X-ray, Lassiter thought. And a dentist. And Demerol. But not in that order.

And not in Naples.

It was a little late, but now he knew why della Torre had played along with the pretext that he'd used: The priest had simply wanted to keep him busy while his room was searched.

There was an urgent knock at the door, and a man's voice, entreating him to open up. "Mr. Lassiter—*per favore*—are you all right?"

"I'm fine," Lassiter shouted, wincing. "Forget it."

"Are you sure, *signore*? The police—"

"Don't worry about it!" Whoever it was, left, muttering in Italian.

A minute later the telephone rang, and for the first time in his life Lassiter was grateful to be in a hotel where there was an extension in the bathroom. He picked it up and shocked the manager by telling him that he didn't want to talk to the police and didn't want to make a complaint.

"But Mr. Lassiter—it's your right. You were assaulted!"

"Just get my car from the garage, and put the bill on my Visa card."

"Are you certain, *signore*?"

"I'll be right down."

It took him almost half an hour to change shirts and pack his bag, and when he was done, it took everything he had left to walk erect through the lobby. The manager was standing in the courtyard at the front of the hotel, looking terrified, dignified, and apologetic, all at once. Lassiter's rental car was idling a few feet away, and the manager, seeing Lassiter, hurried over to it. With a small bow he opened the door and watched his guest ease himself into the driver's seat. That done, the manager shut the door with a practiced firmness, tilted his head and smiled.

"Where's the desk clerk?" Lassiter asked, looking around.

The manager frowned. "Roberto?"

"Yeah. I didn't see him inside."

"He left a little while ago. The asthma."

"Well, tell him I hope he gets better," Lassiter said.

"*Grazie. Il signore e molto gentile!* And after all that's happened!"

"Because the next time I see that sonofabitch, I'm gonna rip him a new asshole."

There was a long silence. Finally, the manager said, "*Scusi?*"

"It's a promise."

—

Lassiter drove to Rome that same night, holding a bag of ice against his ribs and talking to himself as he headed north along the autostrada.

What the *fuck* were you thinking of? he raged. Not that you *were* thinking—'cause if you'd been thinking, you wouldn't have been sucker-punched in your own fucking hotel room. And now, for all you know, you've got a couple of ribs sticking through your lung, and even if you don't, you're sure as shit not gonna sleep on your side for a while—and ohhhhh, Jesus! it hurts.

And not just his body. His pride was as badly beaten as his ribs. Della Torre had kept him in the church for as long as he could . . . first with his fancy speech, then praying . . . *praying!* . . . while his . . . colleague—the Mattress—searched the hotel room. And he might have lingered in the church even longer ("*Fold* him into your heart, Lord!") if the drunk hadn't wandered in and broken the spell. And then the desk clerk, trying to stall him, *If you'd do me the honor* . . . How many hints did it take for him to realize that something was going down— and that "the something" was him?

And finally the room itself . . . *Pronto? Who the fuck are you? Scusi. Bang!*

That's what really hurt—because he was good from the shoulders. He'd boxed in college and done pretty well. He wasn't used to losing fights, and it really didn't matter how big the guy was. Because he knew how to hit. And how not to *get* hit. Or so he thought, at least until that evening.

Still, getting smacked around had an astringent effect that wasn't entirely negative. It woke you up, tuned the senses, and made you think—hard—about how to avoid a recurrence. Which was why Lassiter decided not to retrace his steps to the Hassler. Instead he checked into the Mozart, an obscure hotel on a cobbled street off the Via del Corso.

The hotel occupied the west wing of a down-at-the-heels palazzo that had fourteen-foot ceilings, a dormant garden, and a desolate bar. Though it was almost midnight when he got in, he asked for and was given a suite on the second floor, overlooking the street. A geriatric bellboy led the way, and Lassiter did what he could to keep up with him, clenching his teeth against the pain.

When the bellboy was gone, he double-locked the doors, went to the frigo bar, and emptied two miniatures of scotch into a plastic water glass. Then he sat down at the desk beside the window and took out his "casebook."

Years ago, when he was in Brussels, he'd gotten into the habit of starting a new notebook whenever he began a new investigation. The practice was useful for several reasons, but in particular for a side benefit—the way it helped him retrieve names that if alphabetized would probably have been lost to him. He might not remember the name of a particular investigator, pathologist, or documents' examiner, but he never forgot a case—and he'd remember that the person he was looking for had done some work on it. Once that association was made, it was simple to pick out the right notebook and find the name.

After the first year, he'd taken to using the same kind of journal—an inexpensive three-by-eight spiral-bound reporter's notebook that he could hold in one hand, and which fit easily into the inside pocket of his suit jacket. If they ever stopped making them, he thought, Lassiter Associates would probably go out of business.

When he began a notebook, he entered the names and telephone numbers in the back, starting on the last page. In that way, all of the addresses could be found in a single place and he almost never ran out of room.

He'd followed the same practice in Kathy and Brandon's case as he had in all the others, and there were now quite a few numbers. The first entry was Riordan's, then a few doctors. Tom Truong, the hotel in Chicago. Bepi. Angela. Egloff. And Umbra Domini.

He sipped his scotch and looked out the window. It was a pretty view, with linden trees running the length of the nearly deserted street. Picking up the phone, he consulted his notebook and dialed Bepi's home and office numbers. When he heard the answering machines, he called Bepi's cell phone, but the call didn't go through. Finally, he called the pager number Bepi had given him, and tapped in the numerals for the Mozart. It worried him that twenty-four hours before, he'd gone through this same routine in Naples, and still the kid had not called him back. It wasn't like him, and Lassiter sensed that something was wrong. For one thing, he was too lucrative a client to ignore. And even more to the point, Bepi was deeply in love with technology, boasting that he was never out of touch for more than ten minutes—"no matter if I'm watching Lazio or flying to Tokyo or L.A."

Lassiter had smiled at that; in all likelihood, the kid had never been to Geneva, much less L.A.

He called the office on the chance that Judy might be working late. When he got the switchboard and heard the ruckus in the background, he realized it was the night of the annual Christmas party. The woman who answered was a temp whose name he didn't recognize, and she obviously couldn't hear him very well.

"Wha-aat?"

"It's Joe Lassiter."

"Who?"

"Joe Lassiter."

"I'm sorry, Mr. Lassiter isn't in at the moment."

"No, that's not—"

"And anyway, the office is closed."

Irritated, he hung up and redialed his own voice-mail number in McLean. There were half a dozen messages, but the only one of interest was from Jimmy Riordan—and that message was so filigreed with static as to be unintelligible. Something about *checks*. *You gotta love the checks!* What was *that* supposed to mean?

Lassiter looked at his watch. It was seven P.M. in the States. He tried Riordan's home number but there wasn't any answer. He tried the station.

"Sorry. Detective Riordan's outta town."

Lassiter slammed the palm of his hand down on the desk. The scotch jumped in the glass. He might as well be in a diving bell: he couldn't reach *anybody*.

He asked when Riordan would be back.

"I don't know. Probably the twenty-fourth—'the night before Christmas and all that.'"

"Is there any way to reach him?"

"Depends."

"I'm a friend of his."

"Well, then, he's probably told you: he's at a conference. In Prague." He pronounced the name as if it rhymed with "vague."

"*Prague?*"

"Prague, Prog—he's on a junket, is what he is!"

"You have a number I can reach him at?"

"Hang on."

While he waited, Lassiter remembered Riordan talking about the conference—something about Eastern Europe and democratizing the police. Riordan had even showed him a flyer—and pointed out his own name.

"You still there?"

"Yeah."

"Jimmy's at the fa-bu-lous Intercontinental *Ho*-tel in exotic Prog," the cop said. "Got a whole lotta numbers. First you gotta dial 011. You got a pen? 'Cuz you'll never remember—"

"Shoot."

At the back of the notebook, Lassiter added the number to the others under Riordan's name, hung up and dialed the Intercon. It was almost two in the morning, but the detective didn't answer the phone, and so Lassiter left yet another message.

Then he stretched out on the bed, tipped his shoes off, and with a moan fell into a fitful sleep.

It was almost noon when he finally woke up, and when he did, he was in the same position as when he'd lain down the night before—flat on his back, looking up at the ceiling. Using his arms and elbows, he struggled to sit up, pushed himself to his feet and walked uncertainly into the bathroom, holding his side. Very carefully, he turned to the mirror and raised his T-shirt. The colors on his side made him wince: there was yellow and mauve, purple, black, and a sickly sort of rose.

It took him nearly five minutes to get the water temperature right, and after he'd showered, it took him nearly twice as long to get dry. There were sectors where he could hardly bring himself to touch the towel to the damp skin. He had almost no mobility above the waist: bending down was agony, and sudden moves were something even worse. And so he dressed with infinite patience, taking time out to order coffee and croissants from room service. When the tray arrived, ten minutes later, he was struggling to tie his shoes. It occurred to him that he'd better buy some loafers.

When the bellhop left, Lassiter flicked on the television, using the remote control. Looking for CNN, he snapped his way from one channel to another, until Bepi's face flashed across the screen. He'd already flicked past the channel and had to go back.

The photo was dated, a graduation picture, or something like it. Bepi was smiling in a self-conscious way, and Lassiter saw that his hair was shorter and meticulously blown dry. He looked like a cross between a lounge singer and a choirboy, and the image might have made him smile—if there had been any good reason for Bepi to be on TV.

Lassiter tried to understand what the voice-over was saying, but he didn't get a word.

A moment later Bepi's picture was replaced by a live-action scene. A reporter stood on the sidewalk in front of a large church, talking somberly as a claque of kids gaped and mugged at the camera. Nearby, two police cars and an ambulance idled on the sidewalk.

The voice of the newscaster continued as the camera closed in on a trio of grim-faced men in uniforms, wheeling a gurney. The walkway was rough, maybe cobblestone, because the men were having trouble pushing the thing. It bounced and lurched, and every so often they had to lift it over an impediment.

The camera returned to the studio, and listening hard, Lassiter was able to make out a few of the newscaster's words: "Santa Maria" ... "Polizia" ... "Bepistraversi" ... "Molto strano." Then the newscaster smiled, shuffled the papers in front of him, and shifted to a different story.

Lassiter moved from channel to channel, flipping the remote, but he couldn't be sure what he was watching. A tearful woman in a black shawl was being interviewed about something, but there was no way to know if she was Bepi's wife or a refugee.

Frustrated, Lassiter turned off the set and called Judy Rifkin. Home number. It was seven-thirty in the morning in Washington, and he didn't care if she was awake.

"Joe! Where are you?"

"Rome."

"I was gonna call you this afternoon. The American Express thing is really heating up—"

"I think Bepi's dead."

The line went quiet on the other end. Judy didn't say a word.

"Things started getting a little rough all of a sudden and ... I just saw his face on television. I don't know what they were saying, but there was an ambulance, cop cars, a stretcher."

"You sure?"

"No, I'm not. Maybe ... maybe he's a suspect in something. I don't know what the fuck he is—but I can't get him on the phone, and—" A pain shot through his side and he gasped involuntarily.

"What's the matter?"

"Nothing . . . I got knocked around last night."

"*You?!*"

"Yeah. But, look: the important thing's Bepi. Take a look at the wires—Reuters, AP, whatever. Just run Bepi's name and fax me anything you get."

"Where are you staying?"

He gave her the numbers and hung up. While he waited, he got out the telephone directory, looked up the Associated Press, and dialed the number. They were completely unhelpful. So were the BBC, Westinghouse Radio, and the good folks at the *Rome Daily American.*

Two hours later, there was a knock at the door and an envelope slid into the room. There were two pages inside: a cover sheet on Lassiter Associates' letterhead, and a second page. The cover sheet read:

> *Reuters' story attached. Are you okay? Rifkin.*
>
> Copyright 1995 Reuters, Limited
> The Reuter Library Report
> December 23, 1995, BC cycle
>
> LENGTH: 152 words
> HEADLINE: VICTIM FOUND IN CHURCH
> DATELINE: ROME
> BODY: A private investigator was found slain early this morning outside the cathedral of Santa Maria Maggiore, a few blocks from the Colosseum. According to police, the victim, Antonio Bepistraversi, 26, was tortured before he was killed.
>
> The body was discovered by sixty-year-old Lucilla Conti. She spotted the victim on the expanse of steps leading up the Esquiline hill to the rear entrance of the basilica. In an interview with reporters, Mrs. Conti disclosed that she first thought the figure to be one of the homeless who have long made a base of the nearby Piazza Vittorio Emanuele II. She detoured around the man, for fear she'd be asked for money. Seeing that the figure remained immobile, she approached it and saw that the man's head was enclosed in a plastic bag.
>
> Homicide detectives noted that the incident occurred in "a deteriorating neighborhood," and expressed confidence that the crime would be solved.

Lassiter read the story three times, hoping he'd misunderstood, but it always came out the same. Bepi was dead, and not only that: he'd died badly. Or hard. Either way . . .

Suddenly, it occurred to him that the person he ought to be talking to was Gianni Massina. If anyone could tell him what had happened, Massina could. Flipping to the back of his notebook, Lassiter found the reporter's number and called.

"*Pronto?!*"

"It's Joe Lassiter."

"Yes?"

"We met a few days ago—"

"Of course!" His voice crashed. "You've heard? About Bepi?"

"Yeah. I saw it on television."

Massina heaved a sigh. "I still can't believe it." He sighed again.

"The reason I called . . . I don't know. Bepi—he was still working for me when it happened, and I thought, maybe—with Umbra—since they found him outside a church . . ."

Massina made a skeptical sound. "With Umbra there are always rumors. But this? I don't think so. It's an interesting church, but—there's no connection with Umbra Domini."

"So why do you say it's 'interesting'?"

"Because . . . it is! It's six hundred years old and consecrated to the Mother of God. They say it was built after a snowfall, a miraculous snowfall that fell in a way that . . . it's like a *blueprint* for the cathedral. Right there on the ground! So every year, on the church's birthday, they throw flower petals—white flower petals—from the *duomo*. And there are relics—pieces of wood from the manger! Five of them, eh? What about that?"

"Are they real?"

"How do I know? This is religion. Everything's real! *Nothing's* real. You want to know what's real? The neighborhood the church is in is real."

"Reuters says it's 'deteriorating.' "

Massina snorted. "We call it the Piazza of Shit and Needles! Even the whores won't go there. It's all junkies and crazy people—"

"So what?"

"What?"

"So *what* if it's a lousy neighborhood? The Reuters story said he'd been tortured. So it had to happen somewhere else. You don't torture people on the steps of a church."

"You're right. They dumped him. I talked to the cops . . . off the record, okay? They say he was brought there around five A.M. They don't know where he was before this, but from the way the blood settled, it wasn't on the steps. Not in that position, anyway. Maybe he'd been dead a day before they dumped him." Lassiter and Massina both fell silent. After a moment Massina said, "He's got a kid, you know."

"Yeah, he told me." Once again the line went quiet.

Finally Massina broke the spell. "You know how he died?"

"No. Not really." But he knew, somehow, that Massina was going to tell him.

Massina sucked in some air. "The police don't release this, but . . . They tied his arms and legs behind his back, with the rope around his throat in—I'm not sure of the word—a slide knot."

"Slip knot."

"A *slip* knot. The more he's struggling, the tighter the rope, you know? The police say this goes on for many hours. He starts to strangle—his interrogator frees him. Over and over. Many abrasions around his throat. And his wrists. And the ankles. This means they must threaten him while he's bound up like this—so he can't *stop* from struggling."

"What do you mean?"

Massina sucked in some more air. "They find a plastic bag over his head. With this, you know—you hold your breath, maybe, as long as you can, but then your instinct is taking over—so you struggle! The way Bepi is tied, the rope tightens, you start to black out, and then they take the bag off. They loosen the rope. And they do this many times. Then, the last one, they're putting the plastic bag around his head— only this time they don't take it off. So it's over. He's dead."

Lassiter didn't say anything. What was he supposed to say?

Massina cleared his throat. "What do you think they were looking for?"

"Information."

"But what information?"

"I don't know. Maybe they were just—*fishing*. Maybe they didn't know what they were looking for. Maybe they were trying to find out how much he knew . . . or how much I knew. Or . . . maybe it was recreational—a nut."

"I don't believe in nuts," Massina said.

"Neither do I."

The air hung between them until Lassiter finally broke the silence. "Well . . ." he said.

"*Felice Natale, eh?*"

"Yeah."

"Take care of yourself."

"You, too. Merry Christmas."

21

The moment he put the receiver down, the phone bleated like a smoke alarm, then bleated again. He picked it up as if it was something unclean. "Lassiter," he said in the neutral voice he used when his secretary was on a coffee break.

"Guess who!"

"Jimmy," he said. "I've got a few things—" He was about to mention Bepi and his own troubles in Naples, but Riordan bulldozed right past him with his energetic voice.

"You wouldn't think, you know? Case is stalled, you go off someplace you've never been, but you know what? I think I'm on to something."

Lassiter sat upright.

Riordan cackled. "Got your attention, didn't I?"

"Yes. You did."

"When can you get here?"

"Where?"

"Prague! Where do you think I'm callin' from?"

"Jimmy. Things have been happening. I don't—"

"It's an hour's flight. Just like the shuttle."

Lassiter realized Riordan wasn't picking up the tone in his voice, wasn't really listening to him, because Riordan was really excited about something. "Why don't you just tell me?"

"Because there's someone you gotta meet! So get on a plane, and get *over* here."

"You're sure—"

"*Trust* me. It's important."

Lassiter set down the receiver and tried to think. He felt he should stay in Rome and do *something* about Bepi, but after thinking about it, he couldn't come up with anything useful. Besides, he could be back in Rome in a day. Maybe even less.

—

Five hours later Lassiter stood in the parking lot outside the Intercontinental Hotel in the capital of the Czech Republic, looking up at a
commissar's idea of progress—a glass-and-concrete box whose ersatz
modernity held out the promise of insipid abstracts, stained carpeting,
and Europop. Erected at the height of the cold war, the hotel was
meant to be a plug for the Communist party, an architectural statement that proclaimed to one and all: *We're marching into the future,
doing business arm in arm!* But as so often happens with architectural
statements, this one came out a little differently, so that, today, the
hotel seemed to be saying: *We don't need no stinking AHM-bee-ahnce!*

Inside, Lassiter found Riordan sitting in a booth with a baleful
Czech in a leather trench coat. Dressed in his regulation suit and tie,
Riordan looked like the cop he was, while his companion projected
the image of an out-of-work rock musician, a tubercular genius whose
long and greasy black hair hung down to his shoulders. A packet of
Trumfs lay on the table, surrounded by empty bottles of Pilsner
Urquell. Lassiter dropped his overnight bag to the floor and slid into
the booth. "This better be good."

Riordan did a double take. "Heyyyyy, Joe! Say hello to Franz—"

"Hello, Franz."

"Joe Lassiter, Franz Janacek."

They shook hands. The Czech had a strong grip and hooded eyes,
bad skin and a low, almost subterranean voice that glittered when he
spoke—a gold tooth at the side of his mouth.

"A pleasure," Janacek said.

"Franz is . . . what are you, anyway? Minister of the Interior?"

Janacek grinned. "Not yet." He pulled a business card from inside
his coat and dropped it in a pool of moisture. Lassiter glanced at it
with surprise. Janacek was chief of detectives for the Prague police.

Riordan grinned. "Is this a great country, or what? I love this place!
Lemme get a round," he said, and waved at the waiter as if his chair
were a cruise ship pulling out of port and his family was standing on
the dock, in tears.

The bar was crowded with middle-aged men in dark suits. They
stood in groups of three and four, talking animatedly in what sounded
like half a dozen languages. They all seemed to be smoking, and the
air was heavy with the fumes of cheap tobacco and expensive liquor.

Riordan nodded at them. "Everybody's here! FBI, Secret Service, KGB—even the fuckin' Mounties. Do you believe it? The *Mounties!* Scotland Yard. The *gendarmes*—I never met a gendarme before."

"Pig heaven," Janacek said, lighting a cigarette.

Riordan laughed. "Franz is a hippie."

The beers arrived and Lassiter took a sip. It was delicious, but it stung the cut in his lip and he winced. Janacek grinned. "What happened?" he asked.

"I fell down."

Riordan grimaced. "Seriously."

"A guy broke into my room."

"Then what?"

"He resisted arrest."

"And did he get away?" Janacek asked.

"So far."

"Too bad," Riordan said. "But enough about you. You're probably wondering why I called you here."

Lassiter laughed. "You're drunk, aren't you?"

"Technically, I'm a little past the dew point. So what? The point is, Franz and I are co-panelists."

"On what?" Lassiter asked.

"Cold cases."

Lassiter shook his head. "What's that?"

"Unsolved crime. A homicide or major felony we can't close," Janacek said.

"Because there's no evidence—" Riordan added.

"Or worse than that," Janacek put in, "no motive."

"It's a big problem," Riordan said. "What do you do with a cold case? I mean, besides hoping that someday, somehow, it'll solve itself? Whattaya do?"

"I don't know," Lassiter replied. "What *do* you do?"

Riordan shrugged. "That's why we got a panel. Basically, you go back to the well. Again and again. You reinterview people, and hope for a confession. Or you pray for new technology—like DNA testing. But, mostly, a cold case is a cold case. It's depressing."

Lassiter shook his head, as if to clear it, and Janacek's mouth broke into a lupine grin. "So," Lassiter said, "you talked about my sister's case, *and* . . ."

"Actually," Riordan replied, "we didn't. Because that case is solved.

We just have to find the guy." Riordan lowered his chin and quietly burped. "Again," he added.

"So why am I here?" Lassiter asked. Riordan was beginning to irritate him.

"I'm getting there, but—all right, what happens is . . . at the panel someone asks a question about serial killers."

"This is actually a good question," Janacek said, "because, often, in these cases, we have a body—and no obvious motive."

"Right. Because the killer does what he does—just to do it," Riordan explained.

"He's 'a pure scientist,'" Janacek added. "I think many cold cases are like this."

"So, the guy in the audience—the one who asked the question— wants an example. And Janacek . . . go ahead, tell him."

The Czech leaned forward. "The example I use happened three, four months ago. August. A family near Stromovka Park. Nice neighborhood. Crime is arson, murder. Two dead."

"Now, get this," Riordan said, "the victims are a little boy, two, two and a half, and his mother. It's night, they're sleeping, it's arson. The house is burned to shit."

"They use accelerants, so nothing is left," Janacek said. "Some bones. Teeth. We suspect the husband, but . . . no."

"There's no other woman, no other man, no insurance," Riordan added.

Janacek nodded. "No debts. Nothing."

"Happy family," Riordan said.

"Where was the husband?" Lassiter asked.

Janacek waved his hand as if rubbing out a spot in the air. "At a Sparta game—out of town."

Riordan rocked back in his chair. "Sound familiar?"

"Yeah," Lassiter replied, "it does. When did this happen?"

"September one."

Lassiter frowned. He tried to remember Grimaldi's passport details.

"I checked," Riordan said. "He entered the Czech Republic a few days earlier."

The three of them fell silent and sipped their beers. Finally, Lassiter looked up: "It could be a coincidence."

Riordan nodded. "Absolutely."

"It could be one of those things."

"You think so?" Janacek asked in a neutral voice.

"No," Lassiter said.

Janacek nodded, as much to himself as to his companions.

They were all silent for a moment, and then Lassiter said, "Could I speak with the husband? Would that be possible?"

Janacek frowned. "Jiri Reiner? He doesn't speak English."

"Well, with your help, of course."

Janacek thought about it. "And what purpose would this serve?"

"Well, for beginners . . . I'd want to know if his wife had anything to do with my sister. Or the children? Any point of connection."

"Like what?"

"I don't know."

Janacek shrugged. "Jiri—he's still very . . . disturbed. The doctor—he gives him drugs. Sedation. They still worry he might kill himself. And why not?" His pale eyes swiveled over toward Lassiter. "Anyone might. In one night, he loses—" Janacek slapped his hands together. "—*everything*. His wife, his son, his home." He stared gloomily at the floor.

"Well," Lassiter said, "just a thought."

Janacek drew some air in through his teeth and wagged his head. "Also, Jiri—he is—" Janacek opened and closed his hand several times as if he could catch the right word out of the air. "—he doesn't *communicate* so well, you know? Most of the time, he won't talk at all."

Lassiter nodded.

"Still . . ." Janacek said, drawing the word out, "since the cases are so similar . . . perhaps we could help each other. Do you think I could obtain a copy of the Italian's passport?"

Lassiter and Riordan exchanged a glance. "I'm sure the detective could arrange that," Lassiter said.

"And a photo?"

Riordan nodded. "Sure. No problem."

Janacek drained his beer and stood up. "Okay. I do this. I put the question to Jiri himself, and also his doctor." He shrugged. "Maybe . . ." He stuck out his hand, and both Lassiter and Riordan shook it. "We talk in the morning."

"Thanks," Lassiter said.

The Czech nodded solemnly, began to leave, and turned around. "You know, to have a case that goes from one country to another . . . this is actually very unusual. And this . . . from one continent to another . . . I don't know of any other case like this, except terrorism. And we know this is not terrorism."

"We do?" Riordan asked.

"Of course."

"And how do we know that?"

"Because," Lassiter interjected, "there's no publicity, and no politics."

Janacek nodded and turned to Riordan. "I've got to go." He tapped his head. "When you get back to the States, maybe you can approach your FBI and see if they have anything to match these crimes."

"Absolutely," Riordan said. "I'll call my FBI. See what they have."

The next day, the last session of the conference, both Janacek and Riordan were busy until late in the afternoon. There was a breakfast meeting, followed by discussions, panels, workshops, and a final assembly. In the evening there would be a banquet.

Janacek called to say he was trying to set up the meeting with Reiner. They'd squeeze it in somehow; he'd be in touch.

Which left Lassiter with the day to fill. There were things he wanted to do, but the most important of them was to go for a run along the waterfront and through the streets of the old town. Though it was an understatement to say his ribs were sensitive to the touch, he could still do the miles—so long as he took them slow and easy. The idea was not to bump into anyone, and not to run out of breath. The last thing he wanted to do was gasp for air.

Breaking into a slow jog outside the Intercon, he could taste the pollution in the air. It was cold, and the smoky, metallic taste set his teeth on edge. Prague's legacy from the Communist emphasis on heavy industry—combined with its site in a river valley—had created a serious air pollution problem, especially in the winter.

Still, the heart of the city was ancient and beautiful, spared both the bomb damage and urban renewal that scarred most of Europe's capitals. As he crossed the famous Charles Bridge it began to snow. He loped past one time-blackened statue after another, a phalanx of corroded saints, one after another, every ten, fifteen yards, gazing down from the parapets at the hurrying pedestrians. A few vendors—postcards, photographs, Christmas ornaments, artwork—huddled in front of tiny charcoal fires. An icy wind gusted off the river. On the street corners, bundled-up women stood over plastic tubs full of live carp. He'd been warned about this Christmas custom by Riordan, who'd been standing too close as a patron selected his choice. It was hooked by the gill, laid on a board, and decapitated with a chop that splattered Riordan's best pants with fish guts.

By the time Lassiter had done a couple of miles and turned around to head back across the bridge, the vendors were gone. The wind had dropped and wet snow was beginning to accumulate on the outstretched hands, the bare feet, the sightless eyes of the saintly figures. Before long the sidewalk was awash in slush. Afraid of slipping, he walked the last two blocks back to the hotel. He took short breaths, but it still hurt.

A message waited for him at the front desk, from Janacek: the meeting with Jiri Reiner had been arranged for eight that evening.

After he showered, Lassiter dug out the adapter from his overnight bag, plugged in his laptop computer, and hooked it up to the telephone line. He wanted to run a Nexis search for news stories about arson/homicides similar to the ones that killed Kathy and Brandon, and Jiri Reiner's wife and son. He tapped out the international access number for AT&T and booted the computer into the Nexis/Lexis service. He could have had someone in the office do it, but he found online research an intuitive process—especially when you were trolling for something that didn't really have a name.

Nexis was an expensive database that contained newspaper and magazine articles from literally hundreds of publications, newsletters, and wire services around the world. It was not comprehensive, but it was broad and deep. The search engine was fast, and once you'd defined the terms, it was a simple matter to locate the story or stories you were searching for—whether it was a 1980 bulletin from the Reuters bureau in Sofia, an article about serotonin research in the *Journal of Endocrinology*, or a column about *wadlopen* in last week's *Het Parool*.

The database worked by using logical operators—inclusive terms such as *and/or*, and restrictive ones such as *not*—in conjunction with the key words that defined the story. Lassiter typed: arson *and* homicide *and* child.

The computer screen glowed quietly for a few seconds, and then a message appeared, saying that more than a thousand cities had been found, and so the search had been halted. Lassiter thought for a moment, and then he narrowed the search by adding: *and* 1995.

Within seconds the service reported 214 cities—almost all of which were irrelevant. Most of them were compilations of crime reports, where the arson in question had no relation to either the child or homicide that came later. Redefining his search, Lassiter typed: Kathleen Lassiter *and* arson *and* 1995.

There were nineteen stories in various editions of the *Washington Post*, the *Washington Times*, the *Fairfax Journal*, and the Associated Press. The reports fell into two groups: there were eight articles in the first three days after the murders, a couple of pieces about the grave robbery, and a spate of stories about "John Doe's escape" and the policeman's murder. Since then, nothing.

Scanning the articles was a depressing process, in part because it pumped new life into the horror of his sister's murder, and in part because it made him realize the inadequacy of the net he was casting. While he could certainly configure the search in such a way as to obtain everything about his sister's death that might be found on Nexis, the search terms were too broad to locate similar cases in an effective way. There were dozens of synonyms for *child, arson,* and *homicide*. If he used them all, he'd have to wade through thousands and thousands of stories.

It was also discouraging that the coverage was as short-lived and superficial as it was. Kathy and Brandon's deaths were "a news event" in the Metro section, and the coverage did not persist long enough for any one story to make it clear that the crime was as deliberate and vicious as it was. Neither had anyone in the media paused to consider the implications of Brandon's disinterment, or the possibility that John Doe had an accomplice. The events were reported, but unconsidered.

Lassiter supposed that it was the same in almost any large metropolitan area, where Saturday's double homicide gave way to Sunday's drive-by shooting. Kathy's case had been especially horrible, but even so, the coverage was short-lived and brief.

He ran: Reiner *and* arson *and* Prague. And came up with nothing at all. Frustrated, he returned to his original search and used a browsing feature that went directly to the key words in each of the relevant stories. In the end there was only a single story that might be relevant. It was a short piece in a small daily published in Bressingham, British

Columbia, a hundred miles north of Vancouver. The story told how Brian and Marion Kerr and their three-year-old son, Barry, had perished in a fire that local police said was of "suspicious origin."

Although it wasn't just a woman and a child, as in his sister's case and the Reiners', he ran another search: Kerr *and* Bressingham *and* fire *or* arson.

Since the deaths had occurred in a small town, the story was probably big news. It was. He found eight subsequent articles about the same event, and read them all. Two days after the fire was first reported, police confirmed that it was arson. The blaze had started in three different places, and lab analyses indicated that accelerants had been used. Witnesses reported seeing a man running from the house shortly before the blaze broke out.

The first thing that occurred to Lassiter was that all of the children were boys—at least, thus far. There was Brandon. And the Reiners' son. And now the Kerrs'.

On the other hand, the Kerrs didn't really fit. Lassiter would have remembered if Grimaldi's passport had included a Canadian visa—he was sure it had not. More to the point was the story's dateline: November 14. Grimaldi was still in the hospital on that day. In fact, it was only a few days after Kathy and Brandon's funerals. With a groan, he shut off the computer and called Judy at his office in Washington.

"Hey! Where are ya?"

"Prague."

"Gimme your number; you're supposed to stay in touch!"

He did.

She winced. "Anything new on Bepi?"

Lassiter was silent for a moment. Finally, he said, "No."

"So . . . maybe it had something to do with you," Judy replied, "and maybe it didn't."

"It had everything to do with . . . this case. No question. Everything."

"Then I'd say it's 'flaps up.' Get out of there!"

"I'm not 'there.' I'm in Prague. Anyway—not yet."

"Why *not?*"

"Because there are things I have to do—and a couple of things I want *you* to do. For starters, I want Bepi's family taken care of. Some kind of income. Enough for his kid and whoever's responsible. You know what I'm talking about—enough to handle things."

"For how long?"

"For as long as it takes."

"That could run into a lot of money."

"Judy: I *have* a lot of money."

"Done. What else?"

"AmEx."

"What about it?"

"You tell me."

"They want to know what role you'll play—after the sale."

"None."

"That's not what they want."

"I don't care what they want."

"In that case, they've put an offer on the table for twelve five, plus options that oughta be worth another three million. Catch is: you can't exercise the options for five years. Also, they want a noncompetitive agreement."

"No problem." They didn't want him to go into business for himself.

"The acquisitions guy says: You stay on as CEO, they'll go a lot higher."

"They'll go higher anyway. And tell them I'm not interested in options. I want the money."

"Got it."

"The whole idea is to cash out. And, if I'm gonna cash out, I want to be—"

"All the way out. Okay—so I'll *hondel*."

Lassiter's next call was to Roy Dunwold, the head of his company's four-man London office. Roy was a working-class kid who'd grown up in Derry, or Londonderry, depending on your point of view—but in any case, the hard way. He'd spent two years in Borstal for a series of car thefts, a string of joy rides that finally came to an end when the Porsche he was driving plowed into a hearse at the head of an IRA funeral cortege.

After three months in the hospital and the much longer sojourn in juvenile detention, he was paroled to his aunt's custody in London. A clear-sighted woman who ran a bed-and-breakfast in Kilburn, she pointed out the obvious: Stealing cars was, at best, an avocation. He'd need a trade.

And so Roy set out to acquire one, enrolling in night school and, subsequently, in one of the better polytechnics. A good student, he found work after graduation as a specialist in management information systems. His employer was GCHQ-Cheltenham, Britain's equivalent of the National Security Agency. After a year at headquarters, Dunwold was sent to a satellite base in the Troödos Mountains on Cyprus. After five years in the Aegean outback he'd had enough retsina and one-night stands to last him a lifetime, and returned to England and the private sector. As he told his friends, "I missed the rain, didn't I?" Eventually, Lassiter lured him away from Kroll Associates, offering the same salary, but with a company car of Dunwold's choosing.

He chose a Porsche.

It took Lassiter a while to reach Roy, but when he did, they got right down to business. "I don't know how much you've heard, but . . . I'm working on a private matter."

"Your sister."

"And nephew."

"Right."

"And one of the things I'm looking at," Lassiter said, "is similar crimes . . . arson homicides involving children. I've found a second in Prague, and another in Canada."

"And you're sure they're related?"

"No." A pause. "But they might be. And I thought maybe you could help me . . . find other cases."

"Where?"

"Wherever. You could start with Europe."

"England's more like it."

"Okay, England."

Dunwold was quiet for a moment, and then he said, "Problem."

"What?"

"Well, a great many arsons aren't found out, are they? I mean, they're put down as electrical fires—overturned heater, that sort of thing. Which means we need to look at any fires in which a child's died."

"Okay."

"Bit of work, that."

"I know."

"What's the time frame?"

"Anything after August first."

"Right."

"I was thinking, you might want to try Interpol."

"Sod that lot. Bloody useless. We can do better than that. We've got some interesting databases to play with—and I think the insurance companies might be helpful. They have been in the past. I'll call Lloyd's."

"What about the police?"

"Goes without saying. Of course, I'll check with the police, Europol, the Yard—all the usual suspects."

"Wait a second. I just had an idea." Lassiter pulled out his copies of Grimaldi's passport pages and looked through them for entry stamps in the relevant period. He soon found the one he wanted: "Check São Paolo, will you?"

"Brazil?"

"Yeah. September thirteen to eighteen of last year. Let me know what you find."

"Got it. Do you want a written report?"

"No. Just the information. Judy will know where I am."

"Budget?"

"Don't worry about it. Just do what you have to."

"Right!" They were about to hang up when Dunwold said, "Oh, wait—Joe! Are you still there?"

"Yeah."

"I just had a little thought."

"What's that?"

"This could take a while. I mean—it's Christmas, i'nit? Day after tomorrow. *I'll* come in, but . . ."

"Do the best you can."

"Right, then. Cheers! Happy Christmas and all that. I'll be in touch."

He met Janacek and Riordan in the hotel lobby at seven-thirty, and by eight-fifteen, after a hair-raising drive through the snow, they were in the elevator of the Pankow clinic, somewhere in the outer burbs of the city. A doctor in a white lab coat showed them into Jiri Reiner's ward.

It was stifling in the room, but Reiner, who seemed to be the only occupant, huddled in his blankets. The man was emaciated. His eyes seemed huge in his bony face.

"He doesn't eat," Janacek whispered, running his hand through his hair. The doctor whispered something into the Czech detective's ear, and turned to Lassiter. Wordlessly, he raised a single finger, admonishing them both to be brief. Then he left.

Reiner lay in the bed, staring openly at Lassiter.

Janacek turned to him. "Very well! I will translate. What do you have to say to Pan Reiner? Excuse me—to Mr. Reiner."

"I want you to tell him that on November the seventh my sister, Kathy, and her young son, Brandon, were murdered. Their throats were cut. And then their house was set on fire." He took a deep breath. "Something went wrong, and the man that did this burst through the window of the house with his clothes on fire."

Janacek translated and when he was finished, turned to Lassiter and dipped his chin.

"The man was badly burned, but survived. When the police questioned him, he refused to answer—and no one can find any reason for this crime." Lassiter shook his head. "No one."

He watched Reiner as Janacek translated, and Reiner returned his gaze. As the detective spoke, tears welled up in the patient's eyes. He did nothing to wipe them away. Finally, when Janacek was done, Reiner spoke in an emotion-filled voice, his eyes as wet and huge as a Labrador's.

"He asks," Janacek translated, "was your sister and nephew dead—before the fire? He asks: They did not struggle?"

Lassiter knew what Reiner was after. "That's right," he said. "They didn't die from the fire. They were killed quickly, with a knife." He decided not to mention the multiple stab wounds Kathy sustained, or the defensive cuts on her hands.

The man sat in the bed, davening, rocking back and forth, hands clasped, eyes pressed shut. When he opened his eyes again and spoke, the relief was evident in his face. It was clear to Lassiter he'd been inflicting upon himself images of his child and his wife, trapped, coughing, burning alive. Now, at least, he had another image to consider. He said something to Janacek, and the detective translated.

"He asks: This man—who was he?"

"He's an Italian. A man named Grimaldi. Tell him he's a man with—a bad history. A mercenary. A hired killer."

Janacek translated, and Lassiter watched Jiri Reiner screw his face up at the mention of Grimaldi's name. He bit his lower lip and a bewildered look swept over his face. He shook his head sadly.

Lassiter pointed a thumb to his own chest, then put his hands out wide, and with a baffled look on his face copied Reiner's uncomprehending head shake. Reiner peered at him.

"Grimaldi's passport shows he was here in Prague when your wife and son were murdered."

"I tell him this already," Janacek said in an annoyed voice.

"Tell him again."

Reiner shook his head sadly, then tapped it three times—as if to say there were no answers inside.

They went over things this way, for several more minutes, asking questions back and forth through Janacek. Did the two women know each other? Had Hannah Reiner ever been to the United States or Kathy Lassiter to Czechoslovakia? Lassiter asked Riordan to show Reiner a photograph of Grimaldi, and also one of Kathy and Brandon, but the poor man could only shake his head and mutter, "Ne, ne. Nevim. Nevim." There was no need for translation. Then Reiner brought out from under his pillow a small framed photograph of his wife holding his son. The frame was silver and made in the shape of a heart. Lassiter looked at it and shook his head at the smiling pair. In the end the doctor reappeared, annoyed that the three of them were still there. Reiner spoke in a strong voice, and what he wanted was Joe Lassiter's telephone number and address. Lassiter gave the man his card. The doctor tried to shoo them out, but Lassiter approached the hospital bed, took Jiri Reiner's gaunt hand in his own and clasped it.

"I'll find out," he said in English, looking into Reiner's eyes. Reiner tightened his grasp on Lassiter's hand, pulled it toward him, and pressed it against his chest. He squeezed his eyes shut and said, "Dekuji moc. Dekuji moc."

"That means 'Thank you very much,' " Janacek said.

"Yeah, I got that."

And then the doctor gestured that they should leave. Lassiter looked back over his shoulder, and Jiri Reiner's eyes burned at him. The doctor was preparing to administer a shot to the man, but Lassiter just had a thought and spoke urgently to Janacek. "Just one more question."

Janacek shook his head no, but Lassiter saw Jiri Reiner push the doctor's arm away in a surprisingly strong motion.

"Prosim," he said, gesturing at Lassiter.

"Ask him if his wife ever went to Italy."

Kathy had been to Italy half a dozen times, and Lassiter had begun to wonder if she'd met Grimaldi there—or if Hannah Reiner had. Janacek asked the question, and an odd thing happened.

Reiner looked away.

Maybe Lassiter was reading it wrong, but it seemed to him that Reiner was *embarrassed*. Head down, the Czech muttered something to Janacek, and looked away.

"He says they go there one time only," Janacek said. "On holiday. Now, we must go."

Lassiter nodded, turned, and raised his hand in good-bye. The man in the hospital bed kept his eyes on the framed photograph beside him. "*Ciao*," he muttered. "*Ciao*."

22

In the morning, Lassiter drove Riordan to the airport, threading his way through the Prague traffic, following the blue signs that blazed the way. The detective was uncharacteristically subdued.

"I wanted to talk to you," Lassiter said, "about—"

"Don't shout."

"I'm not shouting, Detective, I'm speaking in a normal voice."

Riordan groaned as Lassiter entered a rotary and, changing lanes, pushed the accelerator to the floor, merging at high speed. Halfway through the rotary a blue sign loomed, and Lassiter plunged across three lanes in the direction of the airport. "Please," Riordan said. "Don't."

"Wages of sin," Lassiter replied without a trace of sympathy. "How many drinks did you have last night, anyway?"

Riordan was silent a moment, as if he were counting. Finally he said, "What's a drink?"

As they drove through the city and into the suburbs, the architecture began to degrade. Slowly, stone gave way to concrete, ornament to empty modernity. Even the windows seemed to change, becoming curiously bland.

Riordan took a deep breath and grunted, as though he'd been punched in the chest. Then he cleared his throat and sat up straight. "Okay," he said, "so what did you want to talk about?"

Lassiter looked at him. "Italy," he said.

"Italy was Campari . . . what about it?"

Lassiter sighed. Where should he start? Bepi. "Well, to begin with, one of the people I was working with—the guy who was helping me in Rome—was killed. Couple of days ago."

Riordan didn't say anything for a moment, and then: "You sure it had something to do with you?"

"I can't prove it, but . . . yeah, I think so. And the night before, I came back to my hotel and there's a guy in my room. Big guy."

"Is this when you 'fell down'?"

"Yeah. I think he woulda killed me, but the maid walked in."

"Jesus Christ . . . what'd he want?"

"That's it. I don't know. When I came in, he was there—my computer was on, and he was looking at it." The street gave way to a broader road that curved to the east, and suddenly they were in the country and all the trees were gone. Sunlight poured through the windshield. Riordan grimaced like Vlad the Impaler, and Lassiter glanced at him. "You look like shit," he said.

Riordan's pink eyes glimmered at him. And when he spoke, it was with the painstaking matter-of-factness of the seriously hung over. "I can't help it," Riordan replied. "They had a banquet. Everybody got up to toast everybody else. One country after another—and then there were liqueurs." He paused for a moment, and added, "I remember . . . there was slivovitz."

"You're a little old for that sort of thing, aren't you?"

Riordan turned the question aside with a weary look. "So, what made this guy think you knew anything?"

Lassiter shook his head. "We were noisy."

" 'We'?"

"The guy I was working with—Bepi. The one who was killed. We went to Grimaldi's old addresses, we talked to his sister—"

"And what did you find out?"

"He had a religious conversion about five years ago."

"No shit?! And what the fuck did he convert *from*?"

Lassiter shook his head. "He was some kind of spook. A paramilitary."

"Yeah?"

"Yeah . . . he killed people."

"And how do you know that?"

Lassiter just looked at him.

"How do you *know* that?" Riordan repeated.

"I have a friend who works . . . for a government agency. He showed me a file."

"Now we're talkin'! When can I see it?"

"You can't."

"Why not?"

"Because the file's gone now."

Riordan growled in frustration, or pain, or both. He started to say something, and changed his mind. Finally he said, "So what did he convert *to?*"

"Umbra Domini. He gave everything to a religious group called Umbra Domini."

"Shadow of the Lord," Riordan said.

Lassiter looked surprised. "You know Latin?"

"No. Sister Mary Margaret knew Latin. I just picked up a couple of words."

"But the strange thing is—you know the wire transfer Grimaldi got?"

"Yeah . . . ?"

"The money came from Umbra Domini."

Riordan chuckled. "Now, that's rich! How'd you find that out? The Swiss wouldn't tell us fuck-all."

Lassiter shrugged. "A friend. It's a onetime favor."

Riordan's foot tapped the floor . . . slower and slower. Then it stopped. "Hey . . . *wait*. The wire transfer. We never released that."

Lassiter changed lanes. "The airport's just ahead," he said.

Riordan sighed. "I knew it was you anyway."

As the car pulled up to the terminal building, Lassiter told Riordan about his trip to Naples and the holy-water bottle that fell out of della Torre's pocket. "It was just like Grimaldi's," he said.

"So what's the point?" Riordan asked. "You tryin' to tell me that this religious group—the Umbras or whatever—paid Grimaldi to kill your sister?"

"And my nephew."

"Get off it!"

"And Jiri Reiner's family. And maybe some others."

"Are you nuts? Why would they do that?" Riordan looked at his watch, then drew some air in through his teeth. He fumbled in his briefcase. "I better write some of this shit down," he said.

"Don't worry about it. I've got a folder for you. Let me park, and I'll meet you inside. Buy you a cup of coffee."

"I'll be in the bar."

Fifteen minutes later Riordan was looking and feeling a lot better. "What do you think does it?" he asked. "You think it's the tomato juice? Or the vodka?"

"I think it's the vodka," Lassiter said, sliding a manila envelope across the table as he sat down. Riordan pulled out his reading glasses and started paging through the Umbra leaflets and news stories. The public address system broadcast a very loud advisory in four successive languages.

"Okay," Riordan said. "Thanks for the lead . . . now all I gotta do is go back and tell my boss the Catholics did it. You have any idea how that's gonna go over?"

"This isn't about 'Catholics,' " Lassiter said. "It's about one organization—*which*, by the way, has a group house outside of Washington. Near Frederick somewhere. You might want to check it out."

Riordan frowned. "All right, I will. But I'll have to blow it by the Federales. Ever since Grimaldi grabbed the nurse, I've had a babysitter from the Bureau." Riordan looked Lassiter in the eye with a stare so intently focused as to make him seem insane. Then he took Lassiter's hand in his own and squeezed it in a manly way. "Derek Watson, Joe. It is Joe, isn't it? We're doing the best we can—I just want you to know that. The very best we can!" Riordan released his hand and closed his eyes. "Derek," he said. "I got Derek when I get back."

"So blow it by Derek. Take him along."

"You'd think they'd have better things to do."

Lassiter shrugged.

"No," Riordan said. "I mean *really*! You'd think they would."

"Yeah, well . . ." Lassiter sipped his coffee, and segued to another subject. "I want to ask you something," he said.

"What?" Riordan asked, swizzling a celery stalk around in his Bloody Mary.

"We talked about it once before, about the nurse . . . Juliette . . . how she just happened to have her car keys in her pocket when she got in the elevator with Grimaldi. It just seems . . . I don't know—so convenient for him. You ever ask her about that?"

Riordan thought about it. "No. Not really. I know I said I would, but . . . she was pretty fucked up when we found her and then . . . Derek came aboard and—he kind of took over at that point. So, I didn't actually speak to her for more than five minutes." He shrugged. "Though I mentioned it to Derek—about the keys—'cause I remember you asked."

"And . . . ?"

"I don't know . . . I guess he blew me off. Said he always kept *his* keys in *his* pockets, so maybe she's the same. But did he *ask* her? That

I don't know." The detective rattled the ice in his glass and signaled the waiter for another drink.

Lassiter frowned. "Will you look into it?"

Riordan made a note on the outside of the manila envelope that Lassiter had given to him. *Juliette: keys.*

"Where did she live, anyway?" Lassiter wanted to know. "Near the hospital, or—"

"No." Riordan shook his head. "Maryland plates. She was way the fuck out there. Hagerstown . . ." A pause. "Emmitsburg."

Their eyes met.

"North of Frederick," Lassiter said.

"As a matter of fact. I remember she said she was looking for an apartment closer to the hospital because the commute was a bitch. Not that she'd done it much."

"Why do you say that?"

"Because she was new. She'd just started working. Coupla weeks before."

"Wait a second. You mean she joined the staff *after* Grimaldi was admitted?"

Riordan rubbed his eyes. "Yeah. She transferred from . . . I don't know where. Someplace. Anyway, it's bad luck. Second week on the job—somebody grabs her. She's still in therapy."

"She never came back to work!?"

Riordan shook his head and yawned. "Too spooked."

"Jimmy . . ."

Riordan put his hand up. "I know what you're thinking," he said. "She's only there two weeks, she's carryin' the keys to her car—"

"And she just happens to live in a town where Umbra Domini has a retreat."

Riordan sighed and nodded. "You're right. I'll check it out. Okay? Just don't get your hopes up." He drained his drink. "So—you coming back to the States for Christmas, or what?"

"No."

"Why not?"

Lassiter shrugged. "I don't want to bring tears to your eyes, Detective, but—what's the point? There's no one left. I don't have anyone. The whole family's dead, except me."

"So where to?"

"I'm not sure. Probably back to Rome."

"Rome! Whatta you talking about, *Rome?* You just told me your partner got blown away. You got a death wish?"

"He was suffocated—and no, I don't have a death wish. No one's looking for me in Rome. I'm safer there than anywhere else. If anyone wants to come after me—they'll look in the States. That's where *I'd* look."

Riordan started to say something, but before he could open his mouth the P.A. system blasted out the announcement of his flight. It was a small airport, and by the time the announcement had been translated into German, Lassiter had paid the bill and was standing with the detective in a line at the security gate. "This thing with your friend," Riordan said. "The guy in Rome?"

"Bepi."

"Yeah . . ." Riordan paused to hand his ticket and passport to the security guard. "The bodies are piling up," he said. The security guard glanced at his documents, stamped his passport, and returned them with a bored smile. A few feet ahead a bald man was removing everything from his pockets, while a blonde waited to pat him down.

"Your sister and nephew," Riordan said, "that's two. Dwayne is three. Bepi. If that's because of you, that's four. And I'm not even counting the lady in Prague and her kid—but that's six." His frown deepened and he cocked his head like a dog listening to a distant sound.

He opened his mouth to say something, but the security guard motioned for him to move on. The bald man was done and Riordan had become a bottleneck, travelers stacking up behind him. Riordan dropped his briefcase on the conveyor belt, threw up his hands and stepped forward. To the annoyance of those behind him, he paused in the frame of the metal detector and turned around.

"Stay in touch, okay? The guy behind this—Grimaldi—*whoever* it is—he's a real triple-sixer, y'know?"

23

Christmas came and went, and nothing happened.

In Italy this was a more tranquil family holiday than in the States. The enormous commercial burden overhanging the season was absent, and without the obligatory frenzy of gift-buying and partying, without the forced immersion in holiday cheer, the mood in Rome was quiet, even peaceful. One day slid seamlessly into the next, and before long it was New Year's Eve.

For Lassiter, it was a strange and disconnected time. He rented a suite in an obscure, residential hotel, just north of the Villa Borghese gardens. He went to the Dental Hospital on the Viale Regina Elena, where an expatriate Brit removed what remained of the tooth that he'd lost in Naples. Two days later he had an X ray taken at the Salvator Mundi International Hospital, where he learned that he'd been shaken, but not stirred: the ribs were bruised but unbroken.

He ate by himself in out-of-the-way trattorias, reading one orange Penguin paperback after another. He slept late and went for long runs in the morning. He might have gone to the police about Bepi, but a brief conversation with Woody put an end to that idea. What could he tell the police? He had nothing but suspicions, and passing those on to the Italian authorities didn't seem like a good idea. At least Woody thought not. Yes, SISMI had been cleaned up. But how well? Grimaldi undoubtedly still had friends there. And who knew how SISMI and Umbra Domini might be twisted up together? Best to keep a low profile and look into it later, when the dust cleared.

And so he waited out the Christmas season with his head down. He called the States every other day, using a pay phone at the train station. There was no news. Even the AmEx talks were on hold until after the New Year. "No one's really working," Judy said. "Everything's backed up." Lassiter told her that he understood. And he did.

He also checked his answering machines. There were half a dozen invitations, twice as many keep-in-touch calls, and holiday greetings from the not so near and the not so dear. Monica left a breezy, affectionate message, Claire a stiff and hostile one. He considered calling each of them, but he had nothing to say.

Some nights, he sat in an old chair upholstered in brocade, thinking about his house in McLean. There had been a big snowfall in D.C., as he'd learned from the *Herald Trib*. A white Christmas. He thought of the driveway and the little bridge, the stream and the trees, dusted with white. And inside the house: the pale, snowlit night, glowing in the atrium windows.

Sometimes, he thought about Kathy, and Brandon. He was beginning to have trouble remembering what they looked like. Thinking about Brandon depressed him. He was . . . he had been . . . a sunny little kid. He would have gotten a kick out of all the snow. In a year or so Brandon would have begun to play soccer, and Lassiter had been looking forward to teaching him the game. Playing catch. And why not? Brandon needed a father, even a surrogate one, and who better than Joe Lassiter, a charter member of the Alliance?

And then Grimaldi. And, after Grimaldi, thermite. *Thermite.*

Lassiter pushed the image out of his mind and turned to safer stuff. The mail would be piling up by now, filling the basket that the housekeeper used when he was away. A mountain of magazines, catalogues, Hallmark cards from law firms in Washington, New York, London, and L.A. None of them would mention Christmas; all of them would send "Season's Greetings." Lying in bed with his eyes on the ceiling, it occurred to Lassiter, for the first time, that he didn't particularly want to go home.

Not today. Not tomorrow. Maybe never.

Nor did he want to "see the sights." He'd tried it for a day or two, visiting the Vatican Library and the Sistine Chapel. Both were impressive, but he was becoming disinterested in everything but Grimaldi. He did the crosswords in the *Herald Tribune*; he drank too much red wine at dinner.

And then it was New Year's Eve, an occasion traditionally set aside for reviewing the past and making resolutions for the future. He waited until eight, then dined alone at a trattoria a block from the hotel, a meal of calamari with marinara sauce, salad with fennel, ravioli stuffed with pine nuts and spinach, and a slice of grilled lamb with mint. He had an espresso with a curl of lemon peel in it, and after that a square of tiramisu and a glass of Vin Santo, on the house.

He drank the wine, which was very good, and left a large tip. Then he walked back toward his hotel, where a few doors down, he found an ancient, underground bar with brick arches and a large television set. The bar was full of workingmen. Their wives were absent— although there were a few women in evidence, flashily dressed types, with mascara and bright red fingernails. Not prostitutes, but party girls. They laughed a lot, but it seemed forced and somehow made him lonely.

Soccer players filled the television screen. Fiorentina and Lazio. A tape. Obviously, Lazio had won, because the assembled anticipated every moment of Lazio glory and every incident of Florentine perfidy, nudging one another whenever something was about to happen, and swearing at the incompetent referee.

It was nearly eleven when Lassiter called the young waiter over and let him know that he wanted to treat the bar to a round of champagne. After the waiter had distributed glasses and, with the help of two of the customers, poured a round of Moët Chandon for everyone, they raised their glasses to him, a loud disorganized cheer, with some singing. He popped for another round of champagne a few minutes later and was thinking of ordering a third when the waiter looked him in the eye and shook his head. Taking Lassiter's pen, he wrote:

> Moët & Chandon: 14,400 lire
> Asti Spumante: 6,000 lire

Then he mimicked expertly that the bar's inhabitants were drunk, the Moët wasted upon them. Lassiter acceded and the Asti Spumante was poured around—with no discernible change in the festive mood. Finally, midnight arrived, and with it an explosion of *abrazos* from the men, and a bit more from one or two of the ladies. When he finally got up to leave—only somewhat less drunk than his companions—the bar got to its collective feet. And there was a round of applause, a series of barwide toasts, which Lassiter did not understand, and a final explosion of "*Buona fortunas.*" And then he left, having tipped the waiter almost two hundred dollars.

—

The telephone woke him at eight A.M., precisely, bleating into his ear. Rolling over, Lassiter felt a moment of panic as he recalled a woman kissing him on the way out of the bar. He hoped to Christ he hadn't brought her back to the hotel, because . . . well, because he didn't speak Italian.

Jesus, he thought, I'm not even hung over. I'm still drunk.

"Hal-lo-allo!" Roy Dunwold's cheery voice burst through the receiver. "Didn't wake you, did I?"

" 'Course not. I was just . . . worshiping."

Dunwold laughed. "Out on the town, were we? Want me to ring back? I don't mind."

Lassiter sat up, and the world shifted dizzily. "No," he said, "no, I'm fine."

"Well, you don't bloody sound it, but—never mind. Reason I'm ringing—finally got something for you. Couple of somethings."

"Ummmm."

"First: Brazil."

"Uh-huh."

"You with me?"

"Yeah—yeah, I'm *with* you."

"On the Rio business. Danny—that's my mate—he's the one who got it." Roy spoke in short bursts. He was obviously scanning something for the highlights. "Two A.M. fire, September seventeenth . . . chichi condo in Leblon."

"What's that?"

"Very swank. Beach neighborhood. Deh deh deh—here we go: child died in the fire . . . just turned four years old . . . Mommy killed. Danish nanny, too. Deh deh deh deh dah . . . fire spread to other apartments . . . no one else seriously injured. Estimated damage to complex . . . sixty gazillion cruzeiros . . . here we go! 'Fire of suspicious origin.' "

Lassiter shook his head. Hard. "That *is* something," he said.

"Little bit more." Lassiter could hear Roy turning pages. "Yeah—officials say it was arson. More on the family. Let's see—wealthy couple. Deh deh deh . . . Name is Peña. Missus was a psychiatrist, and misterrrr isssss . . . a director! Rio Tino Zinc, Sheraton Hotels—it goes on and on."

"The child was . . . what? Boy, girl—"

"Boy. Only child."

"Huh," Lassiter said.

"I'm not done yet! Got another one, don't I?"

"Another what?"

"What d'ya think? Another bloody *crime* that fits your pattern. Another lad—"

"When?" Lassiter asked. "Where?"

"Just October. Matilda Henderson and son Martin. Right here. Right here in London-town."

The flight to London was virtually empty. New Year's Day. Heathrow was similarly desolate. Even so, he almost missed Roy as he came through the nothing-to-declare line at Customs.

Roy had a talent—useful in an investigator—for unobtrusiveness. He was a nondescript sort who described himself as "average-everything, and formerly young." Even so, that didn't explain it. There was something about him that made him almost transparent. Lassiter had remarked upon it once, and Roy nodded in a way that suggested it wasn't the first time the subject had come up. "It's not what you'd call 'a God-given talent,' " he said. "It's how I survived my teenage years."

Suddenly then, as Lassiter's eyes searched the empty terminal, Roy materialized at his elbow, wearing a heavy tweed coat and a lumpy scarf that looked as if it had been hand-knit by a beginner.

"Felicitations of the season," Roy said into his ear, taking his bag and steering him outside.

Roy always parked illegally, but never seemed to get tickets, and his car was right outside, behind a bus. The air was cold and damp and smelled of diesel fuel. Every few seconds a plane shuddered in the air overhead.

Lassiter headed for the right-hand door, and Roy steered him around to the other side. It was a navy-blue Jaguar that Roy had been driving as long as Lassiter had known him. As they drove, Roy told him about the Hendersons.

The woman, Matilda, had been a wealthy woman, thanks to "inheritance *and* a very successful divorce. She was half famous, y'know, in 'highbrow' circles. Wrote novels. Arty sort. Never sold much. Won a few prizes."

"Never heard of her," Lassiter said.

"Right. Well, she was just coming into her own, wasn't she? I read the lady's obituaries, couple of interviews. Said she had the boy at forty-one. According to the *Guardian*, 'avin' the child 'opened the floodgates of fertility in her literary life, as well.' "

"What about the husband?" Lassiter asked.

"No husband. Had the kid on her own, didn't she? Went to one of those places, she did."

"Which places?"

"You know! Where they knock 'em up. Professional, like."

Wait a second, Lassiter thought.

But Roy was off. "It's unnatural, is what it is. Instead of havin' a bit of fun, as what God intended, this is—well, it's *cold*, i'nit? Now, I'm not saying it's wrong, mind you, *buutttt!* Some of these women will go to a sperm bank and look at snapshots! Pictures of the blokes what 'donated'! And then they read about the ones they fancy. Height, weight, IQ, color of eyes, education—they pick out the Da like he's bloody wallpaper!"

It reminded him of Riordan—when Lassiter had said that Brandon had no father. *No father? You tell me how that one worked and you can go!*

Roy was rattling on, but Lassiter was thinking of Kathy, and an idea was beginning to germinate. She, too, had conceived at a fertility clinic. Maybe that was the connection among the various cases. Maybe Grimaldi was a sperm donor. Maybe he'd snapped, and now he was tracking down his own offspring.

"What would old *Darwin* say?" Roy continued ranting. "I'll tell you what he'd say. He'd call it *un-natural* selection, and that would be that."

Lassiter sat back against the seat, half listening to Roy talk as the Jaguar hurtled through the night. He'd discarded the idea of Grimaldi as a lunatic, vengeful sperm donor. That didn't explain Bepi. Umbra Domini. Somebody digging Brandon up and incinerating him.

It was funny the way his mood had flattened out since that morning. Roy's news about the London case was exciting, and ever since the call, he'd been so impatient that he'd taken the first flight out of Rome. And the fertility clinics—there was something there, but he couldn't say what it was. They were a part of it. He was sure of that. And religion—religion was a part of it as well. He could sense that the hard knot of the case was beginning to loosen, but his excitement had faded into an edgy fatigue. Suddenly, he felt deeply tired. His ribs throbbed and all he wanted to do was take a shower and go to sleep.

The Jaguar turned into St. James Place and stopped in front of Duke's. "Here we are. Sorry if I rattled on. Next I'll be on a bloody box in Hyde Park."

"You made some good points," Lassiter said. "No problem."

A doorman in a top hat and tails came over to the car.

"Hang on," Roy said, swiveling around to retrieve a large envelope from the backseat. "Here," he said, "that's the lot of it. Paperwork on the Henderson case, and the one in Brazil. Second: I've set up some interviews for you. Tomorrow."

"Who?"

"Matilda Henderson's sister and her best friend—the boy's god-mother." Roy shifted gears. " 'Round ten?"

As Lassiter nodded and stepped out, there was a sudden flash of lightning, a crack of thunder, and the skies opened. The doorman gave him an annoyed look, as if this was somehow his fault.

24

Matilda Henderson's sister was courteous, but that was as far as it went. Honor was perhaps fifty years old, her gray hair shorn in a crew cut. Heavy earrings and stylish but ugly eyeglasses. She wore baggy trousers with tight bands at the ankle—they reminded Lassiter of the pants worn by the cartoon figures in *Aladdin*, which he'd seen with Brandon. Her flat in Chelsea was decorated entirely in black, white, and gray. She didn't offer them anything to drink, but gestured to uncomfortable matching chairs that seemed to be made out of chicken wire.

"I'm here because we have something in common," Lassiter began. She raised an eyebrow.

Despite the cool response, he hurtled on, talking about how his sister and nephew had died in a manner remarkably similar to *her* sister and nephew. Roy occasionally spoke up while Lassiter went through the entire story—from the day he'd heard about Kathy's death to that very morning. When he was done, the room pulsed with silence. And then she said, "I'm still not sure why you're here, Mr. Lassiter."

Roy Dunwold's jaw dropped, and Lassiter glanced at him. He leaned closer to her. "I just thought . . . *possibly*," he began, "I mean if there's anything in what I've told you that—" He hesitated. "—that reminds you of something about your sister or nephew. . ."

"My sister and her son were murdered in their sleep by a lunatic. He could have been *your* lunatic, I suppose, but what difference would that make?"

Lassiter stared. He didn't know what to say. "You . . . you don't want whoever did it found and punished?"

She blew out a plume of smoke, and shrugged. "He has to live with it," she said acidly. "Like O.J." She stood up. "I'm a Buddhist and I believe all this sort of thing works itself out in time. My sister and I—we weren't close, as I'm sure someone will take pains to tell you. If I hadn't been away in the Bahamas, I'm sure I would have been a suspect."

"Not likely," Roy interjected. "But, there was something about an inheritance."

She glared at him. "I hardly need the money. I suppose I'll put it in a trust and establish a literary prize in Matilda's name. Now if you don't mind"—she glanced at her watch—"I have an appointment."

But Lassiter was determined to get everything there was to get from Honor Henderson—if only so he didn't need to see her again.

"Why would you have been a suspect?"

"My sister betrayed me. We lived here in perfect harmony for years. I painted, she wrote. We were quite happy—until she had this absurd idea to have a child."

"You disapproved."

"Of course I disapproved, and in the end I had to ask Matilda to find her own place. And a good thing! After he was born—Martin, the little boy—Tillie just *gushed* over him. All she talked about was nappies and nipple soreness and toys and making your own baby food. It was impossible to have an intelligent conversation with her." She stopped suddenly and flushed. "It's over. I've done my grieving and I encourage you to do the same, Mr. Lassiter. Now if you don't mind . . ." She began to shoo them toward the door.

On their way out, Lassiter stopped and turned. "Do you know which fertility clinic she went to?"

A big sigh. "Oh Christ, I don't remember. This was quite a quest, mind you. She went to the States; she went to *Dubai*, if you can believe it. She went to half a dozen of those places. She was always babbling about mucus thickness and ovulation cycles." Her face wrinkled up in distaste. "She was continually taking the temperature in her vagina—and then reporting it."

"Did she go to Italy?" Lassiter asked. "Because the man who killed my sister was from Italy." He was standing in the doorway.

"I don't know. We weren't getting along. Now, *please*. I have an appointment."

The door slammed shut.

"Right bitch, that one," Roy said. "She probably did kill them."

———

Matilda Henderson's best friend, Kara Baker, lived on the other side of the Thames, in South London. Roy bludgeoned his way through the heavy downtown traffic with the liberal use of his horn, and finally they were driving across Hammersmith Bridge. Roy's car phone rang just as they got to the other side. He cursed it—"Bloody nag is what it is." Then he picked it up, listened for a while, and in a resigned voice said: "Oh, bugger all. All right then, call me there in an hour."

One of Roy's employees, hard on a case in Leeds, had run into a problem with the local police. He'd have to drop Lassiter off.

Barnes was a villagelike enclave complete with duck pond and cricket pitch. Kara Baker's place was a substantial brick house with old boxwood hedges running the length of the boundaries and a pair of small stone lions—with red velvet ribbons tied around their necks—doing sentry duty on the stone pillars that flanked the walk.

The woman who answered the door couldn't have been less like Honor Henderson—nor could her house have been more different from the achromatic flat in Chelsea. Kara Baker was somewhere in her late thirties and deeply, elementally beautiful, with a tousled mane of curly red hair, bright blue eyes, and a body so curvaceous that a teenaged boy might have drawn it.

Her house was exuberantly and eclectically furnished, antique furniture effortlessly sharing the space with more modern pieces. Old Oriental rugs on the polished floors; art everywhere and of every era. Ropes of greenery—losing their needles—were draped over the mantel, spiraled up the columns in the living room, twisted around the banisters of the double staircases.

It was fairly messy, papers and magazines, books and cups and plates, hats and gloves, scattered around. A red hot water bottle reclined in an easy chair, a bag of potato chips rested on the piano stool.

She apologized for the mess, stopping to kick off her heels, and padded ahead of him in stockinged feet toward the kitchen. "Cup of coffee?"

Lassiter followed her into the kitchen, a huge old room with a row of French doors along one wall. He sat at an old farm table while she made coffee.

"You've been to see Honor, then?" Kara Baker said.

"She wasn't helpful."

"Poor Honny," she said with a sigh. "She acts so hard-hearted, but actually she's quite paralyzed with grief. I'm rather worried about her."

Lassiter hesitated. "Could have fooled me."

"Oh I know; she can be *such* a beast. But take it from me, Tils—Matilda—was the only person in the world she cared about. And Martin."

He tilted his head, as if he hadn't heard her right. "That's not what she told me."

A timer went off. Kara was making coffee in a French press and she pushed down on the plunger, gradually and expertly. "Nonsense," she said, rummaging around for some cups. "That's what I mean about being worried about her. You saw her place, you saw how controlled she is, how compulsive. Wait—I'll show you a drawing of hers." She set the coffee tray on the table—two chipped mugs, an alabaster sugar bowl, and a carton of cream. Kara went to the far wall and returned with a large framed pen-and-ink sketch of Piccadilly Circus. She propped it on a chair and they both looked at it.

"You see," she said. "Just about the most tight-assed drawing you'll ever behold." She flung her hands out toward it. "This—this is what Honny is like."

It was a wonderful big drawing, its composition brilliant, its painterly line engaging, its angled, aerial perspective intriguing. But it was so meticulous and detailed that it reminded Lassiter of the sort of thing that Third World children went blind completing.

"I see what you mean."

Kara stirred her coffee with her finger and then sucked it. "Honor—she's in what the shrinks call 'denial'—only this time she's not denying the murders happened, or that Tils and Martin are dead—she's denying she gives a fig. She doesn't care and therefore the fact that they're dead doesn't matter." She took a sip of coffee and moaned with pleasure.

The coffee was very, very good, and Kara Baker was very appealing. Lassiter felt oddly immune to that appeal—and it bothered him because this was a woman he would ordinarily desire. As it was, his attraction to her was almost intellectual—not physical. He found that disturbing.

"Ummmmmm," she said, holding her coffee mug with both hands. She looked up at him and raised her eyebrows, clearly waiting for him to speak.

"Honor said she kicked Matilda out—because of the child," Lassiter said. "She said they'd been estranged ever since her sister got pregnant."

"*Twad*-dle," Kara said. "Honor was *thrilled* at the thought of a baby. She did hours and hours of *research* on the latest techniques, the success rates of various clinics, grilled half the O.B./Gyns on Harvey Street to ask advice. She ran interference for Tils, made all the setting-up calls, monitored her fertility drugs, her diet. All that stuff."

He shook his head. "This doesn't sound like the woman I saw."

"Look—you needn't take my word for it—you can check." She leaned toward him. "Tils had it *in her will* that Honor was to be Martin's guardian if anything happened to her. As for moving out— that was Tilsie's idea. She couldn't imagine Honor being able to work with a baby 'round the place. But they were looking for a country place to share, for the weekends. And then—"

Abruptly, she broke off, and her eyes filled up with tears. She snuffled and rubbed at her eyes. "I'm sorry. I still do miss Tils so *much*. We were friends forever, from babyhood—and we'd planned to be old ladies together as well. You know, wear outrageous hats and swan around Provence or Tuscany or—"

But then she began to lose control, and really weep. She put her hand over her face, stood up and hurried from the room—"Excuse me. Sorry. I'll be back."

Left in the kitchen, Lassiter thought about the interview with Kara Baker. They were stuck talking about the relationship between the Henderson sisters. He had to bring the discussion around to what he wanted to ask. Why she thought anybody would murder her friend. Suspects, gossip. Tell her his own story—about Kathy and Brandon. See if she noted any similarities.

He cleared away the coffee cups, rinsed them and set them in the drainer. He went toward the refrigerator, to put the carton of cream away.

The refrigerator was enormous—especially for England, where small appliances were the norm. Its surface was entirely covered—two or three levels deep, with papers. It was a virtual museum—of sketches, snapshots, invitations, newspaper clips, recipes, postcards, aging and curled Post-it notes, scraps with telephone numbers but no names, traffic tickets, a child's painting.

The door stuck when he pulled on it, and somehow he knocked against a magnet and a clump of papers fell to the floor. He picked them up and began trying to get them to stick on the refrigerator door—anywhere—when he saw the postcard.

He stared at it, rooted to the floor. He'd received the same postcard from Kathy years before. It was a photo within a photo: the background was of an Italian hilltown, seen from a distance, its jumble of buildings perched on a rocky mount, surrounded by a medieval wall. The photo within the photo was a monocular blowup, depicting the pretty little hotel that had commissioned the card. "Pensione Aquila," it read.

He still recalled the back of the postcard that he'd received, and his mixed feelings at reading it. Not reading, but *looking*, because it was a sketch, one of Kathy's stupid puns. A series of four panels showing a plain door, and a hand knocking on it. From left to right the knocking hand was in a different position. In the first panel the fist rapped at the bottom of the door. In the middle panels, it ascended. In the right panel the fist rapped the top of the door. He got it, all right: *Knocked up*. Kathy had signed with the old sideways A of the Alliance.

Before the trip to Italy, he'd wanted Kathy to give it up. The baby chase. By then, she'd spent almost sixty thousand dollars and three years pursuing motherhood. It was wearing her out, both physically and emotionally. She seemed increasingly fragile. The thought of her going to some obscure clinic outside the country had worried him—although he'd checked up on the place and found it had an excellent reputation.

After he'd gotten the postcard, he worried that Kathy's happiness would end with yet another disappointment. This had happened once before, when her first pregnancy—implanted at a clinic in North Carolina—ended in a miscarriage. Kathy was devastated, almost inconsolable. He hadn't wanted that to happen again.

When Kara Baker came back through the kitchen, he was reading the back of the postcard from her refrigerator:

Dear K—
Beautiful here and so peaceful. Fields and fields of sunflowers, heavy heads droopy. Keep your fingers crossed.
Love—Tils

"Ah—" Kara Baker started, and then closed her mouth in an odd expression, as if she couldn't believe his bad manners. Her mouth smiled thinly but her eyes were cold. "You know—I really think you'd better go."

"I'm sorry," he said. He held the postcard up like a courtroom exhibit. "I know. I'm reading your mail. I—I was putting away the cream and I knocked some papers off, and this postcard—"

She had changed into sweat pants and an old shaggy sweater. She'd been crying hard. Her eyes were red and her face was mottled. She took the postcard from him, read the back, and then flipped it over. She pushed her front teeth down on her lower lip and then took a shuddery breath.

"This is the town. Where the clinic was. Where Tils got pregnant with Martin. That's why I saved it."

"Montecastello di Peglia."

She didn't seem to have heard him. "Actually, I went there to kind of hold her hand. It was beautiful—a perfect little town in Umbria." Another breath. "And she was so . . . *happy*. I'd brought a terrific bottle of champagne, but of course I'd forgotten—she wouldn't even have a sip. So we took a taxi and poured the whole thing out on the lawn outside the clinic."

"How much did Roy tell you?" he asked.

She looked at him sharply. "Roy who?" And then she remembered. "Ah, yes. Your colleague."

"Did he tell you why I'm here?"

She pushed a hand through her hair and frowned. "Something about your sister," she said. "Your sister and her baby." She looked up at him, confused. "Some possible connection . . . to Tils."

"The reason I read the postcard—"

"Oh, never mind," she said. "It's all right."

"You don't understand. My sister sent me *the same postcard*."

" . . ."

"It's where my sister became pregnant. After years of trying—that's where it happened."

"Just like Tils." She swallowed. "The Clinica Baresi." Her eyes widened and she cocked her head. "And you think—what? I can't imagine."

He shook his head. "I don't know what I think. But it's strange, isn't it? Matilda never mentioned anybody named Grimaldi, did she? Franco Grimaldi?"

Kara shook her head. "No."

He asked if he could make a telephone call. She looked at him strangely, then shrugged and waved toward the French doors. "I think I'll have a bath," she said.

He waved at her and watched her go out through the door. It took him more than ten minutes, but he finally got through to Prague. Then he waited again for Detective Janacek to come to the phone.

"*Ne?*" Janacek said.

"Franz. It's Joe Lassiter—Jim Riordan's friend?"

"Of course," he said stiffly. "Happy New Year."

Lassiter filled him in on what he'd discovered. "I have this one question for Jiri Reiner," he said. "Did his wife go to a fertility clinic to get pregnant? And if so, where? I want to know if it was the Clinica Baresi in Italy." He explained why.

"I put it to Pan Reiner," Janacek said. "You call back?"

"You bet."

"Wait. You stay? I'm calling him on another telephone."

"Absolutely."

Lassiter sat with the telephone receiver in his hand for several minutes, turning the possibilities over and over in his mind. If Jiri Reiner's wife had conceived a child at the Clinica Baresi, the pattern would be undeniable: someone was tracking down children conceived there and exterminating them, one by one. A massacre of innocents. But why? He was in the midst of constructing a mental list, one improbable explanation after another, when he heard the thin squawk of Janacek's voice and yanked the receiver up to his ear.

"Hel-lo?" Janacek said. "Pan Lassiter?"

He realized he was holding his breath. "Yeah."

"Jiri—he's not answering me this at first—he's saying, 'Why you are asking this?' "

"Okay . . . so—"

'I'm saying, 'Jiri . . . your family is *murdered*. Answer me this question.' And he's . . . ? He's saying all this about . . . he's feeling bad . . . as a man. Finally he says why he feels bad. It's because his wife not get pregnant just from him. She gets pregnant from a doctor. I have to *insist*, eh? 'What doctor? Where?' I don't trust him, so I don't tell him the name you give me. He can just say yes or no and not mean it. Finally he tells me: Clinica Baresi in Italy."

Lassiter took a deep breath. "Wow," he said. "I'm, ah . . . I don't quite believe it."

"You go there?" Janacek asked. "The clinic?"

"It's my next stop," Lassiter said.

They spoke a little longer, and Lassiter promised to keep the Czech informed. As he hung up, Kara Baker came back into the kitchen, looking polished and clean in a white terry-cloth robe. She touched his arm and gave him a look that told him she was naked under the robe.

He was surprised to find himself shaking his head, and his indifference puzzled him. She was really quite spectacular, but rather than reaching out to her, he told her what he'd learned from Janacek and thanked her for the coffee and the help. Then he stood up to go.

"I can't tell you how helpful this has been. It might have been months—"

"I daresay," she said, in a voice as neutral as sand.

Lassiter looked at her and sighed. "Gotta go," he said. And went.

25

Lassiter stood at the window of his hotel room, nursing a glass of Laphroaig as he watched the rain gust through the courtyard below. The weather had a rhythm of its own, coming at the window-panes in waves, as if the night were breathing, in . . . out . . . in . . . out.

Every so often, the gloom went nova as a bolt of lightning skittered through the sky. Suddenly, the courtyard was as brightly lighted as a stage, and for a long moment he could see the rain drumming on the puddled surfaces, the wet walls gleaming, the faint shapes of the buildings beyond. As the lightning faded, a thunderclap exploded, so loud it seemed to shake the room, its baritone rumble taking a long time to fade.

Lassiter listened to the rain's hiss, rattled the ice in his glass, and thought about what he knew and what he didn't know. Children conceived at a fertility clinic in Italy were being murdered. By a religious fanatic. Who seemed to be working for a strange Catholic cult called Umbra Domini.

But how, exactly, *was* Umbra Domini involved? That Bepi had been investigating the group when he was killed was suggestive, but so what? He might not have been Bepi's only client, Lassiter told himself. Bepi was undoubtedly involved in a lot of things. As for the beating in Naples, Lassiter suspected that della Torre was responsible—but once again, so what? There was no evidence of that responsibility, only his own suspicion. And then there were the holy-water bottles that Grimaldi and della Torre carried. As curious as that was, it proved nothing. Maybe the bottles were given to Umbra Domini's most devout followers, the "Blues." Maybe the water had been blessed . . . by della Torre or the Pope. Maybe it came from Lourdes. In any case, so what?

Which left the wire transfer.

The purpose of the money—and it was a lot of money—was unknown. It might have had to do with Grimaldi's work for Salve

Caelo, buying guns or bribing Serbs. But that was a stretch. The wire transfer took place immediately prior to what had become a string of infanticides. The fact that the murders followed hard on the heels of the wire transfer didn't prove that the one caused the other. What was the fallacy? *Post hoc, ergo propter hoc*—after the fact, therefore because of it. Still . . .

Lassiter sipped his scotch, savoring its smoky, almost medicinal, flavor. He knew a lot more than he'd known a month ago, but it still came to the same basic question: *Why?*

That, he still didn't know—and, worse, he couldn't imagine why anyone, much less a religious person, would go on a killing spree, targeting children. He had no theory, not one.

As for Umbra Domini, why would a religious order—no matter how reactionary—make war on children? The cult's pamphlets spoke out against modern reproductive technologies, and a lot more, but that was hardly an incentive to murder. Something else was involved, something darker. But what?

The night pulsed. Lightning sizzled and, once again, thunder rattled the room. Lassiter paced before the windows, sipping his drink. Whatever the answer was, the most likely place to find it was at the Clinica Baresi. Which meant a flight to Rome in the morning, a rental car, and a three-hour drive to Montecastello. He'd book a room at the Pensione Aquila and take it from there.

Retrieving his computer from the closet, Lassiter wrote some memos to himself about the Henderson and Peña murders, fleshing out the notes that he'd made on paper. He stored the file to the hard disc, encrypted it, connected the hotel's phone to the computer's modem, and sent the file back to the computer in his house. Then an E-mail to Judy, telling her where to reach him for the next few days.

It was almost three-thirty by the time Lassiter drove through the medieval gates of Todi—a lovely and prosperous town perched on a steep hill above the Umbrian plain. He'd been told that he could find a map of the area at the tourist office, just off the main square, and so he headed for it, following the signs for *Centro*. Chased by an impatient taxi, he hurtled up and down a series of increasingly narrow streets until, in the end, he emerged in the Piazza del Popolo.

This was a vast expanse of gray stone, surrounded by a thirteenth-century palazzi constructed of the same material. Lassiter drove past a cluster of tables to a cliffside parking lot that looked north toward Perugia.

An attendant in a green uniform asked him for money. Lassiter shrugged and, like the dumbest tourist, allowed the man to pick lira bills out of his hand. The man took six hundred lira, then delicately pinched a hundred-lira note between two battered fingers. He raised his eyebrows and pointed to his chest. Lassiter understood—a tip— and nodded. The attendant wrote what seemed like a lot of information on a small slip of white paper and stuffed it under the windshield wipers.

"Tourist bureau?" Lassiter asked.

"Ahhhh, *si*," the man said. "*Si, si.*" Whereupon he launched himself into a three-minute peroration of rapid-fire Italian that culminated in a snakelike movement of his wrist. "Shu, shu, shu," he said, turning his palm toward the sky in a gesture of presentation. "*Ecco!*"

It amazed Lassiter that after following these directions, which in fact he had not understood, he arrived directly at the door of the tourist office. The woman in charge spoke little or no English, but she understood what he wanted—and then some. Moving quickly from one wooden filing cabinet to another, she gave him a detailed map of Umbria, a map of Todi and environs—including Montecastello—a list of festivals, a small poster with the city's coat of arms, and four post-cards of the region.

Lassiter thanked her and, taking a pen and paper from her desk, wrote out the words: *Clinica Baresi—Montecastello?*

Seeing what he'd written, the woman frowned and entered upon an elaborate pantomime, her hands swooping up toward the ceiling, then crossing each other and sweeping to the side. She coughed and wiped her eyes. "*Pouff!*" she said.

Lassiter had no idea what she was trying to say, but he smiled and pretended to understand. "*Si, si,*" he said. "No problem."

The woman gave him a skeptical look, but shrugged, and efficiently marked his map, showing both the route to the clinic and a second route to the Pensione Aquila. She marked each location with an asterisk, and handed the map back with a "*Buona sera.*"

Lassiter reclaimed his car from the man in the green uniform, unfolded the map on the passenger seat, and set out in the direction indicated. The road took him down the hill, then out through the gate and into the countryside. After a dozen switchbacks, he found himself on flat ground, running beside a narrow river.

Five miles farther on, he arrived at the central landmark, an Agip gas station. The river was barely fifty feet wide in this spot, but his map identified it as the mighty Tiber, and a sign on the bridge gave its name in Italian: Tevere.

Turning left, he drove a few miles farther, until he passed a nest of blue Dumpsters, and then a tree plantation. It was strange to see trees like that, planted as a crop, in tidy lines. Beyond the trees was a fork in the road. Lassiter pulled to the side of the road and consulted his map. To the right was Montecastello, a walled village clinging to a dome of rock, eight or nine hundred feet above the valley floor. He recognized it from the postcard on Kara Baker's refrigerator—which, in fact, seemed to have been shot from somewhere nearby.

The left fork was the one that the woman had marked on the map. And so he followed it up a gentle rise, past cornfields in winter stubble, groves of olive trees, and a few modest houses.

And then he arrived. On the left were a pair of massive stone pillars, their centers filled with dead vegetation. A sign lettered in elegant cursive swung from a wrought-iron arm: *Clinica Baresi*. Tall, thin cedars lined the long pebble drive that curled up an incline. He drove past the pillars, and half a mile farther on crested the hill.

Then he saw the building, and it was like a blow to the heart.

If the building hadn't been made of the same gray stone as the pillars down the road, there would have been nothing left but blackened rubble. Which, of course, is what the woman at the tourist bureau had been trying to tell him.

Smoke. Fire. *Pouff!*

In so far as it was possible for a building made of stone to burn, the Clinica Baresi had burned to the ground. Where the heat had cracked the mortar, the stones slid to earth in blackened heaps, so that on the right side of the building, nothing was left but a gray chimney surrounded by scorched debris. The west side was more or less intact— but open to the sky. Roofless, and with its windows and doors blown out by the fire, the clinic seemed like a much older ruin than it actually was.

He stepped out of the car and gaped.

The sight of the burned clinic reminded him of that first terrible morning, his arrival at Kathy's house, the smell of scorched plastic and

ping into the sparely furnished marble-floored entry hall, noting the tapestries on the walls, a jet-black grand piano, and a few ancient, Oriental rugs. Behind a huge wooden desk—nothing on it but a round metal postcard rack and a leather-bound ledger—sat a man of about fifty. He had curly gray hair and wore a navy-blue blazer with a gold crest. He was almost theatrically handsome.

"*Prego?*" the man asked.

Lassiter approached the desk, still slightly out of breath from the climb. His ribs pulsed with pain. "Joe Lassiter," he said. He was searching for the Italian word for "reservation" when the man surprised him by speaking English.

"Oh yes. Welcome to the Aquila," he said in a British accent. "Any more luggage? I can send Tonio."

"You speak English," Lassiter blurted.

"Well . . . yes," the man said. "Actually, I *am* English. Originally."

"Sorry. I was surprised."

"Most people are. One doesn't hear the mother tongue much in Montecastello, although . . . in summer . . . we get the spillover from Chiantishire."

Lassiter laughed. "Tuscany?"

"Ummmm. There, you hear nothing *but* English—in August, at least." He smiled. "We don't generally see many tourists—certainly not in January." He hesitated, a genteel pause to allow Lassiter to explain why he'd come to Montecastello at such an unseasonable time of the year. Lassiter returned the man's smile but made no reply. "Well! If you'll sign the register, and let me have your passport for a few hours . . . I'll take you to your room." He turned the ledger around, opened it to the current page, and offered a pen.

The fact that the man spoke English was lucky. He might know something about the Clinica Baresi and the doctor who'd run it. But first, Lassiter wanted a shower, and a little time to think.

He followed the man, who insisted on carrying his suitcase, down a wide corridor. Along the walls were wrought-iron sconces in the shape of eagles, their talons joined to hold fat white candles.

The room was large, high-ceilinged, and furnished with antiques. The man pointed to a worm-distressed armoire: "Telly's in there." However old the room, there were new radiators, and a very modern marble-floored bathroom. There was even a heated towel rack, and a white terry robe hanging on a hook from the door.

"You're surprised," the man said.

"Happy's more like it," Lassiter replied.

The man inclined his head, then opened a curtained set of French doors that led to a small balcony. They both stepped out onto it. It was dark, except for a faint violet smear on the horizon. "If it's clear, like tonight," the man said, "you can see Perugia." He gestured toward a gauzy blur in the distance. "Just there."

They stepped back into the room and the man headed toward the door. He hesitated. "If you require a fax machine, copy machine, we have one, of course. And if that black bag contains a computer, there's a surge protector on the outlet near the desk. Also—" He hesitated. "—will you take dinner? To be honest, unless you're inclined to drive to Todi or Perugia, you probably won't do better. We serve at eight."

"Sounds good."

By the time they were done with their gnocchi, Lassiter knew quite a bit about Nigel Burlingame—the handsome man who'd registered him—and his companion, Hugh Cockayne. Hugh was fifty or so as well, and as homely as Nigel was handsome. Tall and gangly, he was all nose and ears and thinning hair.

As Lassiter discovered, they were two gay Oxford lads who'd come to Italy in the sixties to *paint*. "Well, of course," Hugh said airily, "we were *terrible* at it, weren't we, Nige?"

"Dreadful, really."

"Still, we found each other."

For a time they'd lived in Rome, and then, when Nigel's father had died ("of apoplexy, I expect"), they'd bought a vineyard in Tuscany.

"Sounds wonderful," Lassiter said.

"It was worse than the painting," Nigel remarked.

"Dusty—" Hugh said.

"Sweaty—"

"Do you remember the midges?"

Nigel laughed. "Teeth like broken glass!"

"And the *viperi*!"

"Vipers?" Lassiter asked.

"Mmmm," Hugh replied. "Deadly, you know—although *everyone* has antivenin in the fridge. And they weren't just on the ground. They'd get up in the vines. Pickers were terrified, weren't they, Nige?"

"Mmmm."

"I remember giving a tour . . . you know: 'And these are our *sangiovese* grapes. The vines came from blah blah. We planted them in blah blah blah' . . . and I lifted up a handful of grapes and—my God! I was face-to-face with—hold on!—face to *what*? Face to head?" Hugh turned to his better-looking half. "Does a snake *have* a face?"

Instantly, they were off on a discussion of what comprised a "face," at the end of which Hugh sighed. "Well, anyway, that was the vineyard."

"We were helpless with the field hands," Nigel said. "I mean, you can imagine. And Tuscany was overrun with ex-pats, so the vineyard went—"

"*Mostly* because it was such bloody hard work." Hugh screwed up his face and looked at his companion. "We're *not* hard workers, are we, Nige? I mean, not *really*."

The conversation went on like this, with Hugh clearing the plates from time to time and Nigel serving. The gnocchi were succeeded by grilled lamb chops, and they, in turn, gave way, first to green salad, then to a bowl of fruit, and finally to a *digestivo*.

Throughout, Lassiter was content to listen. He didn't want to ruin the spirit of the meal with his own sad story, but in the end he found Nigel and Hugh looking at him expectantly.

"And now you're wondering what *I'm* doing here."

Nigel threw a glance at Hugh. "Well, of course—we're professionally incurious—but . . . yes. We did wonder."

"Just a bit," Hugh said with a smile.

Lassiter sipped a small glass of Fernet Branca.

"If it's property you're after," Nigel said, "I'd say you won't lose money."

Lassiter shook his head. "Actually," he said, "I was hoping to visit the Clinica Baresi."

Nigel winced. "Bad luck, I'm afraid."

"I know," Lassiter said. "I saw it this afternoon." He paused for a moment, and asked, "When did it happen?"

"It was—what, Hugh?—August? Late July? Tourist season, anyway."

"How did it happen?" Lassiter asked, though he already knew the answer.

"Well, it was arson, wasn't it, Hugh?"

"It wasn't just mischief," Hugh said. "Not kids with candles or

firecrackers or any of that. This was a sixteenth-century building—
the old part of it, at any rate. Converted monastery."

"Survived everything the centuries could throw its way, and
then—" Nigel snapped his fingers. "—it burned straight to the
ground."

"Professional job," Hugh said. "Nothing left but the stones! Well,
you saw it. *Vaporized* the mortar. The fire was so hot, some of the
stone actually cracked. The firefighters couldn't get close."

"Was anyone inside?"

"No. That's the lucky part, if you can call it luck. The clinic was
already closed," Hugh said, lighting a cigarette from the candle flame.

"Why was that?"

"Baresi, the doctor who ran the place, was quite ill. And, when he
couldn't carry on any longer, they just packed it in. It was closed for
months before it burned."

"Do you think I could meet him—this Dr. Baresi?" Lassiter
asked.

Nigel and Hugh shook their heads in unison. "Bit late," Nigel said.

"He passed away a few months ago," Hugh explained.

"Lung cancer," Nigel said pointedly, and with a well-manicured
hand, swept away the smoke from Hugh's cigarette. "We do miss the
clinic, although with Todi becoming so trendy, I expect we'll replace
the business . . . eventually."

Lassiter frowned. "What 'business' is that?"

"Well, the clinic didn't have residential facilities," Nigel explained.
"So the women who went there—stayed here."

Lassiter's surprise was obvious.

"It wasn't exactly a coincidence," Hugh said with a laugh. "I mean . . .
we *are* the only show in town."

"We had an arrangement," Nigel said.

"Dr. Baresi's patients were given a special rate," Hugh added, "and
we looked after them. Had them picked up at the airport, arranged
transport—that sort of thing."

"It wasn't as if they were *ill*," Nigel remarked. "They didn't need
hospital care. I mean: they were healthy women."

"So you knew the doctor?" Lassiter asked.

Nigel and Hugh looked at each other. Nigel wagged his head. "We
were acquainted—but I wouldn't say we were *friends*. Not by any
stretch."

Hugh leaned back in his chair. "What Nigel means is that the good doctor was a bit of a homophobe."

"But his patients stayed at your pensione?"

"Well, yes, but then—in Montecastello, we're *it*. I suppose he could have put them up in Todi—but, really, we're more convenient. As for Baresi himself, we rarely saw him."

Hugh began to put the dishes on a tray, balancing it on one hand and swooping around the table, snatching up each plate and spoon with an exaggerated balletic motion. He paused, tray uplifted. "Actually, I think the famous *dottore* may have been one of us," he said with a knowing grin. He emphasized his points by dipping his chin rapidly, first to one side, then the other. "Never married. No women in his life. Dressed like a dream. Quite a taste for antiques. *Tiny* dog. And—he carefully stayed away from us. It all added up. And that kind is always the most rabidly homophobic."

"What? What kind?"

"The closet kind," Hugh said. He spun on his heel and headed for the kitchen.

Nigel watched him go and then turned his head to Lassiter. "I'm sorry you came for the clinic," he said thoughtfully. "You must be disappointed. Was it—" He hesitated and then changed his mind, shook his head. "I guess I shouldn't really ask."

"Ask what?"

"Well, I mean, was it—your wife? The reason you were coming to the clinic, to check it out first. I mean—were you trying to . . . conceive a child?" He put his hand over his eyes. "Forgive me—appallingly bad manners, I know. Mum and Dad are rotating."

"No," Lassiter said. "No, that wasn't it. I don't have a wife."

Nigel heaved a sigh of relief. "I'm glad. I mean—at least you didn't have your hopes up."

Lassiter was curious. "Was Baresi's clinic . . . I don't know, a sort of last chance? I mean: for most people."

Nigel leaned back in his chair, teetering. "Well, my whole understanding of the mysteries of reproduction is somewhat limited by the lack of relevance, I suppose. But no, I wouldn't say the clinic was a place of last resort. It wasn't like Tijuana or anything. On the contrary, they say the old boy was really quite brilliant. League of his own, so to speak. Patients from everywhere: Japan, South America . . . the four corners. And—most of them left happy."

"Really. What—What was the doctor's . . . special expertise?"

Nigel frowned. "Oh, I don't know. As I said, I didn't have much native interest. But the women talked about it all the time, and apparently Baresi was really quite successful. Some sort of technical breakthrough. With eggs." Nigel frowned. "But there you are: I'm hopeless."

"I *hate* the word 'eggs,'" Hugh said, coming in from the kitchen. "To think of oneself as once an *egg!*" His face contorted. "Like a bloody chicken. A pea-brained, battery-raised, pecking-order-driven chicken." He paused. He grimaced. "Anyway, Nige, they don't call it 'an egg.' It's an *oocyte.*"

"Really?" Nigel looked surprised.

"Among other things, *il dottore* pioneered a method of enabling the *oocyte* to produce this kind of . . . armor . . . which, ordinarily, it only gets once a sperm has penetrated the wall. It's an iron maiden, of sorts, in that it keeps the other sperm out. Because—" Hugh held his hands aloft like a prizefighter. "—the winner has already been chosen!"

Nigel looked appalled.

"Anyway," Hugh went on, "that *armor* stuff doesn't just keep sperm out, it also revs up the whole deal into some kind of superfertile state. It's *ready*, you know, to rock and roll."

"Hadn't realized you were so well *informed* about all this," Nigel said. He turned to Lassiter. "Although his sympathy and handholding qualities were occasionally in great demand from some of the women, poor things."

Hugh nodded, and lighted a cigarette. "Mostly Hannah."

"One of our Czechs," Nigel explained.

"She was so *scared*, and so *cute*. She told me everything, absolutely everything."

"Hannah Reiner," Lassiter said flatly. "From Prague."

"You know her?"

"No," Lassiter said. "I never met her. She died."

26

"I can't believe it," Hugh said when Lassiter finished explaining why he'd come to their pensione. The Englishman sucked hard on a Rothmans Silk Cut and shook his head. Slowly.

Nigel, dumbfounded, looked from one to the other, then rolled his eyes toward the ceiling. "What on *earth?*"

"I was hoping there might be something at the clinic that . . . I don't know—would somehow make sense of things," Lassiter said. "But what about Baresi's house? Maybe he had an office there. . . ."

Hugh shook his head, and explained that Baresi's living quarters had been in an annex of the clinic. And when the clinic went up in smoke, so did his rooms and everything in them. "Nothing left, I'm afraid. Absolutely nothing."

"*Pas des cartes, pas des photos, et pas des souvenirs,*" Nigel added.

"What about the nurses?" Lassiter asked. "They must know—"

"No nurses." Hugh shook his head, and stabbed out his cigarette. "Couple of lab assistants—but I don't think they'd be of much help, really."

" '*Lab* assistants'? You're telling me this guy ran a clinic—and he didn't have a nurse working for him?"

"He was a very secretive man. And it wasn't *that* sort of clinic, anyway. It wasn't a doc-in-the-box, or one of those places with hordes of patients. It wasn't a hospital. It was . . . more of a research facility, wouldn't you say, Nigel?"

"Mmmm."

"I don't think the old boy took more than fifty or sixty patients a year—though from what I'm told, he could have had five times that number if he'd wanted."

"What about the lab assistants, then?" Lassiter asked.

"Well, one was more of a char, really; cleaned up—that sort of thing. The other was a bit more *compos mentis*—but I don't think we've seen her since the fire, have we, Nigel?"

"No. I think the fire spooked her. Someone said she'd gone to Milan."

Lassiter frowned, and thought for a moment. "Was there anyone else? Friends? Relatives? Anyone like that?"

Hugh looked at Nigel. "Don't think so. Not really. *Although* . . . you might talk to the priest."

"Of course!" Nigel exclaimed, "the padre."

"I don't think they were *friends*, exactly—"

"But they played chess, didn't they? In the square!" Nigel said. "Shared a glass—that sort of thing."

Hugh nodded. "Offhand, I'd say Azetti's just the man."

"What's he like?" Lassiter asked.

Hugh shrugged. "Outsider. Suspect. Not much liked by the locals."

"They say he's a bit of a Bolshevik," Nigel added, stifling a yawn. "Which, I suppose, is why he's here."

"Still," Hugh said, "talking to the padre is definitely worth a try. *And*: he speaks English. Rather well, actually."

"I'll look him up in the morning," Lassiter said. "Where can I find him?"

"In the church. In the square. I can give you directions," Nigel said, "or you might just wander around and get lost. Eventually, you'll end up in the square. It's unavoidable, really."

The three of them got to their feet in unison, and Hugh said he'd finish clearing up. Beckoning for Lassiter to follow, Nigel led the way down the hall, snuffing candles as he went. When they entered the lobby, the Englishman went to the front desk and asked if Lassiter wanted a call in the morning.

"I have a clock, thanks."

"Hold on," Nigel said, "there's something I want to show you." Opening a leather-bound book that lay on the desk, he turned through a number of pages, stopped and looked up. "This is our guest ledger. Goes all the way back to when we opened the place— we only had three guest rooms renovated at the time. Hughie had the book specially made in Gubbio." He closed it so Lassiter could see the fine leather work, the spine with its handworked raised ridges, green and gold, and the cover, with its magnificently worked eagle holding in its talons a signboard: L'AQUILA. Nigel ran his fingers over the surface, then opened it to the first page. "June twenty-ninth," he read, "1987. Our first guest. Mr. Vassari. He stayed two days."

"It's a beautiful book," Lassiter said.

"It is, isn't it? But the reason I wanted to show it to you: all of our guests are in here. Name and address, telephone number . . . dates of the visit. I looked for your sister a little while ago, and when I found the entry, I remembered her. She was quiet. Read a lot. And she asked me for my scone recipe." He shook his head sadly. "Here," he said, turning to a page in the first half of the book. "Have a look."

Lassiter did, and there, in a beautiful hand, was the entry for Kathleen Lassiter.

Kathleen Lassiter—**C.B.**
207 Keswick Lane
Burke, VA—USA
703–347–2122
Arr: 21–4–91
Dep: 23–5–91

She'd stayed thirty-two days. He hadn't remembered it being so long. But then, of course, he'd been busy; he was always so fucking busy. "What's that?" he asked, pointing to the notation, **C.B.**

"Clinica Baresi. To keep track of the discount. We have other little notations. **O.T.**—for the tourist office in Todi. **AVM** is the Agencia Viagge Mundial—a travel agency. Like that."

Lassiter nodded, without much interest.

An elegant shrug. "All of our guests from the clinic are in there. You're welcome to look."

Suddenly, Lassiter understood. "So, Hannah Reiner . . ."

"Hannah, your sister—all of them."

Lassiter was thinking that he might be able to identify something that would link his sister and the other victims. Maybe their visits overlapped. . . .

"It's real scut work," Nigel said, "but you *could* work up a list of the clinic's patients—I mean . . ." He shrugged.

Lassiter was thinking how tedious it would be to go through all the names in the book, looking for the C.B. notations—making a list as he went. Just the thought of it exhausted him. But he hadn't any choice.

"Well," Nigel said, turning away and submitting to a deep, shuddering yawn that reflected Lassiter's own level of fatigue.

"One other thing," Lassiter said. "Can you tell me when the clinic opened?"

Nigel frowned. "Oh, I don't know: 'ninety, I should think—or 'ninety-one. Something like that." And with that, Nigel wiggled his fingers in the air, turned and walked off down the hall.

Beginning with the January 1990 entries, Lassiter paged through the register until he found the first of the clinic's guests. This was Anna Vaccaro, a woman from Verona, who'd checked in on May third. She'd stayed at the Aquila for seven days.

A few minutes after he began, Lassiter went to his room, retrieved his laptop, and returned to the lobby. With the register beside him, he created a file called *cbguest.1st,* and started logging in the names, addresses, and dates. Before long he found not one, but several patterns. Almost all of the women stayed five days or a week. But a few, such as his sister, remained at the Aquila for much longer, thirty days or more.

The first of these was Lanielle Gilot, of Antwerp, who'd come to the hotel near the end of September 1990, and left a month later. Lassiter's sister had done the same, and there were probably others in the book as well.

Lassiter was typing Gilot's name into the laptop when Hugh arrived in the lobby, brandy snifter in hand. He looked surprised until Lassiter explained what he was doing and asked why some patients at the clinic stayed less than a week, and others more than a month.

"Different procedures," Hugh said, leaning against a column. He was slightly drunk.

"What do you mean?"

Hugh frowned and looked up at the ceiling, as if he might find the answers there, then down at Lassiter. His focus was a little hazy. His face had the look of sweet concentration of a child thinking hard.

"Different procedures," he repeated. " 'In vitro fertilization' was the quickest. Very efficient. They take one of the woman's eggs and . . . how much do you really want to know? I mean, the ladies did tend to go on about it."

Lassiter shrugged. "I don't know."

"Well, as I said: in vitro fertilization was a short stay. The ladies were in and out in a few days." He closed his eyes, screwed up his face, and thought some more. "And then there were the various . . . *trans-fers*. Gamete transfers. Zygote transfers." He looked amused. "Strange lexicon for baby-making, don't you think? I mean, really!" He paused, then spit the words out: " 'Gamete intrafallopian transfer.' Try to say *that* when you've had a snootful." He looked at Lassiter with a lop-sided grin. "What *is* a bloody gamete anyway? One feels one ought to know. . . ." He swirled the brandy in his glass.

"What about Hannah Reiner?" Lassiter asked, tapping the page he'd been working on. "I haven't gotten to her yet. Which was she?"

Hugh rubbed his eyes. "That's another one," he said. "*Oocyte* dona-tion. Took a month. Your sister was one of those, wasn't she?"

"I think so. I mean, yeah: she stayed for quite a while." He paused. "Do you know why it took so long?"

Hugh started to shrug. "Actually," he said, as if he surprised him-self, "I *do* know. Hannah explained it to me. First of all, old Baresi required this very long stay. Another clinic Hannah had been to, you just went in for an intake visit and they gave you shots and pills to give yourself."

"Shots and pills?"

"It had to do with getting her body synchronized with the donor's body."

"What donor?"

"The egg donor. That's what 'oocyte donation' is."

Lassiter looked completely baffled.

Hugh sighed. "Sometimes . . . a woman like Hannah . . . just cannot get pregnant. Because her eggs . . . are too old."

"What do you mean?"

"Wellll . . . they've got them all—I mean, women do—when they're born. You knew that, of course."

"Of course," Lassiter lied.

"So they have all the eggs they'll ever have—from the very begin-ning. And when the women get older, the eggs get older, and some-times things begin to go wrong. The chromosomes get iffy, you get a lot more genetic disorders, or the eggs don't get fertilized as easily. So this technique was developed. And a woman like Hannah—she can then bear a child. Someone like Baresi removes an egg from a younger woman—the donor—and they fertilize that egg with . . . well, Hannah's husband's sperm . . . and put the fertilized egg in the older woman." Exhausted by this, Hugh took a long sip of brandy, rolled it around in his mouth, and swallowed.

"So . . . biologically speaking . . . it's not really the woman's child."

Hugh flicked his fingernail at the rim of the brandy snifter. It made a little pinging noise. "I disagree. In biological terms, it *is* her child. She carries it to term, she gives birth, she nurses it. But, in the genetic sense, no—they have nothing in common at that level. All the DNA comes from the husband and the donor. I think Hannah was a little bothered by that."

"Why do you say that?"

"Well, he didn't look much like Jiri, did he? The lad, I mean."

"I don't know," Lassiter said. "I saw a photograph, but the child was a baby. But . . . you stayed in touch?"

"Oh, absolutely. For a couple of years we wrote every week. Then it fell off. She did send me a picture of the little chap—and . . . well . . . I suppose he resembled the donor . . . because there wasn't a lot of Jiri in him . . . not that Jiri's any prize."

"What I still don't understand is why it took a month—"

"Well, first it was because of the hormone injections. I was telling you. The woman who received the egg," Hugh explained. "She had to synchronize her . . . *you* know—her *cycle* . . . with the donor's. And then it was old Baresi."

"Right."

"He insisted on having them here, the whole month, as I said—which was not the way at other clinics. Even the local clients he kept here. He liked to monitor the hormones very closely. Also, he didn't like them flying—said it was a mistake . . . something about the air pressure."

Lassiter was frowning. This was . . . a *big deal* Kathy had been through. Yet she'd never said anything about hormone injections, oocytes, or egg donations. But then, Kathy had always been reserved about that sort of thing. She wouldn't have talked about anything so intimate. Even with him. And, maybe, especially with him.

"May I ask you something?" Hugh said.

"Of course."

"Would you keep in touch? About these *murders*, I mean. Nigel teases me about Hannah, but I liked her a great deal." He made a helpless gesture, looked up at Lassiter and yawned hugely. "Well, I'm totally knackered," he said. "I'd better tuck in." He headed off, a bit unsteadily, down the hall.

Lassiter returned to the guest register, running his finger down the pages and pages of names and addresses, his eyes scanning for the tell-tale letters: **C.B.** It was a mindless task, and as he performed it, a thought occurred to him.

Was it possible the murders had something to do with the donors — of eggs or sperm? He found a name, typed it into his computer. There were cases of people pursuing their genetic offspring — men uninformed of their paternity, who later learned that a child of theirs had been given up for adoption. He'd seen a piece about it on "60 Minutes," or something.

It's late, Lassiter told himself. You're tired. Grimaldi on a search-and-destroy mission to eliminate his own offspring? It seemed to him he'd discarded that notion once before — and he'd been justified in doing so. There was no reason to believe that Grimaldi was a sperm donor, and even if he was, why would he hunt down his "children"? Unless he was crazy — and Lassiter had ditched "crazy" a long time ago.

He found another **C.B.** and typed it in.

But what if . . . what if there was an estate, an inheritance? And what if, the heir to that estate knew that the deceased had been a sperm donor? The heir might begin to fear that the donor's offspring would one day seek him out — and lay claim to the estate? Definitely a long reach, Lassiter thought. So much simpler just to destroy the clinic's records — which had been done in addition to killing the children.

His finger fell upon another entry, a woman who'd stayed for thirty-two days at the pensione. She was the fourth, so far. He hadn't reached Hannah Reiner's name yet, but from what Hugh said, she was another. Because Hannah and Kathy had been subjects of an oocyte procedure, he'd taken to marking those names with a double asterisk, in case the longer stay turned out to be significant.

And here was another: Marie Williams, of Minneapolis, Minnesota. She'd checked into the pensione on March 26, 1991, and left on April 28. She and Kathy had had the same procedure, and their stays had overlapped for more than a week. They must have met each other, Lassiter thought.

He continued to turn the pages in the register, writing down the names of the clinic's guests, until he came to yet another oocyte procedure:

Marion Kerr—**C.B.**
17 Elder Lane
Bressingham, B.C.
Arr.: 17–11–92
Dep.: 19–12–92

Lassiter had already typed the entry into his computer and was moving on to the next entry when it hit him. Bressingham. British Columbia. Canada. He'd forgotten the Kerr name—it hadn't seemed important. But now . . . he was stunned. That Nexis search . . . in Prague . . . just before he met Jiri Reiner . . . *arson-child-homicide*, or something like that . . . and one of the hits—the only real hit—had been a story about a family named Kerr.

He didn't remember any of the details, except one, and it was this one detail that took his breath away: the Kerrs' baby had been killed when Grimaldi was in the hospital. And so, he thought, it couldn't have had anything to do with his sister's death and Brandon's. Because if it did, there was more than a single killer—which meant a conspiracy. To murder infants.

The idea was unthinkable, and yet, there it was:

Marion Kerr—**C.B.**
Bressingham, B.C.

He needed a cup of coffee, and knew where he could find one. Walking back to his room, he removed a packet of Nescafé from the frigo bar and boiled a cup of water, using a heating element that the pensione had thoughtfully provided.

He didn't know what to think. The Kerr entry suggested—*proved*—there was more than one killer, and it was impossible not to think that Umbra Domini, Bepi's death, and the beating he'd taken in Naples were all part of the same fabric. But when he tried to come up with *why*, what possible reason . . . his mind went blank.

Nescafé in hand, he returned to the lobby, where his computer waited, glowing in the dark.

For the next three hours he kept going. He knew he was becoming unreliable, and had to force himself to double-check each page. Even so, his mind wandered, and on occasion he caught himself turning a page without ever having focused on it, his concentration dissipated in a mist of fatigue. When that happened, he forced himself to go back through the pages to the last name he'd logged and start over from there.

It was three-thirty in the morning when he realized, dimly, that he'd found a pattern, or the edges of a pattern. But he wouldn't let himself think about it until he'd logged all of the clinic's patients into his computer—because then he'd confine himself to entries that fit the pattern. When he finally reached the end, the sky was beginning to brighten outside the lobby's window.

He was wiped out. He closed the leather cover of the guest register and got to his feet, stretched so hard that something in his ribs actually made a sound. He turned off the light and walked back to his room.

There, he did what he'd not allowed himself to do before— segregate the oocyte procedures, the women who'd stayed at the pensione for a month or more, from the 272 names on the list. The double asterisks stood him in good stead, and with the computer's help it took only a few minutes to compile a list of eighteen names:

Kathleen Lassiter
Hannah Reiner
Matilda Henderson
Adriana Peña
Lillian Kerr . . .

Five that he recognized were dead. And their children were dead. And all of them had died in flames.

He closed his eyes. Brandon rose up in his mind. *Uncle Joe! Uncle Joe! Watch me! I can do a sum-salt. Watch me!* The little body tumbled crookedly over; it wasn't a somersault at all, just a little kid clumsily rolling over on the rug, but Brandon jumped up like an Olympic gymnast, his hands thrust to the sky in victory, his smile beaming with pride.

Lassiter looked at the list again. The women were mostly from the United States and Western Europe, but there were a handful from other places: Hong Kong, Tokyo, Tel Aviv, Rabat, Rio.

He moved the computer to the desk beside the window and plugged the modem into the telephone. Using the N-cipher program, he encrypted *cbguest.1st* and sent it to his office in Washington. Then he wrote a short memo to Judy Rifkin, giving her the names and addresses of the eighteen patients whose names he'd listed. He told her to notify Riordan that at least five of the women on the list were dead, and that all of the others might therefore be in danger. Riordan should contact the authorities in whatever jurisdictions were involved, and have the women and children placed in protective custody. Lassiter planned to return in a day or two, when he'd explain everything.

Meanwhile, he wanted Judy to organize a dossier on the late Dr. Ignazio Baresi, of Montecastello, Italy. Anything she could find on the Clinica Baresi and a fertility technique called "oocyte donation" would also be helpful. Finally, he asked her to backstop Riordan by trying to contact the thirteen women on the list. If the cops were on top of things, none of the women would be available. Which was just the way he wanted it.

The memo was two pages long, and when he'd sent it to Judy, he desperately wanted to sleep. But it was the weekend, and there was a chance that Judy might not check her E-mail until Monday morning. He looked at his watch. It was almost five-thirty in the morning—eleven-thirty at night in Washington. Reaching for the telephone, he dialed Judy's number at home. There were four long rings, and then her answering machine came on. When the long beep sounded, he said, "Judy—Joe. Check your E-mail right away. It's urgent. I'll see you in a couple of days."

He pulled off his clothes and lay back on the bed like a swimmer doing the backstroke. Shutting his eyes against the thin morning light, he listened to himself breathe and waited to lose consciousness.

But his mind was at the races. He saw Marie Sanders, holding her little boy's hand. The kid's eyes were the color of mahogany. Brown and bottomless, and they stared up at him, as if from a well. And then Brandon's carbonized face flashed through his mind, and he heard Tommy Truong's voice: *No blood left in this little boy.* He thought of Jiri Reiner's hopeless gaze. And Kara Baker's tears.

Jesus Christ, he thought, pulling the covers over his head. It's a fucking massacre.

27

It was eleven o'clock when he climbed out of bed, and the first thing that occurred to him was that he needed a good night's sleep—instead of the few hours he'd gotten. But a quick shower took care of that, needling his face with a flood of hot water, massaging his shoulders, rinsing him clean. He didn't want to take the time to shave, but thought better of it. Priests could be funny. Or so he supposed. He didn't really know.

He put on his leather jacket and went down to the lobby. Nigel complained of a hangover, but pointed him in the direction of the square where he'd find the church, "and a café."

It was cold out, maybe forty degrees, and raw with the threat of a rain. He turned left outside the pensione, walking north along a narrow cobbled street. There were no sidewalks and no cars, just a wall of gray stone houses on either side, their shutters and doors closed against the winter air.

He didn't like it, much. In winter Montecastello seemed as menacing as it was beautiful. Over the centuries, the foundations of the houses had shifted, and now they seemed to lean toward each other, crouching above the street. As Lassiter turned down one lane and up a second, it occurred to him that the town was a maze, the kind of place in which it would be easy to get lost but hard to hide.

He passed one unmarked store, and then another. There were no signs anywhere, perhaps because there was no need to advertise: everyone in town must know everyone else, and everyone would know what everyone else was selling. Each of the stores buzzed with fluorescent lights behind doorways strung with strands of plastic beads. With a ripple and a click, an old man stepped through one of the doorways into the street, carrying a bag of vegetables, packages wrapped in butcher's paper, and a loaf of bread. "*Ciao*," he said, with his eyes on the ground, and hurried away.

One more turn and Lassiter emerged from the warren of little streets into the open space of Montecastello's main square, the Piazza di San Fortunato. His destination, the Church of San Giovanni Decollato, occupied all of the north side of the small square. It was a simple, even austere, building, built with the same gray stone that was everywhere else in town. Lassiter was about to climb the steps to the church when the smell of coffee hit him and he turned.

Across from the church was a hole-in-the-wall café with a beaded entrance, and metal tables and chairs in the street in front of it. This was obviously the center for retail sin in Montecastello, combining the functions of a snack bar, newsstand, video arcade, saloon, coffeehouse, and tabacchi—within the confines of a single room. Despite the chill, Lassiter sat down at an outside table and ordered an espresso.

Though the air was cold, it was also quite still—and it might have been quiet, as well, if it were not for the insistent beep of a Pac-Man game filtering out of the café. The square was shielded on three sides by buildings. The fourth side was part of the town wall, a low parapet about four feet high that looked out over the Umbrian plain.

At the next table a pair of middle-aged workmen sat, playing cards. They wore close-fitting, woolen jackets buttoned up over so many other layers of clothes that they had an upholstered look. Sipping coffee and brandy by turns, they cursed quietly, muttered to themselves, and joked about the hands that fate had dealt them.

As he waited for his coffee, Lassiter glanced at the rack of newspapers that stood outside the café. There were at least a dozen papers held in place by metal clips, but nothing in English. A three-day-old *Le Monde*—but he didn't feel up to it. He was trying to decide whether or not to use a pretext in his interview with the priest. And what to say. *Tell me everything you know about Dr. Baresi?* He shook his head.

His coffee arrived, and as he sipped it, he watched the workmen playing cards. The deck was so very old that it had a texture almost like cloth. Left to themselves, the cards would have collapsed in the players' hands, revealing every denomination. So each of the men propped them up with the fingers of his second hand, cupping the cards from behind.

Both men, with their sun-darkened skin and lattices of wrinkles around their eyes, had obviously spent their lives outdoors. They looked vigorous and, somehow, sardonic, eyes and teeth bright in their dark faces.

He tried to imagine a place in America where two such as these might sit outside, minding their business in the daylight hours, drinking coffee and brandy and playing cards. In January. No place came to mind except, perhaps, a beery workingman's bar, and that wasn't the same thing at all.

In the center of the square was a simple fountain, a rectangular stone basin elevated a couple of feet from the ground. Mounted on its single vertical wall was a tattered bas-relief, a lion's head. Its mouth was cracked, so that instead of a stream arching into the basin, a burble of water came out. Even so, the fountain was functional, and more than an ornament. Lassiter watched an elderly woman fill two plastic jugs with water, square her shoulders, and then walk away.

He ordered a second coffee, and wandered over to the parapet while it was being prepared. Below him the land fell almost vertically. It was mostly rock, any earth having long since eroded away; a few scraggly pine trees managed to grow in the stony soil.

In the distance, just above the nearby pines, was Todi, almost floating in the sky. Its walls girdled the mountainside in a series of diagonal planes, climbing the hill to the city itself. There was a messy expanse below that—Todi's urban sprawl—and then order was restored by a crazy quilt of agricultural plots that ran all the way down to the river.

It was a sweet sight, touched with a weird nostalgia for something that, after all, he'd never known. It was a long time since farming had been like this in the United States, if it ever had, and the view of a quilted American landscape was available only from twenty thousand feet. He blamed the nostalgia on Cézanne.

Closer to him, on this side of the river, was the man-made forest he'd driven past, with its geometric lines of trees. He could see where the road forked, one fork heading toward the Clinica Baresi—or what was left of it—and the other to Montecastello. He followed that road with his eyes until it disappeared into the steep configuration of the hill. It emerged a few hundred feet below him, at the little park. He could even see his car—the silver one, right there.

Returning to the café, he found his second espresso waiting and, standing, drank it in a single gulp. Sliding five thousand lire under the saucer, he crossed the square toward the church.

———

Lassiter climbed the steps and went through a heavy wooden door that gave access to a sort of foyer, an anteroom. A wooden wall, with an entryway into the church at either end, separated the world of prayer from that of the world outside. The room was a buffer, and a clearing-house of sorts, containing an old wooden table with tidy stacks of leaflets, and a metal box for donations. He shoved some bills into the box, and walked around the wall into the church proper.

It was surprisingly dark, and at first he could see nothing but the ceiling, high above. Candle smoke and mold filled his nostrils, and he could hear the murmur of low voices, coming from the front of the church where the altar must be.

The only natural illumination came from a row of windows high along one wall. But there wasn't much of it. The winter sun was anemic, and so angled that it lightened the gloom of the ceiling without ever reaching the floor. Nor were the candelabra of much help. There were only a few, and none of them held candles: in their place, small electric bulbs flickered and twitched in the darkness.

They did not look like flames.

Closer to him, halfway up the nave, a bank of votive candles guttered beneath a dark statue. Lassiter took a seat in a pew near the back and waited for his eyes to adjust.

Slowly, the dimensions of the church came into focus. It was surprisingly large. And now he could see that a little crowd was gathered near the altar—vague forms and ghostly patches, bits of white clothing that moved and shifted in the dimness. A baby's sharp wail told him that he was watching a christening.

A few minutes later the ceremony ended and the crowd made its way in a procession down the aisle, led by the mother and her shrieking child. The priest brought up the rear. He was tall, and his head bobbed above the others like a pale balloon. As he passed—a man in his forties with brown curly hair, a strong chin, and an aquiline nose—their eyes met, and Lassiter was reminded of someone. But who? If the priest hadn't been so thin, so very *gaunt*, he might have been handsome. But he wasn't. There was something ungainly about the way his features came together. And then it hit him: the priest was Ichabod Crane, at once haunted and long-suffering.

For ten minutes the anteroom behind Lassiter bubbled with Italian voices and shrieks of laughter, even as the baby screeched, furious and inconsolable. And then, the sounds of departure: the precise smacking of lips that went with the European double kiss of hello-and-farewell. The muffled *abrazos* of the men, their voices raised slightly in departure, a little more formal or jolly than normal.

He heard the door to the church creak open, and a rush of cold air swirled at his ankles. For a moment daylight lifted the gloom. There was the shuffling of feet, the tapping of women's heels, receding voices. He imagined the priest out on the steps, bidding farewell.

And then he heard the door again and, suddenly, the priest was walking past him, down the aisle. Lassiter got to his feet as he heard himself say, in what seemed a booming voice: *"Scusi, padre!"*

The priest turned. *"Si?"*

Lassiter's Italian was exhausted. "Can I talk to you for a minute?"

Father Azetti smiled. "Of course," he said in nearly unaccented English. "How can I help you?"

Lassiter took a deep breath. He didn't know where to begin. "I'm not sure," he said, "but—I'm staying at the pensione and—I was told you were a friend of Dr. Baresi's."

The priest's smile faded and he became very still. He looked at Lassiter with the wariness of an eyewitness. Finally, he said, "We played chess."

Lassiter nodded. "That's what I heard. And . . . actually, I was interested in his clinic."

"It's gone."

"I understand that, but . . . I was hoping we could talk."

The door to the church groaned, and a gust of freezing air rolled across the floor. A woman in black clothing materialized a few feet away, crossing herself as she walked down the aisle. Lassiter and Azetti watched her as she stepped into a pew, knelt, and began to pray.

Azetti looked at his watch and shook his head. "I'm sorry," he said. "I have confession until two."

"Oh," Lassiter replied, disappointed.

"But if you'd like to wait . . . or come back . . . we could talk in my rooms. They're just next to the church."

Lassiter was grateful. "I'll walk around," he said. "See the sights."

"As you like," Azetti replied, and walked toward a dark shape at the end of the aisle. The structure reminded Lassiter of a curtained armoire, but deeper, and when the priest ducked inside, he knew what it was: the confessional.

—

Two hours later Lassiter and Azetti sat in the priest's study, sharing a pasta dish that one of the parishioners had brought to the church. Lassiter decided he must have been wrong about the priest's initial wariness, because Azetti proved a good host. He cut some slices of crusty bread, and poured each of them a glass of wine. He drizzled olive oil onto the bread and sprinkled it with salt and pepper. Meanwhile, Lassiter sat with his back to the electric fire, warming himself.

"So," the priest said, "you came for the clinic."

Lassiter nodded.

"Well, if you've seen it, you know what happened."

"I was told it was arson."

Azetti shrugged. "It was closed anyway. Still, it's a pity. We'll not see another one like him, not in our lifetimes."

"Who do you mean?" Lassiter asked.

"Dr. Baresi. He was a very talented man. I'm hardly an expert, but I'm told his success rate was phenomenal."

"Really?" Lassiter said, encouraging the priest to continue.

"Yes. I think it was because he was not only a physician, but a scientist as well. Did you know that?"

Lassiter shook his head.

"Ah, well! Then you didn't know Baresi! He was many things," Azetti said. "A genius! Even so, I can tell you that I beat him at chess—quite regularly, in fact."

Lassiter laughed.

"I think I made so many mistakes, he couldn't anticipate my moves," Azetti confided. "He used to complain that I was ruining his game. More wine?"

"No thanks," Lassiter said. He liked this man.

"His father, grandfather—the whole family—they were all rich. Politics and construction. Very corrupt—even for Italy. So he never needed money. Didn't need to work. But he studied. Genetics in Perugia, biochemistry at Cambridge. Cambridge!" Azetti poured himself a second glass of wine, dipped a crust of bread in it, and nibbled at its edges. "He worked for one of those institutes in Zurich—won a medal, or some such thing."

"For what?"

"I don't know—research. But, of course, he gave up on all of that—"

"All of what?"

"Science."

"You mean, he went into medicine," Lassiter said.

Azetti shook his head. "No—that was even later. First, he studied theology. In Germany. Wrote a book. In fact, I have it right here." Without looking, the priest reached into the bookcase behind him and extracted a thick tome. He pushed it across the table.

Lassiter opened the book, glanced at the title, and shook his head. "It's in Italian," he said, instantly regretting the stupidity of the remark.

Azetti smiled. "It's called *Relic, Totem, and Divinity.*"

Lassiter nodded and pushed the book to the side.

"He was quite an authority," Azetti added.

"Really," Lassiter said without much interest.

"Oh yes."

"This pasta's delicious," Lassiter said. The conversation was getting away from what he'd come to discuss—the Clinica Baresi—and he wasn't sure how to get it back on track.

"Baresi related the power of relics to certain, very primitive, religious instincts. Animism, ancestor worship, that kind of thing. The same instinct that provoked a tribesman to eat the heart of his enemy—so he'd absorb the man's power—prompted Christians to believe that a saint's bone, or more often, a splinter of bone, carried in a little bag, could protect them from disease."

"Sounds interesting," Lassiter said, without sounding interested.

"Oh, it really is. I recommend it. It's all about sympathetic magic—but then, some would argue, so is receiving communion."

"How's that?" Lassiter asked.

Azetti shrugged. "We eat and drink the flesh and blood of the Lord. To the faithful, that's a sacrament. To others . . . it's something else. Magic, perhaps."

"Sounds controversial," Lassiter said.

The priest smiled. "Of course. But Baresi didn't mind. His credentials were impeccable. And he was well thought of by the Vatican."

"Really?"

"Absolutely. The Vatican used him all the time."

"What do you mean?"

"To test relics. If an artifact was questionable, Baresi was brought in and asked to take a look. Most of the time, it was a simple matter. If a splinter of 'the true cross' turned out to be teak . . . or if a fragment of St. Francis's scalp had the DNA signature of an ox . . . You're familiar with the Shroud of Turin?" the priest asked, referring to the linen cloth that some believed was Christ's burial shroud.

"Sure," Lassiter said. "Everyone is."

"Well, there you are! Baresi was one of the scientists who examined it."

"I read somewhere or other that it turned out to be a fake."

Azetti frowned. "That's what they say. 'A nice piece of thirteenth-century linen.' They say Leonardo made it. They say it's the world's first photograph."

"What did Baresi think?"

"He thought it was a hoax—but a very dark one."

"How do you mean?"

"As he says in his book, the history of relics is actually quite sinister—and the shroud may well be a part of that tradition. At one time relics were so important that if a saint fell sick, people gathered outside his house, waiting for him to die. And when he did, they went into the house and came away with parts—fingers, teeth, ears—whatever they could get—and sold him off, piece by piece."

Lassiter gaped.

"Oh, yes! It's said that within two days of his death, St. Thomas of Aquinas had been boiled down to the bones." Azetti laughed. "Gruesome, isn't it? And sometimes the saints were hastened on their way—with poison."

"But the shroud—it's only a piece of cloth, legitimate or not."

"Yes, but it's suffused with juices—and bilirubin."

"What's that?" Lassiter asked.

"It's a by-product of the blood that's usually excreted. But sometimes, under extreme stress—torture—people sweat bilirubin."

"And it's in the shroud?"

"Baresi found traces of it. And even though he felt the shroud to be a hoax, he feared that someone had been murdered to make it."

"Good God," Lassiter said.

Azetti nodded. "In the thirteenth century, of course, relics were powerful. A church with a famous relic could draw thousands of pilgrims—and pilgrims meant money. Eventually, of course, the Reformation took place, and a lot of the relics were burned."

"Burned," Lassiter repeated. The word reminded him of why he was there. He took a sip of wine. "What I don't understand is: How did he go from relics to medicine?"

"Oh . . . well, he obviously had a calling. I think he was nearly fifty years old when he enrolled in medical school. Bologna. Obstetrics and gynecology." Azetti frowned. "I think it was during his residency that he developed an interest in infertility. And after that, he set up the clinic. Which was quite a surprise."

"Why?"

"Well, it's an emotional subject—as you know. And Baresi was . . . awkward . . . uncomfortable around people—and here he was, asking women to undress! And then, too, he was Catholic. And devout. So there were conflicts."

"Why?"

Father Azetti rolled his eyes. "Cardinal Ratzinger spoke for the Church when he issued his catechism. The Church opposes *any* attempt to interfere with natural conception."

"Birth control."

"No! The Church is just as opposed to fertility clinics as it is to abortion clinics."

"You wouldn't think so."

"Oh yes. They have spoken out directly, and at great length. Children are to be conceived in an act of sexual congress, in the normal way. Just as contraception interferes with God's will, so does reproductive—what do they call it?—technology. Virtually everything that takes place at a fertility clinic is specifically forbidden."

"Interesting. And yet . . . Baresi went ahead anyway. . . ."

The priest looked away. "He felt he had a special dispensation." He sighed. "Besides—he's hardly the only one to ignore the Vatican on these issues. Birth control is forbidden, but in Italy—a country that is still almost entirely Catholic—people have small families, and the population is stable. And yet I can promise you that, as a nation, they do not practice chastity."

Azetti shrugged and refilled his glass. "And now—what are we going to do about your wife? Does she need counseling?"

Lassiter looked at him blankly.

"Is she at the pensione? I'm surprised you came so far without calling ahead. She must be very disappointed. If you'd like me to speak with her—"

"No, Father—"

"I'm a good listener," Azetti interrupted.

"I think there's a misunderstanding," Lassiter said.

"Oh?"

"I'm not married."

The priest looked confused. "Then . . . ?" He turned his palms toward the ceiling.

"I'm here because my sister went to the clinic. Several years ago."

"Ah! Well! Your sister! Was her trip successful?"

"Yes. She had a wonderful baby boy."

Azetti smiled at the news, and nodded. But then the smile faded to a frown. "I don't understand," he said. "I mean, why *are* you here?"

"She died in November."

The priest winced. "I'm so very sorry. And the boy? I suppose it's up to the father now—and you."

Lassiter shook his head. "There wasn't any father. She was raising him alone. And, anyway, the boy died, too. They were killed."

Azetti looked away. After a moment he asked, "And how did this happen?"

"Someone killed them while they were sleeping, and then their house was burned."

Azetti didn't speak for a long while. He cut another piece of bread and dipped it into the wine. Finally, he said, "And that's what brought you here?"

Lassiter nodded. "The man who killed them was Italian. I don't think he and my sister had ever met. And then I learned—"

The priest scraped back from the table and, getting to his feet, began to pace. He seemed agitated, as if by a dangerous idea. He interrupted. "A boy, you said?"

Lassiter nodded, following the priest with his eyes.

"I wonder . . ." Azetti said.

"What, Father?"

"I wonder if you have any idea—you may not know, of course, but . . . I wonder if you know which procedure your sister had? Because there were several—"

"I know there was an egg donor. I think they call it—"

"Oocyte donation." The priest pronounced the phrase as if it was a fatal disease. He continued pacing for a moment, and then he scratched his head, stopped and looked at Lassiter. "But, of course," he said, "these things happen. There's so much violence. Especially in the United States. Did your sister live in a city? These are difficult times."

Lassiter nodded. "You're right. There is a lot of violence. But my sister and nephew weren't the only ones."

"What do you mean?"

"A boy was killed in Prague. About the same time. Same circumstances. Another one in London. Canada . . . Rio . . . God only knows where else. That's why I'm here: they were all conceived at the clinic."

The priest collapsed into a straight-backed chair, lowered his head, and closed his eyes. Then he raised his elbows to the table and pushed his fingers through his hair. For a long while he said nothing at all, and in the silence, Lassiter noticed that rain was beginning to fall.

After a minute the priest straightened in his chair. He placed his hands carefully, palm to palm, and lowered his head until his forehead rested on the tips of his middle fingers. His face was hidden, his chin nearly buried in his chest. He muttered something that Lassiter didn't understand.

"What?" Lassiter asked.

"Well, 'it's God's will,' " Azetti cried. He pushed his palms against the tabletop and looked toward Lassiter. His eyes were wild and unfocused. "Or maybe not!"

"Father—"

"I can't help you," the priest said, turning away.

"I think you can."

"I can't!"

"Then more children are going to die."

Azetti's eyes were filled with tears. "You don't understand," he said, and taking a deep breath, composed himself. "The confessional is sacrosanct. Whatever's said is sealed forever. It's supposed to be sealed forever."

"What do you mean, 'supposed to be'?"

The priest shook his head.

"You know who's behind this, don't you?" Lassiter asked.

"No," the priest replied, and Lassiter could see that he was telling the truth. "I don't. I honestly don't. But I can tell you this: every aspect of Baresi's life is part of what you're looking at—his work as a scientist, his religious studies, his work at the clinic." With that, the priest took a second deep breath and fell silent.

"That's it?" Lassiter asked.

"That's all I can say," the priest said.

"Well, then, thanks for your help," Lassiter replied, his voice thick with sarcasm. "I'll keep that in mind. And if one of the mothers asks why her son had to die, I'll tell her about your oath—about how it's a matter of principle. I'm sure she'll understand." He grabbed his coat and got to his feet.

"Wait," the priest said. "There's something else." Before Lassiter could say anything, Azetti strode from the room and into his study, next door. Lassiter heard him rifling through a desk. Finally, a drawer slammed shut, and the priest returned.

"Here," he said, thrusting a letter into the American's hands.

"What is it?" he asked.

"Baresi sent it to me from the hospital, a few days before he died. I think it will answer some of the questions you have." Lassiter glanced at the letter, which was written in hand on both sides of three onion-skin pages. High overhead, a bell began to toll.

Azetti pulled up his sleeve and looked at his watch. "I have confession until eight," he said. "If you'll come back this evening, I'll translate it for you."

"Couldn't you just—"

Azetti shook his head. "I can't. It's a small town, and by now they're lined up three deep."

"Father—"

"It's waited thousands of years. It can wait a little longer."

28

He needed to think. Or, better yet, to not-think.

The priest had been trying to tell him something without breaking his vows. Something about the different hats Baresi wore and the way they came together. But it didn't make sense. Or, if it did, Lassiter couldn't see it.

He needed to run.

That was what he did when he faced a problem that he couldn't solve. He put his mind into neutral and he ran. As often as not, the solution came to him unbidden, a gift.

But he wasn't going to run in Montecastello. He'd have to circumnavigate the town half a dozen times to cover any distance. Besides, the cobblestones were ankle breakers, even in dry weather, and the streets were so filled with turns that it would be impossible to establish a pace. As for the road leading out of town and down the hill, nothing could tempt him to take it: He might as well throw himself off a cliff and climb back up.

So he did the next best thing. He got into his car and drove aimlessly out of town in the general direction of Spoleto, trying not to think, hoping the answer would come to him. Driving sometimes worked, although as a meditative technique, it was not as reliable as running.

According to the map, Spoleto was forty kilometers away, about twenty-five miles. Which was perfect, Lassiter thought. An hour out, an hour back. Take a walk around town.

But no. What the map didn't show was the mountain range separating the two towns. The road between them was a series of switchbacks on an asphalt track carved into the mountainside. The dropoff at the side of the road was heart-stopping. And while the trip was beautiful, it took him an hour and a half to reach a sign that read,

SPOLETO—10 KM. Even so, he forged on until he found himself behind an underpowered truck that proved impossible to pass, condemning him to climb the mountain in a fog of diesel fumes. Finally, he reached an Agip station about five miles west of Spoleto and turned around. All that was left of the daylight was a faint blush behind the mountains. The dashboard clock read six-fifteen.

"You just missed him," Hugh said as Lassiter came into the pensione.

"Who?"

"Didn't leave his name, I'm afraid. Said he was a friend."

Lassiter looked at him. "I don't have any 'friends' over here," he said. "Did this guy leave a message?"

"No. He said it was a surprise. Then he asked where he might find you, and . . ." Hugh frowned. "I said you'd gone to see the padre."

Lassiter became very still, and seeing that, Hugh winced.

"That was a mistake, wasn't it?"

"I don't know. What did he look like?"

"Big. *Enormous*."

"Italian?" Lassiter asked.

Hugh nodded.

"Is there a back way out?" Lassiter asked.

Hugh blanched, then nodded vigorously. "Yes," he said, and led the way down the corridor, through the kitchen, and into the street behind the pensione.

"I'm terribly sorry, Joe."

"Don't worry about it," Lassiter replied, and started jogging toward the church.

Before long he found himself in a cul-de-sac whose only illumination came from the light that fell from a window high above the street. Overhead, the moon scudded behind a thick blanket of clouds. He knew there was a good chance that the someone—probably the Mattress—would be waiting for him at the church, or in the square, but he decided to meet the priest anyway. It was early; there would still be people around. It was a church, after all. Maybe he'd ask the padre to walk him home.

But somehow he'd taken a wrong turn. He ought to be in the piazza by now. Turning around, he retraced his steps, or thought he did, going deeper and deeper in the maze. Finally, when he was so lost he began to think he'd never find his way, he took a left, and there he was, in the Piazza di San Fortunato.

The air in front of him was a cloud of respiration vapor. He was breathing hard, but not from running. It was adrenaline. His body was flushed with it. He could feel it pouring into his heart like a waterfall, and, knowing what it could do, he paused where he was, at the entrance to the square. Took a deep breath. Held it. Let it go. And again.

Across the piazza three men stood at the parapet, looking toward the lights of Todi. Nearby, the proprietor of the Luna was closing up shop, pulling down a slatted iron curtain over the café's facade. One of the men from the overlook called out to him, something about cigarettes, and the storekeeper muttered in reply. Then he went back inside, and Lassiter looked more closely at the three men.

He'd been mistaken. There were only two. But the second man was as big a house. And as square as a mattress.

His breath was coming normally now, and when the men turned back to the view of Todi, Lassiter crossed the square on his toes, taking the steps to the church two at a time.

Inside, the church was about as well lighted as the night. The votive candles guttered in their blood-red cups, and the electric candelabra glimmered weakly.

"Father?" he said, so quietly that the words barely got out of his mouth. "Father?" he repeated. There was no response, which meant the priest must be in his rooms. Making his way down the aisle in the gloom, it occurred to Lassiter that by now he was more than a little late. The priest must be around somewhere, though. The church wasn't locked.

The men were still at the parapet, smoking, when he came down the steps. He went over to the priest's quarters, just next to the church, and knocked on the heavy wooden door. When no one answered, he tried the doorknob, and when it turned, he went in. The lights were off, but that didn't matter. His eyes had adjusted to the darkness long before. Moving from room to room, he called the priest's name, but got no reply.

Which was odd. It worried him. Where could Azetti be? Retracing his steps, he went back to the church, thinking that the priest might be praying in one of its chapels. Perhaps, when he prayed, the priest's concentration was so complete that he shut off the world outside, and so had not heard him.

Lassiter had no idea what it was to pray. Not really. Once, when Josie had gone on a religious kick—it had lasted about three weeks— she'd insisted that he and Kathy take turns saying grace at meals. And before they went to bed, they'd been made to recite the Lord's Prayer—in her presence and on their knees. He never even thought about the words he was saying. They were sounds to him, but without meaning. Hal-lo-wed be thy name.

Hal-lo-wed.

He called out again, louder this time. "Father Azetti! It's Joe Lassiter." Nothing.

One of the votive candles flared momentarily and sputtered out, leaving a waxy smell that reminded Lassiter of a birthday cake.

Maybe the priest had walked a parishioner home. Maybe someone was ill and he'd gone to their bedside.

He decided to wait. And then he decided to light a candle for the dead. A small sign pointed toward the donation box, and without thinking about it, Lassiter took a bill from his wallet, folded it length-wise, and eased it into the slot. It might have been a dollar, or a hun-dred-dollar bill. It might have been a thousand lire. He didn't know. He didn't really care. There was a strange, free-floating feeling in his head. The men outside. What the priest had said. The spooky town.

For Kathy, he thought, lighting a candle with a length of straw. And then a second candle, next to the first. *For Brandon,* he told himself, feeling as if he were borrowing someone else's ritual—which he was.

He'd wait a little longer for Azetti, and then try to find a way out that would take him away from the square. He'd sit in a pew near the back, and keep his eyes on the door.

Suddenly, his right foot went out from under him and he slipped, staggering sideways two or three steps, finally catching himself by grab-bing the side of a pew.

He looked at the tiled floor where he'd slipped. The darkness robbed everything of color, but he could see a patch of something that looked black but wasn't. Then he caught a whiff of it, and there was no mistaking the meat department smell.

He looked closer, and saw a river of blood seeping along the floor toward the pews. Raising his head, he followed the blood back to the confessional. And though he didn't want to step in it, there wasn't any choice. The only way to the booth was through the blood.

He'd never been inside a confessional, and when he pulled the curtain aside, his heart almost stopped when he found that it was empty. But his relief was short-lived. Glancing around, he saw the partition down the middle of the booth and instantly knew what he'd find on the other side.

The soles of his shoes were sticky, and once again his heart was slamming away inside his chest. Pulling back the curtain on the other side, he found Azetti in his seat, leaning against the partition with his head against the grille. There was a small hole in his right temple, and an exit wound the size of a fist. Without looking, Lassiter knew that the priest's brains were clinging to the wall behind him.

A low velocity bullet, then. Soft point. A bullet that fell apart on impact, flying off in every direction. Dumdums. It used to be that you had to make them yourself, by cutting a cross into the lead point, but now you could buy the same thing, only a lot better.

The priest had been sitting in the booth with his ear pressed against the little metal grille. The killer had entered on the confessor's side and, seating himself, took out the gun even as he'd begun his confession. *Bless me, Father, for I have sinned.* And then he'd fired, point-blank, into the priest's ear, using a bullet that would have killed an elephant.

It took him a minute to maneuver Azetti out of the booth and onto the floor. He wasn't sure why he was doing it. Azetti had looked uncomfortable in the booth. He wished he had a pillow for his head, but . . .

He didn't. He left Azetti in the aisle and went toward the back of the church, past the altar. He fumbled around in the confusing spaces back there, but there didn't seem to be another way out. The back of the church was probably wedged up against another row of buildings which left him with a single choice: he could stay, or he could go. But if he went, it would have to be through the front door.

He opened the door with a gentle push, paused at the top of the steps, and looked out into the square. It was empty and, for the moment at least, brilliantly lighted by the moon. He quick-stepped down the church steps toward the fountain, whose gurgling was the only sound in the square. Moonlight sparkled on the water as it rolled from the lion's mouth, a bright glimmer.

And then he saw the man.

Saw him plain, standing in the moonlight on the corner, where the Via della Felice met the square. A moment later the moon slipped behind a cloud and the man disappeared so completely that Lassiter wondered if he'd imagined him. Turning toward the second street, whose name he didn't know, Lassiter started walking—until the darkness shifted and what seemed like a wall appeared in front of him.

The Mattress.

Lassiter turned on the ball of his foot, and found himself running. With nowhere to go.

"*Ecco! 'Cenzo!*" the Mattress called out softly. His voice was surprisingly high, almost feminine.

Lassiter's eyes swung through the square, taking it in: the fountain, the church, the café, the wall. There was no way out. The Mattress and the smaller man were walking toward him, maybe twenty feet apart, maybe twenty yards away. He could see their teeth in the dark. They were smiling.

Lassiter began walking backward, indifferent to where he was going, so long as it was *away*. The smaller man reached into his jacket and came up with what looked like a Walther with the fat barrel of a suppressor on the end. He tightened the suppressor on its barrel and muttered something to his friend. Lassiter's back touched the parapet, and that was it. End of the road.

As the men came toward him, never hurrying, he could see their faces in the moonlight. The one with the gun was young and ugly. He had the camel-like face of someone whose features had been squeezed with forceps. His eyes were heavy and protrusive, his hair so short it seemed no more than a shadow on his scalp.

The Mattress was made of different stuff—pig iron, probably. Like his body, his face was square, and looked as if it needed to be shaved at least once an hour. His hair was a mat of curls, and even at this distance Lassiter could see the fierceness in his eyes.

I could run at them, he thought. Or go the other way: vault the wall and see what happens. Neither option seemed survivable, but one might be more so than the other. He wanted to turn around so he could calculate the fall: Was it a straight drop to dead-on-arrival, or was there an incline that would break his fall? He couldn't remember, and for the life of him—literally—he couldn't take his eyes off the men walking toward him.

Until the smaller man began to raise his gun, and Lassiter learned that he'd already made his decision. Almost casually, he placed his left hand on the parapet, turned on the ball of his foot, and vaulted into the void. Behind him, and now from above, he heard a popping noise, three shots in rapid succession as he fell, fell through the air for what seemed a very long time.

I'm dead, he thought. Dead. Now, dead. The darkness whirled and, as he fell, his eyes were useless, the images impossible to process. And then, without warning, gravity body-slammed him into the mountainside, ripping the air from his lungs, tumbling him down the slope. He was airborne again, and again a one-man avalanche, entirely out of control. Instinctively he drew his knees to his chest and covered his head with his arms, a human cannonball.

His last coherent thought was that if he hit anything, it would be over. A rock, he thought. Head . . . rock . . . head like an egg . . . the egg cracks . . . brains everywhere. Or a tree . . . even a tree . . . tear me in half. Angle of descent. Science! Increasing velocity of mass.

And then, like a baseball player sliding into second, he found himself using his legs as a brake, stretching them out in front of him even as his hands tore at the ground. A fingernail snapped off at the quick as he knifed through the brush, eyes shut against the lash of brambles. Finally, but abruptly, he came to a stop with his foot against a boulder.

Safe.

Unless he was dead. But he couldn't be dead. He hurt too much. There was a bonfire in the right side of his ribs, where he'd been hurt before, and his ankle felt as if a stake had been driven through it. A soprano kind of pain shot from the inside of his right foot all the way up his leg. He could taste the blood in his mouth, the skin on his cheek was raw . . . and he was afraid to move.

What if he tried to get up and nothing happened? He was hurt and confused, and paralyzed with the fear of being paralyzed. And so he lay there, gazing up at the moon as it played peekaboo with the clouds. The air was heavy with the smell of pine, and the night seemed strangely bright. In the distance he could hear a thousand birds whistling.

What?

Where am I?

Oh, yeah.

He had to get up. If he couldn't move, he might as well start yelling, let the Mattress and his friend put a bullet in him, ending his misery.

With a gasp and a moan he rolled onto his stomach and, reaching for a pine branch, pulled himself to his feet. Swaying slightly, he glanced around and saw that he was on the hillside, just below the town wall, where the ground was relatively flat. The parking lot was a hundred yards away, and just beyond it, the soccer field, ablaze with light. He heard the whistling noise again, and realized what it was: not birds, but people booing, Italian-style. A soccer match, Lassiter thought. There's too much noise and too much light for a pickup game.

As he brushed himself off he searched the ground for a walking stick. Finding a dead pine branch, he tested it against his weight. It bent but didn't break.

He limped toward the parking lot, trying to get a grip on the pain in his ankle. Whatever it was, broken or sprained, he could feel it getting bigger with every step. And there were a lot of steps. It took him ten minutes to get to the lot, and when he arrived, a cheer went up. Someone had scored.

The lot was a small one, filled with cars and bicycles for the match. Lassiter stood in the shadow of a cypress, looking for the car he'd rented, fearful he'd find it blocked. But no, there it was, right where he'd left it, with a clear lane to the road. He was about to walk to it when, fifty feet away, a cigarette lighter flared in the front seat of a black Rover. He couldn't make out the face, but there were two people in the car, and they didn't act like lovers.

He sucked in his breath.

Well, of course. There was only one way out of town. The Mattress hadn't needed to do any heavy thinking: If he hadn't killed himself when he'd jumped, where else could he go but go to his car? What was he supposed to do—roll down the *rest* of the fucking mountain and then hike to Todi?

He could go back, into Montecastello, but it was a trap. He thought about the soccer field. If he could get to it, he might be able to lose himself in the crowd. But no. His clothes were torn and covered with blood—only some of which was his own—his face a lattice of small cuts, and he was walking like Tiny Tim on a bad day. All of which added up to the fact that there wasn't a crowd in Italy large enough for him to get lost in; if people saw him, they'd probably scream. *He* could start screaming; maybe the police would come. On the other hand, if he could get to the police . . . what then? They'd lock him up, at least until they found a translator. He'd be safe then, if only for a while. Unless Umbra Domini or SISMI could get to his jailers—which, this being Italy, seemed likely. In which case he'd no doubt wind up hanging from his belt by morning.

So that was out. And anyway, the Rover was between him and the soccer field, him and the police. Which left . . .

The bicycles in front of him. There was a long rack, crammed with bikes of every kind, and he moved toward them in a crouch. Going from bike to bike, he finally found what he was looking for: a derelict English racer whose owner hadn't bothered to lock it up.

Still, getting out of the parking lot unseen was not going to be easy. But if the Mattress and his friend were focused on his car, they might not look twice at someone on a bike. Then again, they might—and if they did, the whole business would be over very quickly. They'd just shoot him in the head and drive away.

He hesitated, but in the end, there wasn't any choice. If he moved quietly enough, he might get past them. Taking a deep breath, Lassiter swung his left leg over the bike's bar and pushed off with his right, pedaling hard. As the bicycle rolled toward the Rover, picking up speed, it began to make a terrible clatter.

Swip
Swip swip Swip swip swip
Swipswipswipswipswipswipswip

Glancing behind at the noise, he saw the problem: the bike's owner had clamped the ace of spades to the frame, using a clothespin, so that the spokes clipped the playing card as the wheel turned. Making an insane racket. Fuck! The Rover loomed and . . .

Suddenly he was past it, heading out of the lot, home-free. Or so he thought, until he heard the engine turn over with a roar. Looking over his shoulder, he saw the car's headlights flash on, and a moment later the Rover lurched toward him.

He was out of the lot by now, and still picking up speed as he headed downhill, pedaling furiously. The road coiled around the mountain like a corkscrew, spiraling toward the plain below in what, for Lassiter, was a vortex of centrifugal force. He couldn't tell how fast he was going, but the ride was terrifying. Even so, the Rover was far enough behind that all he could see was the light from its headlamps. The car itself was halfway around the mountain, and—the good news—it wasn't gaining.

He touched his brakes from time to time, leaned into the curves and let gravity do the work, praying he wouldn't fly off the mountainside. His heart was pounding, the wind was stinging his eyes, and the playing card was hitting the spokes so quickly that it hummed.

Slowly, the plain began to rise, and he could tell that his descent was leveling off. Soon the ground would flatten out and gravity would start to work against him. He'd lose his speed, the Rover would be on him and—

Suddenly, he was there. On the flat. He came off the mountain like a bowling bowl, flying across the valley floor toward the little tree plantation that he'd seen earlier. It was less than half a mile ahead, but by the time he reached the clearing at its edge, he was pedaling hard and the Rover had him in its lights.

He beat the car to the clearing and pedaled even harder to reach the trees. Vanishing into the darkness of the woods, he coasted for as long as the bike would carry him. When it came to a rest, he let the bike fall and limped even deeper into the woods.

This was an unnaturally tidy place, a deciduous forest in which each of the trees was equidistant from every other, and about the same size. There was no underbrush, and all of the branches were trimmed to about seven feet above the ground.

Turning, he saw the Rover pull into the clearing with its headlights on high beam. It sat for a moment, facing the woods with its engine idling. Then the lights cut out, the doors flew open, and the Mattress and his partner emerged.

Lassiter stood where he was, incredulous at what was happening. He didn't belong here. He had too many connections to wind up hiding behind a tree in somebody else's forest. He had a world of information at his disposal, and corporations trying to buy him out. There were hard men on three continents who'd do anything to work for him—and here he was, scrambling through the woods, having just escaped from church on a bicycle.

Fuck, it's cold, he thought, and with this ankle . . . He could tell it was badly swollen. But it wasn't broken, and either his endorphins were kicking in or the sprain wasn't as bad as he thought. He could walk on it. All he had to do was stand the pain.

In the distance he could hear the river running, and he made for it, thinking the noise might give him cover. And if worse came to worst, he could always dive in, swim downstream, and—

Drown. The water temperature was probably less than fifty degrees.

Behind him, he heard a pile of twigs crunch, and turned. Camelface was coming toward him with his eyes on the ground, walking with the cocky, pigeon-toed gait of a predator. Lassiter stepped behind a tree, maybe thirty feet away, and waited. Suddenly, the man stopped, glanced to each side, and unzipped his fly. With a long sigh he turned against the trunk of a tree and began to relieve himself.

Lassiter could see the steam rising, and knew that the man was at his most vulnerable. If he was ever going to take him down, now was the time. With a deep breath, he stepped from behind the tree and rushed him from behind.

If he'd been able to move normally, he'd have covered the distance in four or five steps and cold-cocked the Italian with a roundhouse to the back of the head. Lassiter had a big swing, and if he'd done it right, Camelface would have gone down with his dick in his hands, facing the wrong way.

But it didn't work out. Lassiter's ankle was too weak to take him anywhere very quickly, and too painful to let it happen silently. By the time he covered the distance between them, the Italian had stepped to the side and turned. And then, suddenly and unexpectedly, Lassiter was on his stomach with his right cheek pressed against the ground. Camelface's right arm was hooked under his right shoulder, with the palm of the man's hand against the back of his neck. The man's left arm held Lassiter's left wrist as he used his head to bulldoze the American's face to the ground.

Lassiter twisted and thrashed, but he didn't know how to break the hold—which was anything but improvised. This guy's a wrestler, he thought, and a good one. He could hear the man's breathing, and smell his sweat.

For a long moment they lay like that, tensed against one another, struggling silently and without motion. Suddenly, the Italian relaxed his grip and let go of Lassiter's left wrist. He reached for something, and as he did, his weight lifted. Lassiter swung an elbow at him, to no effect, and the man grabbed the hair on the back of his head and jerked it backward. The moon flashed in front of Lassiter's eyes and he thought, *He's going to cut my throat.*

The Italian muttered something in a supercilious, almost seductive voice that told Lassiter he had about a second left to live. Almost growling, Lassiter clenched his teeth and lowered his head, resisting the hand pulling on his hair. His chin sank toward his neck and then, without warning, he threw his head backward, driving it into the Italian's face.

The man yelped and rolled away as Lassiter scrambled to his feet. From the clearing a plaintive voice called, " *'Cenzo?*" And then louder: " *'Cenzo!?*" The man in front of him climbed to his knees and shook his head to clear it. With the practiced step of a goalkeeper, Lassiter approached his head as if it were a soccer ball and, with all the malice he could muster, drove his instep into the man's mouth, half expecting to see his head take off for the moon. But Camelface surprised him. He rolled across the forest floor and came up spitting teeth, the knife still in his hand.

Slowly, he came toward Lassiter, holding the knife low, his eyes locked with the American's. There was nowhere for Lassiter to go, and nothing much that he could do. He held his ground until the Italian swung at him, slashing the forearm of his leather jacket. He jumped to the side, and again the Italian swung, a backhanded flick that threatened to empty Lassiter's stomach on the ground.

The voice from the clearing came at them again. " *'Cenzo? Smarrito o qui?*"

Camelface kept his eyes on Lassiter's, circling in for the kill.

"Dove sta, eh?"

It was too much. For an instant the Italian turned his face in irritation toward the voice, and when he did, Lassiter waded in, landing five punches in two seconds. Then he stepped back to let him fall—which turned out to be a mistake, because the Italian lunged at him instead.

The rush took Lassiter by surprise, but even so, he was able to hit Camelface again, and this time the knife flew out of his hands. Lassiter dove for it, came up with it, turned and was flattened. In less than a second he was on his stomach in a paralytic hold that immobilized him from the neck down. The only parts of his body that he could move were his arms, and those only weakly, flailing backward from the elbows in a sort of triceps curl.

But with the knife in his right hand, it was enough. He felt the point of the blade dig into something hard, and Camelface gasped. He pumped his arm again and again, hitting something each time, but never too deeply or hard. Finally Camelface screamed and rolled away. And, as he did, Lassiter swung in an arc with the knife, cutting something that felt like string. Then he rolled to his feet and stared.

The Italian was sitting on the ground, his hands in his lap and a look of surprise on his face. One of his eyes was a socket of gore where Lassiter had stuck him, and gouts of blood pumped from his throat like oil from a can.

Then he fell over and died without a word.

Lassiter got to his feet, panting, and started to limp away, heading toward the river. Fight or flight. In his case, both. He was sky high with adrenaline, and somehow it made him thirsty. But before he could reach the river, a powerful light swept through the woods in an arc, moving left to right, right to left.

Lassiter turned and stared.

The Rover had a searchlight next to the driver's window, and the Mattress was swinging it through the woods, looking for him and his partner. The light was penetrating enough that he would certainly have seen 'Cenzo if 'Cenzo had been on his feet. But he wasn't, and wouldn't ever be again. 'Cenzo was on his back, and as for Lassiter, he was moving at an angle to the searchlight, using the trees as screens.

The Mattress listened for a bit, then fixed the searchlight to point at a spot in the woods. That done, he pulled a handgun from the belt at the small of his back and crossed the clearing to the woods. Lassiter was surprised by his quickness. He didn't think a man that big could move that fast, or that gracefully, outside the NBA. And he was heading directly for his dead partner.

Lassiter didn't think about it. He just started walking, moving as quietly as he could toward the edge of the clearing. It took everything he had not to run, and when the Mattress cried " *'Cenzo!*" in a voice that was filled with shock, Lassiter was all tapped out. He gimped toward the Rover as fast as he could and, reaching it, jumped in, desperate to find the keys in the ignition or a gun on the seat.

He was disappointed.

A bellow came from the woods as Lassiter looked for the keys, pulling the visors down, opening the glove compartment and—

There was another bellow from the woods and, looking up, he saw the Mattress running toward him, lit up like a silo by the searchlight.

And then he glimpsed the keys, lying on the floor. Grabbing them, he tried one, and then another, and then a third, before the engine turned over. By that time the Mattress was at the edge of the clearing and beginning to raise his gun.

Lassiter ground the Rover into reverse and powered backwards toward the road. Even as the Mattress receded in his headlights, he began to fire, with a calmness that was terrible. The first shot took out one of the car's lights. The second put a spiderweb in the windshield, and the third ricocheted off the hood. Lassiter swung the car around and threw it into first as a fourth and fifth shot crashed into the chassis.

Head down, he leaned on the accelerator and roared away, imagining where the road must be. He stayed down for four or five seconds, until he heard a high-pitched noise dopplering toward him and saw the night begin to flicker. Raising his head above the dashboard, he felt his stomach drop as a truck roared directly at him, high beams flashing on and off, horn blaring.

Instinctively, Lassiter ripped the wheel to the right, and when the truck blew past, he let out a long, stuttering breath. Wrong side of the road, he thought.

So shoot me.

29

Todi or Marsciano?

The Rover idled at the stop sign, deep in the middle of nowhere. Left or right? North or south? Impulsively, Lassiter jerked the wheel to the left and headed toward Marsciano—wherever that was. As long as he didn't end up on the mountain road to Spoleto or, worse, heading back to Montecastello.

The town was a trap, a dead end—easy to defend, but hard to escape. And that is what he was doing: *escaping*. From the Mattress, certainly, but also from the police. The priest was dead, and Lassiter knew that by morning he would be a suspect. Nigel and Hugh would hear of Azetti's death, and they'd recall that he'd been on his way to meet the priest—after which their guest had disappeared, without collecting his belongings.

He could go to the police, of course, and explain everything: from Bepi to Camelface by way of Azetti. But driving to police headquarters in a stolen car, with blood on his clothes and ten words of Italian, did not seem like a good idea. At a minimum, he'd be answering questions for days—and, as he'd already decided before he jumped on the bike, he didn't like his chances in the local jail.

Arriving at another crossroads, he turned toward Perugia, heading north. Away from Umbria. Away from Rome. Away from anywhere he'd ever been before.

What he wanted was a telephone, and a place to clean up—which wasn't going to be easy. There were a lot of public lavatories in Italy, but there weren't many that Lassiter could walk into, looking the way he did, without people screaming. A gas station might be okay, but so far he hadn't passed one that was open.

He reached the outskirts of Perugia and followed a sign to the A-1,

Italy's autostrada. This was a toll road with no obvious speed limits, and full-service rest stops that straddled the highway. The rest stops had gas and groceries, telephones and rest rooms. The only problem with them was that they were brightly lit.

Not that he had much choice.

He was hurtling through the dark at ninety miles an hour when a gust of wind rocked the car and, moments later, it began to rain hard. Suddenly, he was driving blind, and yet he felt unnaturally calm—as if all the adrenaline had been drained out of him. Which, he supposed, was probably the case.

Checking the rearview mirror and seeing no lights, he pulled over to the side of the road and methodically worked all of the buttons and levers on the car until he found the one that operated the windshield wipers. Then he got back on the road.

The rest stops were not as numerous as in the U.S. It was midnight before he found one, a few miles south of Florence, and pulled into the parking lot. Most of the cars and trucks were parked as close to the building as they could get, so he drove the Rover to the outer reaches of the lot, where there was less chance of an encounter. Then he flicked on the overhead light and took a look at his face.

It was worse than he'd thought. His shirt collar was soaked with blood, though whether it was his own or someone else's, he couldn't tell. His cheeks were cross-hatched with cuts and scratches from the long fall down the mountain, and there was a gash on the side of his head that he didn't remember receiving. He touched it with his fingertips and quickly drew them away: it was still oozing, and the hair around it was stiff with blood.

Snapping off the interior light, he opened the door and stepped outside, into the freezing rain. A quick glance told him that his clothes were hopeless. There was blood on his jacket, blood on his shirt, blood on his pants. Azetti's blood, his own blood, the blood of the man he'd killed.

What to do? If he stood in the rain long enough, would it wash him clean? No, he thought, it would just give him pneumonia. So he did the best he could. He stripped down to his T-shirt, which was almost clean, and soaked his dress shirt in a puddle of oily water. Though the oil nauseated him, he used the shirt to scrub the blood from his face, and finally from his jacket. That done, he put the jacket on over his T-shirt and opened the hood of the car. The engine was remarkably clean, but there was enough sludge on it to cover the bloodstains on his pants with a mixture of grease and oil.

Then he limped across the parking lot in the rain, and climbed the stairs to the restaurant above the highway. Coming the other way, a businessman gave him an odd look but said nothing. Which was encouraging.

Inside, he came upon a smorgasbord of symbols, pointing toward various services. One depicted a stick man next to a stick woman, and he followed the arrow to a set of doors.

The men's room was vast and—*mirabile dictu*—replete with showers. Seeing him enter, the attendant looked him up and down and jerked his head to the back of the room. Then he raised his hand above his head and signed for showers, trickling his fingers down through the air.

He was a Turk, or maybe a Bulgarian, but stingy with towels, in any case. Lassiter wanted six. He offered two. Finally the attendant frowned and wrote numbers on a sheet of paper—so much for the shower, so much for each towel. He raised his eyebrows and pantomimed shaving, gesturing to a tray of items—packages of soap, disposable razors, aftershave, and something for the hair. Lassiter took what he needed and waited for the attendant to add up the bill. When he presented it, the American gave him twice the amount, and *grazie*.

The shower was sensational until he began scouring his cuts with soap. Then it hurt like hell. He scrubbed the blood out of his hair and washed his pants as best he could, rolling them up in towel after towel to squeeze the water out. In the end the pants were soaked and stained, but it was no longer obvious that the stain was blood.

When he left the men's room, he saw himself in the mirror and thought, *I look like the man who lost the war.*

It was after midnight, and if Roy was home, he was asleep, because the answering machine cut in after five rings. He pushed the card into the telephone and tried a second time. And again.

There was a clatter at the other end of the line, and then: "Dunwold."

"Roy, it's Joe Lassiter. You awake?"

"Mmmmn-hmnn."

"I've got a problem."

"Hunnh."

"Roy—seriously—wake up. I'm in trouble."

"Hunnh! Right. Wide awake! What sort of trouble?"

"There's, uh . . . some people are dead. I can't get to my passport. I'm kind of busted up. And . . ."

"*And?!* There's an 'and'?"

"I'm driving a stolen car."

"Otherwise?"

"Everything's fine."

"Right. And where would you be?"

"I'm on the autostrada, outside Florence. At a rest stop. I'm kind of banged up and . . . I need a way out. To France or Switzerland—someplace where I can go to the embassy and pick up a new passport. What day is it, anyway?"

A pause. "It is Sunday. It is very early Sunday morning."

"Okay. So, Monday, Tuesday at the latest—flaps up."

"You said some people were hurt?"

"I said they were dead."

"Yes, well: *very badly* hurt, then. And you're driving a . . . loaner?"

"Exactly."

"I don't mean to be lukewarm, but the embassy . . . isn't that a *bad* idea? I'm sure I could arrange documents in someone else's name—though by Tuesday? I dunno."

"I'll take my chances with the embassy. The important thing is for me to get out of Italy. *Soon.*"

"Yes, well—give me an hour—two would be better—and ring me back. If you don't get through, ring me up every hour on the hour after that. I'll have someone meet you with a car."

"One other thing."

"Dunwold's here, pen in hand. . . ."

"I'll need some clothes."

"My God! You're *nude?*"

"No, I'm not nude. My pants are wet!"

"My! We *have* had a time of it, haven't we?"

"Roy—just get me some fucking clothes."

"Right. I'll see what I can do."

—

He decided not to wait in the rest stop, but to move on, heading north. That's where the borders were, and if he stayed where he was, he'd just attract attention. Back on the highway, he cranked up the heat in the Rover, turned on the radio and hoped that his pants would dry.

He was five miles south of Bologna, traveling at eighty-five, when a white Alfa pulled even with him, slowed and kept pace. They rode like this for a mile or two until Lassiter, irritated, turned with a scowl toward the other driver—who turned out to be a policeman. Reflexively, Lassiter slowed, and so did the cop—who raised his forefinger and, with a look of expressionless gravity, pointed ahead to the side of the road.

It never occurred to Lassiter to run for it. He was too tired, he didn't know the road, and the likelihood was that he'd get himself killed. So he pulled over, onto the shoulder, and waited to surrender.

The Alfa pulled in behind him, and its driver got out with a hand on his holster. Lassiter kept his own hands in plain sight, on the steering wheel, looking straight ahead, until the policeman tapped on the window. Then he rolled it down.

The cop looked at him without expression, surveying the cuts on his face, the gash in his head, and the fractured windshield. Finally, he said, *"Patente,"* and held out his hand.

Reflexively, Lassiter reached for his wallet, and taking out his driver's license, gave it to the man.

"Grazie, signore," the policeman said, glancing at the license. *"Inglese?"* he asked.

Lassiter shook his head. "American."

The cop nodded, as if this explained something. *"Momento,"* he said, and walked slowly around to the front of the car. He squatted for a few moments, examining the shattered headlight, then got to his feet and ran his hand across the hood, pausing to finger each of the bullet holes. He studied the windshield for what seemed a long time, then made his way back to the driver's side of the car. It's all over, Lassiter thought, and reached for the door handle, thinking he might as well get out, put his hands on the hood, and spread 'em.

But to his amazement, the policeman took out a pad and began writing. When he was done, he tore the page from the book and handed it to Lassiter. "*Parle Italiano?*" he asked.

Lassiter shook his head, disbelieving. "Sorry," he said.

Once again the cop nodded. Then he pointed to the broken headlight, the shattered windshield, and the amount of the ticket. Which was 90,000 lire, or about sixty dollars.

Lassiter pulled 100,000 lire from his wallet and pushed it into the policeman's hands. "*Grazie,*" Lassiter said. "*Grazie!*"

"*Per favore,*" the policeman replied, and removing an oversized, zippered wallet from his coat, put Lassiter's bills inside. Then he extracted a 10,000 lire note and handed it to him.

"*Ecco la sue cambia, signore.*"

Lassiter nodded, wondering if it was a joke.

The policeman touched his cap. "*Buon viaggio,*" he said, and returned to his car. *Is this a great country, or what?* Lassiter thought.

He found the rest stop he was looking for less than ten minutes later. Roy answered on the third ring.

"Hang on, Joe, would you? I'm still on the other line." A moment later, he returned.

"All right, then," Roy said. "I just got something sorted out; tell me if it works. Found a fella in the import-export business. Libertarian, like. Takes olive oil into Slovenia, brings cigarettes out. All very legal—except for the part about taxes. Which he doesn't seem to pay. So he has his ways to cross the border, dun' 'e? Anyway, it won't be cheap, but you can ride along if you want. Excess baggage, like. Innarested?"

"Yeah. No! I mean—where the fuck is Slovenia?"

"Last time I looked, it was in Yugoslavia—upper left."

"How much does he want?"

"Two K—dollars. No checks."

"No problem. Except . . . I don't have that much."

"Not to worry. I'll fix it up on this end."

Lassiter breathed a sigh of relief. "Listen, Roy, if there's ever anything—"

"Oh?"

"Yeah . . ."

"Well, there *is* one thing . . ."

"What's that?"

"You could let me open a Paris office."

Lassiter laughed. "You're kidding," he said.

"I'm not. The work's there."

"We'll talk about it when I get back."

Roy's instructions were simple enough. Take the A-13 north to Padua, and change to the A-4, heading north. The rendezvous would be at kilometer 56, between Venice and Trieste, the only service area on that particular stretch of road. The man he was looking for would be wearing a blue jumpsuit with "Mario" stitched above the pocket. They'd meet at the coffee bar, where Lassiter was to stand with a copy of *Oggi* in front of him. "You can get it everywhere," Roy assured him.

Except you couldn't. The newsstand didn't open until seven, and his meeting was at six.

Lassiter checked the trash receptacles as discreetly as he could, but they'd been cleaned out by the maintenance staff. Barring a foray into town, there was nothing he could do but stand at the coffee bar reading a menu, and hope that Mario wasn't a stickler for tradecraft.

Lassiter was on his fourth cappuccino when a grizzled fireplug swaggered into the bar, wearing a workman's blue jumpsuit. He had a package in one hand, a cigarette in the corner of his mouth, and "Mario" on his chest. Coming up to the bar, he glanced at Lassiter, ordered an espresso, and looked away.

Lassiter gave it a minute and turned to him. "*Scusi,*" he said, exhausting his Italian. "*Scusi!*" Mario turned his back toward him and gave a little wave, as if to say, *Don't bother me.*

Lassiter thought about it for a moment, then tapped him on his shoulder. "You know where I can buy a copy of *Oggi?*" he asked. Mario shook his head. "Because what I'm looking for," he said, "is *Oggi!* The Italian newspaper? 'OH-GEE'? Ever heard of it?"

Mario turned to him slowly, with a look of angry amazement, and a question in his eyes that didn't need translating: *Are you out of your fucking mind?*

"It's too early, *signore*," the barman said, giving Lassiter a warning look. "You have to wait."

Lassiter shrugged as Mario tossed some money on the bar, picked up his package, and, without looking back, walked to the men's room. The American stayed where he was for a long minute, then followed the Italian back to the lavatory. Inside, Mario shoved the package into his arms and rolled his head in the direction of the stalls.

"You speak English?" Lassiter asked.

"No."

Interesting.

The package was wrapped in brown paper and neatly tied with twine. Inside was a jumpsuit, just like the one Mario wore, except that the name on the pocket was "Cesare." He stripped off his pants, put the jumpsuit on, and considered the result. His legs were three inches too long, and the tassel loafers that he wore were about as appropriate as a pith helmet at the opera. Still, it was a uniform, and any uniform was a good disguise. A FedEx guy, a nurse, a cop—in this case, a Smurf. People saw the uniform and never looked at the face. Anyway, Lassiter thought, the jumpsuit was a lot more comfortable than his pants—which he stuffed in the trash. At least the jumpsuit was dry.

Mario's truck was a dwarf semi, bigger than a pickup or a step van, but smaller than anything else you'd see on an American road. And it was wired for sound, with fifty-watt speakers in the doors.

Unfortunately, Mario's taste in music ran to Europop, and very old rock and roll. Worse, he was a singer, though Lassiter had to admit that he had every breath and intonation—every hesitation—down.

"All the little birds on Jay-bird Street . . ."

Someone was shaking his arm. He came to a semblance of consciousness in the front seat of the truck, holding his leather jacket in his lap. His face stung. His ankle throbbed, his head hurt, and his ribs were raw. Otherwise, he was fine, except for the fog he was in.

"*Attenzione!*" The voice made him jump. He turned.

Oh yeah, Mario. In the seat next to him, the little guy in the blue jumpsuit gave him a serious look and pressed a finger to his lips. "*Niente*," he said, in case Lassiter didn't get the message.

The radio was playing "The Wanderer."

"Go 'round and 'round and 'round . . ."

A sign at the side of the road told him they were near Gorizia, wherever that was. Soon afterward, they pulled up at a border crossing, where there was yet another sign: SANT' ANDREA ESTE. A uniformed man emerged from a small wooden building, smiled, and waved them on.

They drove slowly. Mario tapped his arm again and, steering with his knees, cocked his head, put his palms together, and briefly shut his eyes. Then he made a snoring sound, sat up, and pointed decisively at Lassiter.

He got it.

The American leaned against the door, relaxed his muscles, and closed his eyes. Mostly. They passed a sign that read N. GORICA, and soon afterward came upon a second building. Cinder block, this time.

A man in a gray uniform emerged, and gestured for Mario to come inside. It was obvious that he wanted both of them to get out of the truck, but Mario shook his head and, with a pitying look, nodded toward the apparently sleeping Lassiter. A string of Italian followed, and finally the guard shook his head and shrugged. With a *grazie*, Mario jumped from the truck and followed the other man into the building. Lassiter watched through narrowly parted eyelids as Mario joined several other men, sitting at a table, playing cards.

It was strange, listening to them talk without understanding a word—it made him alert to every nuance and mannerism, so that the half-glimpsed scene in front of him seemed unusually vivid and complex. What was that supposed to mean? And that! And that!

This went on for twenty minutes, as Mario drank, first, a cup of coffee, and then an aperitif.

And then another.

Lassiter gritted his teeth as the men joked and smoked. From time to time paroxysms of laughter burst from the building. Finally, they all stood up and, one by one, exchanged *abrazos*. Moments later Mario emerged, climbed into the truck, and, with a wink, drove off.

A sign announced that they were in Slovenia. Seeing it, Lassiter gave Mario the thumbs-up. Mario grinned and gave a little shrug. Nothing to it.

The road ran beside a narrow river that cut through a valley in the mountains. There were orchards and vineyards on either side, and limestone outcroppings everywhere. An inch of fresh snow lay on the ground, and everything seemed prosperous and in good repair. At the crossroads there were signs for places Lassiter couldn't pronounce: Ajdovscina, Postojna, Vrhnika, Kranj. The only place he'd ever heard of was their destination, Ljubljana, the capital.

It took them an hour and a half to reach it, but when they did, it was all at once. There were no suburbs, just a beautiful city in the middle of a beautiful country. Mario pulled to a stop in front of the railroad station and turned to Lassiter. "Loob-yana," he said. It was the first time the American had ever heard the name pronounced.

Lassiter shook his hand and was about to climb out when the Italian touched his sleeve. Pinching the fabric of the jumpsuit between his thumb and forefinger, he said something that obviously translated as "Give it back." With a look of surprise, Lassiter turned his palms to the roof. Then he crossed his hands in his lap and looked frantically from side to side.

The light dawned—no pants. With a grin, Mario put the truck back into gear and drove them to what turned out to be a Sunday market in the oldest part of town. Though most of the stalls sold vegetables and food, there were a few that sold clothes. Lassiter found a pair of jeans in his size, and a T-shirt with the words: I ♥ Ljubljana.

He changed clothes in the back of the truck and, after shaking hands with Mario, got out at the Grand Hotel. "*Arrivederci,*" Lassiter said.

"Catch you later," Mario replied and, with a grin, pulled away from the curb.

The desk clerk was a bald man with a handlebar mustache and a bright red nose. Lassiter asked for a room, and the man nodded crisply. "Passport?"

The American shook his head. "Sorry," he said. "I have to get a new one in the morning."

The clerk looked at his face and frowned with concern. "You have been in a crash?" he asked, patting his fingertips gingerly against his own cheeks. "In your car?"

It sounded good to Lassiter. "Yeah—"

"Ohhhh," the man crooned. "I am so *sorry* for you. Would you like a doctor?"

Lassiter shook his head. "No, I'm going back to the States tomorrow. All I need right now is some rest."

"Of course," the clerk said, and gave him a registration card to fill out.

In the morning Lassiter found a men's store in the old part of town, where he bought an Italian suit and everything else he needed. While the trousers were being taken in for length, he breakfasted on coffee and croissants, read the *Herald Tribune*, and bought a cane at the local pharmacy. Then he went back for the suit and other clothes that he'd bought.

It was barely noon when he returned to the hotel. Changing quickly, he went out again to have some passport pictures made. Then he walked to the American embassy on Prazakova Street and lied through his teeth. He'd gone to the casino last night. There'd been a girl. And then an argument with one of the locals. When he woke up, he was back at his hotel, but his passport was missing—and it looked to him as if he'd lost a fight. (Though he didn't remember being in a fight, not really.)

The clerk looked about twenty-three, and had "Bennington" written all over her. "Do you think it was stolen?" she asked.

"I don't know," Lassiter said. "The night's kinda hazy."

"Well . . . did you report it to the police?"

"No."

"Why not?"

"Because I don't think my wife would understand."

"Oh."

To his surprise, he was taken at his word. And to his relief, there was nothing in the embassy's computers to suggest that anyone in Italy was looking for a killer tourist named Joseph Lassiter. In the end, no alarms went off. The red tape was next to nothing, and within an hour he had a temporary passport, good for a year.

And so it went. He found an Air Adria flight that took him to Paris that same afternoon. There, a bus carried him from Orly Airport to Charles de Gaulle, where he boarded a United flight for Washington. Easing himself into a seat in the First Class cabin, he asked the flight attendant for a Bloody Mary, sat back and closed his eyes.

Listening to the sounds around him, it was almost as if he was already back in the U.S. of A. The flight attendants were so wonderfully midwestern that Lassiter wanted to tip them just for talking.

Finally, the 747 rumbled into position on the runway, revved its engines to a roar, and rolled toward the horizon. Moments later they were airborne, climbing over the Bois de Boulogne. The landing gear thumped. The seat belt sign pinged off. And one of the flight attendants came by with his Bloody Mary.

"Migosh," she said, setting the drink on his tray, "what happened to you?"

"Actually," Lassiter said, "I fell off a cliff."

She gave him a radiant smile, a bag of peanuts, and a playful slap on the forearm. "Oh, you!" she said.

"No—really."

"Well, how did you do that?" she asked, taking the seat beside him and crossing her legs with a zip of static from her panty hose.

Lassiter shrugged. "It was easy," he said. "I just let go." Then he tapped the rim of his glass against the plastic window and toasted Roy Dunwold. "To the wild blue yonder," he said.

"Clink!" she riposted. "Clink clink!"

30

"Very bad storm, sir! Very bad. A true blizzard!"

"Yeah, I can see that," Lassiter said, hoping that Freddy had remembered to have his driveway plowed. "It must have been something."

"Oh, yes, sir! I don't mind telling you! I am writing home about 'the Storm of 'Ninety-six.'"

"And where's that?" Lassiter asked, gazing out at the drifts of snow, glowing in the moonlight.

"What, sir?"

"Home."

"Oh—Pindi, sir. But that is what the television people call it, you know: 'the Storm of 'Ninety-six.' Very dramatic."

"You want to go left up here."

"May I ask, sir? Have you traveled far?"

"Italy."

The driver nodded. "And did they rob you?"

Lassiter shook his head. "No. They did everything else, but they didn't rob me."

"Then I congratulate you."

"For what?"

"For traveling so light! Even as an immigrant—"

"Left at the corner."

"Very good—even as an immigrant, I brought many more things to America. But I can see that you practice nonattachment, sir—an extra jacket. No more! You are very wise."

"Thank you. I am very unattached."

"I can see that, sir."

"It's the driveway on the right."

"The very big house?"

"That's it."

"My goodness! It is so modern—"

"Thanks."

"I am reminded of Leonard Nimoy."

Lassiter gave the driver two twenties, declined a receipt, and told him to keep the change. With a little wave, he turned and climbed the steps to the front door.

And then he hesitated. The house was dark, completely dark—which wasn't the way he'd left it. Whenever he traveled, he made a point of leaving on a light or two, not so much to discourage burglars as to welcome himself home. But the only light that he could see was the red diode on the alarm system, winking steadily in an aluminum panel next to the door.

At least the alarm's on, Lassiter thought, recalling that it came equipped with a battery that kicked in whenever there was a power failure.

With his house and office protected by state-of-the-art security systems, Lassiter knew that leaving a key outside was truly stupid. "You don't know how easy those keys are to find," he'd been told. "They use metal detectors, they surveil places. . . ."

So Lassiter didn't tell anybody about the key, but he was glad he kept it there. The key wouldn't do anybody much good, in his opinion, not without the alarm code. He trudged through snow that was almost up to his hips and then ducked under the deck. He kept the key in one of the joists, where it was impossible to see and could be located only by touch. And there it was. Stepping inside, he groped for the keypad that controlled the alarm and tapped in the code that turned it off.

Then he closed the door behind him and stood in the darkness, listening to the house. After Naples he'd become more cautious about his entrances. But there was no one, and nothing. Just the soft light of the snow, seeping through the windows. He tried the light switch on the wall, but it wasn't working. Neither were the lights in the hall—and now that he thought about it, the heat was off as well.

Lassiter sighed. The temperature in the house was only forty-five degrees or thereabouts, but even so, he wouldn't have to go to a hotel.

There was a fire laid in the study, and a leather sofa that pulled out into a bed. He'd sleep there, and if the lights were off in the morning, he'd move to the Willard until they were fixed.

The phone still worked, of course, and Lassiter used it to report the power outage. The woman who answered laughed at the report and asked, "Where have *you* been? There hasn't been any power in McLean for three days! But we should have it back pretty soon."

And so they did.

When Lassiter awoke, the fire was out, but the heat was on, and the house had gone from cold to cool. Padding across the carpet to the bath, he found enough hot water to take a lukewarm shower, and dressed quickly. He was thinking that he had a lot to do at the office, when he heard it—a low hum on the way out of his study.

The computer was on. Sometime during the night, when the electricity was restored, it must have rebooted. Lassiter went to the desk, where the monitor was glowing, and shut it off. Then he thought about it.

If the computer rebooted, it must have been on when the power went off—three days ago. Which meant one of two things: either he'd forgotten to turn off the computer when he'd left for Italy, nearly a month ago, or someone had broken in.

"I didn't leave the computer on," Lassiter muttered. "I never do." Which meant that someone had entered the house while he was gone. But that didn't make sense, either. The alarm was working, and it was a good one. If someone had managed to bypass it, he'd have to be a pro. And yet, Lassiter thought, glancing around, nothing had been taken. There was a $2,000 Breitling wristwatch sitting on his dresser. The stereo was intact, and the liquor was untouched. In a corner of the study a small glass cabinet sat undisturbed, holding first editions valued at more than $25,000. The lithographs in the living room were worth even more.

And yet, none of it had been touched. Except the computer.

Lassiter sat down in front of the machine and hit the Enter key three or four times. The *autoexec.bat* file went through its routine until a word appeared in the middle of the screen: *Password?*

This was, in fact, not a word at all, but a combination of case-sensitive letters, numbers, and punctuation marks—gibberish—that was unguessable precisely because it was neither a word nor a phrase. Until the combination was keyed into the computer, the hard disc remained inaccessible: no operations were possible, and no information could be obtained. Still . . . a very talented someone had bypassed the security alarm and gone directly to the computer. How likely was it that the password had stopped him? Lassiter didn't know. But that's what passwords are for, he told himself: to keep people out. Right, he replied, and that's what alarms are for, too.

Reaching down to where the CPU sat on the floor, Lassiter felt for the On/Off switch. It took him a second to find it, and looking down he saw why: the computer had been moved—not far, but definitely. There was an indentation in the rug where the machine had rested for more than year. Now it sat about an inch away.

You're hallucinating, he told himself. You probably left it on when you went to Italy. That would explain everything.

Except, of course, it wasn't true. And he knew it wasn't true.

"Hey, Joe—"

"What happened to *you*?!"

"Welcome back, Mr. Lassiter!"

"Good to see you again."

There were exclamations and waves, smiles and looks of real solicitude as Lassiter made his way past the cubicles and watercooler to the sanctuary of his own office. Closing the door behind him, he tossed his coat and cane onto the couch, picked up the intercom, and told his secretary, "See if Murray Fremaux's around."

"You mean the computer guy?"

"Yeah."

"I'll check, but you've got about fifty calls—"

"That's okay—just get Murray in here."

Two minutes later Murray came into the office with a cup of coffee in his hand and a worried look in his eyes.

"What's the matter?" Lassiter asked.

"I've never been in your office before."

"So? Sit down."

"Okay, but . . ."

"What?"

"I don't know . . . I mean, am I going to be fired?"

"No."

"Good," Murray replied, flopping into a chair. "I just bought a Camry."

"Congratulations. Now listen: I think someone broke into my house while I was out of the country."

Murray frowned. "I thought you had an alarm."

"I do. They bypassed it."

"*Bypassed* it?" Murray asked.

"Yeah."

Murray thought about that for a moment, and asked, "They take anything?"

"No. Nothing I could see. But . . . I was thinking, maybe they got into the computer."

Murray nodded. "Could be," he said.

"Thing is—I don't see how they could have gotten into anything. I mean, there's a password—"

"Passwords suck."

"—and anything that's really sensitive is encrypted."

Murray looked skeptical. "What do you use?"

"N-cipher."

"Good program," Murray said.

"So . . . they didn't get anything. Right?"

A shrug. "I don't know. Did you notice anything else?"

Lassiter thought. "Not really," he said. "Well . . ."

"What?"

"I think . . . maybe they moved the computer."

"Why do you think that?" Murray asked.

"Because . . . well, because it *was* moved—I went to turn it off, and it was a couple of inches away—I mean, from where it usually is."

Murray nodded again, and said, "Sounds like they took you to the cleaners."

"What!?"

"My guess is: they took the hard drive out of the case. Copied the contents, and put it back. If that's what they did, the password was useless. It's in the boot sector."

"And the encrypted files—"

With a regretful look, Murray shook his head. "Depends. Where'd you keep your key—on a floppy or the hard disc?"

"Hard disc."

Murray winced. "Big mistake," he said.

"So they got everything—"

"Probably."

Lassiter groaned. He was thinking of the messages he'd sent from Montecastello, listing the women who'd had procedures at the Clinica Baresi, tasking Judy to contact Riordan, and so on. Fortunately, those messages had been sent from his laptop—so at least they were safe.

"You look relieved," Murray said.

Lassiter nodded. "I sent some E-mail from Italy. It was pretty sensitive."

Murray averted his eyes.

"What?!" Lassiter asked. "What's the matter?"

Murray shook his head. "They probably got those, too."

"What? How? That's impossible."

"Not really. Let me ask you a question. When you log on to the Internet, what do you do?"

Lassiter shrugged. "Nothing much. It's all automatic. Basically, I just hit Alt-E. The computer does the rest."

Murray nodded. "That's what I thought. You use an automatic log-on procedure—a macro, right?—with your password built in."

"So what?"

"So whoever broke into your house has that, too."

Lassiter shrugged. "I'll just change the password."

"Good idea," Murray said, instantly regretting the sarcasm. "But it only works one way. By now they've gotten at your old E-mail—no matter what computer you used."

Lassiter stared at him.

"It's archived on your local Internet server," Murray explained. "Anyone who's got the password can get into your old messages."

Lassiter leaned back in his chair and closed his eyes. So that's how they knew, he thought. That's how they knew where he was. In Montecastello. At the Aquila. After a moment he opened his eyes again. "Thanks," he said, "you've been a big help."

Murray clambered out of the chair and shrugged. "Sorry," he said, and turned to leave.

"Not your fault. But Murray . . ."

"Yes, sir?"

"When you go by Judy's office, ask her to see me for a second, would you?"

Murray hesitated in the doorway. "Judy?" he asked.

Lassiter looked up from his desk. "Yeah. Judy Rifkin. She's your boss."

Murray gulped. "I don't think she's in."

Lassiter looked puzzled. "Why not?" He looked at his watch: ten-thirty.

"I don't think she gets out of the hospital until this afternoon."

"*What* hospital?"

"I think it's Sibley."

Lassiter looked blank.

"She had an accident," Murray said.

"What accident?"

Murray rolled his eyes. "There was some kind of celebration—I don't know what it was about. But . . . *apparently*, she was opening a bottle of champagne . . . and . . . she shot herself in the eye."

Lassiter was dumbfounded. "With what?"

"The cork."

"You're kidding."

"Uh-uh. I know what you're thinking: it's the ultimate yuppie injury, but . . . I guess it was actually pretty serious. Mike said they had to sedate her so she wouldn't move her eye. They were worried about the retina."

Lassiter was nonplussed. "When *was* this?"

"Friday night," Murray said, and with a little wave, closed the door behind him.

Lassiter remained where he was, looking at the objects on his desk, trying to decide what to throw. Not the netsuke, not the scarabs—he liked them too much. Maybe the stapler, or the tape dispenser. Or the scissors! The scissors might actually stick.

In the end he didn't throw anything. He got to his feet and, forgetting his cane, limped down the hallway to Freddy's cubicle, a six-by-six-foot box dominated by a huge poster of Fritz Lang's *Metropolis*.

"Hey, boss! Welcome back!"

"Thanks," Lassiter said, dragging a chair over to Freddy's desk. "You got a minute?"

Freddy sat back, crossed his arms, and waited.

"There's something I want you to do. Right away."

"You heard about Judy?"

Lassiter nodded. "Yeah, that's why I'm here. I sent her a memo over the weekend. I guess she didn't get it."

"I guess you're right."

"Murray knows how to get at everything. Tell him I want him to download a two-page memo that I sent her. . . ." Lassiter calculated. "It would have been Friday night, your time."

"Okay."

"When you get it, I want you to drop whatever you're doing. There's basically two things: a list of women—I think there's thirteen—who have to be contacted right away. And a pull-together on a scientist named Baresi—books, articles, whatever you can find."

Freddy nodded. "Got it. But . . . which is more important?"

"The women."

"I'll ask the research guys to do the pull-together, and check out the women myself."

Lassiter thanked him, and walked back to his office. He wanted to call Judy, but before he did that, he needed to talk to Riordan. And the Aquila.

He left a message on Riordan's voice mail asking the detective to call him as soon as he could, and then placed a call to the pensione in Montecastello.

"*Pronto!*"

"Hugh?"

"No. This is Nigel."

"Nigel! It's Joe Lassiter."

"Oh." There was a long pause. "How *are* you?"

"A little banged up, actually."

"Yes, well, we've had rather a time of it ourselves."

"I know."

"You've heard about Father Azetti?"

Lassiter nodded, forgetting that Nigel couldn't see him. "I was the one who found him in the church."

"Well, they've found a second victim—"

"In the woods. Below the town."

The pause was even longer this time. Finally, Nigel said, "That's right."

"He wasn't a victim," Lassiter said. "He tried to kill me. But, look: I'm going to get in touch with the Italian embassy, give them a statement—"

"Before you do that . . . I think you may want to speak with a lawyer."

"Why's that?" Lassiter asked.

"Well, because . . . when the man was found in the woods . . . Hugh and I were certain he must be you. I mean, you *did* say you were going to see Azetti, and all. And then, of course, we heard that a body had been found. And when you didn't return to the pensione . . . I'm afraid we went to the police."

"Don't worry about it."

"I can't tell you how relieved we were . . . I mean, when we saw it was someone else. But now . . . I think the police want you to help them with their inquiries."

"I'm not surprised," Lassiter said as line two began to blink. "Hold on for a second." He punched the Hold button and switched to line two. "Lassiter."

"Joe! It's Jack!"

"I'll get right back to you," Lassiter said, and returned to line one. "Look, Nigel, I gotta take this call. Tell the police I'll be in touch with the embassy. In Washington. And while you're there, I think it might be a good idea for you to give the police your guest register."

"The register? But . . . why?"

"Because the people who killed Azetti may come after it. You'll be safer this way."

"Very well. I'll take your advice."

"Gotta go," Lassiter said, and hit line two. "Hi."

"I got some news," Riordan said.

"Good or bad?"

"Good as it gets. We got your boy."

"Who's 'my boy'?"

"Grimaldi."

"What?!"

"We're picking him up in an hour. You want to ride along?"

Twenty minutes later Lassiter was sitting next to Riordan in the detective's unmarked Crown Victoria, heading north on the Beltway toward

Maryland. A red light revolved on the dashboard as the car cruised just below ninety miles per hour.

"When we get back to the office," Lassiter said, "I've got a list of names for you."

"Oh, yeah? What kinda list?"

"A hit list. Women and children. You're gonna want to contact the local police, get 'em in protective custody."

Riordan reached into his jacket pocket and pulled out a photograph. "Look at this," he said, handing it to Lassiter.

It was a picture of Grimaldi, standing on the porch of an old Victorian house. Though one side of his face was a blur of scar tissue, it was clearly him. Lassiter smiled. "Where'd you get it?" he asked.

"Surveillance shot. Long lens. You can see the grain. FBI took it, day before yesterday."

"How'd they find him?"

"Remember the nurse?"

"Yeah."

"Turns out—where she lives? It's a group house, north of Frederick, not far from Emmitsburg."

" 'A group house,' huh? Let me guess—"

"You don't have to. Just say 'I told you so' and leave it at that."

"So what is it? A monastery?"

"I don't know what they call it. Some kinda retreat. Basically, it's just a big house in the boondocks."

"And it's Umbra Domini?"

"Yeah. According to the assessor's office, the place is owned by Umbra Domini."

Lassiter sat back with a sigh, and the two of them rode in silence for another six or seven miles. Finally, he couldn't help himself. "Well," Lassiter said, turning to Riordan, "I told you so."

Twenty minutes later, they turned the corner of a tree-lined street on the west side of Emmitsburg, where five unmarked cars, an ambulance, and a communications van waited behind a line of yellow tape. A second van, matte-black and heavily armored, sat in the middle of the street, while a helicopter hovered overhead, beating the air with its rotors. Nearby, a pair of Emmitsburg policemen joked with a gang of kids on BMX bicycles.

The focal point of everyone's attention was a large Victorian house, set in a clearing amid winter gardens and leafless oaks. On the lawn in front of the house, surrounded by snow, was a statue of the Virgin Mary, holding the baby Jesus in her arms.

Riordan parked at the curb and, together with Lassiter, walked over to the communications van. An earnest-looking man in a blue windbreaker was sitting in the front seat with the door open, talking on a cellular phone. Seeing Riordan, he raised his chin in silent hello. A dozen other men stood in groups around the van, waiting for something to happen. All of them were wearing windbreakers with FBI on the back.

"That's Drabowsky," Riordan said. "He's like the number-two guy in the Washington field office."

"What happened to 'Derek'?"

Riordan narrowed his eyes and faked a double take. "You've got a good memory," he said.

"So?"

"I don't know. He was reassigned, or something. Now I got Drabowsky. He's a lot more senior."

"I'm sure he is, but what's he doing here?"

"Well, offhand, I'd say he's running the show."

"I can see that, but *why?*"

"Armed carjacking. Bureau's got jurisdiction."

"I don't mean that. What I'm wondering is: since when does someone like him make apprehensions?"

Before Riordan could answer, Drabowsky tossed the phone onto the seat beside him, swung his feet out of the van, and jumped down.

"Okay, lissen up!" he said, clapping his hands to get the agents' attention. "They're coming out in three minutes! Eight people! One by one! That's eight! *Ocho!* Everybody got that?" The agents murmured assent. "Once they're out, LaBrasca and Seldes will ID them in the van. When I give the go-ahead, and *only* then . . . the Special Unit's going to enter the house and clear it, room by room. When that's done, we'll execute the search. Any questions?" Drabowsky looked around. "Okay—one other thing. Remember! This isn't a crack house. It's a religious community! Only one of the people in there is accused of a crime—so keep your cool, gentlemen! Okay? All right! Let's go!"

The agents suddenly came alive, taking up positions behind the cars and other vehicles, while Drabowsky strolled over to shake hands with Riordan. "Nice of you to stop by," he said.

Riordan shrugged. "I was in the neighborhood. Anyway, I want you to meet someone. Joe Lassiter—Tom Drabowsky."

Drabowsky frowned, but shook hands.

"Joe's sister was—" Riordan began.

"I know," Drabowsky said. "You aren't going to do anything that would make the news, are you?"

Lassiter shook his head. "No. I just wanta see the sonofabitch."

"Good, because—"

"Whoops!" Riordan said, with a nod toward the house. "Here we go!"

The door to the house swung open and a middle-aged woman stepped out with her hands on top of her head. She was followed by a kid of college age, who couldn't help smirking, and an old man, pushing an aluminum walker. One by one the occupants of the house filed up the garden path to the street, where FBI agents took each of them by the arm and led them to the back of a van, there to be ID'd.

"There she is," Riordan whispered as the nurse walked out, keeping her eyes on the ground. Then a stocky Korean, closely followed by a postal worker in full uniform, a well-dressed Hispanic man, and a young woman in a smock.

And then, no one.

"Where is he?" Lassiter asked, after a long, edgy minute.

Riordan stamped his feet in the cold and shook his head. "I don't know," he said, glancing toward Drabowsky, who was speaking into a portable phone with quiet intensity. Suddenly, there was movement at the side of the house, as three FBI agents ran in a crouch toward the front and back doors, ducking under the windows. One by one they edged their way into the house, triggering a long and pregnant silence on the street.

Lassiter expected to hear a fusillade of shots. But there was nothing. One minute passed, and then another. Then a third. Finally, the agents came out with a collective shrug, shaking their heads as they holstered their guns. "Okay," Drabowsky called out, "let's take a look around." Immediately, he and two other agents began walking up the path to the house.

Lassiter turned to Riordan. "I thought Grimaldi was supposed to be inside," he said.

"So did I," Riordan replied.

"They took a picture of him. He was right over there."

"I know."

"So what the fuck?!"

"I don't know!"

Together, Lassiter and Riordan followed Drabowsky up the path. As they mounted the front steps, an FBI agent stepped in their way. "You can't go in there," he said.

Riordan brushed past him, flashing his ID. "Fairfax police. It's our case." Reluctantly, the agent stepped aside.

The scene inside the house was one of determined simplicity. The walls were white and mostly empty, the hardwood floors polished to a high sheen. There was no television or stereo that Lassiter could see, and very little furniture—all of it old. The only "ornaments" were crucifixes above each of the doors, and an eight-by-ten framed photograph of Silvio della Torre, smiling benignly from one of the walls in each of the rooms.

The common areas of the house were functionally spartan, and of very little interest. The dining room held a long, pine table with wooden benches on either side—and nothing else. In the kitchen, cabbage soup simmered atop a porcelain stove that had seen much better days. The living room held eight straight-back chairs, arranged in a circle, as if the room was dedicated to group discussions—which, in fact, it probably was.

Most of the FBI agents were in the bedrooms, searching through drawers. Lassiter and Riordan went from one room to another, looking for Drabowsky. Finally, they found him.

He was going through a dresser in a room whose only other furniture was a mattress and a standing lamp. There was a jar of Silvadene next to the mattress, and a wastepaper basket half full of gauze bandages.

"This is his room," Lassiter said, picking up a copy of *L'Osservatore Romano*. "He was here."

Drabowsky looked over his shoulder. "We missed him," he said.

"Bad luck," Riordan replied.

"You should see the bathroom down the hall," Drabowsky

remarked. "It's like a field hospital. She was taking real good care of him."

"Can I ask a question?" Lassiter said.

Drabowsky looked at him. Shrugged.

"How the fuck did he get away?"

Drabowsky shook his head. "There's no need for foul language," he said primly.

"He was under surveillance!" Lassiter came back. "How the fuck does he get away with you guys sittin' on his doorstep—"

"He wasn't under surveillance," Drabowsky replied.

"Bullshit!" Riordan exclaimed.

"I saw the picture!" Lassiter said.

"We terminated the surveillance last night."

Riordan gaped. "You *what*?"

"Whose fuckin' idea was that?" Lassiter asked.

"Mine," Drabowsky answered.

Lassiter and Riordan exchanged glances.

Riordan shook his head. "Tom—for chrissake—why did *that* seem like a good idea?"

"Because it's a rural area!" Drabowsky shouted. "Maybe you noticed. We had half a dozen people coming and going out of the house, and the van's sitting outside like a spaceship! I didn't want to spook him, okay?"

" '*Okay*'? No, it's not 'okay.' The sonofabitch took off," Lassiter said.

"It would *seem*," Drabowsky replied.

Lassiter turned on his heel and walked out the door, with Riordan close behind. "This is wrong," Lassiter muttered. "Something about this is really fucked."

"I know what you're saying."

"It doesn't even make sense!"

"I know."

"I mean: so *what* if Grimaldi made the surveillance? What's he gonna do—*dig* his way out?"

"I don't know. I don't know what was on their minds!"

As they left the house, striding down the path to where the cars and vans were waiting, Lassiter saw the nurse talking to an FBI agent. Her hands were cuffed, but she was smiling—beatifically—as she answered his questions.

Lassiter hesitated.

"Don't," Riordan said.

But Lassiter couldn't help himself. He walked up to her, grabbed her by the arm and spun her around.

"Your friend butchered my family. You know that, don't you? Killed them in their sleep. Real tough guy—"

"Hey," the G-man yelped, pulling Lassiter's hand away. "Hey hey hey! That's enough of that."

Juliette looked up at him with soulful brown eyes. "I'm sorry," she said. "But . . . what did you expect?"

Suddenly, Riordan waded in like an Irish Mahatma Gandhi, bouncing his palms in the air. "C'mon! C'mon! Let's go! No problem!" Taking Lassiter by the arm, he pulled him away from the nurse and led him toward the Crown Victoria.

"What did I *expect?*" Lassiter muttered. "What did I fucking *expect?!*"

It was Thursday before Judy returned to the office, and when she did, she wore a black patch over her left eye.

"It's over," she said, closing the door behind her.

Lassiter looked up. "What? Your career as an umpire?"

Judy stopped and cocked her head: "No," she said, "your career as a P.I."

Lassiter leaned back in his chair. "Oh?" he said, hating himself for trying to sound so cool and disinterested.

"Yeah. That's what I was celebrating. We've got a deal. In principle, anyway." She dropped into a chair and crossed her legs. "As soon as their lawyers draw up the papers and our lawyers look 'em over— you're outta here."

"Good. How's the eye?"

"The eye's gonna be fine. You interested in how much you're getting—or should I just give you what's fair and keep the rest?"

"No," Lassiter said with a laugh. "I'm actually pretty interested."

"I thought you might be. Bottom line? Eighteen five."

"*Really!?*"

"Of which you get to keep twelve, with the rest going to minority shareholders."

"Such as you."

"Such as me. And Leo. And Dunwold. And everybody else. Even Freddy's got a share or two. Enough to buy a car, anyway."

"It's called profit-sharing."

"I know what it's called—"

The interoffice phone rang, and Lassiter answered with a soft "Yeah . . ." He listened for a moment, then put his hand over the mouthpiece. "Speak of the devil," he said. And then, "All right, send him in."

Judy gave him a quizzical look.

"It's Freddy—do you mind?"

"No," Judy said, starting to get up, "I'll come back."

Lassiter shook his head. "Stay where you are. This will only take a second. I want to talk to you about how we break the news."

There was a short knock on the door, and Freddy came in, looking glum. Seeing Judy, he said, "Hey, Jude—I heard about the accident. Glad you're okay." Then he turned to Lassiter. "I've been running those names you gave me—"

"You can probably wrap that up. I've already given the list to Jack Riordan."

Freddy shook his head. "I'm all done."

"You're *done?*'"

"Yeah, pretty much."

"And . . . ?"

"They're dead."

Lassiter looked at him for a long moment, as Judy's gaze shifted from one man to the other. Finally, Lassiter said, "What?"

Freddy gulped. "I'm sorry, but . . . what I said was: they're all dead."

31

Lassiter was speechless. They're all *dead*?

Well, then, he thought, it's over. There's nothing left to do, and in the end there was never any point to it at all.

The pensione's guest book, and the list it generated, had led him to hope that some of the women and children might still be alive. If they were, his investigation might have served a larger purpose than revenge, or the satisfaction of his own morbid curiosity. So long as there were survivors, he could *save* them. And they, in turn, could help him to discover why Kathy and Brandon had been killed.

But now . . . there was no one, and the realization left him stranded and cut off, with nowhere to go.

The truth is, every one of us is staked out and helpless, Lassiter thought. Cars crash, planes fall, disease spreads, and innocents are caught in the cross fire. It's a wind-shear, guinea-worm kind of world—with an undertow. That's why people prayed, took vitamins, and crossed themselves. It's why they knocked on wood and wrote letters to the editor. It was all a way of maintaining the illusion that life was fair, or if not fair, somehow survivable—you could protect yourself and the ones you loved if you took the right precautions, or had the right mojo. Except, you couldn't. Because the vitamins didn't work, the letters went unread, and no One seemed to be listening to the prayers.

Why Kathy? Why Brandon? *Why not?*

"Uhhh . . . Joe?" Freddy was looking at him. "You okay?"

"Yeah," Lassiter said. "Sorry. I was just . . . surprised."

"I could tell. Anyway, like I was sayin', I'm pretty much done with the list—"

Lassiter raised his hands. "Wait a second: What do you mean, 'pretty much'? Are you done, or aren't you?"

"There's one I haven't found," Freddy said. "Not yet. So I can't be sure she's dead, but—"

"Which one?"

"Marie Williams. Minneapolis."

Lassiter thought about it. "How hard did you look?"

Freddy shrugged. "Not that hard. Just what we did for the others."

"Give me an idea."

Freddy pulled a folder out of his briefcase and slid it across the desk. He tapped it with his fingertips. "There's a report on each of them. Jody did half and I did half, and we subbed out a couple of the ones overseas. Routine stuff, mostly. I mean, it wasn't like we were looking for the Unabomber. It was real basic."

"Like what?"

"Well, first we called the telephone number, if we had one. And if we didn't, we got it from the Criss-Cross, using the address. Most of the numbers were kaput, but a coupla times we got the husband. And we talked to neighbors. The current stuff's online, and we have CD-ROMs that go back about eight years. You key in the address, and it gives you the people on either side, across the street—wherever. So we called them and . . . one by one, they told us what happened. Same story, each time, with a couple of variations. Mother and kid were killed, sometimes the whole family. Always in a fire."

"And there were kids in every case?"

"Boys. They were always boys, and none of them was older than four."

"What about Tokyo, Rabat—you chase them down, too?"

"We used subs, but—yeah, same thing."

"I want to be sure. How much of this was actually confirmed? And how much is just—"

"Hearsay?"

"Yeah."

"None of it's hearsay. We got a date for every incident, and checked it with the local paper. We talked to insurance investigators, fire departments, funeral homes—they're all dead."

"Except for what's-her-name . . ."

"Yeah. Except for her. Maybe."

Lassiter opened the file folder and glanced at the dossiers. None of them was longer than a page.

Helene Franck
302 23 Börke SW
Vasterhojd, Sweden
B: August 11, 1953 D: September 3, 1995

August Franck
same address
B: May 29, 1993 D: September 3, 1995

Cause of death: Smoke inhalation assumed

Confirmation of death:
1. National Registry (#001987/8), Stockholm
2. Annelie Janssen of Vasterhojd
033–107003 (neighbor)
3. Mäj Christianson of Stockholm
031–457911 (mother/grandmother of deceased)

Investigator:
Fredrik Kellgren
Agentur Ögon Försiktig
Stockholm, Sweden
031–997–444
3 Feb. 1996

Lassiter paged through the forms until he got to the sheet for:

Marie A. Williams
9201 St. Paul Blvd. #912
Minneapolis, Minn.
Tel: 612–453–2735 (Until 9–9–91)

"What about the one you couldn't find?"

"She was one of mine," Freddy said. "Let's see. I called the number—it's dead." He held up a finger. "No, wait—that's not right—I got a fax tone. So I redial about thirty times in a row and finally somebody picks up and says the obvious: 'This is a fax number.' I'm like—wait, wait, I know that, don't hang up. Anyway, it's an insurance agent, he's had the number for a couple of years."

"Which means she moved at least two years ago."

"Two years, plus. So I look up the address in the Criss-Cross, and turns out they got two hundred telephones hooked up to the place."

"So it's an apartment building."

"Right. 'The Fountains,' or something. Anyway, I get the super on the line, and he checks for me. Says Marie Williams lived there for a couple of years. Left in 'ninety-one. No forwarding address. In fact, the super says they still have her security deposit—so she must have left in a hurry."

"Did he remember her?"

"No. He's new. So are the neighbors."

"And that was as far as you took it?"

"Yeah. I guess . . . I mean, she was the second one I looked at. Jodie was just starting on her list. Nothing from the foreign subs. So, at that point, I figured some of them would just, you know—answer their phones. So I didn't press it. I mean, I didn't even run a credit check." Freddy paused. "You want me to do that?"

Lassiter didn't answer. Instead he got up, went to the fireplace. "No, Freddy. You did a good job. I thought this was going to take a couple of weeks."

"Tell you the truth, I was surprised, too. But when you think about it—most of these women were forty, forty-five years old. They were all doing okay, nobody's dodging the bill collector. Most of them were married. Stable people. Ordinarily, you take a dozen people—hell, a third of them will be at least a *little* hard to locate. You know—they moved, they got married, the husband was transferred. These women were easy to find. Good citizens. Lotsa footprints."

"Except for Williams."

"Yeah," Freddy said. "Except for her."

Lassiter picked up the poker and moved some wood around until he got a flurry of sparks. "Well," he said, "I'll take it from here."

"I kinda thought you would," Freddy said. "But . . ."

"What?"

"I wouldn't get your hopes up, because . . . whoever did this was pretty *diligent*. I mean—why should she be the only one to survive?"

Lassiter shrugged, but what he meant was: *Why not?*

He spent some time matching the birthdates in the dossiers with the dates on the pensione's register. It was just as he expected. From their dates of birth, it was clear that all of the children had been conceived at Baresi's clinic. Marie Williams—she would have been a few months pregnant when she left her apartment in Minneapolis.

He stirred the fire some more and looked out the window. The streets were still a mess from the fourth big snowfall of the season. It was now a week since the last one, and nothing had melted yet, thanks to record-breaking temperatures, unheard of in D.C. Single digits, night after night. Along the curbs, mounds of snow and ice entombed invisible cars. One of the owners was out there now, across the street, sticking a small American flag into the top of a frozen, gray mound. Lassiter watched him as he spray-painted CAR, in huge red letters, on the dingy snow. When the job was done, he stood back, like an artist examining his work. Finally, he walked off, satisfied that his effort would keep the plows, if they ever came, from mangling his buried car. The District was strapped for cash, and half its snowplows awaited repairs that somehow never got made. So the streets had dwindled to the width of alleys, and the sidewalks to lumpy, trodden paths.

The whole city needs an angioplasty, Lassiter thought as he stood at the window, watching a new snow begin to fall.

The intercom buzzed. "Detective Riordan," Victoria said in her musical voice. "Line one."

He started to tell her that he wasn't in, then changed his mind. "Put him through."

"So?" Riordan said. "You call Conway?"

Lassiter sighed. "Yeah," he said. "I was just about to call him."

"You're acting like a chump—you know that, don't you? After what happened in Italy—"

"I've been busy."

"Don't give me that, all right? You're kidding yourself. You got Grimaldi out there—I don't know what *he's* doin'! You got—I don't know what you got! So do me a favor. Don't make me put a coupla guys on ya—'cause I will, Joe, honest to Christ. Get yourself some protection. You can afford it."

"All right," Lassiter said. "I'll call."

"You promise? I swear to God I'm gonna call Terry—I'm gonna check."

"I promise."

"Okay." Lassiter heard Riordan thump his desk. "That's good."

"So . . . what's the news?"

"About Grimaldi?" Riordan gave a little dismissive snort. "Nothing. Zilch. The guy's Houdini."

"Well, he had *help*, didn't he?"

"Yeah," Riordan said, "and we're talking to her."

"I don't mean the nurse. I'm talking about the surveillance."

"What can I tell you? Drabowsky's a fuckup. Obviously."

"You sure about that?"

Riordan was silent for a moment, and then he asked, "What—you think the Bureau *helped* him?"

"I don't know what I think," Lassiter said. "But . . . forget that. I've got some news for you."

"About what?"

"The list I gave you. From the pensione's register."

"Oh yeah, the women who went to what's-his-face's place. The clinic. We're just getting started with that."

"Don't bother."

"Why not?"

Lassiter looked out the window. It was snowing harder. "They're dead."

"Who's dead?"

"The women. And their kids."

There was a long pause, and then: "All of them?"

"Probably. There's one we haven't been able to run down. Marie Williams. Middle initial A."

"I'll see what I can do at this end," Riordan said, "but—just a second." Someone was screaming in Spanish, and another voice was screaming back at her, not far from the telephone. Lassiter heard Riordan put his hand on the mouthpiece, muffling the sound, and then Riordan screamed, too: "*Hey! Shut the fuck up, all right?*" The silence was instantaneous. A moment later the detective said, "Keep me apprised, okay?"

"Whatever you say, Jim. I will keep you apprised."

"And call Terry Conway—like you promised."

"I will."

Riordan paused and when he spoke again, his voice was pointed and hard. "Lemme ask you something."

"What?"

"You think it's *over*, don't you? They're all dead, except for what's-her-name, who's probably dead, too. So you figure that's it. Am I right?" The detective didn't wait for an answer. "You bet I'm right. But lemme tell you something: We still don't know what the *fuck* it's about, do we? So *we* don't know when it's over; only *they* know that."

"I'll call Terry."

"You do that," Riordan said, and hung up.

—

But he didn't call Terry. Not immediately.

Instead he flipped through his Rolodex until he found the card for his favorite information broker—the bucket shop in Florida.

"Mutual General Services." The woman answered the phone on the first ring, which was one of the things he liked about the firm. They were efficient; they were fast; they were discreet. And you didn't get voice mail.

"It's Joe Lassiter at Lassiter Associates. We have a standing account?" He read off the numbers.

"What can we do for you?"

"I want a credit report on a Marie A. Williams. Last known address was Minneapolis." He gave her the address and asked, "How far back can you go?"

The reply was immediate: "About as far back as you can afford—remember Bridey Murphy?"

Gateway Security was run by a nice guy named Terry Conway, an ex-NFL tight end with a law degree and a good head for business. He was making more money now than he ever did in football, which was saying something, because Terry had been all-pro until his knees went.

Gateway was a niche company in the security field, providing bodyguards for the rich, the famous, and the infamous—diplomats and politicians, celebrities and CEOs, their families and properties. He did not compete with Wackenhut or any of the rent-a-cop agencies, but specialized in executive protection services. The people he hired were professionals, not bouncers.

Even so, Lassiter hated the idea of hiring bodyguards. It amounted to placing himself under surveillance—in effect, paying through the nose to invade his own privacy. And they were annoying, as well, precisely because they were always *there*. With their code words, cell phones, and static.

He knew what it was like because he'd arranged the same service for a number of clients. At first they were grateful to feel "safe," and flattered to be at the center of so much effort. But after a while, they began to whine. And then to plead. Is this *really* necessary? How much longer is it going to go on?

In the end, he placed the call with a grimace, and when Terry came on the line, he described the assignment in a nutshell: "I got a CEO in Washington—civilian, no family, thirty-five—"

"Government ties?"

"No. Anyway, there's been some pretty credible threats on his life—"

"Such as?"

"People shooting at him."

"That qualifies."

"So we were thinking, maybe it would be a good idea—"

"Who's the client?" Terry asked.

"Me."

A long silence ensued. Finally, Terry said, "Now, that's bad news: you get killed, I lose one of my best customers." He paused again. "Tell you what," he said. "I'll send Buck over. He's got a light touch—you'll like him."

"Is that Buck like the dollar, or Buck like the deer?"

"Very funny. I'll have him at your office around six—and we'll send someone over to your house to take a look at the perimeter. In the meantime, I think you should get a hotel—just for the night. You and Buck."

Lassiter muttered to himself, and said, "Yeah, well, let's hope I *do* like him."

As Lassiter hung up, the fax machine trilled, and he turned to it. The top of the letterhead fed through first, and he saw it was from Mutual General Services. Headed, *Williams, Marie A.*, he was delighted to see that it was the credit report he'd requested, and that it included her date of birth (March 8, 1962) as well as her social security number.

With a name, address, DOB, and Social, he could locate and access bank accounts, medical records, mortgage agreements, tax documents—and a lot more, if he wanted. Even the Social itself was embedded with information. From the first three numbers he could tell where she'd been born, which might help him to find her.

He pulled a copy of *The Open Sourcebook* from the shelf and opened it to the chapter on social security data. There, he found a list of numbers and locales: 146 was Maine. He put the book away and turned back to the credit history itself. Immediately, he was struck by several peculiarities.

For one thing, her record was immaculate: there were no slow-to-pay entries, *ever*, and no bounced checks. Not one. That was unusual, but what was strange was the fact that the credit history didn't begin until 1989. Which meant that, if her DOB was correct, she'd paid cash for everything until she was twenty-six years old, at which point American Express had given her a Platinum Card. There were a couple of Visa cards issued at the same time—both with huge credit limits—but nothing before then.

How do you do *that*? Lassiter wondered. It was as if she'd sprung full-blown from the forehead of the Great Creditor. Where had she come from?

And where had she gone? The credit cards were allowed to lapse in 1991, and her bank accounts were closed at the same time. Since then, nothing. No mortgages, no liens, no comments. In effect, she'd disappeared.

Nor was that all. Credit reports always included a list of inquiries. If you wanted to rent an apartment, the landlord would request a credit check, and that request would be listed on future reports. So, too, if you applied for a charge account at Macy's, bought a car for something less than cash, or went looking for a job—a credit check would probably be made, and it would be listed on subsequent reports. Indeed, his own inquiry—or, more accurately, Mutual's inquiry—was now a part of the record. It was automatic.

But, with a single exception, Marie Williams's credit record hadn't been checked since 1991—which meant that she'd vanished from the economy. And while that was possible, it wasn't likely: even bankrupts went out of their way to obtain ersatz credit cards, paying cash deposits to offset future charges. Otherwise, they found it almost impossible to rent a car, make reservations, or cash a check.

Moving abroad wouldn't explain the lack of activity on Marie Williams's credit history, and neither would a marriage. Joining a cult might, and so, also, would living by barter. Maybe she's a Moonie, Lassiter thought, or trades potatoes for Pampers. Or maybe she just doesn't need to rent a car, make reservations, or cash a check.

Whatever the truth, it wasn't obvious from the report.

The exception to all this was a credit inquiry dated October 19, 1995. Two weeks before Kathy and Brandon were killed.

According to the report, the inquiry originated in Chicago with a firm called Allied National Products—which, judging by the name, was probably a bucket shop like Mutual.

It didn't mean anything, of course, but it was odd. If there had been a cluster of inquiries, Lassiter would have assumed that Marie A. Williams was picking up her old life after a long sabbatical. But that wasn't the case. There was just that one, in October—and then nothing until Lassiter weighed in.

He put the file to the side and buzzed Judy.

"*What?*" she shouted.

"Uh . . . it's Joe Lassiter. I own the place?"

Judy giggled. "Sor-ry, Joe, my desk's on fire. How can I help ya . . . ?" She laughed again. "Come on, come on—whattaya want?"

"A subcontractor in Minneapolis. We got one?"

"Of course we do. The Cowles case—remember? Guy out there did marathon legwork. George something . . . Gerry?" Lassiter remembered the case but he didn't remember a subcontractor. Judy was already pulling it up on her computer. "*Gary.* Gary Stoykavich. Twin Cities Research." She rattled off the telephone numbers and hung up.

With a name like Stoykavich, and a base like Minneapolis—which had to be the white-bread capital of the world—Gary Stoykavich's voice was a surprise.

"Good after-*noon*," he boomed. "Twin Cities Research." He spoke in a gravelly baritone like Fats Domino's; his voice was unmistakably African-American. "You're speaking to Gary."

"It's Joe Lassiter—you did some work for us while back—"

A rich chuckle. " 'Course I did, 'course I did. Whole lot of work as a matter of fact. For Miss Joo-dee Rif-kin."

"Right."

"So what can I do for you, Mr. Joseph Lassiter? I take it you're the big boss—or are we in the presence of a massive coincidence?"

"Nope—I'm the one."

Stoykavich laughed, a long rumbling chortle. "Well, then," he said, "I'm listening."

"I'm looking for a woman who lived in Minneapolis—1991." He dictated the details.

"I have a question," Stoykavich said. "This Marie Williams: Did she move, or is she 'missing'? And if she's missing, is she hiding?"

Lassiter thought about it. Good question. "I don't know," he said.

"Because that could make a big difference in the budget."

"I realize that, but . . . Mr. Stoykavich? What I think you're going to find is that Ms. Williams is dead."

"Oh."

Lassiter said he'd fax the credit report, and recounted the steps that Freddy had taken. Stoykavich said he'd check with the DMV, the newspapers, and the courthouse.

"One other thing," Lassiter added. "I think she may have been pregnant. In fact, I know she was. About four months."

"I might be able to do something with that," Stoykavich said. "Anything else come to mind?"

"Not at the moment."

"I'm full-tilt, then," Stoykavich said.

Lassiter was going through the preliminary contracts for the sale of Lassiter Associates when Victoria buzzed and said there was a Deva Collins to see him. From Research.

"Send her in."

Deva Collins was young and nervous. She shrugged back her long blond hair and took off her glasses. Then she stood at attention, holding a stack of documents. He told her to sit down, and she did.

"This is the initial material," she said, "a pull-down from online sources."

"What material are we talking about?"

She looked startled and somehow exposed. She jammed her glasses back on and seemed a little more comfortable. "Ummm—the Italian doctor: Ignazio Baresi."

"Looks like a lot."

"Oh, it's mostly secondary sources—references to his work by other academics and research scientists. I weeded through them. The second half of the stack—from the yellow sheet down, those are fairly inconsequential references—just his name or someone citing one of his publications. I only saved them because I thought—I don't know—just in case. You might want to call the writer or something."

"What about Baresi's own publications?"

"That's going to take a little longer, although, as of today, I've tracked most of them down." She hesitated. "Well, not me personally, but all of us. Some of the material is available in university collections, but it's scattered all over the place because he worked in two different fields. I knew about him, actually."

"Really."

She blushed. "Well, his biblical scholarship. I was a comparative religions major, and he was footnoted all over the place."

"That's terrific, that should help out—with the research." He wanted to encourage her, but she only seemed embarrassed.

"Maybe a little," she admitted grudgingly. "At least I know where the major collections are. But the genetics was a problem. We had to call Georgetown for help."

"That's good."

She began to brighten, and took off her glasses again. "Anyway, most of his work, the articles, we can get through interlibrary loans. But you're going to have to have it abstracted—unless you want it translated."

"What would that take?"

She seesawed her head. "The abstracts would take . . . I don't know. The translations could take forever. I mean, it's not like translating a short story. It's hard science."

"What about his book?"

"It's in a number of university libraries," she said, "but so far, I can only find the Italian language edition. It *was* published in English, but it's kind of tough to get a copy. I'll keep trying, and if I can't get it, maybe I can find a review somewhere."

He glanced at the dossier on his desk. "Well, thanks, Deva. It sounds like you're doing a good job." He stood up and shook her hand.

She blushed for the second time, and for a moment he was afraid she was going to curtsy.

When she'd left, he picked up the first document in the stack on his desk and looked at it. It was an article published in the *Journal of Molecular Biology*. By somebody named Walter Fields, Ph.D.

    The Role of Repressor Proteins in Ribonucleic Acid Polymerase Transcription: Comments on published findings of Ignazio Baresi, Ezra Sidran, et al., as presented at the Annual Conference on Bio-Genetics in Bern, Switzerland, April 11, 1962.

Lassiter struggled through the first paragraph, and found that he understood not a single sentence. Frowning, he set the document aside and picked up the next one in the stack.

Eucaryotic Gene Regulation: A Colloquium
(Under the Auspices of Kings College, London):
Remarks

Impenetrable.
And another:

Sex-Linked Traits: X Chromosome, Recessive Alleles, Kline-felter's and Turner's Syndrome. Comments on recent studies by I. Baresi, S. Rivele, and C. Wilkinson.

This one was actually intelligible for more than a page, though it became increasingly technical as Lassiter went on. Frustrated, he tossed the paper on the desk, sat back, and closed his eyes. The problem, he thought, was more complicated than it seemed. To begin with, he needed a rabbi—someone who could explain the science to him, in terms that an English major could understand.

He made a note. *Rabbi.*

But even that might not be enough. Baresi's published papers might well be incomplete. What if, after "leaving genetics," he'd actually continued his researches on his own—in his clinic, underground. The newspapers were filled with articles about the ethical dilemmas posed by genetics research. What if Baresi had come up against something of that sort, and . . . The hell with it, Lassiter thought. This isn't getting anywhere: it's just speculation. And bad speculation at that: there wasn't any evidence that Baresi had continued his researches.

With a growl, he turned to the stack of articles and began to arrange them into two piles, separating Baresi's research in genetics from his later work in theology. It occurred to him that he might actually be able to read one of the latter. Such as:

Early Christian Communities and Kerygma: an analysis of textual similarities to regional sources contemporaneous to the Gospel according to Mark. By I. Baresi, *Journal of Comparative Religion*, Vol. 29, August 11, 1971.

Victoria buzzed. He put the document down on his desk. Maybe theology wasn't going to be any "easier" than the material on genetic research.

"Yeah?" he said.

"Have we been sold?" Victoria asked.

"*What?*"

"*Business Week*'s on line one."

"Tell 'em no."

"No-we-haven't-been-sold, or—"

"No-I'm-not-in."

"Oh-kayyy. Also: a Mr. Stoykavich is on line two."

"I'll take it." He picked up. "Hey—Gary—what do you need? You got a question?"

"Oh no," he boomed. "I don't have a question. What I have is an answer."

"In two hours—you're going to tell me you found Marie Williams?"

"Oh no, not that one, not yet. Remember when I asked you did this woman want to be found or not? That's the one I know the answer to."

"And what is it?"

"She most definitely does not want to be found."

"Where are you going with this, Gary?"

"It hurts me to tell you this—because I was ready to put in a *large* number of billable hours. But this is a no-brainer, my friend. Marie Williams took off on September nineteenth because, on September eighteenth, her identity was revealed."

"What are you talking about—her 'identity'? What identity?"

"Marie Williams is Callista Bates! How '*bout* that?"

"You're kidding," Lassiter said. A tabloid photo flashed in front of his eyes: Callista at Cannes. Callista at Le Dôme. Callista in Seclusion. The actress hadn't made a picture in seven or eight years, but her face—always beautiful—still looked out from the tabloids in the supermarket racks. Like Garbo, she was an icon precisely because she'd walked away at the apex of a brilliant career, exchanging glamour for obscurity. But it was even more mysterious (and sinister) than that. Like "Lindbergh" or "Sharon Tate," when you said "Callista Bates," you alluded to a story—and everyone knew the details.

An inmate at the state prison in Lompoc, California, a man serving an eighteen-year sentence for malicious wounding, burglary, and rape, had become obsessed with Callista midway through his sentence. He'd written to the studio for photographs, joined her fan club, and recorded her comings and goings in an ever-thickening scrapbook—until, in the end, his cell had become a cinder-block shrine dedicated to his One and Only, Sweet Callista Bates.

Paroled in 1988, the man had taken a bus to Beverly Hills, where tour guides pointed out her house. In the months that followed, he haunted the neighborhood, while leaving a string of unwelcome "gifts" at the front gate to her estate. Among them, Lassiter recalled, were an S&M video filmed in Germany, and a snapshot of a weightlifter with pierced nipples, wearing a black hood and nothing else. It was creepy stuff.

And it got worse. Night after night the speakerphone buzzed at Callista's front gate, though no one was ever there. And while her unpublished number was repeatedly changed, the telephone rang at all hours, and the voice and the message were always the same: "Callista, you cunt—let me *in*."

Twice, the man climbed the wall that separated her property from the street, only to be chased off by the excited barks of her aged Lab, Kerouac. Once, on retrieving letters from her mailbox, she found them soaked in blood. On another occasion, as the gates to her property opened, the stalker materialized beside her car, yanking furiously at the door handles, screaming to be let in.

The police were polite, concerned, and ineffective. For a month or so there were increased patrols—squad cars rolled past the house in the late night hours, shining their searchlights into the trees and bushes. But nothing ever came of it. At the cops' suggestion, she arranged for a telephone service that identified incoming calls, but the stalker always used pay phones. After months of false alarms, or real alarms with no apprehensions, the police shook their heads and shrugged. *Kids*, they said, as if that explained the blood, the porn, and the lunatic yanking at the car door.

The night he killed the dog and forced the door, she was in the living room, reading. She heard the animal's low-throated bark, the agonized yelp that followed, and then the sound of breaking glass. Her breathless call to 911 was played on every news broadcast for a week thereafter: "This is Callista Bates . . . 211 Mariposa . . . there's a man . . . with a knife . . . he killed my dog . . . now he's standing in the living room . . . and . . . this is not a kid."

To their credit, the police arrived in less than four minutes, but not before he'd slashed her twice—severing the tendons in her right wrist.

The last footage of her was taken on the steps of the courthouse, after the man's sentencing. She was impossibly beautiful in an ice-blue suit, and all she had to say was, "That's all, folks."

She gave an occasional interview after that. There was talk of returning to work. But the tabloids were right when they said she was a woman in withdrawal from the world. Over the course of the next year, she sold her house and furniture—and disappeared.

She was never seen again—or, rather, she was seen everywhere, and often in different places at the same time.

In the equations of popular culture, then, Callista Bates was part Marilyn and part JFK—an image spray-painted on the sides of bridges and buildings. A piece of work.

And there was something else, something about her . . . For a moment Lassiter felt a surge of adrenaline, a momentary alertness. It was on the tip of his tongue—and then it wasn't. It was gone. Something he'd remembered. Something he'd forgotten.

"No, Mr. Lassiter, I am not kidding. I found the previous super-intendent, the man who worked at the apartment building. Lives in Florida. And when I called him about Marie Williams, he says, 'You from that paper?' And I say, 'What paper?' And he says, 'The *Enquirer*.' So we're off and running. He says, Marie Williams is the one tenant he *does* remember—and you coulda knocked him over with dust—that's what he said—when he learned she was Callista Bates. Why, he himself was in the paper, showing the reporter around her apart-ment—and would I like to see the clips?"

"Gary," Lassiter began, his voice heavy with skepticism, "the *Enquirer* isn't exactly—"

"Wait a second! Wait a second! I know what you're going to say. But hear me out: I *remember* that story. *You* wouldn't remember it because you don't live in Minneapolis—and because it seems like someone spots Callista Bates about once a week, somewhere or other. Didn't I see somethin' the other day, sayin' she was on Norfolk Island, or someplace weird like that?"

"Yeah, and she weighed sixty pounds and had leukemia."

"Right—that's the one where they morphed her picture, made her all bony and wasted-looking. But what I'm saying is, Minneapolis is my hometown. And I remember the lady who spotted Callista being interviewed on television and all. I just didn't pay it much mind. And I didn't remember the name 'Marie Williams.' "

"So what makes you think it was her?"

"Because I talked to the reporter."

"At the *Enquirer*?"

"Yes."

Lassiter scoffed.

"Hold on, now! Those boys are a lot more careful than you'd think. They have to be, 'cause they're sued every other day." The detective paused. "You listenin'?"

"Yeah, I'm all ears."

"Okay. Now, here's the way it worked. Somebody called in a tip to the Callista Bates Hot Line—"

"There's a Callista—"

"That's what I'm saying! Someone dimed the hot line at the *Enquirer*: 'I saw her!' they said. 'With a real estate agent. Century 21!' It was some nosy woman, you know, out in the suburbs."

"I thought she lived in an apartment building. Downtown."

"She *did*—but now she was buying a place. Comfortable house. Nice neighborhood. All cash. Realtor said it was a done deal. Then some stringer from the *Enquirer* shows up and finesses Williams's name out of the receptionist. Next thing, he's banging on her door at the Fountains—knock knock! Who's there? The *Enquirer*! That's it— she *gone*."

"Good story. The only thing is, how do you know it was Callista Bates?"

"The stringer—guy named Michael Finley—takes pictures. Before he goes to the door, he's sittin' out front in his car, takin' pictures. She's comin' and goin', comin' and goin'. I seen the pictures. Now, I admit—her hair is brown, cut different. Sunglasses. But it looks like her. No question."

" '*Looks* like her.' "

"I'm not done! I called Finley. And he told me he *knows* this was Callista Bates."

"And how's that?"

"He ran a credit check. Tried the same Social with a different name: Callista Bates. And he got everything! Turns out, this Callista thing was a stage name, something her agent came up with when she came to California. Something that would stand out on the marquee, you understand? But she didn't mess with her social security number—why should she? No matter *what* she's calling herself, she's still got withholding taxes. So she used her own number."

"Wouldn't that show up in a lot of places?"

"Not really. And besides, she wasn't hidin'—*then*. Her agent paid her through a loan-out corporation—and get this, she called it 'A Large American Firm'—with a capital A?—so she could say she was chairman of a large American firm! Real sense of humor. Anyway, all the agent had was a federal ID number. Callista—she did her own books. And she did her own taxes. So *my* guess is, her Social didn't come up a whole lot."

"So let me get this straight. Her real name is . . ."

"Marie Williams."

"But she changed it to Callista Bates when she started to act."

"And when she left California," Stoykavich said, "she went back to Williams." The P.I. paused for a moment, and then went on. "You know, this was a helluva thing she pulled off, especially when you think how well known she was. Talk about a chameleon. This woman is one . . . terrific . . . actress."

"What happened to Finley?"

"Oh, Finley did fine! Don't *worry* about Finley. Finley got her damn charge records. He's still living off the stuff. *You* know: 'Callista's Favorite Restaurants!' 'Callista Hits Rodeo Drive!' 'Callista's Secret Getaway Spots!' That kind of thing."

Lassiter felt a twinge of panic. He could see the headlines at the Safeway: *Serial Killer Stalks Callista and Her Secret Love Child.* There'd be a special on "America's Most Wanted." Scenes of Riordan plugging away at his phones, the camera zooming in to an open file on his desk. A long look at Grimaldi's ruined face. A grisly parade of slaughtered infants, murdered moms, torched houses. And a hotline number: *Call 1-800-Calista (1-800-225-4782). Help us find her before They do!*

"Uhhh, Gary, let me ask you something: How much did you tell this guy? I mean, did my name come up, or what?"

"No. It did not. I told him I'd been hired by a help group—women who've been stalked. I also had to give him two hundred bucks before he'd talk about anything."

Lassiter thought for a moment. "That's good," he said, "but . . . I'm not sure what to do at this point. It seems to me, if she was hard to find before—"

"She's gonna be even harder now. I agree. But we got some leads. The super said she did volunteer work at the library. Took some classes at the community college. And then there's the pregnancy bit. She may have taken Lamaze classes, joined some kind of support group, you know, like that. I could check."

"Yeah, why don't you do that? See what you can find. And while you're there—give me the reporter's number. What's his name? Finley."

Stoykavich recited the number. "Just one thing," he said.

"What's that?"

"When you call Finley? Hang on to your wallet." And then the black Minnesotan laughed. Like rolling thunder.

Callista Bates.

It was like a good-news/bad-news joke in which the news was the same in either case. The fact that she was hard to find made her hard to warn—but it also made her hard to kill. And if *he* couldn't find her, Lassiter thought, no one could. Of that he was sure.

He stood up and went to the window. It was twilight, and so cold that the snow had stopped. Behind the Pentagon the sky was a rare and deep sapphire color that glowed with almost supernatural clarity. The floodlit dome of the Capitol shone with cold brilliance, its ridges and curves and details so precisely cut that it reminded him of the ivory carved and sold in Chinatown. Above the dome an attenuated moon hung amid a jumble of stars. The stars glittered with such vitality that it was easy to imagine the universe enclosed by a gigantic dome— visible only where the metal had been pierced to allow a glimpse of heaven's glory.

He felt his mood lift; he felt almost good. Maybe she was alive, after all. Maybe—

The intercom buzzed.

"What's up?"

"There's someone here to see you," Victoria said, in a voice heavy with disapproval.

"Who's that?"

" 'Buck.' "

32

The man who came through the door was about five feet five inches tall, maybe forty years old. His hair was slicked back into a ponytail, and his skin was a deep chemical bronze. He had no neck to speak of, just a column of flesh that seemed to be an extension of his shoulders. He looked like a character in a bad action film.

"I'm Buck," he said, extending his hand.

"Thanks for coming," Lassiter replied as the smaller man crushed his hand in his own.

"You mind if I look around?" he asked.

"Help yourself."

Almost idly, the bodyguard moved through the room, turning his head this way and that, taking everything in, but without ever evincing real curiosity. "What's in there?" he asked.

"Shower."

Buck opened the door and glanced inside. "Nice," he said. Moving to the windows, he studied the street for what seemed like a long time, then pulled the blinds closed. Turning back to the room, he surveyed it with a restless, unfocused gaze, remarkable in its neutrality.

Finally, he sat down on the edge of the Barcelona chair next to the fireplace and cracked his knuckles. "Terry already briefed me, so you just go ahead with whatever you're doing. I'll just . . . observe." And with that, Buck pulled a book from his briefcase and began to read. Lassiter glanced at the title: *Intermediate Japanese*.

Returning to the papers on his desk, Lassiter continued sorting them into two piles, one concerning Baresi's career as a scientist, the other his career as a religious scholar. When he finished, it was five-thirty. He asked Victoria to get the woman from Research on the line. "You think she's still here?"

"I'm sure she is, but . . ."

"What?"

"Who *is* that man?" She giggled.

"You mean Buck? Buck's my baby-sitter."

Buck kept his eyes on the page.

"Oh," Victoria said, and paused. "You mean a *bodyguard?*" She sounded thrilled. "I'll try Deva Collins."

Momentarily, the researcher was on the line, asking what she could do. "I need a rabbi," Lassiter said.

"Excuse me?"

Deva wasn't familiar with the in-house slang. "Rabbi" was Judy's term for the individual often consulted at the very beginning of an investigation. Usually a journalist, sometimes an academic, the rabbi acted as a tour guide through the terrain that made up the background of an investigation: the garment industry, the metals trade, the AMA. In this case Lassiter needed someone who could talk about molecular biology in plain English. He explained this to Deva.

"Oh," she said. "Of course. I'll find someone."

"Good. And I was hoping maybe you could brief me on the religious material. There's a lot to read. Maybe you could organize it in terms of who's who, Baresi's contribution to the field—that sort of thing."

She laughed nervously. "I don't know . . . I'm not an expert or anything."

"I don't need an expert."

"Well, then . . . I'll give it a try, if you like. Do you want a memo?"

"Or we could talk."

"Oh, no," she said, sounding flustered. "I always like to organize my thoughts on paper."

He told her that would be fine, and asked her to have someone in Research do a pull-together on Callista Bates.

"All right," Deva said, doubtfully. She paused, trying to contain her curiosity. "Is this for a different case?"

He hesitated. Finally, he said, "No."

"Oh . . . well . . . I'll have the memo for you by tomorrow night. Will that be okay?"

He told her that would be terrific. When he hung up the phone, Buck turned a page of his book and said, "Callista Bates . . . now that was a *fox.*"

—

An hour later Lassiter was sliding into the cramped passenger seat of a gray Buick that waited at the curb outside Lassiter Associates.

"Pico—he'll be the driver after tonight," Buck said as he easily maneuvered the car through the icy streets. "Pico *loves* this baby. Me? I'm afraid to step on the gas pedal too hard. There's a hell of an engine under there."

Soon they were on Memorial Bridge, crossing the frozen Potomac. Buck filled him in on the car's features as they hurtled past the Pentagon, heading south on Shirley Highway.

"People talk about bulletproof? They don't know what they're talking about. This here's half-inch Lexan," he said, tapping on the side window. "Good stuff. Stop anything—*almost*. But if they want you bad enough? They'll use C-4."

The car looked normal from the exterior, but it was cramped on the inside, and so well insulated that when the doors closed, Lassiter's ears had popped. The reason the interior was so tight, Buck explained, was that a lot of the space in the standard model had been sacrificed to armor-plating, an outsized fuel tank, and hydraulic devices that could raise the chassis for off-road driving.

"I feel like James Bond," Lassiter said.

Buck smiled. "Everybody says that."

They stopped at a 7-Eleven to get a twelve-pack of Bud Light, and then at a Blockbuster store to rent a couple of Callista Bates videos. When they arrived at the Comfort Inn, Lassiter waited in the car while Buck registered. Sitting there, while the car was *parked*, was like sitting in a bank vault.

Finally, Buck walked gingerly across the icy lot and climbed into the car. "I got adjoining rooms," he said, "and a VCR." Taking the car around to the back of the inn, he led Lassiter up the stairs to the third floor.

"We could have stayed at the Willard," Lassiter said. "I would have popped for it."

Buck shook his head. "This place is better. Someone's looking for Joe Lassiter, he's not going to start at a Comfort Inn in the burbs."

Their rooms were at the end of the corridor, across from the stairwell. Connected by a door in the adjoining wall, they were relatively large and nicely furnished, with king-sized beds and a panoramic view of the traffic on Interstate 95.

"I got a Triple A discount," Buck said proudly. "Sixty-four dollars a night! And that's *with* taxes *and* breakfast." He went to the windows and pulled the drapes closed. "The thing is," he said, "a hotel like this, security's pretty good. They lock the doors at midnight—you have to get buzzed in. Also, there's an armed guard, right in the lobby. A big hotel like the Willard, they got a doorman." The bodyguard shook his head. "Like *he's* gonna help."

Lassiter stretched out on the bed and read the blurb on one of the video boxes.

> *Fast Track*—Comedy—114 minutes, 1987. Callista Bates. Dave Goldman. Harvard hijinx as grad students plot to make a killing on the stock market.
>
> "Callista Bates's timing is better than a Rolex—four stars!" *New York Times*
>
> "We sprained our thumbs laughing!" Siskel & Ebert
>
> Blockbuster says: *If you liked this movie, check out* A Fish Called Wanda. *Available for rental at all locations.*

The second video was a sci-fi film.

> *Piper*—SciFi—127 minutes, 1986. The Pied Piper story, updated and reset in Hamlin, Ohio. In her Oscar-nominated role as "Penny," Callista Bates is a punkish panhandler whose blues-harmonica saves the town from an infestation of rats infected with a deadly virus. When the aldermen renege on their promises, they soon wish they'd paid this Piper.
>
> "Stunning." *New York Daily News*
>
> "Terrifying!" *Premiere*
>
> "Callista's irresistible. You'll want to follow her, too!" *Rolling Stone*

He remembered the buzz about *Piper*, remembered wanting to see the movie, even remembered watching the Oscars with—who was it? *Gillian*. Gillian rose up in his memory—dimpled smile, milk-white breasts. Whatever happened to her?

The Academy Awards were an interminable bore, but Gillian had insisted. He'd given in with bad grace and endured a night of nudge-nudge jokes, hokey sets, and overproduced musical pieces—made all the more intolerable by Gillian's annoyed resistance to seduction. She'd been glued to the couch, bouncing at times, rooting for her favorites. When the "Best Actress" award was finally announced, the camera followed the winner as she made her way to the stage, and then returned to Callista Bates. Gillian had been outraged that Callista didn't win, but she—and Lassiter and everyone else—was charmed when the actress impishly pulled out a harmonica and played it for the camera, the deep mischievous look in her eyes reminding everyone that "Penny" knew how to deal with being stiffed.

He never did see the movie, and he barely remembered 1986. That was the year he'd incorporated the firm. He'd been hiring people like crazy and leasing space, and there was more business than he could handle. He remembered working sixteen-hour days, but apart from that, the whole year—and Gillian, too, he guessed—had dissolved into a blur of work.

Buck was on the telephone, ordering pizza from a local place that boasted of "a real brick oven" and free delivery.

"Buzz me up from the desk; I'll come down to get it. Don't forget the salads."

Then Buck called Pico and Chaz—the rest of the "team." They were checking out Lassiter's house in McLean. After a brief conversation Buck let out a surprisingly high-pitched laugh. "No," he said. "They don't. Look—I'll call you in the A.M." He hung up and turned to Lassiter. "You live in the country?"

Lassiter shook his head. "Most people don't think of McLean as the *country*, exactly."

"Pico saw a deer. Scared the shit out of him." He laughed. "You know what he asks me?"

Lassiter shook his head.

"Do they *bite*?"

They sat on the sofa and watched *Fast Track* and ate pizza. The beer was cold, the salad crisp, the pizza better than it should have been.

And the movie was funny, very funny—but every once in a while Lassiter could see how close to the edge it really was. A director with a heavier hand, actors less gifted, and the whole thing could have been a disaster.

It was Callista who held it together. She had a genius for comic timing, and made the most of a role that turned a cliché on its head. She wasn't a dumb blonde, but a scheming one who knew how to play dumb when it was to her advantage.

Buck seemed to know the movie by heart, signaling bits in advance by elbowing Lassiter. "This is where they go to the World Trade Center—look at the little guy in the background!" And then he'd lose it.

About halfway through the film Lassiter was alerted to one of these high points by a smack on his arm. "Oh this, oh man, look at this."

Dressed in a dark suit and a pillbox hat with a lacy black veil, Callista is posing as a mourner at a funeral home. Surrounded by banks of flowers, her partner-in-crime reclines in an open coffin, pretending to be dead. Slowly, Callista walks up the aisle and, kneeling at his side, begins to pray. Or so it seems, until the camera dollies in and it's clear that she and "the corpse" are arguing with each other through gritted teeth.

"Give me the key," she demands.

"I can't! They'll see me move."

"Then which pocket is it in? I'll get it myself!"

"And leave me here? I don't think so!"

To the alarm of the nearby funeral director, and the consternation of other mourners, Callista begins to go through the dead man's pockets.

"I swear to God, Walter, if you don't give me the fucking key, I'm going to kill you!"

"You can't kill me," the corpse says, rising on one elbow. "I'm already dead! That's the whole point!"

Whereupon the funeral director faints, Callista seizes the key, and—

"*Hold it!*" Lassiter said. Grabbing the remote control, he stopped the film and punched Rewind.

"Oh *man!*" Buck complained. "What are you *doing*? This is one of the funniest parts!"

Lassiter stuck his hand in the air and made a distracted, shushing sound. Buck gave a sudden, sage nod as he recalled that Lassiter's interest in Callista Bates had nothing to do with entertainment. "I'm gonna hit the can," he said, looking hurt. "Maybe I'll get some ice."

Lassiter nodded without listening, rewinding the film, then reforwarding it to the frame he wanted—where the camera closed in on Callista's veiled face. He hit the Pause button, and the close-up shuddered on the screen.

He stared at it, and there was no mistake. *This woman had been at Kathy and Brandon's funeral.*

Callista Bates.

Standing in the Comfort Inn, his eyes on the jittery TV screen, Lassiter remembered the funeral as if it, too, was a movie.

The polished wooden coffins, small and large, Kathy's and Brandon's, resting in the deep, rectangular pits that had been dug to receive them . . . each casket bearing an artful scatter of white roses, dropped there by the mourners. One final rose falls in cinematic slow motion, bouncing slightly on impact.

A man—it is Lassiter himself—stands at a discreet distance, waiting to receive the muttered condolences of those gathered to pay their respects. The first of them is, as so many of them are, unknown to him: an attractive blonde, dressed in black, wearing an old-fashioned hat with a gossamer veil.

For a moment Lassiter came out of his reverie and stared at the image on the television screen. Then he closed his eyes to revive the memory.

At the funeral, the woman looks familiar, but he can't place her. One of Kathy's neighbors, maybe, or a mom from Brandon's preschool. The boy is about Brandon's age, with dark curly hair and Mediterranean skin. He's embarrassed that he can't remember the woman's name, and he sees himself lean forward. "Don't I know you?" She shakes her head: "I met your sister in Europe—"

Suddenly, the television lurched into sound and motion as the pause mechanism released its hold upon the woman on the screen. Callista stuffed the key in her pocket and pushed her way past the mourners and—

The sound seemed much too loud, as if someone had turned up the volume inside Lassiter's head. He snapped off the television and tried to think. At Kathy and Brandon's funeral, she must have introduced herself to him—and her son—but although he was certain of this, he couldn't remember the names. Not for the life of him.

With a sigh, he sat down on the couch and popped open a beer. Callista Bates, Marie Williams, whoever she was—she and her son had been alive in November. But were they still, and if so, where?

Buck pushed through the door, carrying a plastic bin of ice. "Hey," he said, gesturing to the dark screen, "thanks for waiting. I appreciate that."

They finished the pizza, most of the beer, and watched the rest of the movie. Lassiter scrutinized the film intently for a few minutes, but soon he was into the movie again, just laughing, and waiting for Buck to jab him in the arm.

When it was over, Lassiter showered while Buck made telephone calls. They watched the news together, then a few minutes of the Knicks, pasting the Bullets. Finally, Buck got to his feet. "Well," he said. "I'm gonna hit the sack. But I'll be right next door, so . . . toodle-ooh."

Toodle-ooh. Woody used to say that. And thinking of Woody reminded Lassiter of something—or almost did. Whatever it was, he couldn't quite remember; and there was something else, as well. Something about Callista's "Marie Williams" identity. And then it hit him:

What if it was Grimaldi? What if Grimaldi was the source of the other inquiry on Marie Williams's credit report?

Lassiter climbed out of bed and went to his briefcase. Removing a file, he opened it to Williams's credit report and looked at the last page:

Inquiries: 10.19.95—Allied National Products (Chicago).

Chicago. "John Doe's" old base.

If it hadn't been for Grimaldi's telephone call to the Embassy Suites, where he'd rented a room as "Juan Gutierrez," the Italian's identity might still be a mystery. Lassiter looked at the date of the credit check and saw that it was made about two weeks before Kathy had been killed.

Which didn't prove that Grimaldi was behind it—after all, Lassiter thought, he had run his own inquiries through an information broker in *Miami*. Still . . . if someone were looking for "Marie Williams," and all he had to go on was an old address, a credit check would be a useful first step. If he got lucky, it might generate a new address, and even if it didn't, he'd have her credit card numbers. And once he had those, Grimaldi could trace her comings and goings—unless she was running away. Which she was. And because she was, she'd ditched her credit cards—and that had probably saved her life.

The driver, Pico, was a handsome Cuban of few words, and he got them to Lassiter Associates in record time, negotiating the clogged and icy downtown streets as smoothly as Michael Jordan going to the hoop.

While Buck sat in the outer office, flustering Victoria by his presence, Lassiter asked Research to run a credit check on Kathleen Anne Lassiter, who was formerly of 132 Keswick Lane, Burke.

There was a moment of silence, and then the researcher asked, "Isn't that—"

"Yeah."

"Okay . . . I'll do it right away."

Then he called Woody.

At some point during the night he'd remembered what it was that made him think of Woody—or not Woody, but one of his brothers. Andy or Gus. Or Oliver.

When Joe Lassiter and Nick Woodburn had been students at St. Alban's, Woody's family was famous. Not famous in the way that Lassiter's was—but because of its size. Its *sheer* size.

There were eleven children—seven boys and four girls—a number so out of whack with the norm in D.C.'s private schools that, wherever the Woodburns went, a mantra followed them. "They have eleven kids— *and they're not even Catholic—not even Catholic!—not even Catholic!*"

It was popular among Nick's friends to speculate about why Mrs. Woodburn was constantly pregnant, and also to tote up the tuition fees every time another Woodkid toddled into Pre-K at Sidwell, St. Albans, or National Cathedral. Lassiter spent half his childhood at Woodburn's house in Georgetown—a house that came with its own name, its own "grounds," and enough siblings, friends, and sidekicks to play Capture the Flag on a monumental scale.

When Lassiter telephoned him at the State Department, Woody took the call, but only to say, "I can't talk. I'm in a meeting."

"It isn't you I want to talk to," Lassiter said. "It's one of your brothers."

"Normally it would amuse me to guess, but—"

"The one at the tabloid."

"*Gus?* Gus would have been dead-last on my list. Wait a sec'—here you go."

It was harder to reach Augustus Woodburn, the managing editor of the *National Enquirer,* than it was to contact his brother, who was merely the head of one of the most secret components in the American government. In the end, Lassiter had to settle for a secretary's promise that "A.W." would be given the message.

Gus had always been in love with journalism. He'd edited the St. Alban's *Bulldog*, interned at the *Post*, and reported for the school paper at Yale—until his senior year, when he dropped out to marry a professional water-skier. Moving to Florida, where his wife worked at Cypress Gardens, Gus found a job on the *Enquirer*.

In any other family he might have been seen as a black sheep. But the Woodburn clan was large enough to be forgiving, and as Woody put it, "You wouldn't *believe* who that kid can get on the phone."

What made Lassiter think of Gus was that he'd seen the kid on television once, while he was flipping through channels. It was one of those round-table shows where a predatory moderator orchestrated a shouting match among a group of pundits and reporters. Lassiter would have blown right by except that the sneering host was introducing "Mr. *Augustus* Woodburn, managing editor of the *National Enquirer*. The topic: Media Ethics."

Obviously, it was someone's brilliant idea to have Gus on the show as a whipping boy for the virtuous men and women from *Harper's*, the *Washington Post*, the *Times*, and NPR. But it was Gus, a good-looking guy in his thirties, with a chiseled jaw and piercing blue eyes, who sucker-punched the stars. Taunted about "the sleaziness of tabloid journalism," he launched a frontal attack on the establishment.

With a mixture of measured perplexity and cool glee, he reminded his colleagues that the *Enquirer* earned its income in the traditional way—from the sales of newspapers, rather than from the advertisements of liquor and tobacco companies. As for the newspaper's contents, it was true that the *Enquirer* had never won a Pulitzer Prize—but then, the prize itself had lost a lot of credibility as a consequence of the Janet Cooke scandal. Which raised the issue of journalistic ethics. Naming panelists and their benefactors, Gus questioned the likelihood of a journalist reporting evenhandedly on a subject— say, gun control or health care—when the same journalist had been paid $30,000 for a speech to the NRA or the American Medical Association. "We don't give speeches at the *Enquirer*," Gus said. "In fact, we don't even cover them."

By the time the show ended, the audience was on its feet, and Gus had a standing ovation.

When Gus returned his call, it was almost two P.M. Lassiter started to explain who he was, but Gus cut him off.

"I remember you. Elizabeth Goode dumped me for you when I was a sophomore and you were a senior."

"I'm sorry."

"I got over it," Gus said, and cut to the chase. "So what's up? I can't imagine."

It was a little uncomfortable, but Lassiter said he hoped he could count on Gus's discretion.

Gus laughed. "You know, I go through this about ten times a day. And the answer is: yes. You can count on it. Bulldog honor."

"It's about Callista Bates."

"My favorite movie star. What about her?"

"I'm looking for her."

"You and everyone else. We get more tips on Callista than anyone except Elvis. Though, personally, I hope she stays lost. Because if she turns up, it's big news for a week—and then she's just another actress looking for a deal."

Lassiter joked that if he found her, he'd keep the news to himself. He explained something of *why* he was interested in the actress, that it was personal, that he couldn't really say more, but that if the paper had any leads about Callista's whereabouts, even leads that didn't seem to check out . . .

"I'm flattered. An investigator comes to *me*." He sighed. "But Callista Bates? To tell you the truth, I don't think there's been much at all since she took off from Minneapolis. A lot of 'sightings,' if you know what I mean, but—it's what, almost six years now?"

"Well, if you hear anything—"

"I might. Then again, we've got a stringer who's made a career out of Callista—"

"Finley?"

"Yeah—what? You already talked to him?"

"Not me. A guy who works for me—"

"Well, I hope he was discreet, because Finley is a pit bull. But listen, I'll tell you what: I'll have someone take a look at the archive, check out the hot line, see what we've got. I'll say we're doing an update, and—I'll put Finley in charge. That'll keep him busy. Hell, we'll probably *run* the thing, eventually. Anyway, I'll take a look at what we get, and if I see anything interesting, I'll be in touch."

"Thanks, Gus. I owe you one," Lassiter said.

"Two. Don't forget Elizabeth Goode."

—

Later that afternoon an envelope arrived from the Research department, containing the credit report on Lassiter's sister. It was six pages long, but he went directly to the end, where the other queries were listed. And there it was: *10–19–95 Allied National Products.*

That sealed it. The same broker in Chicago who'd run "Marie Williams" had run his sister—and he'd done it on the same day. It had to be Grimaldi.

He drummed his fingers on the desk. Now what? He thought for a moment, and called Research. "I want to get a birth certificate," he said, "for a woman named Marie Williams. Middle initial A, as in . . . Alabama. The DOB's March eighth, 1962. I don't know the place of birth, but it was somewhere in Maine. Get a sub in the state capital—I'm sure they've got a Bureau of Vital Statistics or something like that. Ask them to fax us whatever they can get."

Which, at a minimum, would be her parents' names and place of birth. And while Callista might not have gone home, she might still be in touch with her parents, or failing that, with some of the people she'd grown up with. What the hell, it was a lead.

But there wasn't much else that he could do. He had Gary Stoykavich poking around in Minneapolis, seeing what he could learn about Callista's two years there. He had Gus Woodburn culling leads from the *Enquirer's* archive, and someone in Maine looking for Callista's birth certificate. Deva Collins was writing a memo on Baresi's religious studies and, if she hadn't forgotten, looking for someone to explain what Baresi had been doing as a geneticist.

He was mulling this over when one of the kids in Research called to say that "a ton of stuff is on the way from Katz and Djamma—"

"What the hell is that?" Lassiter asked.

"They're the P.R. firm that handled Callista Bates."

"Nice of them to help," Lassiter remarked.

"They're pretty motivated. The guy I talked to said if we can locate her, it's big bucks. Tristar wants her for a bio-pic on Garbo, and Nicky Katz says he can get eight figures. So I had to promise that we'd let 'em know if we found anything."

He spent the rest of the day in staff meetings and in consultations with lawyers, going over the fine print in contracts for the company's sale. Wherever he went, Buck remained exactly two steps behind,

scanning the office as if it were Dealey Plaza. That his presence un-
settled people was clear from the worried glances he inspired, and yet,
Lassiter made no effort to explain him, taking perverse pleasure in the
fireplug's improbable presence.

When Deva Collins stopped by around six o'clock and, with a little
flourish, set a paper on his desk, he was tired.

"Ta-daa!" she said.

"What's this?"

She looked crestfallen. "My brief."

"Your 'brief'?"

Her face reddened. "On Ignazio Baresi—his contribution to religious scholarship."

"Oh, yeah," he said, rubbing his eyes. "Right. Great!" He tried to
sound enthusiastic, but his heart wasn't in it. At the moment all he
wanted to do was go home, have a drink, and watch Callista Bates
movies with his new pal Buck.

He looked at the memo. Five or six pages.

The truth was, his interest in solving the mystery—which turned
upon Baresi's relevance to Umbra Domini and the murders—had
begun to recede the moment that he'd started watching *Fast Track*.
The important thing now was to find Callista Bates and her child.
Dead or alive. Once that was done, he could return to his search for
Grimaldi, and for the *reason* behind it all.

Still, the young woman in front of him had worked hard on the
report, and he didn't want to seem unenthusiastic. So he sat down
with the memo and, chin in hand, started reading.

Ignazio Baresi (1927–1995):
Contributions to the Field of Biblical Scholarship
Report Prepared By: C. Deva Collins
Biographical data and list of publications.

Lassiter glanced quickly through this section. Baresi had enrolled at
the Sorbonne, a thirty-seven-year-old "undergraduate" taking courses
in philosophy and comparative religion. After a year he'd gone on to
study at the University of Münster, in Germany. Later, following a
year as a visiting professor at Harvard's School of Divinity, Baresi
retired abruptly from the field, in 1980, to return to his home in Italy.
Despite the brevity of his career . . . blah blah . . . Baresi's influence
was still felt in the field, etc.

This was followed by a chronological list of Baresi's published work. Lassiter skimmed through it, his eyes catching only a few titles: *The Essential Humanity of Christ: Doctrine or Dictum?* (1974) . . . *Goddess Worship and the Virgin Mary* (1977). And his single book: *Relic, Totem, and Divinity* (1980).

Biblical Scholarship and Christology. Deva described the nature of this discipline, which she said had been focused for the last 150 years on what she called "the search for the historical Jesus." Essentially, this was an attempt by scholars to strip away myth, hearsay, and doctrine imposed after the fact on "the salvation event," and to find out what parts of the gospels were "verifiably true." As increasingly sophisticated modern methods were brought to bear on the matter, the answer to the question, "What could be absolutely verified about the life and death of Jesus?" was: *hardly anything.*

Baresi's work. Baresi's master's thesis was in the field of doctrinal analysis and concerned the influence of exterior events on church doctrine. Baresi pointed out that the insistence of doctrine on the human, carnal, fleshly nature of Jesus was not from gospel, but to counter the belief of another Christian sect that Jesus was entirely divine. In the gospels themselves, there was little mention of Christ's birth—Mary was barely referred to—and not much emphasis on his suffering, either. The doctrinal insistence on a Jesus who was born like a man, died like a man, and felt pain like a man could be traced also in the visual record of Christian religious art. Although there was no early Christian art—early Christians came from a Semitic tradition that forbids depiction—once it began to evolve, renditions of Christ changed rapidly: from a glowing, happy "solar" youth, surrounded by radiance (fourth century), to a suffering Christ nailed to the cross and bleeding from his wounds (seventh century).

Deva pointed out that although this initial paper was within the tradition of biblical scholarship, after that, Baresi's work veered off sharply.

Relic, Totem, and Divinity. In his only book, Baresi researched the development of the cult of martyrs and saints within Christianity, which led to the popular belief in the power of relics—and how this almost certainly had its roots in ancient totemic and animistic belief systems.

Totems and fetishes differ from relics in that although both confer power upon their possessors, totems and fetishes are symbolic, whereas relics are the actual material remains of holy persons after their death, or objects sanctified by contact with the "corporeal body."

Totems and fetishes are often connected with animals—and both honor and transfer the strength of the animal to a tribe or individual. In Baresi's opinion, ancient cave paintings were totemic in nature, both honoring the animals and in some sense "capturing" their power.

Baresi related totemic beliefs and faith in relics to very primitive rites—in which the blood of the lion, for example, was ingested as a means of absorbing the animal's strength. Cannibal ritual also often involved the ingestion of blood and organs of the vanquished enemy, a means of absorbing his strength and conquering his spirit. Baresi discussed the totemic power of ritual objects in many religions—and explored the shift of such power in some cultures from objects to the more abstract: words, incantations, and, especially in Judaism and Islam, letters and numbers.

The second half of Baresi's book concerned relics, and especially the role of the relic in Christianity. By the fourth century the belief in the magical power of Christian relics to cast out demons, to cure illness, and so on, was well established. As a representation of power easily understood by the common man, it was not surprising that relic popularity grew. By the ninth century there was a specialized business, centered in Rome, that sold holy relics all over Europe. By the Middle Ages, nearly every tiny church had its bones, fingernail parings, teeth of various saints and martyrs, often kept in elaborate reliquaries. So avid was relic gathering, and so strong the belief in their power, that relic mongers watched over likely saints and martyrs, especially sick ones, and moved in as soon as they died, boiling the bodies down to the bones.

The most powerful relics were those of Jesus and Mary. Jesus' foreskin was preserved in jeweled reliquaries in half a dozen churches, as was hay from the manger, hair, his umbilical cord, his milk teeth, his tears, his blood, his fingernails. Mary's hair was here, there, and everywhere, as were vials of her breast milk and even chips of rock upon which her breast milk had fallen, turning the stone white. As for relics of the Passion, there were innumerable nails, thorns from the crown of thorns, the *entire* crown of thorns—at the Sainte Chapelle in Paris—three examples of the Spear of Longinus (the lance that pierced Christ's side), and various cloths impressed with Christ's sweat, including the vera icon and the famous Shroud of Turin. There were shards of the marble slab from Christ's tomb, burial linens and sandals, and every imaginable artifact that had come into contact with the body of Christ. (No bones or teeth, of course—the normal relics of saints—since these had ascended into Heaven.)

Baresi listed some of the miracles attributed to these various relics and traced their lineage. Although there were obvious hoaxes—enough splinters of the True Cross to build any number of barns—the belief in the power of relics was so ancient and instinctual that it defied common sense to believe that there were *no* relics of Christ. If modern-day peoples, Baresi argued, easily came to believe that something as immaterial as a vision of the Virgin might pinpoint a source of curative waters—as witness the pilgrims to Lourdes—then how likely was it that none of Jesus' many followers preserved actual relics of what was, after all, a living god?

He finished by arguing that the ritual of the Eucharist, wherein the symbolic wine and wafer are transformed into the blood and body of Christ, is a practice *based* on primitive animistic belief in the power of relics. Transubstantiation is nothing more than a spiritual transformation of the symbolic relic (the wine) into the actual relic (the blood).

> (Note: Mr. Lassiter. Most of this information came from a Georgetown student's doctoral thesis, written in 1989. The student's name is Marcia A. Ingersoll, and I have her address if you want it. Deva.)

33

In the week that followed, Lassiter's "progress" was mostly negative.

The subcontractor in Augusta reported that no one named Marie A. Williams had been born in Maine on March 8, 1962. "She might have had a change of name," the sub suggested, "but if she did, there's nothing we can do about it. Change of names aren't cross-referenced, and *no*, I can't pull up all the girls who were born March eighth, 'sixty-two. What I could do—and did—was look for a *Mary* Williams, in case you got the first name wrong."

"And what did you get?"

"I came up with seventeen since 1950, and four of them have a middle name that begins with A. But don't get your hopes up: none of them are the one you're looking for—the birthdates are all wrong. Wrong year, wrong everything."

So that was that. As for Gus Woodburn at the *Enquirer*, and Gary Stoykavich in Minneapolis, nothing had been heard. Indeed, the only new information that he'd received was delivered to his office by a kid from Research, who walked in with a cardboard banker's box in his arms. This was a pull-together on Callista Bates, supplemented by materials from the Katz & Djamma agency. All in all, it was a chaotic compilation of online research, newspaper and magazine clips, videos, photographs, fanzines, screenplays, and transcripts. Callista's testimony in the stalking trial was there, verbatim, and so were copies of interviews with *Rolling Stone, Premiere*, and "60 Minutes."

The kid was apologetic. "We tried a couple of different ways to organize it, but without knowing what you're looking for ..." He shrugged, and added, "We just put it in chronological order."

"That's okay," Lassiter replied. "I don't know what I'm looking for, and I won't until I've found it. So, I guess I'll just have to do my own reading."

And so he did. He read everything about Callista Bates, from deconstructionist reviews in *Cinema Aujourd'hui* to the tabloids' breathless (if speculative) accounts of her love life. He learned how much each of her pictures had grossed, her favorite flower (Queen Anne's lace), favorite charity (PETA), and where she stood on organic food (she preferred it). He could recite chapter and verse of sightings that put her everywhere from a music studio in Muscle Shoals to an opium den in Chiang Mai—and most points in between. (She's dying of a disfiguring disease in a Swiss clinic! No, she's living as a Poor Clare on the streets of Calcutta!) In short, while there was still a great deal left to read, it seemed to him that he knew everything about Callista Bates—except where she was born, where she was living, and what she was calling herself these days.

In the evenings, he worked his way through the videos. He'd seen them all by now, watching them with Buck and Pico, stretched out on the living room floor. With the streets buried in snow and ice, running had become a virtual impossibility, and so he'd taken to doing abdominal crunches with his baby-sitters. It did not make him happy.

One thing about Callista's acting—she was a chameleon, and that, obviously, was one of the main reasons she'd been able to disappear so successfully. Whoever she was on screen, you thought, that's the *real* her, that's what she's actually *like*—no matter what she wore, or whom she was playing.

Maybe that made her a great actress, maybe not. There was a lot of hype where Callista Bates was concerned, and the truth was, her star didn't go nova until, like so many other artists, she was suddenly gone— another brilliant flame-out in the constellation of the prematurely dead.

Or missing.

Still, Lassiter thought, in Callista's case the hype was almost true. She had amazing authority as an actress, and that authority only became apparent when the film had ended. You never saw the wheels turn or had the sense that you were watching "a performance"—until it was over, and you suddenly realized that you hadn't taken your eyes off her for two hours. And it wasn't just her beauty that held you. On the contrary, her attractiveness was often obscured by the roles she chose—the punked-out, junkie minstrel in *Piper*; the rabbity housewife in *Daylily*; the buttoned-down scientist in *Meteor Shower*.

Which reminded him: he had to call a scientist named David Torgoff. According to Deva, Torgoff was a consultant whom the company had used as an expert witness in investigations involving DNA evidence. "A walking oxymoron," he was a famously plain-speaking professor of microbiology at MIT. As such, he was eminently suited to guide Lassiter through the polysyllabic fog of Baresi's researches into genetics. The operative words being "plain-speaking."

He searched his desk for Torgoff's number, and just as he found it, Victoria buzzed him on the intercom. "There's a Mr. Coppi calling? From Rome?"

Lassiter hesitated, wondering who Coppi might be. Finally, he said, "Put him through."

A moment later a man's voice came on the line. "Mr. Lassiter? Mr. Joseph Lassiter?"

"Yes?"

"Forgive me, but . . . I must be certain that I have the correct person. Are you the Mr. Joseph Lassiter who was recently a guest at the Pensione Aquila in Montecastello di Peglia?"

The silence hung between them for a long while, as the adrenaline surged in Lassiter's chest. "Who is this?" he asked.

"I apologize, Mr. Lassiter. My name is Marcello Coppi. I am a lawyer in Perugia."

"Mm-hmnnn," Lassiter said, doing his best to keep his voice in neutral.

"Yes. And, uhhh, I was given your telephone number by an associate—in the carabinieri."

"I see. And what's it about?"

"I am afraid that I have some unpleasant news."

"Mr. Coppi . . . please."

The Italian cleared his throat. "The police will soon petition the court for your indictment in the murders of . . . a moment, please . . . Giulio Azetti and . . . Vincenzo Varese."

Lassiter felt the breath go out of him. "That's insane," he said. "If I was going to kill Azetti, why would I tell people I was on my way to the church? He was dead when I found him!"

"I have no doubt of your innocence, Mr. Lassiter, but I would caution you not to discuss details of your defense on the telephone. The purpose of this call is only to suggest that it is in your interest to have representation in this matter—here, in Italy . . . and to offer my services."

Lassiter took a deep breath and blew a stream of air toward the ceiling.

"I can assure you that I have the highest references, Mr. Lassiter. If you will contact the American embassy—"

"This is unbelievable," Lassiter said.

"Yes, I agree. It is quite unusual. Normally, the police would make an effort to arrange an interview in Washington, but in this case . . . I am told they will seek extradition as soon as the court issues its indictment. It is very unusual."

Lassiter thought for a moment, and asked, "Why would they do it that way?"

"I don't know. Perhaps there is pressure. . . ."

"Yeah," Lassiter said, "and I can guess where it's coming from." He paused. "Look: this isn't what you'd call a convenient time for me to be extradited anywhere—"

"This is a joke?"

"Yes. The point is: if you represented me over there—could you delay this thing?"

"I don't know," the Italian said. "It is possible, of course, *but* . . ."

"You'll need a retainer."

"Well . . . yes, of course."

Once an amount had been settled upon, Coppi promised to keep Lassiter informed of every development, and Lassiter, in turn, said that he'd find a lawyer in Washington to represent him in the States. When they'd exchanged particulars, Lassiter hung up the phone, sat back in his chair, and muttered *fuck,* over and over again—until Victoria knocked and leaned in through the door.

"Joe?"

"Yeah, c'mon in."

"This just arrived." She came to his desk, and handed him a Federal Express envelope. "It's from the *National Enquirer.*"

"Oh! Great. Thanks."

As Lassiter began to open the envelope, Victoria turned toward the door, then stopped. "Ummmm . . . ?"

Lassiter looked up from the envelope. "What?"

"I was just curious."

"About what?"

"Buck."

Lassiter snorted. "We're all curious about Buck—what's on your mind?"

"Well," she said, "I was just wondering if . . . well, is he married?"

Lassiter frowned. "I don't know," he said. "It never came up. You want me to ask him?"

"No," Victoria replied, blushing. "It's not important." And with that, she closed the door behind her.

Lassiter put his head in his hands. Italy was a disaster. It wasn't a question of prevailing in the courts. He was confident of doing that—if the case ever came to trial. But it wouldn't, that was the point. If I'm extradited, Lassiter thought, they'll kill me in jail—no question.

Unless I beat them first.

He looked up, sat back, and drummed his fingers on the desk. What to do? Stay cool, he told himself. Until it gets hot. Then run like hell.

The envelope from Gus Woodburn contained a note and an eight-by-ten photo of a woman, laughing as she knelt to zip up the parka on a little boy. They were standing outside a McDonald's, somewhere cold: piles of dingy snow lay on the ground, and there were parked cars and mountains in the background. Lassiter looked at the woman and thought, That's her. That's definitely, probably her. But he couldn't be sure. She was in three-quarter profile and slightly out of focus. The photograph was obviously a blowup of a snapshot taken with a cheap camera, and . . . it could be her, or it could be someone who looked like her.

Still, it was definitely her—or her sister—because there was no mistaking the boy: he was standing in front of the woman with a ski cap in one hand, and a Big Mac in the other. His hair was a tangle of dark curls, and he seemed to be looking at the camera from the bottom of a well.

And this is Jesse, she'd said. Lassiter remembered now, and remembered, also, that she'd told him *her* name as well. Standing there, a few feet from Kathy's grave, she'd introduced herself. Her name was . . .

Gone. Absolutely gone.

With a growl of frustration, Lassiter turned to the note that accompanied the photo, and began to read:

Joe—
    The Callista-watchers think this is the real thing, but what do they know? It came in a year ago, and the cover letter went up in smoke, somewhere between the mail room and my desk. So we don't know who took it or where, but if it's of any use . . . great. (Looks like she's got a kid! Love child? Terror Tot? If you find out, let me know!)

Gus

There was a magnifying glass in Lassiter's desk, and he used it to look more closely at the photo. Callista and Jesse were in the foreground, with the restaurant just behind them. To the left were a couple of parked cars, and in the distance, mountains.

If the angle had been a little different, it would have been possible to see the license plates on the cars—and that might have allowed him to guess the state in which the picture had been taken. But the photographer had framed the photo in such a way that only the upper parts of the cars could be seen.

Even so, there was a clue of sorts: using the magnifying glass, Lassiter could see that one of the mountains in the background was crisscrossed with ski trails. With forty people in the Washington office, there was a chance one of them would recognize the place. He called Victoria on the intercom and asked her to come in.

"We're having a contest," he said, handing her the photo. "A weekend for two in New York, all expenses paid, for anyone who can tell me where this was taken."

Victoria squinted at the photo. "How are they supposed to know that?" she asked.

"If I knew that, Victoria, I wouldn't have a contest," Lassiter said. "But I was thinking: maybe you should mention the ski slope in the background. Maybe somebody'll recognize the pattern."

Victoria looked doubtful. "What ski slope?" she asked.

"Right there," Lassiter said. "Behind the restaurant. You can see the trails."

"It's a blur."

"It's not a blur. A skier would probably recognize it in a second."

"I'm a skier," Victoria said, "and I'm telling you, it's a blur."

Lassiter grimaced. "Look, just get some copies made—and pass 'em out, okay? You never know."

Victoria shrugged. "Oh-kayyy," she sang, and went off to the copy room.

That night, Lassiter ate Chinese takeout in his study, and washed it down with too many Tsing-taos. He watched *Meteor Shower* for the third time, and fell asleep, thinking, *I'm going to need a lawyer.* He corrected himself. *Another* lawyer. Someone to join the contingent of corporate lawyers retained to represent the firm, someone to supplement the efforts of the special legal talent finalizing the fine print of the AmEx deal, someone to handle the stateside end of things in tandem with

Marcello Coppi—in short, he needed a *criminal* lawyer. It was a bad sign, he knew, when the lawyers in your life outnumbered your friends.

In the morning, they stopped at the cleaners on the way to work, and Lassiter picked up his shirts and leather jacket. To his surprise, and chagrin, an envelope was pinned to the pocket of the jacket— and inside was Baresi's letter to Father Azetti. In the escape from Montecastello, he'd forgotten completely about it. He glanced at it briefly and shoved it into the jacket's breast pocket.

As the Buick rolled down the GW Parkway toward the Key Bridge, Lassiter sat in the back, reading the *Washington Post*. Pico and Buck were in the front, talking quietly, when Buck suddenly turned around.

"We got a problem," he said.

Lassiter grunted. "No shit."

"I mean it," Buck said. "We've had a tail for two days now."

Lassiter looked up from the newspaper and reflexively glanced over his shoulder. There were a thousand cars behind them. "I don't see anything," he said. "It's *rush* hour."

"Buck's right," Pico said. "There was a car outside the house last night."

"*All* night," Buck corrected.

"And when we went to the cleaners, they pulled into the gas station across the street. I think they've been with us since yesterday morning," Pico added.

Lassiter put the newspaper down. "Why didn't you call the cops?" he asked.

Buck shrugged. " 'Call the cops'? They *are* the cops."

"What do you mean?"

"Bureau plates," Pico said. "The city issued 'em all at once—so they're all in sequence. You can spot 'em a mile away. It's like they're wearin' a bell."

Buck provided the sound effects: "Bong! Bong!"

Pico laughed. "Avon calling! Except that isn't what they say. What they say is: 'Washington field office!' "

Lassiter took a deep breath, closed his eyes, and let it out.

"Is there something we ought to know?" Buck asked.

Lassiter shook his head. "I've got a problem in Italy. I think this is probably a part of that."

When they got to the office, Pico parked the car in the garage beneath the building, while Buck accompanied Lassiter to the ninth floor. As the elevator doors opened the bodyguard pushed the hair back at the sides of his head and, apropos of nothing, said, "That Victoria—she's something, huh?"

As soon as he entered his office Lassiter went to the window and looked out. Across the street a blue Taurus sat in a No Parking zone, begging for a fifty-dollar ticket. He couldn't see if anyone was in the car, but a curl of smoke was rising from the tailpipe. Gritting his teeth, he pulled the drapes and went to his desk.

Where a package wrapped in butcher's paper was waiting. He glanced at the return address—Institute of Light—and tore it open.

Inside was a fine, but not mint, copy of *Relic, Totem, and Divinity*. There was no dust jacket, and a number of pages were dog-eared. Still . . . it looked interesting. There were a number of black-and-white plates, reproducing such obscure paintings as *Abgar's Messenger Receives from Christ the Linen Bearing Christ's Likeness*; *The City of Hierapolis*; *Mary Breast-feeding Jesus*; and *The Massacre of the Innocents*.

This last, attributed to the "Pomeranian Master (Danzig?)," and dated 1490–97, was part of something called *The Jerusalem Triptych*. According to the text, the painting stressed the sadism of Christ's tormentors, while illustrating the metaphysical wedding of Christ to St. Veronica.

Lassiter leafed through the pages of the book.

The first chapter discussed the origins of relic worship and icon cults. In it, Judaism was contrasted to Greek culture, which Baresi characterized as polytheistic, sedentary, and iconic—by which he meant that the Greeks organized their lives around city-states and representational art. Judaism, on the other hand, was defined by "linguistic monotheism." It was a religion of nomads, oriented toward the Word rather than the image. Christianity was seen as a Jewish sect, or schismatic tendency, that became increasingly iconic as the centuries passed—until, in about A.D. 325, portraits of Christ began to appear.

A second chapter, entitled "Blood and Gnosis," was devoted to the question of the cultural attitudes of Christians and Jews toward nature, and in particular toward menstruation or "female flux." Lassiter was reading this when Riordan called.

"Something's come up," the detective said.

Lassiter set the book aside. "What? The nurse is talking?"

"No, the nurse is not talking. The nurse is *praying*. One rosary after another."

"So . . . *what*? You've found Grimaldi?"

"No. But I think I know how he got loose. And it ain't good."

"What do you mean?" Lassiter asked.

"We got a copy of the toll calls from the house in Emmitsburg. Over the last six months. See who they're talking to, y'know? Maybe we'll get a lead on where Grimaldi's gone."

"Good idea."

"Right. So I get a list, and I'm going through the numbers with a Criss-Cross—and there's a couple of hundred numbers, and guess what?"

"Jimmy . . ."

"C'monnnnn—guess."

"They're doing phone sex."

Riordan made a sort of nasal bleat—*Nyannnh!*—in what was really a pretty good imitation of a TV game show signaling the wrong answer. "Wrong! There's all these calls from Emmitsburg to a house in Potomac. Now, I won't make you guess whose house it is—"

"Thank you."

" 'Cuz you'd never guess. This particular house belongs to your friend and mine, Thomas Drabowsky."

Lassiter was at a loss. He sat there for a moment, rubbing his eyes with his thumb and forefinger. Finally, he said, "The FBI guy?"

"Right!"

"So . . . you think Grimaldi was calling Drabowsky?"

"No no no! The calls I'm talking about are *way* back—before Grimaldi's even on the screen. August, September, October—they *stop* about the time Grimaldi's arrested."

"Then . . . what's the point?"

"Almost all of the calls are on weekends, or at night. So I figure this guy's got some personal business with the people in Emmitsburg. You with me?"

"Tentatively."

"So Derek and I go out to see 'em—"

"Derek?!"

"Yeah, Derek's back on the case. Anyway, we go out there, and I'm talkin' to 'em one on one. And about the fourth person I talk to, this mousy guy, says, 'Oh, yeah, those are my calls. I was talking to Thomas.' And I say, 'Oh? And can you tell me what the calls were about?' And he says, 'Sure. We were talking about the outreach program. Thomas helps us on weekends with the shelter and the soup kitchen. Thomas is a saint,' he says.

"And I say, 'Oh, really? And who *is* this guy, Thomas—I mean, *really*?' And *he* says, 'Oh, he's just a member—like everyone else.' 'A member of what?' I ask. And he says, 'Umbra Domini. Thomas is a numenary.' 'And what,' I ask, 'does Thomas do in real life when he's not helpin' the poor?' And the guy says, 'I don't know. We don't talk about our secular lives.'" Riordan exploded into laughter. "He's talking to a homicide detective, and he says, 'We don't talk about our secular lives'! Do you believe that?!"

Lassiter didn't say anything for a long while. Then: "So what do you think happened?"

"I know what happened. I can't prove it—but I know. When Grimaldi's in the hospital, the word gets out. The next thing you know, Juliette's working the burn ward at Fairfax General. Time comes to transfer Grimaldi, she helps him escape and he winds up in Emmitsburg."

"We already knew that."

"Lissen up! Potomac ain't the only place they're calling. I got toll calls to Italy. Emmitsburg to Naples—it kind of jumps out at you. And guess who they're calling?"

"I don't have to guess."

"Right, Grimaldi's calling home. He's calling Umbra Domini headquarters. I checked."

"Isn't that . . . I don't know—kind of risky?"

"Nah. Why's it risky? This is their house—if they got to call headquarters once in a while, what's wrong with that? No, the interesting part is the timing. The first call comes the day after Grimaldi blows the hospital—so I figure he's reporting in."

"Okay."

"The next call comes a couple of weeks ago—right after the surveillance goes in."

"Emmitsburg calls Naples?"

"Yeah. I figure they must have spotted the surveillance. Which wouldn't be difficult—I mean, it's not like there's a lot of traffic out there."

"So Grimaldi called Naples and—"

"Bibbity bobbity boo! Drabowsky takes over. *Thomas* takes over, and he does some *outreach*, all right. The surveillance disappears. And so does Grimaldi."

Lassiter thought about it. Finally, he said, "What are you going to do?"

"What am I going to *do*? I'll tell you what I'm gonna do. I'm going to crawl inside a mummy bag and zip it up. Then I'm gonna mail myself to Mars, that's what I'm gonna do."

"I'm serious."

"So am I. Look at it from my point of view: I'm gettin' out in thirty-four days. I don't need this shit. And not only that: I can't prove anything, anyway. It's all speculation."

"It's not! You've got the toll slips."

"Right—as if the toll slips told us what was said. Except they don't! We're guessing. And as for Drabowsky—you can't use the guy's religion against him. Think about it. What am I gonna say? 'Arrest that man, he's feeding the homeless.' Are you kiddin'? Not to mention, this guy ain't exactly a foot soldier in the Bureau. He's more like a brigadier general. You fuck with him, you're in a world of trouble." Riordan sighed as the two of them fell silent. Then he asked, "What about you? You got anything for me?"

"No," Lassiter said, and then he remembered. "Well, maybe."

"Maybe? What's 'maybe'?"

"I have a letter . . . from Baresi."

"He *wrote* you?"

"No," Lassiter replied, "it's a letter to a priest. When I get it translated, I'll send you a copy."

When Riordan rang off, Lassiter sat back in his chair and thought about Drabowsky. And what he thought was: *This is trouble. If anyone can find Callista Bates, the Bureau can. And if someone in the Bureau wants to fuck me up, he's got the resources.*

The intercom buzzed, and Victoria said, "Dick Biddle's outside—can you see him?"

"Sure," Lassiter said. "Send him in."

Biddle was an older man who'd retired from the State Department five years before. Tall, thin, and patrician, he was partial to dark gray suits, burgundy ties, and expensive cuff links. He was also a chain-smoker who had the disturbing habit of letting the ash on his cigarette grow to the point that those around him were distracted by the question of when it would fall.

Entering the office with a cigarette in hand, he laid an eight-by-ten glossy on Lassiter's desk and sat down, crossing his legs. The cigarette fumed in his hand, a few inches from his ear. Lassiter noticed that the ash was almost an inch long. How does he walk with it? he wondered.

"I've always liked the Lowell," Biddle said, "but I hear nice things about the Peninsula. Either one will be fine."

"For what?" Lassiter asked, glancing at the photo. It was the *Enquirer's* picture of I-think-it's-Callista, standing outside the McDonald's in God-knows-where.

"My weekend in New York. I'm claiming the prize." He took a drag on his cigarette and Lassiter watched, fascinated, as gravity tugged at the ashes.

"You know where it is?"

"I do." Smoke curled toward the ceiling.

"And . . . do you want to share that information?"

"Absolutely. It's somewhere . . . Mainey."

Lassiter gave him an incredulous look. " 'Somewhere Mainey'. . . Like what? Lillehammer?"

Biddle smiled. "No. Like Sunday River. Or Sugarloaf. One or the other, but definitely Maine." He took another drag, and the ash hung in the air like a fallen parenthesis.

Lassiter looked at the photograph. "How can you tell?"

"Well, there's the snow, to begin with. That's a clue."

"Ye-ahh . . ."

"And there's a ski resort . . . which, of course, Maine has."

"Right . . ."

"And then, there's the bears."

Lassiter looked at the picture again. "What bears?" he said. "There aren't any *bears.*"

"There are bears," Biddle replied, and nodded toward Lassiter's magnifying glass. "Polar bears."

Lassiter picked up the magnifying glass and applied it to the photo. "Where?" he asked.

"On the window of the van."

Lassiter looked. A veneer of salt and dirt was caked on the rear windshield, on which someone had scrawled *Clean Me!* and *Go You Bears!!!* "You mean the graffiti?" he asked.

"I mean the polar bear," Biddle said. "In the lower right-hand corner."

Lassiter moved the magnifying glass closer to the photo, then pulled it back. There was an oval white spot on the window. "The white dot?" he asked. "You can't tell what that is!"

"It's a polar bear. Galloping."

"How do you know?"

"Because I went to Bowdoin. It's my alma mater. I *know* the bear."

"But lots of schools have bears as their . . ."

"Totems," Biddle said.

"Thank you," Lassiter replied, glancing around for an ashtray. The long parabola of ash trembled at the end of the investigator's cigarette.

"But those are brown bears or black bears or grizzly bears—or some such thing. And besides, when the students cheer for them, they say, 'Go Bears!' or 'Yoo-rah-rah Bears.' But not at Bowdoin. We say 'Go *You* Bears.' No one else says that."

"C'mon—"

"We've practically patented it. Which is why I can tell you that the white dot you're looking at is definitely, unquestionably, *Ursus maritimus.* Trust me on this."

Lassiter sat back and laid the magnifying glass aside. "That doesn't prove the van's *in* Maine. Just that it's *from* Maine. At most, that's what it proves."

Biddle tapped his forefinger against the cigarette, and smiled as the ash crashed to the carpet. Lassiter winced. "I take it you're looking for the woman in the picture?" Biddle asked.

Lassiter nodded.

The older man moved his right leg in an arc, brushing the ash into the carpet. "Do you have any reason to believe she's anywhere *other* than Maine?"

Lassiter shook his head. "No," he said. "In fact, she was born there."

"Really?" Biddle said, getting to his feet.

"Yes."

"Well, then," he said, turning toward the door. "Should I make a reservation or not?"

Lassiter picked up the magnifying glass and looked at the photograph for the hundredth time. Finally, he put the magnifier down and said, "Yeah. Enjoy yourself."

As the door closed behind him, Lassiter walked to the window and looked out. The blue Taurus was still there.

He went back to his desk and roused Victoria on the intercom.

"Send Buck in, would you? And tell Freddy I'd like to see him." Then he dialed the number Deva had given him for the genetics guy in Boston. The phone rang once at the other end, and a man answered, *"Was ist?"*

Famously plain-spoken, my ass, Lassiter thought. "Dr. Torgoff? David Torgoff?"

"Da-ahh!"

Buck and Freddy came into the room, and Lassiter waved them to sit down. "This is Joe Lassiter . . . in Washington."

"Oh," Torgoff said. "Sorry about that. I thought you were my racquetball partner."

Lassiter smiled with relief. "Is he German?"

"No," Torgoff answered. "That's just something . . . we do. It's kind of hard to explain. I guess you'd have to be there."

"Actually, I will be—that's why I'm calling. I'm coming up to Boston this afternoon, and I was hoping . . . if you have any time on Saturday—"

"I'm afraid I don't—but I could see you on Sunday. Is the afternoon all right? Two-ish?"

"Two's fine." Lassiter wrote down Torgoff's directions and hung up. Then he turned to Buck and Freddy. "Is Pico downstairs?" he asked.

Buck nodded. "Yeah, sure. He's waiting in the garage. You want him up here?"

"No. I want the three of you to get in the car and take it out of the garage—fast. Don't kill anyone, but when you hit the street, hang a right, and *floor it.*"

"Where do you want us to go?" Buck asked.

"I don't care where you go, as long as the Taurus across the street follows you."

"You want me to ride with them?" Freddy asked.

"Yeah," Lassiter said. "I want you to sit in the back. Like a decoy."

Freddy nodded thoughtfully. "Is that a decoy, like an optical illusion . . . or is that a decoy, like a sitting duck?"

"More like an optical illusion," Lassiter replied, getting up from the desk. He went to the coat tree, grabbed his overcoat, and tossed it to Freddy. "Put this on," he said, "and see if you can borrow a hat."

Buck shook his head and frowned. "I don't know about this, Joe . . . Terry said I should stick to you like white on rice."

Lassiter nodded, pulling on the leather jacket that he'd gotten back from the cleaners that morning. "When you see Terry? Just tell him I said the Buck stops here." Freddy groaned. *"Floor it,"* Lassiter repeated, and pushed the two of them out the door.

Returning to his desk, he stuffed Baresi's book and a handful of the Callista articles in his briefcase, turned off the light, and walked to the window. Standing to the side, he looked out at the street. There were a few pedestrians navigating the icy sidewalks, but very little traffic. A minute went by, two, three—and suddenly the Buick exploded out of the parking garage, leaped the curb, and pancaked as it hit the street. Swinging to the right, it fishtailed away, accelerating into and through the intersection. A moment later the Taurus arced out of its no-parking space and, tires spinning on the snow, roared off after the Buick.

Briefcase in hand, Lassiter shut the door behind him and walked toward the elevators at the end of the lobby. Seeing him, Victoria called out, "Joe?"

"What?" He pressed the button for the elevator.

"There's a federal marshal downstairs at the reception desk," she said, holding her hand over the telephone receiver. "And a man from the Italian embassy. What do I tell them?"

"Tell 'em to come up," Lassiter replied. Victoria spoke into the phone as her boss waited for the elevator to arrive. When it did, he remained where he was, holding the doors ajar, his eyes on the indicator above the second elevator.

4 . . . 3–2–1 . . . 2–3–4–5 . . .6— In a few seconds it would be here.

With a little wave, Lassiter stepped into the elevator, turned toward Victoria and released the doors. "Tell 'em I stepped away from my desk," he said. "Tell 'em I'll be right back."

34

He registered at the Marriott Long Wharf as Joe Kelly, paying cash in advance, along with a fifty-dollar deposit to cover any telephone calls he might make. It wasn't like he was on the run, not really, but he wasn't strolling, either. If Umbra Domini wanted him indicted in Italy, he was sure they could get it done—if they hadn't already. The only reason a marshal would come to his office with someone from the Italian embassy would be if the Italian police wanted to talk to him—and thought he was dangerous.

And so, in the interests of prudence, he'd decided to be discreet, at least until he found Marie Williams.

There was a day to kill, and nothing much to do, before his appointment with Torgoff. So he trudged through the snowbound Boston streets until he found a hole-in-the-wall that sold falafel sandwiches. Ten minutes later he was back in his room, sitting on the couch with his feet up on the coffee table, reading from a stack of clips about Callista Bates.

There wasn't much that was new. After a while the press recycled its own stories, repackaging them with a different headline and different photos. Lassiter went through half a dozen stories without encountering a single detail he hadn't read somewhere else. It was drudge work but, in the absence of anything better to do, or any other leads, it was a way to kill the afternoon.

He picked up the transcript of an interview from a defunct late-night talk show called "Reel Time." In the late eighties the show had enjoyed a reputation as low key and hip, although in the end it proved too intellectual for commercial success. He remembered it fairly well. Stark sets, and one-on-one interviews with actors, directors, screenwriters, and critics.

The date on the transcript was April 27, 1988, when Callista was promoting a noir thriller called *Rose Red*. Her interviewer was Valery

Fine, and she was obviously determined to do more than flack Callista's new flick.

VF: So—an Oscar in your pocket for *Lost Horizon*, the new movie's a hit—you're pretty high-flying, aren't you? What's it like?

CB: Like? I don't know. (Laughs) High-flying? I guess it's like catching a thermal.

VF: You seem so . . . *unfazed*—is that a real word? I mean, it's been a pretty wild ride for you, and yet—you seem so . . . *together*. You choose your roles carefully, you turn down a lot of work . . . you seem immune, somehow, to the glitz.

CB: I wouldn't say that.

VF: I would. You're so . . . amazingly *level-headed*. And I wonder: Did you ever do anything really . . . *stupid*?

CB: (Laughs) Of course. God—*level-headed*. How boring is that?!

VF: Well, "level-headed," considering that you're everybody's love goddess. I mean—you're sitting there—you're Callista Bates! But at the same time you're so much the girl-next-door.

CB: (Laughs) Where are you *going* with this? You make me sound like Betty Crocker—with boobs!

VF: Well, hardly. For one thing, you're much too elusive for Betty Crocker. Tell us about yourself—about the real Callista Bates.

CB: No.

VF: "No"?!

CB: Unh-unh. I *want* to be elusive.

VF: But why? I know the ground rules—we won't talk about your family or childhood or any of that. But why do you want to shut people out? You're a bright, intelligent woman. You read, you have interests. Why shouldn't people know about that? It would give you—more dimension.

CB: But I don't *want* them to know that about me.

VF: Why not?

CB: (Sighs) It's like this. You know how when there's a camera around—at some news event—or maybe a sportscaster is doing a stand-up after a game? And, in the background, there's always a bunch of people, jumping up and down, waving at the camera, trying to get on TV?

VF: (Waving) You mean—Hi, Mom! Hi, Mom!

CB: Exactly. And if they actually make it onto the news or something, they're *thrilled*. It does something for them. It makes them part of another world—the Televised World—and somehow they think that's *more real*.

VF: You know what's really weird about that—this has happened to me. I mean, I don't have to tell anybody to watch me because, of course, everybody does already. (Laughs) But, what you were saying? *Friends* tell me to watch, all the time. "Heyyyyyy, Val—if you catch the Laker game on the tube, look for me! I'm six rows back of the bench and off to the right."

CB: Yes! Even though this is your *friend*, you know, and you see her all the time. Life-sized. In the flesh. So you don't have to watch her on television. But she *wants* you to see her on television.

VF: Actually, this was a guy.

CB: (Laughs) Anyway—that's one reaction to the camera, but there's another one, too. There *are* people who don't want to be on television, who don't want their pictures taken—because it makes them *less* real. You know the cliché—about the tribesman who doesn't want his picture taken because he thinks the camera will take his soul?

VF: Of course, but—wait a second! We're supposed to be talking about *you*!

CB: (Laughs) I'm getting to me! My point was—I'm a little bit like both of those examples. When I'm *acting*, I'm jumping up and down like *crazy* and I want *everybody* in the world to see me. But in real life, *me*, the real me? No. Then, I'm like the guy in Borneo. I don't want to talk about my personal life because, when I do, it makes me feel bad. It makes me feel like I lost a part of my soul.

VF: Come on, now—isn't that a little . . . *pretentious*? I don't want a piece of your *soul*. Just a story. Something about Callista the Person—instead of Callista the Star.

CB: (Sighs) You don't understand because you're not—I mean, you're the one asking the questions.

VF: Okay. Fair enough. Ask me a question. Go ahead. Anything.

CB: Okay. (Clears throat) Tell me—how often do you masturbate?

VF: (Screeching and laughing) That's *not fair*! I didn't ask you anything like that!

CB: A radio shock-jock would.

VF: But then you'd just refuse to answer, right?

CB: Yes—but then people would say I'm being *elusive*. Or not a good sport. Look—I'm not trying to be difficult. I used to blab all the time about myself.

VF: Not really.

CB: All right, not really. But even what I *did* say—it got so it kind of creeped me out.

VF: What do you mean?

CB: Well, I'd meet somebody. And he'd know everything about me—or think he did—and it was just . . . lopsided. After a while you just stop talking about a huge part of your life because, once you share it, it's not yours anymore. It's gone. I mean . . . I'm not explaining this very well.

VF: But those are the wages of fame, aren't they? If you want people to pay six bucks to go and see you—don't you owe them something?

CB: I don't think so. I mean, they're paying to see the movie, not to find out who my favorite Laker is or what I looked like when I was five.

VF: So you're not going to help me out?

CB: You're relentless!

VF: Pleeeeze! Just one thing—one dumb thing!

CB: (Sighs) All right. But only because it might stop someone else from making the same mistake. Although it won't, of course. Who am I kidding?

VF: Come on, come on. We're waiting!

CB: Okay, but it's really stupid. Not foolish or funny, but dumb—as in dangerous. (Sighs) When I first came to the West Coast, I was nineteen years old, I had almost no money, and I drove all the way out here by myself, in Gunther—

VF: Who's "Gunther"?

CB: Gunther is a VW van. An *old* VW van with bald tires, bad brakes, and a temperature problem. He's always overheating, and I practically had to push him over the Rockies. Not a safe car. And to save money, I slept in it— sometimes by the side of the road, sometimes in parking lots. I still can't believe I did it.

VF: So—did something terrible happen to you?

CB: No, but that's not the point. Most people were unbelievably nice, but things happened that could have been . . . I don't know . . . dangerous.

VF: Like what?

CB: Like the guy who tried to drag me into his car. Or the guy who climbed on top of the van and wouldn't get down—totally stoned.

VF: But still, you made it, right? Isn't that what counts?

CB: No. I was lucky. Someone else might not be.

VF: Good point. But I have to ask: Who *is* your favorite Laker?

The interview went on for another page or two. When Lassiter was finished with the piece, he put the story aside and reached for another article. But then he changed his mind. The story about the VW van . . . there was something about it that connected to something else. But what?

And then he remembered. There was an article in *L.A. Style* about the time she disappeared. The headline was "Th-Th-Th-That's All Folks! Callista Bows Out!"

Did he have it with him? He'd left most of the "Callista" material in D.C., bringing only what he hadn't read and a few key articles that he'd culled along the way. The *L.A. Style* piece ought to have been there, and so it was. He pulled it out of the stack from his briefcase and flipped through its pages, looking for the detail he wanted.

The article was an interview at the Beverly Hills Hotel, where Callista had stayed after selling her house. It was a stylized piece that was as much about the writer as it was about the actress. Irrelevant but precisely observed details crowded every paragraph. Callista's eyes were "a bruised indigo." She answered questions "with the syncopated cynicism of a lover who's been badly burned." What does *that* mean? Lassiter wondered.

The prose was arranged around a photograph of the star. She sat, in shorts and a blouse, with her bare legs crossed ("the only sign of tension an occasional impatient twitch of one toe").

> She was casting off the imprint of the city. That much was clear. The house was gone, the furniture sold, the Bentley sent back to the studio whence it came. In the hallway to her suite, a single suitcase waited by the door.
> I asked her what she was planning to do. She sat awhile in the tent of silence that she's inhabited since the trial, then shook her great mane of hair and said, "I'll think of something." As she spoke she swirled her straw and watched the condensation slide down the outside of her glass toward the table.
> "Isn't there anything you've kept?"
> She shook her head.
> "No clothes? No pictures? What about the Mercedes?"
> "I sold it," she replied. Behind her a lizard streaked up the sun-struck bungalow wall, so fast it seemed an hallucination. Callista grinned. She put on her sunglasses and stood up. It was clear that

the interview was over. "I thought I might as well ride out on the horse I rode in on," she said. And then she turned, and she was gone.

Lassiter put the article down and frowned. He was disappointed. He'd thought there was more to it. But still: *the horse she rode in on.* Well . . . that was Gunther. If you took her literally, the horse she rode in on was a VW van. That's what brought her to California: *Gunther.*

He got on the phone and called Gary Stoykavich in Minneapolis. "You got anything for me?" he asked.

"Nope."

"Well, let me ask you something: Can you find out what kind of car Williams drove when she was living there?"

"I already know that," the detective said. "And there were two cars— not one. She had a Honda Accord that she bought local, and a VW."

"A bug?"

"No. A van."

"Really!" Lassiter said.

"Yup. And the funny thing is—when she left, that's what she took. I mean, she *abandoned* the Honda. Left it in her parking slot and took the damn van. Of course, maybe she had a lot of stuff. So maybe the van was more useful. That's what Finley thinks, anyway."

Lassiter's heart sank. "So Finley knows she had a van."

It was a statement, not a question, and Lassiter felt empty, as his short-lived excitement crashed and his new "lead" began to fade into just another dead end. If Finley knew she'd left in a van, he'd have tracked it to the ends of the earth.

"Oh, hell, yes," Stoykavich said. "Finley ran Marie Williams and her Social through every DMV in the United States—including Alaska."

"And he came up empty?"

"I think he found a whole lot of Marie Williamses, but none of 'em owned a VW van. Or, if they did, he checked 'em out and they weren't her. They were some other Marie A. Williams."

Fuck, Lassiter thought.

"Did I just rain on someone's parade?"

"No," Lassiter lied and, thanking him, hung up.

In fact, the parade ground *was* a bit wet. The simple truth was that Grimaldi and his friends had a three- or four-month lead in trying to locate Callista. And while they had no doubt concentrated their efforts on eliminating those who were easiest to find, three or four months was a long time. On the other hand, Lassiter thought, I'm probably better at this than they are. And if *I'm* having this hard a time, Grimaldi isn't likely to be doing much better.

Unless Drabowsky and the FBI are helping him. In which case . . .

He walked over to the window and looked out at the gray urban landscape. Sleet ticked steadily against the pane, until the wind gusted and a cloud of ice crystals rattled the glass.

He rubbed his eyes and sat down. He tried to imagine "Marie Williams"—or whatever she was calling herself—driving the van into the woods somewhere. Letting it disintegrate. Or maybe she'd abandoned it on a city street, walking away from the car as she'd walked away from so much else.

But no. If she'd wanted to walk away from it, she would have walked away from it. But she didn't. She rode out on it—*and she was still riding.* Which meant, what?

If she still had the van, its registration was probably in her new name. Whatever that was. Wherever she might be.

He took a deep breath and exhaled. He realized that he was operating almost entirely on instinct. Simply because the woman had been born in Maine, and a photograph had been taken of her in Maine—or, at least, of someone who looked like her in what Dicky Biddle claimed was Maine—did not mean that she *lived* there.

On the other hand . . . why not? She had to be somewhere, and even if the evidence was thin, it was at least more likely that she'd be found in Maine than . . . Finland.

Lassiter reached for the phone. There were only a million people in Maine, so how many VW vans could there be—and how many of those would be owned by women? He got the number for the Department of Motor Vehicles in Augusta and dialed it. But, of course, it was closed. He'd have to call back on Monday morning.

With a sigh, he picked up the next article from the "Callista" file. It was a story about "palmistry" from a women's magazine in which the handprints of four celebrities were reproduced and analyzed by a team of chiromantists. According to the team, Callista suffered from "an excess of melancholy."

—

The next day he caught the T to Cambridge and got out at the stop across from MIT. Immediately, he wished he'd taken a cab. The sidewalks and gutters were a mess. Tons of salt had melted the snow, but there was nowhere for the water to go. It sat in lagoons beside the curbs, forcing pedestrians into long detours and occasional, athletic leaps.

Torgoff's office was in the Biology Department of the Whitaker College of Health, Science, and Technology. Torgoff was waiting for him—a compact young man with black hair and a cheerful smile. He was casually dressed in blue jeans, hiking boots, and a red T-shirt that sported identical images of Roy Orbison under a banner that read, ONLY THE CLONELY.

"Sorry I'm dressed like this," Torgoff said as he got to his feet to shake hands. "But then, I always am."

The office was small and piled high with stacks of books and papers. The walls were covered with charts and lists, a Tibetan calendar, Post-its, and cartoons about mad scientists. A dusty and battered model of the double helix, constructed of green garden twine and pieces of white poster board, hung from the ceiling like homemade flypaper. An easel stood next to the desk, and on the desk itself, amid piles of papers, was a Rubik's cube—an object Lassiter hadn't seen for years. Torgoff gestured to a chair as he fell back into his own, an ergonomic masterpiece in green corduroy.

"How much do you know about genetics?" Torgoff asked.

Lassiter looked at him. Shrugged.

"It's not a trick question," Torgoff said. "If I start talking about lac operons and RNA polymerase transcription—I might lose you. Which wouldn't be good. So why don't you just, you know . . ." He tapped the side of his head. "Whatcha got?"

Lassiter thought for a moment. "Mendel. There was a guy named Mendel. There's heredity—"

"Good! Heredity's big!"

"Dominant and recessive genes."

"Can you explain them?"

"No, but—I used to be able to. And then—" He rolled his eyes toward the ceiling and, seeing the homemade DNA molecule, said, "The double helix."

"You know what it is?"

"It's DNA," Lassiter said. "Though, actually, I guess I know more about DNA *tests* than I do about DNA. I couldn't tell you what DNA is. Per se."

"Give it a shot."

"Well . . . each of our cells contains something called DNA. And the DNA from one person to another is unique. Somehow. Like fingerprints."

"Thank you, O.J.! What else you got?"

"That's about it. I wouldn't know a chromosome from a Pontiac."

"Uh-huh, uh-huh, uh-huh!" Torgoff was nodding his head like a golf pro who's asked to see a few swings and, having seen them, suddenly realizes that the lesson is going to have to start with the words, *This is a golf club . . .*

"Okay," he said, "we've established that what you know about genetics is precisely bupkis. Which is fine. No problem." Torgoff made a clacking sound in the back of his mouth and pressed his hands together. "The next question: your assistant said you're interested in Baresi."

"Right."

"So which is it? Are you interested in genetics, or are you interested in Baresi?"

"Mostly . . . I guess I'm interested in the research that he did."

"Okay! So we can forget Mendel. Except . . . maybe not. Because Mendel and Baresi were a lot alike. Both of them were asking basic questions. And both of them were way ahead of their time."

"How so?"

"Well, when Mendel was in the garden, making notes about peas, everyone else was hung up on Darwin. Who, as you may have heard, made the case that organisms evolve in response to environmental pressures—though he couldn't tell you how they do it."

"But Mendel could."

Torgoff shrugged. "Not really. But he figured out a couple of things. Like the fact that hereditary characteristics are passed from one generation to the next, independently of one another. In other words, some people with blue eyes are color-blind—and some aren't. It's called the 'Principle of Independent Assortment.' And he understood dominance, too. He saw that when you breed tall plants with short plants, you get tall plants—not medium plants. It's only when the hybrids are rebred with one another that the recessive genes kick in—and then you get short plants and tall plants. You with me?"

"Check."

"Well, this is a big deal. What Mendel did was to set out some of the rules of inheritance. In effect, he solved one of the oldest mysteries in the universe—not that anyone noticed. They were all looking at Darwin, and they *continued* to look at Darwin for another thirty years! Until some *other* scientists undertook the *same* experiments and, searching the literature, discovered that what they'd actually done was reinvent the wheel. Mendel was there before them.

"Which is pretty much what happened to Baresi," Torgoff continued. "When Baresi was doing his best work, everyone was looking at Watson and Crick." The MIT professor picked up the Rubik's cube and began to twist it as he talked.

"He got his doctorate in biochemistry when he was what— twenty-two? Something like that. Anyway, it was 1953. Which, to a geneticist, is like 1776 or something. It's a *big* year! There was tremendous excitement at the prospect of some basic problems finally yielding to solution. And DNA—this enormous molecule that's present in the cell of every living organism—was at the heart of it all.

"By then, everyone knew that DNA was the key to inheritance. But how did it work? How did it regulate chemical actions within the cells? Because that's what it does. It synthesizes proteins." Torgoff paused. "You with me?"

"In a sense," Lassiter said.

"Never mind. The point is that DNA regulates some extremely complicated processes. And before any of them could be understood, someone had to figure out the molecule's structure. Which they did. In 'fifty-three a couple of guys named Watson and Crick put together a physical model of DNA. That's it up there." He raised his eyes to the double corkscrew of twine and poster board hanging from the ceiling. "A double helix. Twisted ladder. Whatever you want to call it.

"So we're talking about a very exciting time to come out of the university with a doctorate in biochemistry. Because once the structure of DNA was understood, however primitively, it became possible to imagine that we might one day understand how DNA makes copies of itself, how genes work, and a lot more.

"Now, at the time, Baresi was working at the LeBange Institute—"

"Where's that?" Lassiter asked.

"Bern. Switzerland. It's a hotbed for this kind of thing. Always has been. Anyway, he started out in a fairly conventional way, working with *E. coli*—"

"Bacteria," Lassiter interjected.

"Exactly. It's a very simple organism that's easy to culture and reproduces like crazy—so it's popular in labs. Like everything else that's alive—except certain viral organisms and these wacky little things called prions—*E. coli* is made of DNA, same as you and me. So it's more or less ideal for the purposes of study. Not that Baresi stuck with it. After a year or two he shifted to blood studies—"

" 'Shifted'?"

"It's not that different. When we talk about 'blood studies,' in this case, we're talking about red blood cells. And the thing about red blood cells is that they're like bacteria in two very important ways. One, they don't have nuclei. And two: they're easy to get. We're making them all the time.

"Now, this was cutting-edge research that Baresi was doing, but it was nothing like the next step that he took. And before I tell you what that was, you need to understand that Baresi wasn't just a genius—he was an inductive genius—someone capable of forming extraordinary hypotheses. And like most inductive geniuses, he was more or less indifferent to prizes and the opinions of his colleagues. He didn't rush after 'the next big thing.' He just did what he wanted. Which is to say that he took off in directions that were entirely his own."

"What does that mean?" Lassiter asked.

"In Baresi's case, it means that he abandoned the blood studies to work on nucleated cells."

"Why was that so revolutionary?"

"Because it was so hard to do, especially at that time. We have some cell lines now that are pretty dependable, but in the fifties? No. Nucleated cells are difficult to culture and they don't always live so long. This would have been a real problem, because if old Baresi had a cell line die out on him prematurely—and this was not at all unlikely—Baresi would have had to toss out months of work. I'm still not sure how he managed it." Torgoff paused. "But I can tell you why he did it."

"Oh?"

"Sure. He was after the mother lode."

"And what's that?" Lassiter asked.

"Cellular differentiation. And you can't investigate *that* without working on nucleated cells. Because differentiation isn't something that happens in single-celled organisms. It happens only in cells with nuclei." Torgoff sat back, looking content.

After a moment Lassiter said, "This is going to come as a shock, Doc, but I don't know what 'differentiation' means. Not exactly." He thought about it for a moment, and added, "Not at all, in fact."

Torgoff smiled happily. "Ah, *well*—differentiation. I'll explain." He took a deep breath. "As I'm sure you've heard," he began, "we start out as a fertilized egg—a zygote. Which is a single cell. Now, inside the nucleus of that egg is a tangle of chromosomes, which are strands of DNA to which specific genetic information is attached—in the form of genes. In case you're wondering, the number of chromosomes found in the cells is the same within each species—dogs have seventy-eight. Fish have ninety-two. You and I each have forty-six—half from Mom, and half from Dad. Half from the egg, and half from the sperm that penetrated it. Got the picture?"

Lassiter nodded, and Torgoff continued. "Our genes—and there are hundreds of thousands of them—are scattered around on the two pairs of twenty-three chromosomes. One gene for eye color, another for blood type, and so on. It's not really that simple, but . . . you get the point. It's all there, right from the beginning, in that one fertilized cell. And then the cell starts to divide." Torgoff put his hands together and pulled them apart. "The next thing you know, there are two cells—and then four, and so on. And each of these cells, the early embryonic cells, contains the same genetic material—DNA, chromosomes and genes in the same amount. And it's this *stuff* that decides who the little guy's gonna be. You, me, or Babe Ruth.

"But pretty soon, when the embryo grows to eight or sixteen cells, the cells begin to differentiate. Which is to say that, *somehow*, they begin to take on specific roles; they become brain cells, liver cells, nerve cells, and so on. Even though each of them has the same DNA, they activate or 'express' different genes—and the genes they express determine the enzymes they produce, and that, in turn, determines the kinds of cells that they become.

"So it's an interesting conundrum: since they contain the same genetic information, one would think they'd have the same genetic capabilities. But they don't. An early embryonic cell is *totipotent*: it can generate an entire organism—a person, a cat, a giraffe—from a single cell. But a nerve cell can only make another nerve cell. How come?" Torgoff looked at Lassiter.

"You don't expect me to answer that, do you?"

"No. But that's what Baresi was working on: the differentiation process, and the mechanisms that control it. Which put him about thirty years ahead of the curve." Torgoff took a deep breath, exhaled, and looked around. "Why don't we get some coffee?"

"Good idea," Lassiter said.

"There's a place on the corner." Torgoff glanced at the Rubik's cube, thought for a moment, and twisted it three times in rapid succession. When he laid it down on the desk, it was perfectly aligned. Together, the two of them got to their feet. Torgoff pulled a scarf from the coatrack in the corner and wound it around his neck. Then he hunched into a battered pea coat and settled a watch cap on his head. "Let's go," he said.

The air outside was freezing, and as they walked single file on a path through the snow, Torgoff continued his lecture.

"You follow the O.J. trial?"

"No," Lassiter replied. "Did it get much coverage?"

The professor laughed. "Remember how hard they worked to muddy up the uniqueness of the DNA prints? Using statistics?" Torgoff affected an aggressive, pontifical voice: " 'So you can't *say* this DNA belongs to Nicole Brown Simpson, isn't that right? You can only *say* that there's a statistical *probability* that it belongs to Nicole Brown Simpson, isn't that right? Yes or no.' 'Yes, that's true, but, uh—we'd actually have to go to eight *billion* samples before we'd find another like it. And there aren't that many people on earth, so—' " Torgoff stuck his hand in the air. " 'Objection, your honor, witness is not answering the question. I asked if it was possible to state definitively that this DNA sample belongs to Nicole Brown Simpson. Yes or no?' " " 'But, but—' " " 'Yes or no, sweetcakes. Yes or no.' "

The coffeehouse was a long and narrow room behind a plate-glass window, white with steam. An Italian flag was draped across a wall of exposed brick, and the air was heavy with the aroma of freshly ground espresso. Torgoff and Lassiter took a table near the window and ordered lattes. Nearby, three young men sat at three different tables reading three different books. It occurred to Lassiter that all of them looked like Raskolnikov.

"So," Torgoff continued, "we got DNA. And the DNA we got? It's identical in every single cell of our body. Which is why a bit of semen, a drop of blood, a hank of hair, a patch of skin—any of them can be used to identify an individual by comparing it with a blood sample from the same person. Each cell, no matter what *kind*, contains the individual's DNA—and that DNA is unique, from one person to another."

The coffee arrived, and Lassiter watched in amazement as Torgoff stirred about four tablespoons of sugar into his cup.

"Basically, the DNA in a differentiated cell 'tells' the genes that this particular cell is going to be hair: so it can forget about traits like eye color, blood type, and so on. Think of the DNA as a piano with a hundred thousand keys, and each of the keys is a genetic trait. In a differentiated cell, most of the keys are covered. They're off. They don't work. But even so, a lot of the keys are still operational: with hair, you've got curliness, pigmentation, thickness— like that. But that's it. Everything else is *off*. And once it's off, it's off for good."

"Forever?"

"As far as anyone knows. Once the DNA expresses a particular gene, there's no going back. A nerve cell is a nerve cell. It can't become a blood cell. It can't become a brain cell."

"So how does that work?" Lassiter asked. He was becoming interested in the subject, though he didn't see how it could possibly relate to his sister's murder or the deaths in Italy. "How does a cell *decide* what it's going to be?"

"I don't know. No one does. That's what Baresi was trying to find out—thirty or forty years ago."

"And did he?"

Torgoff shrugged. "Not that I know of. Not that anyone knows of." He paused, and then went on. "The problem is: he stopped publishing. At some point he stopped submitting articles for peer review— though how long he continued working in the field is uncertain. It may have been months. It could have been years. The last I heard, he was in Germany, or some such place, studying—"

"Theology," Lassiter said.

"That's right!" Torgoff looked at him. "That's right. You knew that. Well . . ." Torgoff glanced at his watch and frowned. "I've got to pick up my son. . . . Look," he said, "biology is the hottest science in the world right now. And the hottest area in biology just happens to be what Baresi was working on, way back when."

"Differentiation?"

"Exactly. He was studying the totipotent cells in frog embryos. Judging from the last papers that he published, he was dividing the embryos at the four- and eight-celled stage, using what must have been some very primitive equipment. And then he was culturing the divided embryos to see if he could develop identical organisms."

"He was cloning frogs?"

"No. He was 'twinning' frogs."

"What's the difference?" Lassiter asked.

"Well, even identical twins get their genetic material from two sources: Mom and Dad. Clones get it from one: Mom *or* Dad. So if you wanted to create a clone, you'd have to remove the genetic material from the mother's egg—"

"The nucleus—"

"—and replace it with the nucleus from a totipotent cell. A cell that's in the earliest stage of embryonic growth. Then you'd have a clone, with all of the genetic information coming from a single source."

"And they can do that?"

"Yeah. They've done it with sheep at the Roslin Institute. In Edinburgh."

Lassiter thought about it. "And if they can do it with sheep, they can do it with people, right?"

Torgoff shrugged. "Theoretically."

"I mean, if they wanted to, they could clone *me*."

"No," the scientist said. "They couldn't."

"Why not?"

"Because *all* of your cells are differentiated. The last time you had a totipotent cell in your body, you were smaller than a freckle. What we could do, though—theoretically—is clone a *child* of yours. But only if we got to him in the earliest embryonic stage. When he was a cluster of totipotent cells. Four. Eight. Sixteen, max."

"And that's possible?"

Torgoff raised his eyes to the ceiling and rocked from side to side. "Maybe. Somewhere. They could probably do it at Roslin, but if they did, they'd go to jail."

"Why?"

"It's illegal to clone people in the British Isles—not that it's come up much. But getting back to Baresi: we've come to take a lot of this for granted. Today, embryos are created all the time in fertility clinics. Back in the late fifties and sixties, it was a different matter. What we in science call 'way out.' I mean, if you think of the technical innovations that Baresi had to make, just to deal with the nuts and bolts—what's the matter?"

Lassiter shook his head. "It's just that . . . you know how Baresi ended up, don't you?"

"No," he said, "the last I heard he was writing about religion."

"Yeah, well . . . the beat goes on. He abandoned religion and enrolled in medical school—this was when he was, I don't know, fifty years old or something. Specialized in gynecology and obstetrics. Wound up running a fertility clinic."

Torgoff raised his eyebrows and sipped his latte. "Well," he said, "he certainly had a lot of experience making embryos. He was probably pretty successful."

"Yeah, I think he was."

Torgoff sighed. "Still," he said, "it's sad."

"Why do you say that?"

"Because he was a terrific research scientist, and if you look at what he was doing, and what he was after . . . it seems a waste."

"What do you mean," Lassiter asked, " 'what he was *after*'?"

"Well, the whole point of the differentiation studies was to find a way to reverse the process—to restore the totipotency of differentiated cells."

"Why? What good would that do?"

"What *good* would it do?" Torgoff said. "It's the Holy Grail."

"How so?"

"Because if you could do that . . ." Torgoff frowned. "The mind boggles," he said. "It would be worth . . . trillions. And the money would be the least of it. If you could reverse differentiation, you'd change the world forever."

"How?"

"Because . . . then we *could* clone you. And anyone else. Hell, you could dig up Beethoven, Custer, and Elvis and have *them* for children. Or your own mother. Or you could grow replacement parts, cannibalizing the clones whenever you needed a new lung, a liver, a heart. You can imagine the ethical issues, and the social ones: What happens to adoption when people can order copies of themselves—or anyone else—by mail? And when you combine cloning with recombinant DNA technology, it's easy to imagine clones that *aren't quite human*—fungible look-alikes, useful as cannon fodder, gladiators, or slaves. Instead of organic farms, *organ* farms. Disposable people."

Lassiter scoffed. "I think you're out there, Doc."

Torgoff laughed and shook his head. "But I'm not. All you'd need is a nucleated cell with the DNA intact—a little bit of blood, a follicle of hair, a piece of flesh. Almost anything would do. Once the differentiation was reversed and the cell's totipotency restored, you could use it to generate a whole new organism. All we'd have to do is insert the nucleus in an egg whose own nucleus had been removed. And then we'd culture it. Nifty, huh?"

Lassiter thought about it. "What do you mean, you'd 'culture it'?"

"Well, if it was a person, we'd treat it as an oocyte procedure." Lassiter blinked at the word, and Torgoff started to explain. "That's when we—"

"I know what it is," Lassiter said. "My sister had one."

"Oh," Torgoff replied. "Well . . . then you know about it." He looked at his watch again, and scraped back in his chair. "I really gotta go," he said. "There's a twelve-year-old kid and hockey tickets involved."

"Just gimme a second," Lassiter asked. "If Baresi had done this . . . I mean, if he'd found a way to reverse the differentiation of cells—we'd have heard about it, right?"

"Absolutely," Torgoff said, getting to his feet. "That would be as big as . . . what? The invention of the wheel? You'd have heard about it, all right. Unless . . ."

"What?"

Torgoff tightened his scarf and drew the pea coat's collar close around his neck. Then he pulled his watch cap down over the top of his head. "I don't know," he said. "Unless he had *doubts*. Maybe he scared himself. I mean, he *did* get religion, *didn't* he?"

As he rode back to the Marriott on the subway, Lassiter didn't know what to think. Baresi saw God in a molecule and turned to the study of theology? Maybe. But what did that have to do with Umbra Domini and a string of murders from Tokyo to Washington?

As the train rattled along Lassiter became increasingly impatient with himself. Why should he assume that Baresi's passions for science and religion were important to the case? Because the priest said so?

Yes.

But obviously, the key to it all was the clinic, Lassiter thought, not science, and not religion. *The fertility clinic.* That's what held the victims together—that's what they had in common. And now that he thought of it, why was he chasing phantoms when he might have been interviewing women who'd actually been at the clinic? He had the names and addresses. They were the ones whose visits had lasted about a week, rather than thirty-two days. None of them had had the oocyte procedure, and none of them—so far as he knew—was dead. There were at least a hundred of these women, and he hadn't talked to a single one.

But Freddy and Riordan had. And what they'd learned could be summarized in a single sentence: *Ain't life grand?* It was clear to Riordan, clear to Freddy, and clear to him, that none of these women were in danger. Even so . . .

He bent over, ran his hand through his hair and groaned. It must have been a loud groan, loud enough so that when he looked up, the man across the way was giving him a hard, but weary, stare. Lassiter could read his mind: *This is all I need, another fucking psycho.*

And then Lassiter had another thought, a thought that jolted him so hard that his body twitched involuntarily and he sat up: What if Baresi had actually done it? What if he'd used the fertility clinic to clone . . .

That's where it all broke down. To clone what? Or whom? Lassiter growled with frustration, and the man across from him got up with a curse and moved toward the end of the car.

But what if he did? Then what? Lassiter asked himself. What happened then? Did Baresi have a change of heart? Did he have the children murdered?

The answer came back instantly: This is insane. And anyway, the boys at the clinic *couldn't* be clones. They didn't look alike. Brandon didn't look like Jesse, and neither of them looked like any of the other children he'd seen in photographs. Not Martin Henderson. Not Jiri Reiner's boy. They were all different.

So clones were out, Lassiter thought, unless . . .

Unless what? Unless they were clones of a group.

But which group? The College of Cardinals? A.C. Milan?

I don't think so, Lassiter told himself.

It was ridiculous. Even if Baresi had been able to do something like that, why would he? It wasn't as if the children were part of an experiment. The women came to the clinic, got pregnant, and went home. It was all very ordinary, and as far as Lassiter could tell, Baresi had never even asked for a picture of the kids, much less followed their progress. It was a fairly simple medical procedure, and that was that.

Except it wasn't.

Because all of the patients had been killed.

35

It didn't get this cold in Washington.

Sitting in a rented Taurus outside the DMV in Portland, Maine, Lassiter held his hands in front of the car's heating ducts and second-guessed himself. He shouldn't have used his credit card at Hertz. He should have paid cash. Except they wouldn't take cash, and so he didn't really have a choice. And what did it matter, anyway? So long as he paid for his gas with cash, the car could be anywhere.

Despite the stream of hot air that blew across his hands, his fingers were still frozen after scraping the frost from the windshield, using the sports section of the *Portland Press-Herald*. I'm not equipped for this, Lassiter thought. This is the kind of cold, the kind of *industrial* cold, that you found in Minnesota or Saskatchewan. A leather jacket just doesn't cut it, and neither do these very expensive gloves from Bergdorf Goodman. I need electric mittens, he told himself. And a space suit.

The dashboard clock read 8:56. Four minutes until it opens, Lassiter thought. And then: I should have gone to Sunday River, and showed her picture to everyone who worked there. The people who rented condos, the technicians who sharpened skis, the instructors and day-care minders. But . . . what good would that have done? A zillion people came and went every weekend at Sunday River. The picture was two years old, and besides, it wasn't as if she was *at* the resort. It wasn't as if she was *skiing*. She was outside McDonald's, with the mountain in the background, off in the distance.

But it *was* the mountain. It *was* Sunday River. There were tourist brochures at the Ramada, and he'd compared the mountain in the photo with the one in the brochures, and they were obviously one and the same. Which meant that she was in Maine, or at least that she *had* been in Maine. Two years ago.

Lassiter snapped on the radio and watched as a pear-shaped woman emerged from the DMV, carrying two flags. Skirting the ice in the parking lot, she went to the flagpole and unceremoniously hoisted the Stars and Stripes. The Maine state flag, which consisted mostly of a pine tree, followed a few seconds later. Then the woman retraced her steps through the parking lot, hurrying back inside.

A voice on the radio announced that it was six degrees—"and getting wahm-ah!"

At nine A.M., precisely, the woman unlocked the doors to the DMV and a dozen engines died. One by one, early birds in Thinsulate parkas clambered out of their cars and headed toward the building. Lassiter followed suit, and soon afterwards found himself in front of a window marked INFORMATION SERVICES.

It had always seemed to him that the police—and only the police—should be able to trace a license plate. But that was a very old-fashioned idea, formulated in an age when privacy was still possible—because people were thought to own the facts about themselves. In the Information Age, time wasn't money—data was. And so Maine was in the demographics business, which is to say that somewhere along the line it had joined the other states in selling information to anyone who would pay.

As Lassiter well knew, there were companies that retailed specialized lists, tailored to the customer's needs. If someone wanted a compendium of childless home owners whose household income exceeded $100,000 and who lived in a particular zip code, the information could be assembled in an instant. And if the customer wanted that same list refined to white males with a history of late payments, that, too, could be done.

Maine's Department of Motor Vehicles was just as capable of tailoring its lists. Thanks to the computer, the service was available at any branch. And so, when he filled out a form requesting the names and birthdates of the registered owners of Volkswagen vans, model years 1965–75, the chirpy clerk had a single question:

"Do you want that as a printout or mailing labels?"

"A printout's fine," Lassiter replied. He handed her a hundred-dollar bill and then three tens (to cover the cost of expediting the request).

"You can pick it up in the morning, anytime after ten."

Which left him with a day to kill, and he murdered half of it on the road, driving nowhere in particular. He liked Maine. There was something about the rocky land and the snow and the pine trees that seemed particularly clean and spare. And while franchised America and shopping malls were still too plentiful for comfort, he passed through a dozen small towns and villages that seemed to be organized around ice rinks and newsstands, boatyards and bookstores. These were towns that seemed as if they had soda fountains in them. And if some of them were blighted by empty buildings or restored to an artificial quaintness, he still felt a connection to them. It might be false nostalgia, but these places seemed a much better bet for sustaining civilized life than the subdivided sprawl replicating up and down the coast.

It was five o'clock and dark when he got back to his room. Settling into an armchair, he tilted back and, with his feet up on the desk, began reading from a handful of articles about Callista.

He'd been working his way through the collection of papers provided by the P.R. agency in reverse chronological order. By now, he was all the way back to 1986. Instead of churning out the usual avalanche of personal details, with a parade of past-life relatives and friends weighing in with self-important anecdotes, the ten-year-old coverage of Callista Bates consisted of wild speculation about who she was, where she'd come from, and why she was so secretive about her past.

She'd burst/exploded/emerged on the Hollywood scene in 1984, with the release of a remake of *Lost Horizon*, a "little" movie that unexpectedly took off. Most thought its surprising success due to the captivating and unknown actress who'd played the female lead. Simply put, she lighted up the screen. The movie might easily have been a kind of hokey, new-age melodrama, with soaring music and idealized landscapes, but Callista's mischievous persona rescued the film from its perpetrators, revealing the casting director to be a genius.

By the time she disappeared, in 1990, the star's resolute stance on not talking about her past was accepted; no one really bothered about it anymore. But in 1986, of course, it was still grist for the tabloids' mills. The actress was quoted to the effect that there was a fine line between freedom of the press and the right to privacy, and those who crossed it would no longer have their calls returned. Reactions varied widely. Some publications took her at her word and avoided questions about her background, while others took the opposite tack, assigning reporters to investigate her past. It was all a front, anyway, they reasoned: Without publicity, her career would die on the vine.

She said okay, that was fine, they had their work, she had hers—and if they chose to dig into her past, that was okay, too. Just don't expect her to be complicitous or forgiving. Soon afterward, *Piper* was released, and when it went nova, a tabloid called *Startrak!* published a rumor, based on an interview with Callista's private secretary.

CALLISTA'S SECRET TRAGEDY: SHE'S AN ORPHAN!!!

The actress never denied the story—and neither did she confirm it. She simply dismissed her secretary and told her successor that calls from *Startrak!* were to be ignored.

It took a while for the tabloids to realize how serious she was. For two or three years speculative pieces continued to appear, hinting about a youth so wretched that the actress couldn't bear to recall it. At least a dozen parents came forward to claim Callista as their only child, while rumors zipped through the grapevine like so many Pachinko balls: there were rumors, some of them published, of a tragic childhood in which she'd drowned her baby brother, starred in pornographic films, and suffered convictions for mail fraud, shoplifting, and arms-dealing.

One magazine went so far as to put Callista's photograph on a *Wanted!* poster. There was a hot line with an 800 number, and a series of eccentrically morphed photos that purported to reverse the aging process, depicting the actress as she might have been—at sixteen, twelve, eight, four, and birth.

A headline asked: DO YOU KNOW THIS LITTLE GIRL? while another begged: CALLISTA'S MOMMY—WHERE ARE YOU?

It was ridiculous, annoying, and hurtful. And eventually it backfired. The *New Yorker* made her the centerpiece of a twelve-thousand-word essay on the "metastasis of celebrity" and its malignant effects on the private lives of public figures. Other journals followed suit, applauding Callista's stance even as they quoted Andy Warhol on the inevitability of it all.

From an investigative standpoint there was nothing to be learned from any of the stories. Callista might be an orphan or she might be a quint. There was no way to tell. The tabloids' sources were either anonymous or suspect, and usually both. But one thing was abundantly clear: when the time came, Callista Bates was not going to thank him for tracking her down.

That night he went to a place called the Muddy Rudder, where he washed down a lobster with a bottle of Pilsner Urquell. "They're sweetah in the wint-ah," the waitress enthused. It took him a minute to understand she meant the lobsters.

At ten P.M. he was back in his room, reading the *Boston Globe*. The big stories were mostly old news—things he'd overheard on the radio while driving along the coast that afternoon. There was an update on a plane crash, an update on Bosnia, and stories about interest rates, the primaries, and counterfeiting in the Middle East.

He usually skipped the local news when he was traveling—what did he care about political maneuvers in Boston, or welfare fraud in Foxboro? Even so, there was an interesting story in the *Globe* about a writer named Carl Oglesby. Turning to the jump page, where the story was continued, Lassiter was stunned to see a picture of Silvio della Torre, smiling out at him.

The accompanying article was headlined: OVERFLOW CROWD HEARS LATIN MASS

> BROCKTON—Despite treacherous roads and temperatures near zero, more than a thousand worshipers flocked to Our Lady Help of Christians Catholic Church Sunday to hear Father Silvio della Torre recite the mass in Latin.
>
> With his back to the congregation, the traditionalist leader addressed the altar in a powerful voice that rang through the church, moving many to tears. While some praised the "power and beauty of the ceremony," others spoke of an almost mystical bond to generations of Catholics who have celebrated the mass in this same, ancient language.

In his sermon, the English-speaking della Torre called for "a more muscular Catholicism," while urging the assembled to "stand fast against the abominations of science."

The traditionalist leader is the Italian head of the rapidly expanding lay order Umbra Domini. He arrived in Boston Friday for a ribbon-cutting ceremony at the group's new hospice in Brookline.

Umbra Domini's charter rejects many of the changes imposed by the second Vatican Council, while affirming the rights of Catholics to worship in the traditional way. The doctrinal variation was approved by the Vatican some years ago.

A spokesman for the group said that della Torre's American itinerary is "flexible and open-ended."

Lassiter read the article with a racing heart, and when he was done, he read it again. Then he poured a scotch from the minibar and, gazing at the priest's photo, downed it in a gulp.

In the morning, Lassiter drove to the DMV with his eyes half closed, squinting against the flat light that came off the snow. The sky was dense with clouds, and while the temperature was higher than the day before, so also was the humidity. The result was a raw cold that reached inside your clothes and made you think about Florida.

The clerk at "Information Services" handed him a manila envelope. He took it to a long table against the wall, where a blond girl with bad skin was filling out a form, using a pen attached to the table by a short chain.

The printout was about ten pages long and listed every VW van, circa 1965–75, registered in the state of Maine. The information was alphabetically organized and included the owner's name, address and date of birth, the license plate number of the vehicle, and its year of manufacture. The DOB was particularly important because Lassiter could use it to narrow the list to women in their thirties.

Callista had been born in 1962.

He'd anticipated a tedious process. Once the men had been eliminated, and the list narrowed to women of a certain age, he'd visit them one by one—and doorstep them. Moving through the list, from to A to Z, he'd put checks next to seventeen names. And then he saw it:

Sanders, Marie A.
DOB: 3–8–62
P.O. Box 39
Cundys Harbor, Maine 04010
Volkswagen (van): 1968
EAW–572

The first thing that jumped out at him was "–62"—and then *Marie*. He stared at the entry. March 8. Was it March 8? He was sure it was.

Jesus Christ, he thought. I've found her.

He slammed his fist onto the table, and the girl with the bad skin turned and stared at him with a look so sour it startled him. Shoving the list into his jacket pocket, he ran out to the car, nearly losing his footing on the ice.

It had to be her. What were the chances that there were two women named Marie in the state of Maine who'd been born on March 8, 1962, and owned an old VW van?

He yanked open the glove box, pulled out the map, and glanced at the index. Cundys Harbor: K–2. His finger skated through the empty pinkness of Quebec, across the border into Maine, down through a tangle of lakes and towns, coming to rest finally on a small dot next to the coast, a little south and east of Brunswick.

An hour later he passed through the pines of Bowdoin College (thank you, Dicky Biddle), and turned right at a sign for

ORRS ISLAND

Even under the lowering sky the landscape was appealing, with slate-gray boulders and dark green pines stark against the clouds. There was a special richness to the light, an intense gray that hinted at the nearby sea. As he followed the road on the map, he passed one business after another that was closed for the winter—a shore restaurant, a shack advertising lobster rolls, a gift shop. The road forked to the left, becoming narrower as it arced toward a dead end in the hamlet of Cundys Harbor. Seeing a flag, he headed for it, and pulled into a small parking area next to a post office that doubled as the general store.

There, he saw a blue VW van, and even without looking at the plates, he knew it was hers. One bumper sticker read FRODO LIVES, and the other VISUALIZE WHIRLED PEAS. In between the two was the license plate itself:

EAW-572

Now what? he asked himself, standing on a ledge of rock next to the little building no more than a hundred feet from the sea. He had to assume Callista . . . *Marie* was in the store. She'd been stalked, she'd been followed. He didn't want to spook her.

And while she might recognize him from Kathy's funeral, that wasn't necessarily positive: the connection might unnerve her. Lassiter wandered down to the water's edge, thinking about what to do. He'd been concentrating so hard on finding her that he'd never even considered what his approach would be. And so he stood beside the water, stranded with indecision, staring out to sea.

Cundys Harbor was a postcard, but it wasn't a museum piece. It was an old fishing village where the men still went to sea. There were barnacle-encrusted wooden wharves, stacked with lobster traps and other equipment, and a motley collection of boats riding at anchor in the snug harbor. A rusting trawler, bristling with winches; some funky old lobster boats; a couple of shiny new crafts with center cockpits.

At the moment, the tide was out and the expanse of mud flat and rocks and yellow seaweed was littered with ice that had formed on the surface, and then lay fractured and cracked where the receding water left it. The sky was streaky and getting darker, and when the raw wind kicked up a notch, Lassiter couldn't stop shivering. He really ought to buy an overcoat, he told himself. Or get inside.

The post office/general store was an antique tinderbox with racks of dry goods and groceries, and an old-fashioned cooler holding milk, eggs, and beer. A gray-haired woman looked up from her newspaper as he came in. "Howdy," she said, pronouncing the word as if it were a warning. Lassiter smiled, and went directly to the wood stove, where he warmed his hands and looked around. The store was packed with tidal charts, maps, fishing lures, pocketknives, flashlights, groceries, penny candy, electrical supplies, Hostess cupcakes, newspapers, and pretzels. Along the opposite wall was a miniature post office with a slot for mail, a counter, and a bank of fifty little bronze mailboxes.

But there was no Callista Bates, and no Marie Sanders.

Finally, the gray-haired woman spoke up in a thick Maine accent: "Can I help you, dee-ah?"

What the hell. "I hope so. I'm looking for Marie Sanders."

She made a little clucking sound. "Oh dee-ah," she said, with a stricken look that sent Lassiter's own mood plummeting.

"Isn't that her car outside?" Lassiter asked.

"Ay-uh! That's it, all right. But she isn't he-ah. You a friend of hers?"

Lassiter nodded. "When do you expect her?" he asked.

"Month. Six weeks, maybe."

Lassiter shook his head, perplexed and disappointed. "I thought she lived here," he said.

"Well, of course she does. Not he-ah, but he-ahbouts."

"So . . . is she traveling, or—"

The woman's pale blue eyes widened behind her glasses, and then she giggled—a surprising sound that made her seem almost like a teenager. "My lands," she said. "I must sound like I'm talking in riddles. Let me show you." She shrugged into a huge blue sweater, and beckoned for him to follow her out the door, which she closed with a thrust of her hip.

The wind was blowing just enough to make them lower their heads as they walked out onto the wharves. "There," she said, pointing out to sea where a chain of islands hunkered on the horizon. "They're out on the last one."

Lassiter blinked. "They *live* out there?"

The old lady cackled. "Ah-yuh! On a clear day, you can see the smoke from her wood stove." Then she shivered. "Come on inside, de-ah. I'll make us a cup of tea."

Together, they returned to the store. "She must have a radio, or something," Lassiter said.

"Cell phone."

"Well, then—"

"Doesn't work, though."

"You're kidding."

The woman shook her head, and moved behind the counter to plug in an electric kettle. "No. Jonathan tried to raise her just before the last big storm. Got a lot of static, but that was that. Could be a battery problem—it's happened befo-ah. Look he-ah," she said, coming around the counter to a large map that was posted on the wall. It was a mariner's chart, the land mass a featureless blond expanse, the water dense with data and details about currents, depths, and features of the sea floor. She put a finger on a scimitar-shaped harbor.

"We're he-ah," she said, then moved her hand to one of three islands, out to sea. "And your friend's way out to here."

"Sanders Island," he read. *Sanders* Island? That must be her real name, then, her family name.

"That's the name on the chart, de-ah, because when Cap'n Sanders bought the island—oh, a long time ago—he wanted that name on the charts, and by golly he got it. Still—you won't find anyone here call it anything but Rag Island—which is the old name, going back to I don't know when."

"Why'd they call it that?"

She moved behind the counter and switched off the electric kettle. "Look at the shoreline. That island has more jigs and jags than you can shake a stick at. And right down from it—Dutchess Island—the shoreline's so smooth, you can hardly find a place to tie up your boat."

Lassiter looked absently at a display of penny candy. Mary Janes, Tootsie Rolls, atomic fireballs.

"Sugah?" she asked. "Cream? Well, Half and Half?"

"Both. Please."

"Just like me. Pale and sweet." After a moment she put two cups of tea on the counter, each in a delicate china cup resting on a saucer. "Don't care for mugs," she confided.

He devoted fifteen minutes to drawing out the woman ("Maude Hutchison—and I'm nothing like that TV Maude, let me tell you") on her likes and dislikes, how long she'd lived there ("forever, dear") and local history. While they talked, a couple of men came in for cigarettes, a woman to check the mail. By the time Lassiter brought up the subject of Marie Sanders again, he and Maude were on their second cup of tea. "So—Marie actually stays on that island all winter, by herself?"

"Her and the boy." She stirred her tea. "First year—I don't think anybody'd been to the place for twenty-five ye-ahs! 'Course I remembered Marie from way back when, not that I recognized her after all that time."

"You mean . . . you knew her when she was a child?"

"Oh, show-ah! Knew both her parents. Used to be the whole

family'd go out to the island. Even her brother, who was sickly. They used to wrap him up in blankets and carry him out to the boat. And old John Junior? He was quite the sailor. They'd be out there every weekend of the summer—and vacation, too. 'Course—she was just a twig of a thing. Maybe five years old. Now she's out they-ah with her own boy."

"Do her parents live around here?"

She shook her head. "Oh, Lord no. They've been dead for yee-ahs. Marie didn't tell you?"

"No."

"Well, it doesn't surprise me. She's one for keeping her business to herself, bless her heart." She drew in her breath sharply. "John Junior got to drinking down in Portland, and Amanda went to get him. Well, John Junior said he could drive all right, and I guess he did—for a few minutes. At least, until they got to the railroad tracks. Lawyers said the signal was broke, but they never proved that, and the truth was—John Junior was wicked impatient. I can just see him, racing the train." She shook her head. "Well, Amanda's sister took Marie in. Lived down in Connecticut. Last we saw of her until—"

"She just showed up."

"That's right! Pretty as a picture and bold as you like, and next thing you know she's got workmen back and forth to the island, putting in septic, insulation, a proper bathroom, wood stoves, a dock, I don't know what all." She sucked in her breath and shook her head. "Talk of the town is what it was—mostly about how foolish it was. Because she'll never get it back if she ever wants to sell."

"Why not?"

"No electricity out there, likely never will be." She drank the last sip of her tea. "How times change!"

"Why do you say that?"

"Used to be, people came down here to the shore, or out to the islands—the whole idea was to get back to basics, away from the workaday life. Just go out into the woods—no telephones or toasters, just candles and cookstoves, and water from the springs and rain barrels."

He mentioned something about the Boy Scouts, the back-to-nature movement.

"Back when Cap'n bought—" She smiled and dipped her head. "—*Sanders* Island, why the islands would have been the pick of all the places. Back then, the more remote, the better. But nobody wants to *rough* it these days; they just want to bring their regular life someplace different. The old places out on the islands are just falling down—because nobody really wants to get away from it all anymore."

"They want to take it all with them."

She giggled. "Right. Lord forbid they should miss '60 Minutes' or a Red Sox game."

"So she's out there all winter—without electricity."

"She spent the summer, one year, then May to November. This is the first year she's stuck it out." The old woman frowned. " 'Course, there's some that don't approve, not at all, never mind that we used to be well known hereabout for keeping out of private business."

"Why don't they approve? Because it's so remote?"

" 'Remote' isn't what gets to folks. Some—and these would be the men—are wicked disapproving. Because she cuts her own wood, sets her nets, minds her business . . . Men plain don't like to think a woman can do all that without 'em. Now, the women—they worry about the boy."

"What about you?"

She shrugged. "I used to be one of them, worried about Jesse, but he's such a sweet child, and so happy. She truly dotes on that boy. And I get to thinking, well, what's he missing? Cartoons, video games, and Wal-Mart."

"Still, if there was an emergency . . ."

She sighed. "I agree! We've all talked to her about it, and she just says, 'Well, we've got a flare gun. If there's ever a problem, you'll know about it.' Even so, I'd be a lot happier if she had a proper boat."

"She doesn't have a boat?"

"Oh, she's got a boat, all right—but it isn't much. Not something you'd take out in the winter. Not in that water." She paused for a moment. "So," she said, "how do you know Marie?"

There was a disinterested tone in her voice that Lassiter sensed she didn't feel, and it occurred to him that perhaps she suspected he was Jesse's father.

"I met her at my sister's funeral," Lassiter said. "And when I came up to Portland on business, I thought I'd stop by to see her. She never mentioned anything about an *island*." He grinned and shook his head.

"I wonder," he said, as if the thought had just occurred to him. "Is there anywhere around here I could rent a boat?"

"Oh, no dear. No one I know would rent a motorboat, this time of ye-ah."

"Why not? Because of the ice?"

"Oh no. Ice isn't much out he-ah. We don't freeze in but once every few years. There's too much water. Even then, it's just sea ice — not much more than slush, really."

"Then why not a motorboat?"

"Oh, it's too cold, de-ah. Small boat's not safe. You'd need something with a cabin and some heat. Elsewise, just a little engine trouble — shear a pin — something like that — you'd freeze up like a Popsicle. It's wicked cold in an open boat, you know — you're making your own windchill. And if you go overboard, well . . . that's that. I don't expect you'd last more than a minute or two."

"So no one goes out in the winter?"

"Lobstermen, urchin divers, are the only ones crazy enough, and they wouldn't do it neither — 'cept for the money."

"What's an urchin diver?"

"Sea urchins. They like the cold water, and the Japanese like them. So I'm told. Personally, I won't touch them."

"You think one of the divers or the lobstermen would take me out?"

She looked doubtful. "The lobstermen? No. It's only the big boats go out in win-tah. Urchin divers? They might do. But it'd cost a penny."

"Even so," Lassiter said. "You know where I could find someone? I mean . . . it wouldn't hurt to *ask*."

"Well, you could check down to Ernie's — that's the marine supply store, fishermen's co-op. There's usually someone down there."

Lassiter thanked her, and told her what a pleasure it had been.

She was pleased and a little embarrassed and fiddled with the cups. "I don't believe you'll be goin' out today, though. We're due for some more weath-ah."

Ernie, the proprietor and also the harbormaster, echoed that thought, shaking his massive head. They were surrounded by marine gear, huge pink mooring balls, what seemed like thousands of fittings in little bins, charts, flares, life vests, everything. A radio rasped in the background, an unintelligible voice speaking in between stretches of pure static. "Weather channel says another nor'easter's on its way. Not s'posed to get here till the morning, mind you. But me? I don't like the way the air feels. I wouldn't recommend anybody going out. Nossir."

"Well, I was hoping I could speak to someone—"

Ernie nodded toward a door in the back. "Try if you like," he said. "There's a coupla fellas in they-ah. You're welcome to ask."

"You just don't want me to leave because you need a fourth for pinochle," Roger said to the men at the table. "But I was going out anyway. Urchins are a hundred dollars a pound in Tokyo, and if I don't find some pretty quick, the mufflah on my truck's gonna get even loudah."

He was a big, good-natured guy with long black hair and a salt-and-pepper beard, heavy brows over bright eyes, and snow-white teeth. He wore bright yellow overalls and giant boots that made him look like a Down East Paul Bunyan. Lassiter had just agreed to pay him $300 to take him out to Rag Island and pick him up the next day.

One of the men at the table shook his head. "Storm comin'," he said in a don't-say-I-didn't-warn-you voice. "Check the barometah."

"There's not even small-craft warnings yet," Roger said. "Besides, if we get a storm tomorrow, that'd stir the bottom wicked, and I'd be shit-outta-luck till the weekend."

"Your passenger's gonna want a wet suit."

"How 'bout yours? You aren't goin' anywhere." Roger turned to Lassiter. "You want a wet suit? Keep you warm."

"I don't know," Lassiter replied. "Whatever you say."

"Well, you don't *really* need one—it's not like you're goin' swimmin'. Plenty of good places to put ashore." Roger turned his massive head toward the wall, where the pendulum on a tidal clock ticked from side to side. "We'll have plenty of water, too. Other *hand*! If the wind kicks up, you turn out to be a clumsy bastard—" He cocked his head. "—you might wind up core-froze and there goes my license."

"Core-froze!?" Lassiter repeated.

Roger nodded. "Ah-yuh. But I think you could probably use my old gear. You're a pretty big fellah."

One of the men at the table laughed. "Your old gear? Last time I saw it, the butt was ripped. Why'd you even save it?"

"It *does* have a rip—but this man's not going to be *diving*, is he? It's just gonna keep him warm in the boat. And if he happens to slip when I'm setting him down, he won't freeze up, will he?"

"Rodge is right," said a man in a Red Sox cap. "You don't need no H-bomb to kill no fly, and you don't need a perfect wet suit to take a little boat ride."

They worked out the details as Roger fetched the wet suits and thermal underwear from a storage area in the back room. "Don't smell too good," he said with a sniff, tossing a pair of long johns to Lassiter. "Sorry."

Lassiter shrugged, stripped, and redressed. When he was done, he folded his own clothes into a little pile and pulled on his leather jacket over the wet suit. Retrieving his wallet from his pants, he began to put it in the breast pocket of his jacket—but something was already there.

Baresi's letter.

"Somethin' the mat-tuh?" Roger asked, seeing the look on his face.

"No," Lassiter said. "I keep forgetting something." Shoving the letter back in his pocket, he stuffed his wallet next to it and buttoned them in. Then he put his clothes in a plastic grocery bag and knotted it shut. The deal was that Roger would take him to the island that same afternoon, and return for him at high tide the next morning. "Weath-ah permittin', of course. Never can tell what the weath-ah's gonna do."

Lassiter knew that his plan was risky—to trespass on an island owned by a woman who was scared to death of stalkers. But Marie Sanders would probably recognize him from Kathy's funeral, he thought, and he was confident that he could explain everything. The fact that it would be impossible for him to leave until Roger returned might even be a plus. She couldn't just slam a door in his face; she'd have to take him in.

Besides, he couldn't wait a month or six weeks for her to come ashore. If he'd found her, so could they—and with Drabowsky helping, it wouldn't take long.

He followed Roger out to the dock, which was attached to a ramp that angled down to a float on the water. It was the winter dock, Roger explained, the ramp and float easily pulled out in the event of a bad storm. Together, they climbed down to the ramp, which rose and fell as a wave swept under it.

"Wait he-ah," Roger said, "I'll be right back."

He picked up an inflatable red dinghy and tossed it into the water. Hopping in, he rowed out to a gleaming white boat with *Go-4-It* written on the stern. Roger pulled the dinghy aboard and lashed it down. A minute later the engine turned over with a growl and the boat swung slowly around. With practiced ease, Roger brought it to the dock, jumped out, and steadied the boat so Lassiter could climb aboard.

The cockpit was crowded with equipment: diving tanks, masks, lines, marker buoys, and other equipment whose purposes Lassiter couldn't guess. Suddenly, the boat surged forward as Roger pushed off and leapt on board. Then Lassiter followed the big man into the cabin, where a little heater glowed on the floor.

Roger talked about urchin fishing as they maneuvered out of the tiny harbor. "It's dangerous work," he said, "but I can bring in a thousand pounds on a good day. That's urchins—not roe. Urchins pay about a dol-luh twenty-five a pound."

"Why winter? It's freezing," Lassiter said, raising his voice above the engines. The boat was in open water now.

"That's the season: September to April. If you harvest them in summuh, the roe's about three percent of the body weight. Win-tuh-time, it's ten to fourteen. So win-tuh's a lot more efficient."

"And it's the roe you're after?"

"Ay-uh. That's what they're payin' for. Japs call it *uni*."

Lassiter was enjoying the ride. The boat was well designed; it seemed to skim along sweetly on top of the chop. Behind them, Cundys Harbor had shrunken to toy size.

"So . . . do you like it?" Lassiter yelled.

"Like what?"

"The roe?"

"To *eat*?"

"Yeah"

"Oh, God, no," Roger said, wincing. "Thing about the Japanese— *watch it!*" He flung his arm in front of Lassiter as he wrenched the boat violently to the left. There was a dull thump, and the boat shuddered under their feet. *"Fuck!"* Roger said, gritting his teeth. Then he cut the engines until the boat began to pitch and roll on the swells.

"What's the matter?" Lassiter asked.

"We hit a log," Roger explained.

"How can you tell?"

"They float on the surface, you can see 'em. They sink, that's okay, too. But when they get just the right saturation . . . they hang there, just below the surface. So you can't see 'em, no way." He revved the engine, and listened. It had a ragged sound.

Roger cocked his head. "Sounds like I just nicked it," he said. "Might be able to sand it down." Suddenly, he slammed his hand down on the console above the ignition and gears. *"Fuck!* That's the third propeller this *ye-ah!"* A big sigh breezed through his lips as he swung the boat around, set course, and eased the throttle forward. A moment later the boat was pounding through the waves.

"What was I sayin'?" Roger shouted. "Before we were so rudely interrupted?" He laughed at his joke, a big, confident ha-ha-ha.

"The Japanese!" Lassiter replied, forcing his voice above the engine noise.

"Right! I think, whatever's hard to do, or contrary—that's what they like. Take those bonsai trees. A tree wants to grow big, so they like to grow 'em *small.* And look at their gardens—bunch of rocks! And urchin roe's another example because it's naturally disgusting. And some of the other things they eat—blowfish? Do it wrong, and it'll kill you in a heartbeat."

Roger looked around—and frowned. "I think we might be getting that storm a little early. Look at that."

Lassiter looked, and saw that the waves were bigger now. The wind was stronger, too, and there were whitecaps everywhere. Still, the boat could handle it.

"If this gets any worse, I may just let you off and have back," Roger said. "It's been a bitch of a win-tuh."

"If it's a problem landing—"

"No problem, there," Roger said dismissively. "There's a good spot on the lee side of the island. What's a *problem* is diving. I will not dive in rough water. Not by myself."

He flipped open a metal-framed section of the windshield and stuck his head out. Instantly, the cabin was wet and freezing cold. A second later he drew his head back in and snapped the window shut.

"It's blowing up good all right." He heaved his huge shoulders. "I think after I set you down, I'll just head back. Best take a look at that propeller."

Roger was bummed enough that he no longer wanted to talk. He picked out a cassette and popped it into the tape deck. It was one of the old Little Feat albums, and listening to it, Roger dipped his shoulders, right and left, boogying in place. He was six-four, if an inch, but a graceful dancer. Listening to him sing along, Lassiter realized that he had a good voice, too.

"You should have been in rock and roll," Lassiter shouted. The boat was thudding over the waves at thirty to thirty-five knots.

Roger smiled, and waved a big hand toward the left. "Pine Island," he said. Then he dipped, spun, and clapped his hands.

"*If you'll be my Dixie chicken*," he sang, with absolutely no self-consciousness.

Lassiter stared out at the water through the salt-streaked windshield and thought about what he was going to say. Like . . . *Don't shoot!* And . . . *We met at my sister's funeral.*

"Dutchess Island!" Roger yelled, gesturing seaward.

Lassiter nodded, and thought, I'll think of something.

Another song came on: Dire Straits, doing "Sultans of Swing." Roger tapped him on the arm as the opening guitar licks rolled out into the air, then pointed ahead, and to the left. "That's Rag Island, comin' up to port. See it?"

Lassiter followed the Mainer's gaze toward a dark mass of rocks and trees. He nodded and smiled.

Roger turned his attention back to the music, singing along with Mark Knopfler, into it, his huge eyes half closed, as if he couldn't afford any distraction from the tune. This might have worried Lassiter if he'd thought about it. But he did not.

Instead he listened to the driving bass and syncopated licks and relished the moment for what it was: exhilarating, loud and perfect. He was snug against the blistering cold, slamming over the waves toward a damsel in distress, surrounded by music and water. The boat was pure fiberglass joy. He could all but feel the white curls of foam falling away from the prow as it cut through the water. And Roger, his boon companion, the Bunyanesque urchin diver, with firm opinions about Japanese culture and a really terrific voice, was there at the helm, piloting the pair of them toward . . .

A wall of rocks.

The island loomed, and as they rushed toward it, Lassiter turned to his new friend with a questioning look, thinking a joke was in the works, then blanched to see the panic in the diver's face as he spun the wheel to no avail.

"God damn!" Roger cried, his voice cracking as he slapped at the throttle in a vain attempt to slow the boat before it crashed.

The last thing Lassiter heard before the boat slammed into the rocks was Mark Knopfler, singing:

"The band plays Dixie, double-four time . . ."

And the last thing he thought, improbably enough, was, Hunh . . . two straight songs with the word "Dixie" in them.

An instant later the moment expanded as the *Go-4-It*'s hull powered into a mass of seaweed-clad boulders, ripping its bottom apart with a long, low, fiberglass shriek that slammed Lassiter into the console. Suddenly, water was pouring in from every side as the cabin shattered with a bang, sending a cascade of ear-splitting cracks and pops and tearing noises through the back of his head.

The lights went out. The dark rushed in. The water rose. A hand reached for him in the night and took him by the arm. Then the floor heaved as a wave lifted the boat off the rocks. For a moment it was as if gravity had failed. The boat, and all the world around it, seemed suspended in the air, hanging weightless at the apogee of its destruction—and then, as suddenly as the boat had risen, it slammed back down on the rocks.

This time his head was driven into something hard. A flashbulb went off behind his eyes, and a bright red seam arced through his vision. The hand on his arm was torn away, and then he was in the water, dazzled, tumbling, hurt.

Something was happening inside his head. The noises were all wrong—distant, fizzy, carbonated, *wrong*.

For an instant he felt the ground beneath him, and just as quickly it was gone. Instinctively his feet began to bicycle in the water. Which was cold. Freezing. And slicing into the rip in his wet suit like a knife made of ice. He could feel the warmth seeping away from him, and knew that he had less than a minute, and then he'd be dead, smashed against the rocks, drowned or core-froze. The thought pulled a gasp from his chest. His eyes flew open and, through the salt burn, he saw a ring of orange flames, shooting this way and that in quick, exuberant zips.

We are the sultans . . .

A wall of sparkling black rocks loomed out of nowhere as the cold took him by the chest and squeezed, tearing the air from his lungs. For a second he felt something under his feet and, with surging heart, he took a step, and then another. Suddenly, the water fell away from his chest—dropping to his waist, his knees, his ankles. There was a clatter of stones at his feet as a million pebbles rushed toward the sea on a tide of phosphorus and foam. For a moment he was rooted to the spot, and turning around, looked up in dread to see the Wave, like a dark house falling toward him out of the sky.

36

"Mommy—I think he's awake!"

"Are you *sure* this time?" A woman's voice, a little distracted but still sweetly indulgent.

"Uh-huh. You want to know why?"

"No."

"Be-*cause* . . . heyyy! You said *no-o*." A chuckle. "You do want to know why, Mommy!"

"You're right, I do."

"Because his eyes are closed but underneath they moved. Really fast, like they jumped."

Lassiter could feel faint puffs of air against his cheek. The sweet smell of a child's breath. Brandon? And then the woman's voice: "Just because he moved, that doesn't mean he's awake. It's a reflex. He probably heard me drop that pan, even in his sleep, and it startled him."

"What's a 're-fless'?"

"Re-*flex*."

"What's that?"

"It's when your body reacts all by itself. Say . . . if I poked my finger toward your eye—really fast. Even if you didn't want to, your eyes would squeeze shut."

"Except I know you won't *really* poke me, so I could keep my eyes open."

"No, that's what a reflex is—you can't help it. When something's coming toward your eye, your eyes slam shut so they won't get hurt."

"You *try* that—poking my eye." A little laugh. "Only not *really* really."

"Let me finish the dishes first."

"Okay." The child began to hum a sweet little tune.

From his strange, removed space, Lassiter was beginning to remember something: music, a wave, drowning. . . . His eyes fluttered open and a blurry little face, not a foot from his own, jerked back, startled.

"Aaaaaa! He opened his eyes!" The child chuckled, happy and scared. "Mommy! He woke up!"

"Oh, Jesse," the voice said, moving closer. "You stare at him so long, you *want* him to wake up so much—"

"Nuh-*uhhhh*. He looked at me. *Really*."

The light hurt his eyes, and Lassiter closed them again, but this time he couldn't slide back into that cool dead space.

And then the woman's voice was floating down from the air over Lassiter's head. "Jess-*ee*—he's still asleep."

"I thought . . . maybe it was just a *reefless*."

"Oh, you," she said indulgently. "How did you get so smart?" Then she must have tickled him, or swung him around, because the child giggled, a deep, rolling, belly laugh of pure delight.

"Do that again!"

Lassiter was thinking: *double-four-time . . . double-four-time*. What was double-four-time? And then, *core-froze*. And *maybe I'm dead*. His eyes snapped open.

The woman was holding the boy under his arms, swinging him in a circle, head back, hair flying. Once, twice: the whirl began to slow as the woman pulled the boy toward her and then settled him on his feet. The child swayed, giggled, and waited for the room to stop moving. Then his eyes met Lassiter's and a look of great solemnity came over his face.

"Look," he said.

The mother turned to where the boy was pointing and stared.

"I *told* you," the boy said.

The woman's carefree expression faded into a cautious one. "You were right, Jesse," she said carefully. "He *is* awake."

"We saved you," Jesse said, his huge brown eyes fixed on Lassiter. "You even stopped breathing until Mommy put her breath into you. *I* had to count—it was very impor-tant—and then you spitted up water." An apologetic look. "We cut your diver suit off, and we can't ever fix it. How—"

He heard the woman say, "Shhhh."

Little fingers touched his forehead and stroked it. "You'll be all right," the boy said.

Lassiter heard his own breath, ragged and loud.

"You've been unconscious," the woman said. "For two days."

Lassiter groaned.

"It took a long time to get you up here, up from the beach—"

"You were cold," Jesse said. "You were blue. We saved you."

There was another sound in the room, and Lassiter frowned as he tried to place it. Finally, it came to him. Rain on the roof. The wind moaning. Lassiter opened his mouth to speak, but nothing came out.

The woman said, "Jesse, get a glass of water."

"All right," the boy said cheerfully. Lassiter heard him march off, heard the scrape of a stool.

When the boy returned, the woman lifted Lassiter's head to the glass, while the boy held it. He managed a few sips, and then fell back, exhausted. "There was another man," Lassiter said. What was his name?

The woman frowned, and shook her head, slowly. "We only found you."

Roger. His name was Roger.

We are the sultans . . .

Suddenly, it all came back to him in a rush that made his body jerk. Kathy. Brandon. Bepi. The priest. So many dead. "Callista," he said.

The woman gasped, and her eyes hardened. Reaching for Jesse, she pulled the boy back from the bed. For a long moment there was only the storm. When she finally spoke, there was no tenderness in her voice, none at all. "Who are you?" she asked.

When he woke for the second time, it was night. The cabin glowed with the buttery light from a pair of kerosene lanterns, hanging from the wall. As he looked around, he saw that he was in a large, pine-paneled room, post and beam, open to the rafters. A mammoth field-stone fireplace took up most of the far wall, maybe twenty feet away. Inside the fireplace, flames danced behind the glass doors of a wood stove. He didn't see the woman or the boy, but he heard a voice, a low murmur, somewhere behind him.

I have to get up, he thought, and, leaning on his elbow, swung his feet from the bed. Pushing himself into a sitting position, a tremor of weakness ran through him, followed by a wave of nausea. The room pulsed hot and cold as he took a deep breath, and stood, swaying like a drunk in a breeze that wasn't there. Then his eyes rolled up, the room fell away, and he crashed to the floor, pole-axed.

"Are you crazy?" she asked, pivoting his legs up onto the bed again. He sank back down. "You were *unconscious* for two days."

"Is my face messed up?"

"No . . ." She stopped, tossed her brown hair, surprised by the question. "What kind of a question is that?"

"It's not what I meant," he said. "I meant . . ." She was more beautiful than he'd remembered. Even in the flickering light he could see the difference. The waif was gone. She was older now, stronger and more womanly. "I meant . . . do you recognize me?"

"No," she said, more wary than curious. "Who are you?"

"You came to the funeral," he said, "in Virginia. My sister's funeral. Her son's funeral."

She stared.

"Kathy Lassiter," he said, "and Brandon."

Her brow wrinkled, and something moved in her eyes.

"It was November. You wore a hat with a veil. And your hair was blond."

He could see the recognition in her eyes, although she tried to hide it. He could tell what she was thinking. She was thinking, *He's here for a reason. And that isn't good.*

"You met her in Italy—at the clinic."

"What?" She stepped from the bedside and, nervously, pushed back the hair from her face.

"This isn't about Callista Bates. I was looking for a name in the ledger—"

"What 'ledger'?"

"At the pensione Aquila. I was looking for 'Marie Williams.' And I found out . . . she was *you.*"

She returned to the bed and sat down beside him, just out of reach. "I don't understand . . . why did you go to the clinic?"

It took him an hour to tell her the story, and twice his voice gave out, and she brought him water. The kerosene lamps sputtered into smoke, their fuel exhausted, and she replaced them with others. From time to time she got up to feed the wood stove, and when he was done, she said: "I don't get it."

"What?" Lassiter asked.

"Any of it. Why would anyone do that?"

Lassiter shook his head. "I don't know. But there were eighteen women and eighteen children—and you're the only ones left."

She threaded her fingers into her hair and pushed it up on top of her head. She looked so vulnerable, he wished he could take her into his arms and comfort her. But of course he couldn't do that at all. Finally, she said, "How do I know you're not lying?"

"Because you remember me. You know you do."

She let her hair fall down and walked away from the bed. A moment later he heard the door of the wood stove creak, and the thump of a log thrown on the fire. Then the door creaked shut and he watched her shadow as it slid across the ceiling, huge in the weak light of the lanterns. Finally, she dropped into a rocking chair and tapped her foot. Nervously.

"You could check," he said. "Call the pensione. Talk to Nigel, talk to Hugh. Or you could call Jimmy Riordan in Virginia—he's with the Fairfax police. Or you could call—"

"The phone doesn't work," she said. "And, anyway, Jesse and I are safe here. I *feel* safe. No one's going to find us here."

"Why not? *I* did."

She glared at him, and changed the subject. "The storm's winding down," she said. "The Coast Guard will be out, looking for you in the morning. They'll take you back to the mainland, and you can forget about us. I mean—it's horrible about your sister and the others and—I mean, *thank you*, I appreciate your concern—but . . . Jesse and I, we'll be fine."

He sighed. There wasn't anything else that he could do. "Look," he said, "if you won't let me help you, maybe you can help me."

She looked puzzled. "How?"

"I started on this because I couldn't understand why someone would kill Kathy—and I still don't. But maybe . . . if I could ask you a couple of things . . ."

"Like what?"

"I don't know, but . . . why did you go to the Baresi Clinic? I mean, why there, rather than somewhere else?"

Callista—*Marie*—shrugged. "The same reason Kathy did," she

said. "I researched it. The clinic had a good track record. Baresi was well respected. And it was one of the first clinics to offer the procedure I was interested in. The only thing against it was that it was in a foreign country, but even that was an advantage. I got to go back to Italy."

"Back?"

"I lived there when I was a kid. Near Genoa."

"You grew up in Italy?"

She shook her head. "Three years was all. My aunt got sick or I would have graduated from high school in Arenzano."

"But—"

"My uncle worked construction," she said. "I guess he was pretty good, because we lived all over the place. Pakistan, Saudi—here in the States, too. I spent the third grade in Tulsa, five through seven in Wilmington, Delaware, then Tacoma—I didn't even go to school in Tacoma. And then . . . eight through nine in Houston. Italy was after that. And actually . . . I lived there longer than anywhere else."

"The woman in the store said your parents died when you were little."

"My aunt and uncle took me in. I don't think they wanted to, really—but she was actually the only blood relative I had."

"And their name was Williams?"

She nodded. "Aunt Alicia and Uncle Bill."

"Did they adopt you? I mean . . . legally?"

The question made her bristle. "What's that got to do with your sister?"

"It has to do with *you*. Because if they adopted you, there's a paper trail. Somewhere. In one courthouse or another."

"They wanted my name to be the same as theirs. I remember Aunt Alicia saying it would be less *confusing* if we all had the same last name. Otherwise, it took too long to go through Customs." She shook her head and laughed. "So they adopted me because it was more efficient that way, not because they loved me, not because it would make us a family. Because it was less hassle." She paused, and laughed again. "No wonder I was such a mess."

"They actually put it that way."

She pressed her lips together. "Umm-hmmm." She sighed. "I shouldn't complain. They were both in their fifties, and they were taking on someone in kindergarten. They treated me well enough."

"Why do you say you were a mess?"

"I was a ratty little thing—and really, *really* shy. My parents were killed, and right before that, my brother died. Moving around was hard, and Aunt Alicia and Uncle Bill—they pretty much ignored me most of the time. So I became . . . I don't know. Withdrawn. And except in Saudi, I didn't even go to English-speaking schools. Most of the time, I found that the best thing was to be unnoticeable. So I got pretty good at that."

Lassiter gave her a skeptical look. "I should think you'd have been pretty noticeable, even as a kid."

"No. It's true. I was a real ugly duckling. My ears stuck out, my nose was too big, my eyes, my mouth—everything was too big. Even my knees. And my feet were massive. It was like I was a puppy or something."

Lassiter laughed.

"My aunt used to look at me," she said, "and shake her head, and say 'Maybe she'll grow into it'—but she sounded doubtful, and you could tell she didn't think I would." She laughed, and just as suddenly, she frowned. Then she sat up straight and gave him a wary look. "This can't possibly help you. I think it's time—"

"I just thought maybe there was something *different* about Dr. Baresi's clinic . . . I don't know."

"Well, he didn't let you pick. That was one thing. And I guess most people thought it was a minus, but not me. I thought it was a plus."

"What do you mean 'pick'? Pick what?"

"Sperm donors. Egg donors."

"You can *pick*?"

She nodded. "Most places. I went to a clinic in Minneapolis—just to see what the deal was. And, of course, they 'counseled me' about the procedure, all the steps you go through. They asked questions like—are you married? Will your husband's sperm be used to fertilize the egg? No? Well, look through these—and they handed me a three-ring notebook with blurbs about the donors! I couldn't believe it." Her voice segued into the smarmy pitch of a game-show voice hyping a prize. "Donor 123 is an aerospace engineer with an athletic build, 1500 SATs, and *perfect pitch*. Donor 159 is six feet six inches tall and weighs in at . . ." She shuddered and let out a restrained fake scream. "I mean: ahhhhhhhh."

He laughed. "A little too master-race for you?"

"Just a little. But there wasn't any of that at the Baresi Clinic. They wouldn't tell you anything about the donors. Nothing at all. Which was fine with me. I didn't want to know." Once again her voice turned into someone else's—this time, a low growl with an Italian accent. "Mah-ree-uh! *Carissima!* It will be *una sorpresa piccola!*"

"What's that?"

" 'A little surprise.' Except, to me, he spoke Italian." She smiled at the thought. "I liked him very much."

She seemed more relaxed now, so he tried again. "I know you don't want to hear this," he said, "but it really isn't safe to stay here."

Tired of the argument, she rolled her eyes and looked away.

"Look," he said, "these people have a lot of money—and not just money. Contacts, too. People in the FBI. If I can find you—"

"How *did* you find me?"

"Gunther."

She looked puzzled for a moment, and then: "You mean, my car?"

"Basically . . . yeah."

"I don't call it Gunther anymore."

"That's not the point."

"I know, but—"

"Let me ask you something: How did you do it, anyway?"

"Do what?"

"Create a new identity. Because you didn't do such a bad job . . . I mean, for an amateur."

"Thanks . . . I guess. Anyway, I just bought a how-to book. From this place in Colorado? They have all kinds of strange books: How to blow things up, how to forage for food, how to build your own mortar? I think they're kind of big with the militia types."

"And you just followed the directions?"

"Yeah. Something like that. They told you how to go to a cemetery to get a name off a baby's gravestone. But I already had a name, a name I hadn't used for twenty-five years—so I didn't have to do that. I even had the birth certificate. And, by then, I was already pregnant, so I was kind of in a hurry."

"This was the Marie Sanders birth certificate."

"Right. *My* birth certificate. It was in an old manila envelope that I'd been carrying around ever since I was eighteen and my uncle gave it to me. It had a couple of my baby teeth, a wedding photograph of my parents, a newspaper clipping of my grandfather at a ship launching, and some U.S. savings bonds which my parents had bought for me when I was a baby. That's how I got to California—I cashed in the savings bonds."

"But—"

"Look," she said, abruptly getting to her feet. "What I think is: we should get some sleep now—especially you." And with that, she blew the lanterns out, one by one, and disappeared.

That night, he slept like the dead, and in the morning woke to hear Jesse calling to his mother. "It's so *warm*, Mommy. I don't even need my mittens. Can I take them off? Pleeeze?"

"Well . . ."

"It's almost *hot*, Mommy. You come out—you'll see. It's *hot*. And foggy, too. You can't even see Bear Island!"

Lassiter heard the door close, and opened his eyes. Seeing that he was alone, he sat up, pulling the blankets around him. Then he swung his legs from the bed and, getting slowly to his feet, shuffled across the room to a chair beside the wood stove.

A minute passed. Then a second and a third. Then the door burst open and Jesse came running inside. Seeing Lassiter, he skidded to a stop. "Hey!" he cried. "You're up! Will you play pickup sticks with me? Mommy's tired of it. Pleeeze?"

And so he did. He played pickup sticks and Candy Land all morning. Marie dug out some old clothes from a trunk in the loft, and he put them on. They were ragged and musty, but they fit.

Lassiter was amazed by the little family's self-sufficiency. They had a root cellar, fishing gear, and eel pots. There were strings of dried fruit, braids of onions and garlic, ropes of dried red peppers, and bundles of herbs hanging from the beams. There were containers filled with staples—rice, beans, dried milk, and powdered eggs. Flour, sugar, oatmeal. There was water from a well that Marie, and even Jesse, standing on a stool, hand-pumped in the kitchen. "Sometimes it freezes," Jesse confided, "but we have a *lot*—I mean *really a lot* of bottles. And rain barrels, too. Want to see?"

The kid was irresistible, and Lassiter caught his mother, several times, looking on with an expression he remembered seeing on Kathy's face: a mother's love and pride. *Isn't he wonderful?*

They had lunch, and afterward Marie gave Jesse a reading lesson. Lassiter sat in an old Adirondack chair on the porch, watching the ocean, listening. When the lesson was done, Jesse ran back outside, eager to show him how they moved heavy objects—the boat, the dock—to and from the water. "It's just like the 'Gyptians," he said, dragging a crude sled from under the porch.

The sled was actually a piece of corrugated iron with a two-by-four nailed to one end. Holes had been drilled in each end of the wood, and a rope threaded through them, so the whole thing was easy to pull. To demonstrate, Jesse placed a rock on top of the sled, then took the rope in his tiny fists and pulled, lifting the contraption onto the first of two small logs. Slowly, and with a great deal of huffing and puffing, he began to drag the device and its burden toward the water's edge, stopping every few feet to move one of the logs from the back of the sled to the front.

"This is how they moved all the rocks to build the pyramids," Jesse said. "Because they didn't have wheels."

At dinner Marie said that if the fog cleared, the Coast Guard would almost certainly come by in the morning. "And Mr. Lassiter will be able to get back to civilization."

"Can't he stay?" Jesse asked. "It's funner with him here."

"It's more fun," Marie corrected. "No, of course he can't stay, Jesse. He has his own life to get back to. Don't you?"

Lassiter looked at her for a long moment. Finally, he said, "Oh, yeah, absolutely."

It was a lie, of course, and he thought about it afterward, washing the dishes while Marie read to Jesse in the other room. The truth was, now that he'd found them, it still wasn't over—and it wouldn't be over until . . .

Until I know what happened, and why.

When Marie returned from putting Jesse to bed, the two of them sat in front of the fireplace. She seemed sad, and he said so.

"It's just that . . . with you here . . . Jesse's so excited . . . and it makes me realize . . . how selfish this is."

"Living on the island?"

She nodded. "But it won't go on forever. He goes to kindergarten in the fall, so . . . we'll have to find a house in town."

"Aren't you afraid someone will recognize you?" Lassiter asked.

She shook her head. "Not really. It's so out of context, and . . . I was different then."

"You mean, the way you looked?"

"No. I mean the way I felt. Somehow, all that doesn't seem so important anymore. What's important is Jesse."

Lassiter nodded. "Right. And that's exactly why you've got to get out of here."

She threw him an impatient look. "I thought that was settled," she said.

He sighed. "All right, so it's settled. But do me a favor: when the Coast Guard comes, tell them you haven't seen me."

"Why?" she asked, glancing at him suspiciously.

"Because the same people who are looking for you are looking for me, too. Which—trust me on this—is not good for you. Because if the Coast Guard takes me back to the mainland, someone's going to have to write a report—and that report's gonna have my name on it. And because a local guy got killed, the papers are gonna pick it up. And the next thing you know, you've got people in town that no one's ever seen before. And guess what? They're asking things like, 'He rented a boat? To go out in a storm? Where was he going? Who was he going to see?'" He paused and took a breath. "It's a big problem. Better I get to the mainland on my own."

"How?"

"You've got a boat. You could take me to shore."

She pulled her knees up to her chest. "And then what? Just drop you off on the rocks somewhere?"

"Yeah."

"That's crazy. What would you do?"

"Don't worry about it."

She shook her head. "The boat's not even in the water yet. The *dock's* not even in the water."

"What do you mean, 'The dock's not in the water'? Where is it?"

She looked at him. "You have to pull it up in winter—because the ice would take it out. The cove freezes once or twice a year."

"Yeah, but if something's tied up—"

She laughed. "We're talking *tons* of ice. When that starts to melt, and the tide goes out—"

"There isn't any ice out there—"

"Not *now*, but . . ." She heaved a sigh. "I guess we could put the dock in. And then . . . I suppose I could take you to shore."

"That's all I'm asking."

"All right. That's what we'll do."

They fell silent for a moment. Lassiter looked away, and then turned back to her. "Can I ask you something?"

"Jesus!" she said. "You're as bad as Jesse."

"No, seriously—about the clinic. All of the people who died had the same procedure, and I was wondering . . . why did you have it?"

"What . . . the oocyte donation?"

"Yeah. I mean, at your age . . . it's unusual, is all. The other women were like Kathy . . . they were older. I mean, I thought that's what it's *for*, it's . . ." He looked up at the ceiling. "I guess I'm getting kind of personal."

"Why not?" she said in a what-the-hell voice. "I'm telling you everything else. In my case it wasn't because I was infertile. I could have children. And I really, really wanted to carry a baby to term. But it had to be someone else's genetic material. Not mine."

"Why?"

"Duchenne's syndrome."

Lassiter gave her a blank look. "What's that?"

She stared at the fire. "There's a gene . . . women carry it, and pass it on—though it doesn't affect them. It affects males."

"And what happens?"

"It's an X-chromosome disorder, like hemophilia—except it can't be treated. Everyone who has it, dies young. My brother was only thirteen."

Lassiter remembered Maude talking about the brother being carried out to the boats, wrapped in blankets. "I'm sorry."

She sat back down in the chair and told him in a detached tone what the illness was like—a progressive, wasting disease of the muscles. It begins just below the calves, and moves slowly upward. Walking is awkward, at first, then difficult, and finally impossible. The leg muscles atrophy and, still, the disease moves higher, until the diaphragm is afflicted—and it becomes difficult to breathe, and impossible to cough. In the end, the victims get pneumonia or some other infection. And then they die. "I had the test in my twenties. And I found out I'm a carrier."

He didn't know what to say, and so he asked, "Would all of your children get it?"

She shook her head. "It's fifty-fifty, every time. Which means there's a one-in-four chance that you'd have a boy with Duchenne's."

"That doesn't seem so bad—"

"You'd do better at Russian roulette. And the thing is, it's someone else's life you're playing with—and it's someone you love more than anything in the world." Her hands flew up and floated down.

"I keep wanting to say I'm sorry," Lassiter said, "but—"

"It doesn't matter. I have Jesse . . . and there's no way in the world that I could ever love anyone more than I love him."

"I can tell."

"And it's not like I was devastated when I found out about the disease. I mean—I wasn't involved with anyone, I wasn't thinking about having a baby. It was a door that closed, but I wasn't even knocking on it."

"What made you change your mind?"

She shrugged. "I was living in Minneapolis. I had this kind of secret life. It was all so . . . lonely and disconnected. And I knew if I had a baby, it wouldn't be that way—and I thought of adoption, but . . . with Callista and all that, it was just too complicated, it wouldn't have worked. And then I saw an article about this new technique, using donor eggs—and I was galvanized. Two months later I was on a plane to Italy, and two months after that I was pregnant."

When the Coast Guard came, late the next morning, Lassiter and Jesse were on the far side of the island, "exploring."

It was unseasonably warm, almost springlike. Fog hung in the trees as Lassiter followed the boy on a narrow path through the woods, treading on a thick carpet of pine needles. Their first stop was "the dock," where two boats sat on a rocky ledge, high and dry amid a litter of broken clamshells. The boats were upside down, resting on their gunwales, secured by lengths of rope to the trunk of a red pine. One of the boats was a skiff, about fifteen feet in length; the other a dinghy. Nearby was a small shed and in it, "all of our boat stuff." There was an Evinrude outboard, resting on a wooden brace; gas tanks, oars, life jackets, moorings, anchors, fishing tackle, and more.

The dock itself was new, and painted gray. One part was permanently attached to the ledge, extending out over the high-water mark like a plank suspended out to sea. The rest of the dock, consisting of a raftlike float and a short ramp, were pulled up onto the ledge until it came time to hook them up.

He followed Jesse from one cove to another. They liberated a pair of crabs from one of the eel pots, and Lassiter was duly impressed when Jesse showed him an oak tree growing up through a discarded iron bedstead, the thick trunk nearly engulfing the metal. Their last stop was a cove at the end of the island, where the old boathouse was, and the slivered remains of an old dock. "They used to keep the boats in here in the winter," Jesse explained, "but now—" The little boy cocked his head and held up a finger.

Lassiter heard it, too: the low drone of an engine.

"Coast Guard," Jesse said. The engine grew louder and then cut off. Soon afterward they heard the whine of another, smaller engine. "That's their little boat," Jesse said. "It's a 'flatable." He peered at Lassiter. "Did I show you my fort yet?"

"No."

"Come on," he said, and taking Lassiter by the hand, led him up a spongy path to "the fort"—a clearing bounded by a tangle of small spruces and firs. There, in the clearing, Jesse had created a series of small "rooms" by dragging pieces of deadwood into a sort of floor plan. Leading Lassiter into the fort's "living room," the boy seated himself on a rotten log—"the couch"—and with Lassiter beside him, recited a fable about a lost seal and the people who were looking for him.

It was a strange story, and the moment it ended, a soft whistle came to them, undulating through the woods. Lassiter recognized the tune and knew what it meant: ollie-ollie-in-come-free. The Coast Guard had come, the Coast Guard had gone.

"What about Roger?" he asked.

Marie shook her head. "They didn't find him. But they will—eventually. The current takes everything down past the Nubble, so—"

"Did they ask about me?"

She nodded. "They said Roger was taking someone out to see me, and that they'd found a car in Cundys Harbor."

Lassiter turned his head and muttered to himself. *Fuck.*

"And then they asked if I knew a man named Lassiter."

He groaned with exasperation. "So why didn't you tell them I was here?"

"Did you want me to?"

"Of course not."

"Because . . . it just didn't feel right. They should have had a salvage boat, to begin with, and anyway, I could tell: they weren't all Coast Guard."

"What do you mean?"

"Two of them were wearing suits."

"And what did *they* look like?"

Marie shrugged. "Big."

"You think they were cops?" Lassiter asked.

"They could have been."

"But maybe not."

"Right," she said. "That's what worried me."

Lassiter sighed. "What did they want to know?" he asked.

"Well . . . about you. And if we'd seen the boat go down, and—oh, yeah, they wanted to know where Jesse was. 'Where's the little guy?' "

"And what did you tell them?"

"I told them we were asleep when it happened. And the next day, when we found the boat, there wasn't anyone. And I said Jesse was taking a nap."

"You think they believed you?"

She nodded. "Yeah. I'm a really good actress. Used to be, anyway."

Later that afternoon, when they'd had lunch and the tide was an hour from high, they began to put in the dock. It was a complex operation that took almost three hours to complete. When it was done, Lassiter paddled the float around while Jesse and Marie lowered the ramp with pulleys and ropes. Finally, Lassiter snapped the fittings together, and sat back.

"I can't believe you do that by yourself," he said.

Jesse was insulted. "She *doesn't*."

The dinghy was light enough to lift, and with Jesse's help, Lassiter carried it to the water. Then he and Marie rolled the skiff down toward the dock on three wooden poles. Every few feet Jesse yelled "Okay!" and they stopped, waiting for him to drag each bypassed pole up to the front and reposition it under the bow. When they reached the water's edge, they flipped the boat over onto some planks and pushed it into the sea. Going into the shed, Lassiter emerged with the outboard in his arms and a look of amazement on his face: that she could lift this deadweight by herself was astonishing. Together, they clamped the motor to the transom of the skiff and hooked up the gas tank. Meanwhile, Jesse, looking like the Michelin man in an enormous life vest, clipped the fuel line, first to the motor, and then to the tank. Then he squeezed the rubber bulb four or five times and, with his mother looking on, pressed the electric starter. After a few tries the motor caught and roared, churning out a cloud of dense, blue smoke.

That night, when Jesse had gone to bed, they sat in front of the fire, Marie in the rocking chair, her knees pulled up to her chest.

"Do you have any money?" she asked suddenly.

Lassiter was taken aback. "I do okay," he said.

Marie smiled. "I don't mean that. I mean *with* you. So when you get to shore . . . you won't be stranded."

Lassiter nodded. He thought he'd been making progress, but . . . she obviously couldn't wait to get rid of him. Slowly, he got to his feet and crossed the room to where his leather jacket was hanging on a peg. "I think I've got enough," he said. "The real problem is, what do we do about you?"

Marie shook her head. "Don't worry about us," she said. "We'll fade away in a day or two. I've got money. We can set up somewhere else. This time, I'll do it right."

"I could help you with that, y'know. I used to be a pro at it." He reached into the pocket of his jacket and pulled his wallet out. A soggy envelope fell to the floor, and he stooped to retrieve it. *Baresi's letter.*

"You could take Gunther," she said. "It needs work, but—"

"You read Italian, right?"

"What?"

"Can you read Italian?"

"Sure," she said, "but . . . ?"

There were three or four onionskin sheets inside the envelope, still damp and stuck together. Returning to the fireside, he sat down at Marie's feet and pulled the pages apart, very carefully. "Thank God for ballpoints," he said.

"What are you talking about?" she asked. "What's that?"

"It's a letter that Baresi wrote to the priest in Montecastello. The priest gave it to me before he was killed, and—here," he said, handing the pages to her. "Tell me what it says."

Reluctantly, she took the pages in hand, and began to read, haltingly at first, and then almost fluently. "August second, 1995. My dear Giulio . . .

With death so near, I write to you with an open and joyful heart, secure in the knowledge that I will soon stand in the presence of our Lord, there to be judged.

I see now that I came to you in my weakest hour, seeking through confession not only the forgiveness of the Church, but its complicity as well. The enormity of my life's secret, and the profundity of what I then believed to be my sin, seemed so great that I could no longer bear the weight alone—but felt that I must share it.

And so I did, and that was wrong.

They say you closed the church, and went to Rome. And that you stayed for days. Oh, Giulio . . . how I must have worried you!

But now I know that it was only through the lens of false pride that God's will could ever have been mistaken for my own achievement. I know now what you, as a man of God, have always known: that we are all instruments of the Lord, and that what we do is neither more nor less than the working out of His will.

The calamitous discovery that I made, by which cells could be returned to . . .

"I don't know what that is," Marie said, pointing to a word. Lassiter looked. "Totipotency," he said. "It's a word in genetics." Marie continued:

> . . . by which cells could be returned to totipotency, was inevitable in the great scheme of things. If Ignazio Baresi had not done it yesterday, another would have done it tomorrow. If not in Zurich, then at Edinburgh.
>
> And it is precisely in this, in the inevitability of what I did, that God's hand can be seen. Because that's what "inevitability" is and must be: God's plan, hard-wired into the world around us.
>
> How else, my friend, if not by reference to such a plan, can we explain the circumstances that brought a microbiologist to the study of relics? Relics! What are they, but magic tokens, fetishes and rabbits' feet? A sort of "visual aid" for the unsophisticated, making complex, metaphysical doctrines accessible to the common man. This nail pierced the hand of Jesus! This splinter stung His flesh! He walked among us. He was real.
>
> And yet . . . almost against my will, I found that when I placed these objects in a microscope, they swarmed with possibilities. The patronizing point of view with which I first approached the subject soon gave way to a more profound understanding. After fifty years of scholarship, I realized what

every peasant knows by intuition —that these objects are vital and tangible links to God.

As you know, this is not a point of view that's encouraged in Rome. The Vatican would prefer to forget when the trade in relics was most intense—when fortunes were paid for bits of flesh or wood, and relic mongers poisoned saints, the sooner to sell off their bones. The Vatican has always seen relic worship as a threat. When powerful relics have found their way to remote dioceses, pilgrims have followed with their wealth. And the Vatican is all the poorer for it.

As a consulting scientist in the Vatican's employ, my task was simple: to discredit the spurious, and reserve comment on the rest. And so I did: I revealed that "St. Anthony's clavicle" was only a fragment of a lamb's rib. And that "the cloth that mopped Christ's brow" had been woven in the fifteenth century.

In truth, a great many of the objects that I examined were, as the Vatican suspected, counterfeits. But not all. There were objects that simply could not be discredited: their provenance seemed likely, their age appropriate. They might be what they claimed to be—or might not.

It was then that I turned to medicine, stunned by the realization that I might serve as midwife to God—and that, indeed, this was my life's work.

Marie looked at Lassiter. "What's he talking about?" she asked. Lassiter shook his head. "Just keep reading . . ."

It wasn't difficult. My medical studies were comparatively brief. The clinic was easily established, and women came to me, mysteriously, from everywhere in the world—all of their own accord. Using DNA materials taken from a dozen of the most likely relics, I created an immaculate conception for each of eighteen patients.

Who knows, old friend, what will come of this? Perhaps these children will be no more than a strange band of peasants, resurrected from antiquity to no good purpose. Or perhaps I will, indeed, have begotten Christ anew. I will never know. You will never know. But, surely, we must hope.

And so, my friend, I bid you good-bye with the hope that I have set your mind at ease. I knelt before you in doubt, it's true— but that was only human. Christ, too, knew doubt—though I no longer do.

This matter is in God's hands. And always has been.

Ignazio.

"Joe?" There was a tremor in her voice. "What's he talking about?"

Lassiter was silent for a moment, and then: "Do you have anything to drink?"

Marie got to her feet, went to the cupboard, and returned with a bottle of cognac and two glasses. She poured one for each of them, and repeated her question. "What's he talking about?"

Lassiter took a long sip. "Jesse," he replied.

"What about him?"

"Well . . . Baresi . . . what he was doing—he was trying to clone Jesus."

"*What?!*"

Lassiter sighed. "Maybe Jesse . . . maybe Jesse is Jesus."

They stayed up late as Lassiter related what he'd learned from the professor at MIT.

"So that's it," he said, pouring his third cognac. "He took a scraping from a likely relic, isolated one of the nucleated cells, and returned it to its totipotent state. After that, all he needed was an egg and a woman who wanted to have a baby."

"*Una sorpresa piccola,*" Marie said.

"Once he had the egg, he replaced the nucleus with the one from the relic, implanted it, and . . ."

The fire popped, sending a spray of sparks across the floor. "I don't believe it," she said. "How could he *know,* after two thousand years, if a relic was genuine? There's no *way* he could know that."

Lassiter talked about Baresi's painstaking historical research into the provenance of relics, his ability to conduct DNA tests, his scientific credentials—but Marie continued to shake her head.

"All you're saying is that he was in a better position to guess than anyone else. But even so—it was just an educated guess." Lassiter was about to reply, but she held up a finger. "Wait a minute," she said. "Your nephew Brandon—did he look like Jesse?"

"No, he—"

"And the others?" she demanded, "did they all look exactly the same?"

"I didn't have the pictures of all of them, but . . . no."

"Well, there you go," she said, as if everything was settled. "They can't be clones then, can they? Not if they're all different. So Baresi was just guessing, that's all he was doing. If the children were not identical, the most you can say is that there's a remote possibility that maybe *one* of them was produced from a true relic. The rest of them would be . . . whatever—the butcher, the baker, the candlestick maker." Her hands flew up in the air. "So what you're suggesting—it's crazy!"

Lassiter agreed with her that obviously, Baresi could not rely on the provenance of any single relic; that was almost certainly why he multiplied his chances by using DNA samples from a collection of likely relics. "Maybe *none* of them is a true relic—but that doesn't make any difference."

"How can you say that?"

"Because it doesn't matter who Baresi cloned. It doesn't matter if he cloned Jesus or Al Capone."

"I just don't—"

"As long as there's a possibility that even a single relic was the real thing—well, someone's unwilling to take a chance on that. That's why my sister died, and Brandon, and all the others. That's why you've got to get out of here."

"I can't believe anybody would *do* that, kill a bunch of children on the off chance . . ."

"Well somebody has, and what's more, they've taken an extra step and made sure that none of the DNA survives. That's why the children are burned—to eliminate that possibility. They're *exorcising* it. With fire."

"Oh, come on—"

"When Brandon was killed, the man who set the fire was caught. Something happened. He fucked up. The combustion was incomplete, and you could still recognize the kid—barely, but you could recognize him. So they dug him up, and burned him *again*."

"But . . . they're *children*. They're just babies. They're . . . they're just more souls for the Church."

"This isn't about the Catholic Church. It's about Umbra Domini. Christian ultras who've bombed abortion clinics, waged a crusade against Muslims in Bosnia, and—" Lassiter threw up his hands. "Look: in *Umbra's* view, what Baresi did was an abomination."

"But *why*?"

"Because he turned the *Bible* inside out: God creates man in his image, not the other way around." Tears rolled down her cheeks, and Lassiter knew that, at last, she'd accepted that he was right. "Let me help you," he said, "because they won't stop until they find Jesse."

"But how? If it's what you say, how can anyone help?"

"When I was in the army . . . I had a funny kinda job." She looked at him as if he were insane, but he plunged on. "I ran the central cover staff for the ISA."

"What's that?"

Lassiter shrugged. "Intelligence Support Activity. It's like the CIA, except they know what they're doing. Anyway . . . the point is: I can build identities for you and Jesse that no one can ever break. I can have them backstopped from here to Mars—and I can promise you, you won't be traced. Ever. But you have to trust me. And you have to leave."

"Mommy?" Jesse was standing in the doorway, in his pajamas, rubbing his eyes.

"Hi, sweetie," Marie said, her voice full of love. "What's the matter?"

He stumbled toward them, clumsy with sleep. "I had a bad dream."

"Oh noooo," Marie said. He climbed into her lap and put his head on her shoulder. She stroked his hair and kissed him. "I'm sorry."

"Bad men," Jesse said.

She made a sympathetic sound, a sort of coo, and asked, "Should I read you a story?"

Jesse lifted up a chubby finger and pointed it at Lassiter. "No," he said. "Him."

"I'm not sure—"

"I'd love to," Lassiter said. "Want a piggyback ride?"

Marie caught his eye as he knelt down so that Jesse could climb aboard, but he couldn't read her expression.

"Heyyyyyy," Jesse said as Lassiter straightened up. "This is *high*." Lassiter grabbed his feet.

They strode toward Jesse's room, ducking under beams and doorways, as Jesse reached up to tap the ceiling. Sitting down on the bed, Jesse said that he didn't want to *hear* a story, he wanted to read one— to Lassiter.

"Okay," Lassiter said. "Hit it."

The boy pulled a book from under his pillow and, with a look of immense gravity, said, "Dr. Seuss." Then he opened the book to the first page and, dipping his body toward the words, said:

"One fish—"

Slowly, his little body rocked back, away from the book: "Two fish!"

And forward again: "Red fish!"

And back—but this time with a deliberately goofy look on his face, wide-eyed and grinning at the ceiling: "Blue fish!" Then he toppled onto his back with a belly laugh as big as the moon.

37

Lassiter was kneeling on the dock, untying the dinghy, when Jesse said, "Look, Mama—a boat."

Turning to where the boy was pointing, Lassiter raised his eyes to the horizon, squinting against the blowing mist. There wasn't anything that he could see, except the slate-gray sky, the rocks, the pines, and the heaving ocean. And then—there it was: a white motor launch riding up the back of a dark swell. The kid's eyes were amazing.

"Who is it?" he asked.

Marie cupped a hand above her eyes and grimaced into the wind. "I don't know," she said. "I've never seen it before."

Lassiter cursed, and retied the dinghy to its cleat, looping the line into a clove hitch. They'd been just about to row out to the skiff and take off, but that was impossible now. Or at least it was not possible without being observed by whoever was in the white boat. "You have any binoculars?"

Marie nodded, and lifted Jesse into her arms. "In the cabin," she said, and started running. Lassiter followed, squinting against the drizzle.

The binoculars were hanging from a hook next to the big bookcase. Raising them to his eyes, Lassiter looked out to sea and turned the focusing knobs. Although the boat was still too far away to make out the men's faces, he could see there were three of them.

"Is it them?" she asked, coming to his side.

"I can't tell." He forced his eyes to focus on the shuddering faces— and then it happened. In the stern of the boat a block of muscle got to its feet and pointed toward the cabin. Lassiter didn't need to see the man's face to know who it was. "It's them," he said as their features coalesced. "The big guy. Grimaldi. And della Torre."

Marie sucked in her breath and pulled Jesse closer.

"We can't stay here," Lassiter said. "Is there anywhere else?"

She thought for a second. "We could go to the boathouse. They don't know the island. They might not look there."

"All right," Lassiter said. "Get a flashlight." Then he crossed the cabin to the closet where she kept her rifle. "Where do you keep the ammo?"

"In the bread box," Marie replied.

He should have known. Grabbing the gun, he went to the bread box and opened it. Inside he found a loaf of sourdough, a couple of corn muffins, and, in the back, a box of ammunition.

Which was surprisingly light.

Lassiter tore open the box and, with a groan, found a single cartridge. "Where's the rest?" he asked.

Marie looked crestfallen. "I don't know. I guess . . . maybe I used it up."

"Doing *what*?" Lassiter asked.

"Practicing," Marie explained, and seeing the reaction on Lassiter's face, added, "Well, it's not like there's a lot to do in the winter!"

He couldn't believe it. "What am I supposed to do?" he asked. "Tell 'em to stand in a row?"

It was too much. Marie's face crumpled with unhappiness, and seeing this, Jesse rushed to console her.

He threw his little arms around her legs in what was meant to be a protective embrace. "Don't cry, Mama," he said, "don't cry."

Lassiter threw up his hands. "I'm sorry," he growled. "I'm really sorry. Just take Jesse to the boathouse—I'll meet you there in a few minutes."

Marie nodded, started to leave, and turned back. "But . . . what are you going to do?"

"I don't know," Lassiter said. "*Pin 'em down!*"

He pushed Jesse and Marie out of the cabin and watched them as they vanished into the woods. Then he loaded the single round of ammunition and went outside. Kneeling on his right knee, he steadied the rifle on the porch railing and closed his left eye. Slowly, he swung the gun in an arc until the motor launch swam into view.

The scope was a masterpiece. Della Torre loomed in the bow of the boat, swathed in a black cassock, oblivious to wind and rain, a clerical Odysseus. The motor launch was two hundred yards offshore, and though the shot was a difficult one, Lassiter knew he couldn't miss. He took a deep breath, letting it out in a slow stream as he settled the crosshairs of the scope on the priest's chest.

One shot, and it would all be over, he thought, and felt his finger tighten on the trigger. Killing della Torre would be like decapitating a snake. The body might live for a while, but it would be blind and aimless, thrashing in the dirt.

Or maybe not.

He moved the barrel an inch to the left, until the crosshairs came to rest just below the Mattress's right eye. The Italian was shouting to della Torre, unaware of the fact that his life hung by the weight of a single finger. And though the boat was yawing, Lassiter had its rhythm and knew for sure that he could take the big man out.

Take the shot, he told himself. Take it! You don't want to dance with this guy. He tried to kill you twice. He shot Azetti, and probably killed Bepi. It was a persuasive argument, but even as he made it, he felt the rifle slide to the left for the second time. And suddenly Grimaldi was in his sights.

He sat in the stern, grim as the rain, staring straight ahead. By now the boat was barely a hundred yards from shore, and heading directly to the dock below the cabin. In spite of the weather, Grimaldi's features were so clear in the scope that Lassiter could tell he needed a shave. Do it, he thought. Do it for Kathy and Brandon.

Jesse and Marie.

Jiri. Me.

If I pull the trigger, Lassiter told himself, the bullet will go through his skull like a high-speed drill, tunneling through the brain until it blows out the back of his head. His finger tickled the trigger.

But no, he thought. They're not looking for me. They don't even know I'm here. And if they find the cabin empty . . . who knows? Maybe they'll leave.

It was an unconvincing argument, but it had the force of an only hope. In any case, he had nothing to lose by backing away. It wasn't as if he had an M-16 with a full clip; he had a bolt-action Roberts with a single round. There was only so much damage he could do with the gun, and once that damage was done, so, in all likelihood, was he. Better to wait.

With a sigh that came out like a growl, he lowered the rifle and got to his feet. The motor launch was almost at the dock, and its occupants were standing, eager to come ashore. Almost tentatively, he took a step backward, and then another, and another—until he rounded the corner of the cabin and found himself on the path that Jesse and Marie had taken.

The woods were dim, the twilight dying. Ground fog lay on the path like smoke from a fire, and, everywhere, rain dripped, dripped, dripped from the trees. There were patches of snow in the lee of boulders, and fiddleheads poking out of the ground. The air was dense with the smell of resin.

Lassiter ignored it all, striding through the forest in dead silence, his footsteps cushioned by a mulch of pine needles.

And then, too soon, he was there.

The path opened onto a ledge of rock at the very edge of the sea. There, a low, dilapidated building crouched by the water's edge, its stone foundations lapped by the waves at high tide. Twenty years earlier the building had provided winter storage for half a dozen small boats and canoes. Today it was a gray wreck with a bowed roof and broken windows.

Lassiter looked one way and then the other, hoping for a better place to hide—but there was nothing. Just the rain, which was heavier; the sea, which was higher; and the woods, which were darker.

Crossing the ledge to the boathouse, he pulled the door open and stepped inside. "Marie?" he asked. The building was pitch-dark until, quite suddenly, a finger of light stabbed him in the eyes, blinding him. "Jesus!" Lassiter exclaimed, his heart lurching.

"Jesse!" Marie cried. "Turn that off!"

Instantly, the flashlight went out, and once again Lassiter was standing in the dark. Blinking. "Where are you?"

"I let him hold the flashlight—"

"It's okay."

His eyes swam with colors, as if his vision had been marbleized. And then, very slowly, shapes began to materialize in the room. A boat's cradle. A pile of lobster pots. Some fishing nets, hanging from the walls.

"Are we going to be okay?" Marie asked. She was huddled in a corner of the boathouse, holding Jesse in her arms.

"Yeah," Lassiter said, "we're gonna be fine."

"You're sure?"

Why lie? "No," he said. "Not really. The path goes right from the cabin. If they follow it . . . isn't there anywhere else?"

Marie thought about it. Finally, she said, "No."

"There must be somewhere."

"It's a small island . . . maybe they'll think we're gone."

Lassiter shook his head. "The wood stove's warm. They'll know we're here. You and Jesse, anyway."

The flashlight on and off.

"Jesse," Lassiter whispered. "Don't."

"I'm sorry," the boy sang.

Lassiter sat down below a broken window, next to the door, cradling the rifle in his arms. He was thinking of the three men that he'd had in his sights. I should have killed one of them, he thought. Della Torre or Grimaldi, Grimaldi or the Mattress.

"What are we going to do?" Marie asked.

Lassiter shook his head. "I'm not sure."

The minutes passed slowly, but they passed. The wind was blowing now, a low howl that made the rafters moan. It wouldn't be easy for della Torre to look for them at night, Lassiter thought. Not in weather like this. Not if he was smart. If he was smart, he'd go back to the mainland, and try again in the morning. It was the only sensible thing to do, Lassiter told himself. And then he sighed. Sensible as it was, he couldn't even sell this line of reasoning to himself.

He was hoping against hope, and he knew it—knew it for a fact when he heard the voices coming through the woods. At first he couldn't make out the words, and then, when he could, he couldn't understand them.

"*Franco? Dove sta?*"

Lassiter waited with the rifle. Across the room, Marie sat on the floor, holding her breath—and Jesse. "Don't worry," Lassiter whispered as the rain drummed on the roof and the wind moaned.

The men were outside now, walking around the boathouse. Lassiter's heart was a drum.

Suddenly, a flashlight's beam sliced through the darkness, sweeping the walls from left to right and back again, casting enormous shadows. It came from the window above Lassiter's head, and in a second it had them. Like startled deer, Jesse and Marie were caught in the light, petrified.

"*Ecco!*"

With a crack, the door exploded on its hinges, and a huge shape materialized in the void, shoving the splintered wood out of the way.

Standing in the ruined doorway, the Mattress hesitated, savoring the effect of his entrance on the terrified woman and child. Then he took a step toward them, and Lassiter murmured, "Hey—big guy!"

The Italian turned with a roar, and as he did, Lassiter fired. The bullet slammed into his face and, hitting the cheekbone, somersaulted through his brain, lifting him into the air before it blew off the top of his head. The noise of the gunshot filled the room. Marie yelped. And the Mattress dropped to the floor like an armload of wet laundry.

Lassiter dropped the rifle and scrambled on his hands and knees over to the Italian's body. As he searched for the gun that had to be there, he glanced at the dead man's face, which now wore a look of permanent surprise. And then, quite suddenly, it was Lassiter's turn to be surprised.

"*Ciao.*"

The voice was atonal, above and to the left. Without looking, he knew who it was, but turned his head nonetheless. Grimaldi was standing just outside the broken doorway, looking down at him. He had a Beretta in his hand, and no obvious sense of compassion.

Now I'm dead, Lassiter thought. We're all dead. This is how I die.

Grimaldi said something over his shoulder, speaking in Italian, and della Torre came to his side, holding a flashlight. "Why, Joe," he said, shining the light in the American's eyes. "What luck to find you here." Slowly, the flashlight's beam traveled to the body on the floor, where the Mattress lay in a slush of blood and brains. Della Torre made the sign of the cross, and stepping into the boathouse, moved the light in a slow arc, from one side of the room to the other, until it held Jesse and Marie in its glare.

"Do you know who they are?" the priest asked. When Lassiter didn't reply, he answered the question himself. "They're bad company, Joe," he said. And then, "All right—everyone get up. We're going back to the cabin, where it's warm."

Grimaldi asked a question in Italian, and della Torre shook his head. "No—*portali tutti,*" he said, and moments later the five of them were walking through the woods.

Jesse and Marie led the way, guided by the eerie beam from della Torre's flashlight. Lassiter came next, just ahead of Grimaldi and the priest. Though the gunman was five feet away, Lassiter could feel the barrel of the Beretta pointing directly at his spine, as if the handgun were a phantom limb. If I break for the woods, he thought, they'll kill me right away. And if I don't, they'll kill me later. Either way, Jesse and Marie are dead. There's no way out.

Unless they make a mistake.

Which, however unlikely, was their only hope, and so he clung to it, and kept on walking.

By the time they reached the cabin, they were soaked. Grimaldi herded them over to the kitchen table and gestured with his gun for them to sit, while della Torre lighted a kerosene lamp and stoked the wood stove. After a moment the priest came over to the table with the lamp and sat down, across from Jesse and Marie.

"Well," he said, clapping his hands lightly together, "here we are!" With a glance toward Grimaldi, he muttered something in Italian, and nodded toward the wall, where a coil of rope was hanging from a nail. Then he looked directly at Marie, who was holding Jesse in her lap, and said, "Tell me something, Joe. Do you know who Lilith was?"

Lassiter shook his head. "No. Never heard of her."

Grimaldi came to the table with the rope and gave the Beretta to della Torre, who leveled it at Lassiter. Then Grimaldi turned to Marie and, looping the rope around her waist, began to tie her to the chair. Instinctively, she started to get up, and as she did, Grimaldi reached for her wrist and, with a twist, forced her to sit down. Then he said something to her in a low snarl that needed no translation.

When Grimaldi finished tying her to the chair Jesse climbed back into his mother's lap. "It's all right, Mama," he said softly. "It's all right."

Della Torre cleared his throat. "Lilith was Adam's wife—before Eve."

"Listen," Marie said, "if you'll leave Jesse alone, I'll do anything you want."

Della Torre turned to her. "You should listen to this," he said. "It concerns you." Then he turned back to Lassiter. "When Lilith left Adam—and this will amuse you, Joe: they disagreed about who should be on top!—angels begged her to return."

Lassiter was thinking, *The kerosene lamp has possibilities.* But what he said was, "And did she?"

Della Torre shook his head and looked regretful. "No," he said. "She didn't. She was so unhappy with Adam, and with God, that she went to live with Satan. Eventually, she bore his children." The priest reached over and, with a smile, tousled Jesse's hair. "They were demons, of course."

Lassiter nodded. "You see a lot of that these days. I blame it on MTV."

Delle Torre clicked his tongue against his palate—*tsk tsk tsk*—and, leaning forward, said, " 'And the ten horns which thou sawest upon the Beast, these shall hate the whore, and shall make her desolate and naked, and shall eat her flesh, and burn her with fire.' " Sitting back, he added, "Revelations, 17:16."

Then he turned to Grimaldi and spoke to him in Italian. Grimaldi spread his hands and shrugged.

"They're out of rope," Marie explained.

Della Torre looked surprised. "You speak Italian?"

"Chi lasci andare, Padre."

Della Torre pretended to consider the idea. Finally, he said, "I can't do that," and beckoned to Grimaldi. When he came over, the priest whispered in his ear. Grimaldi nodded and walked back to the kitchen. There, he searched through one drawer after another until he found a pair of kitchen knives. Returning to the table, he gave the knives to the priest, who handed him the gun.

Marie blanched, and Jesse held her closer.

Della Torre turned to Lassiter. "Give me your hand," he said, picking up a chef's knife with a six-inch blade.

Lassiter stared at him, disbelieving. After a long silence, he said, "Unh-unh." Della Torre nodded to Grimaldi, who stepped behind Lassiter.

He expected to be hit, hard, but all he felt was the lightest touch—the edge of Grimaldi's hand against the back of his head, slightly to the right of center. And then he heard a click and suddenly, he knew why Grimaldi was holding his hand like that: He wanted to shield himself against the spatter when he fired.

Lassiter took a deep breath, muttered an obscenity, and held out his hand to della Torre. The priest received it in his own, and turning it over, gazed at the palm. With a gentle touch, he pushed the hand down on the table and, taking the chef's knife, touched the point to the middle of Lassiter's palm.

"Have you ever had your palm read, Joe?"

Lassiter shook his head and, in a rasping voice, said, "No. Never did." He was trying to control his breathing, and it wasn't going well.

"You see that line?" della Torre asked. "The short line, just there? That's your lifeline." And with that, the priest drew back and brought the knife down with all his force, driving the blade into and through Lassiter's palm, nailing his hand to the table.

The pain was so sudden and piercing that Lassiter's head flew back, reflexively, and a gasp burst from his mouth toward the ceiling. He heard Marie scream, faintly, as if she were far away, and then Grimaldi wrestled his other hand down to the table. Somebody straightened his fingers out and, a moment later, the point of a paring knife was driven into the palm of his right hand. This time he shouted something that sounded like a string of vowels that, once again, ended in a gasp.

He dropped his head to the table and groaned through gritted teeth. He lay like that for what seemed like a very long time, but probably wasn't. When he finally looked up, della Torre was watching him with excited eyes, while Jesse cried in a weird and stertorous way. Marie was white as phosphorus.

He looked at his hands, impaled against the table. There was surprisingly little blood, but still, he felt his stomach sway. Taking a deep breath, he leaned toward della Torre. "You psycho fuck—what's the matter with you?"

"We had to improvise."

Grimaldi heard the word, and chuckled. Lassiter's stomach heaved, and suddenly he felt very cold. *I'm going into shock*, he thought. And then: *Don't.*

"You don't understand what's at stake," the priest said.

"I know exactly what's at stake," Lassiter replied.

"I doubt that," della Torre said, and just as he spoke, lightning pulsed through the room. Then thunder exploded like a grenade, and suddenly the rain began to gust against the windows, hitting them in waves. With a worried look, della Torre glanced around the room. "I wonder," he said, "with all this rain . . ."

Lassiter wasn't listening. He was looking at his hands, and asking himself if he had the courage to upend the table. If he did, as the table fell over, gravity would tear the knives loose from his hands.

Della Torre shook his head. "You're not paying attention."

Lassiter looked at him. "I'm a little distracted," he said.

The priest nodded. "You're the wrong person to ask, in any case." Then he turned to Grimaldi and muttered something in Italian. The gunman nodded, zipped up his coat, and went outside, into the rain.

Della Torre turned back to Lassiter. "You think you know what's at stake, Joe, but you don't, really. You can't. Because unless you believe in God as much as you do in science—and you have to believe *in both* to *really* understand—you never will. Do you know who that boy is?"

"I know who you *think* he is," Lassiter said.

The priest cocked his head. "Really? And who is that?" he asked.

"You think he's Jesus Christ."

Della Torre pursed his lips, thought for a moment, and shook his head. "No," he said. "I don't. Because . . . if I thought he was Jesus Christ, I'd be down on my knees. *Of course.* But he's not. He can't be."

"You're sure of that?"

Della Torre gestured vaguely. "I'm sure that God made man in His own image—and not the other way around. The child's an abomination. And the abomination has a name."

"His *name*," Marie said, "is Jesse."

"His name is Antichrist!" The priest was glaring at her, but then he seemed to soften. "You know," he said, "Baresi's achievement was really quite spectacular. He accomplished in a few years what all the world's magicians had failed to do in as many centuries."

"What's that?" Lassiter asked, thinking, *All you have to do is throw yourself forward. It'll only take a second. The table will go over, and . . . I can't,* Lassiter thought. *I just can't.*

Della Torre was looking at him, as if he guessed what he was thinking. Finally, he said, "He conjured demons from blood."

A gust of cold air blew through the doorway as Grimaldi returned with a jerry-can of gasoline. Coming into the room, he asked della Torre a question, and the priest nodded.

Suddenly, della Torre seemed out of breath, and perspiring. "I'm a little nervous," he explained, seeing Lassiter's eyes on him. "I've never done anything like this before."

"Come on, come on, come on," Lassiter muttered to himself and gritted his teeth in search of the gumption he needed to overturn the table. His brain was screaming at his legs to stand, but his hands wouldn't let them do it.

"There's no choice where they're concerned," della Torre said, nodding to Jesse and Marie. "But . . . we could make it quicker for you."

Lassiter's fingers curled and uncurled around the blades of the knives as Grimaldi unscrewed the top from the gasoline can. "No thanks," Lassiter muttered.

"Well," della Torre said, getting to his feet. "It's time." Leaning forward, the priest dipped his finger in the blood that ran from Lassiter's right hand. Turning to Marie, he traced the number 6 on her forehead, then grabbed Jesse by the arm and, twisting it, did the same to him. Replenishing the blood, he wrote the same number on Lassiter's forehead, and stood back to admire his handiwork.

For a moment Lassiter was nonplussed, but then he understood. Himself, Jesse, and Marie:

666

The Beast.

Turning from them, della Torre reached into his cassock and produced a holy-water bottle that Lassiter recognized immediately. Removing the stopper, the priest snapped the bottle toward each of the four corners of the room, mumbling in Latin as droplets of water flew in every direction.

Suddenly, Grimaldi stepped behind Jesse and Marie. Inverting the can, he poured the gasoline over their heads, filling the cabin with an explosive smell. Lassiter began to struggle to his feet, realizing it was now or never—when Marie made the decision for him. Leaning back in her chair, she put the ball of her foot on the edge of the table and, using the leverage it gave her, pushed the table over.

Lassiter cried out in pain as the knives tore away from the table and the kerosene lamp crashed to the floor at della Torre's feet, igniting his cassock. With a bewildered look, the priest bent to slap at the flames, while Marie screamed for Jesse to run, and Grimaldi bellowed at everyone and no one. Suddenly, the room was a dance of shadows as the cassock flared and della Torre became a torch, running toward the door—the outside, the rain—with a terrified wail.

Grimaldi took a step to help but before he could reach the priest, Lassiter blindsided him. Slamming into Grimaldi's back, he sent the gas can flying at the priest. In an instant the blaze went nova; a little line of flames zipped along the cabin's floor. Lassiter drove Grimaldi into the wall, and the air burst from the man's lungs with a sound like a cough. Turning the Italian around, Lassiter grabbed Grimaldi by the lapels and drove his own forehead into the bridge of Grimaldi's nose. Something snapped—it made a sound like plastic cracking—and Grimaldi seemed to sag. Without thinking, Lassiter swept his legs from under him and, as the Italian hit the floor, drove the point of his shoe into Grimaldi's chest.

And again. And again, searching for his head, until the Italian rolled away from him—and came up firing.

Three shots in the same second, a panicked fusillade that slapped harmlessly into the ceiling, wall, and door. Lassiter launched himself at the gun and, in the darkness, crashed into Grimaldi's side, sending the Beretta flying. Like child psychopaths bent on murder, they scrambled through the smoke and gloom on their knees, sweeping their hands across the floor in search of the gun.

A moment later lightning showed them where it was, and seeing it, they dove, landing side by side. Lassiter's reach was longer. But as the American's hand closed painfully around the grip, Grimaldi slammed him in the mouth with his elbow and rolled onto Lassiter's back. In an instant the Italian had the American's throat in the crook of his arm and, flexing with all his strength, slowly began to crush his windpipe.

He was incredibly strong.

Lassiter resisted, and resisted, thrashing beneath Grimaldi's weight. But it was no use. The tension began to fade from his muscles; his vision was flaring; he knew that any second the life would go out of him. So he pulled his arm back in an arc across the floor, and when the gun stopped against something hard, he fired.

Grimaldi screamed as the bullet exploded through his knee, and Lassiter rolled away, scrambling toward the wall, trying to breathe. Then the lightning blazed and Lassiter saw him as if he were on a stage, sitting on the burning floor with his knee in his hands, rocking back and forth, almost keening.

Seeing him that way, with his face contorted in so much pain, Lassiter was reminded of St. Sebastian in the famous painting by what's-his-name.

He shot him anyway, a single shot that made a small, wet hole just above his left eye.

Then Marie called to him, and turning, he saw that the fire was only a few feet from her chair. Jesse was beside her, doing his best to untie the knots, but his fingers were too small and weak. Going to her side, Lassiter undid the knots and, skirting the fire, led them outside.

Where a smoldering bundle lay in the rain on the path below the cabin, quivering.

"Jesse—don't look," Marie said, pulling the boy close to her.

Lassiter knelt beside the priest, and winced to see that della Torre's face was a carbonized ruin. His hair and eyelids were entirely gone, and a strange fluid leaked from the orbits of his eyes. Lassiter was certain he must be dead—until he stirred, and groaned.

"We have to get him to a hospital," Marie said. "We can use their boat. C'mon!"

Lassiter looked at her as if she were insane. "We can't do that," he said.

"He'll die!"

"Of course he'll die! I *want* him to die."

"Well, you can't leave him like that. It's freezing. He's burned!"

Lassiter stood up. "Look," he said, "if we take him to a hospital . . . it won't stop there. There are a million people—they think just like he does. And when they find out you and Jesse are alive—and they will— they'll come after you. We can't take him to a hospital. We have to get out of here."

Marie shook her head. "He's a person," she said.

Lassiter stared at her for a long time. Finally, he said, "Okay. Take Jesse to the boat. I'll bring him along."

Taking Jesse by the hand, Marie turned and started running toward the motor launch. She was almost to the dock when she heard a shot on the path behind her and, without turning, knew they wouldn't be going to the hospital.

EPILOGUE

She wouldn't talk to him for days afterward, and in the end it was a month before she finally agreed that the coup de grace had been just that—as merciful as it had been necessary. By then the three of them were traveling as a family, while Lassiter worked all the magic that he knew to establish new identities for each of them.

It wasn't just a question of changing names, but of creating a legend—a fully backstopped *past*, replete with job and medical histories, school and credit records, legitimate passports and social security numbers that seemed to have been issued years before. The entire process took three weeks, and $50,000, to complete, and when it was done, he didn't want to tell her.

"I'll be out of your hair in a couple of days," he promised, "as soon as the bank signatory card comes through from Liechtenstein." That was where their money had finally come to rest, after bouncing like a roulette ball from one funny venue to another, courtesy of Max Lang.

"A couple of days" turned into a couple of weeks, as Lassiter knew they would—and then it was spring, and then he kissed her.

The name on the mailbox was Shepherd.

It stood at the end of a long driveway in the North Carolina Piedmont, in the foothills of the Blue Ridge Mountains. The drive wound through a hundred acres of rolling pastures, ending at a stone barn not far from a big, old farmhouse that needed work. About a mile of white board fencing enclosed the property, which was patrolled by an Arabian mare and her foal.

It was a beautiful part of the country, but a little too far from Raleigh, or anywhere else, to commute. So most of the people who lived in the area were self-employed, one way or another.

Mr. Shepherd was no exception: he bought and sold rare books and first editions, conducting his business entirely by mail. It was yet another odd profession among many in the area, and so drew little notice from the neighbors. Indeed, within a mile of the Shepherds' place, there lived: a world-famous mandolin maker, a couple that raised ostriches, a woman who made culinary wreaths for Smith & Hawken, and a man who built dry stone walls. There were also a (suspected) marijuana grower, two novelists, and a game designer.

The Shepherds lived modestly, at least for the moment, slowly improving their house, and doing much of the work themselves. The plan had been that they would stay together for a while, divorce, and go their separate ways. It was a sensible plan, and one that would go a long way toward bolstering the legends they'd created. But the plan came undone as their affection for one another grew amid the pleasures of simple country life. Within a short time their proverbial marriage of convenience seemed more like a marriage made in Heaven.

The past intruded only once. Two years after they'd left Maine, "Unsolved Mysteries" ran a docudrama called "Doom Island." Lassiter and Marie watched in horror as Robert Stack took the audience through a lurid reenactment of the events leading up to their flight from the island.

It began with a blue Taurus driving into fog-shrouded Cundys Harbor. An actor who looked nothing like Lassiter was seen negotiating with an actor who looked nothing like Roger Bowker—after which, the two men boarded a boat that looked a lot like the *Go-4-It*. The real Maude was interviewed, as was the real harbormaster: "We knew there was a storm comin'," he recalled. "Rog-ah was stubborn!"

The boat's spectacular crash was not reenacted, but reprised by Stack's narration. This was followed in rapid succession by photos of Lassiter Associates' Washington office, Lassiter's home in McLean— "Nice," Marie remarked—and Lassiter himself. This last photo was a copy of the one that he kept in his office as a joke.

"It doesn't look like you," Marie said. "Not at all."

"I know."

The narrator explained that Lassiter's disappearance coincided with the takeover of his company, and then asked, "Why did Joe Lassiter come to the island? Was he investigating something? Yes, he was."

This remark was not immediately explained. There were three commercials, and then another reenactment. A black Mercedes pulled into the marina on Bailey Island, and three men stepped out. Soon, the men were poring over nautical charts and muttering in Italian as they traced a route from the marina to Rag Island.

Then the narrator was *on* the island, standing in front of the burned-out cabin. This was followed by a series of shots—the boathouse, the dock, the rocks on which the *Go-4-It* had crashed, ending in a close-up of the sun, sinking into the water.

Interviews with the Brunswick police chief, a Coast Guard captain, and an attaché from the Italian embassy led Stack to ask, "What were these men doing here?" Photographs of della Torre, Grimaldi, and the Mattress filled the screen. "One—a prominent Catholic cleric. Another—a triple murderer. The third—a thug, well known for violent mischief in his own country. Why were they together? Why did they all come to this remote island? These questions await answers.

"And what of the mysterious woman, who lived with her child on the island? Curiously, no photographs exist of either." A sketch artist's drawing came on camera, as Maude clucked about Marie's decision to live "out they-ah." Happily, the drawing was entirely generic, resembling Marie only in that she had the correct number of eyes and ears.

The narrator concluded the piece standing on the dock. "The fire that destroyed Marie Sanders's cabin wasn't the only one that night. Witnesses report that a second fire was seen at sea, later that same night. Police are convinced this second fire consumed the boat that Father della Torre had rented earlier that same morning. If so, experts agree that no one could have survived a swim to shore at that time of the year. And yet, when forensic experts combed the island, the remains of a single individual were recovered: and that individual was Franco Grimaldi.

"What happened to the others?" A montage of faces flashed across the screen: Joe, Roger, the Mattress, Jesse, Marie, and della Torre. "Maybe the water has claimed them; maybe they're buried on the island. Or maybe ... just maybe ... Marie Sanders and her child escaped in *this* little boat"—a picture of Marie's dinghy filled the screen—"found the next morning, beached on the mainland."

The piece ended with an aerial shot, and Robert Stack intoning, "All we know for certain is that seven people came to Doom Island— and none were ever seen alive again."

—

Nothing came of the show. If anyone saw it, they didn't connect it to the Shepherd family. Which wasn't surprising: By then the Shepherds were a part of the community, and there were some who would have sworn that they'd always lived in the area. Marie took classes in speech therapy at the local community college, and Joe coached a seven-and-under soccer team.

As for Jesse, his was the only first name that they hadn't changed. They called him Jay most of the time, though, and his friends had doubled that to "J.J."

He had a lot of friends, as it turned out, and was well liked at school. At the parent-teacher conference his teacher remarked that he seemed to be a natural leader—and something of a peacekeeper, too. "Maybe he'll work for the U.N. someday."

At the moment, his diplomatic skills were being put to use on the school bus, where he was a safety patrol.

Joe liked to watch him, from the window of his study on the second floor, as Jesse walked up the long drive to where the school bus picked him up—the Day-Glo orange band of his patrol belt visible even when he was mostly obscured by the willow tree. On this day, Joe was surprised to see Jesse stop halfway, set down his lunchbox, and race back toward the house. He pushed in through the front door.

"What'd you forget?" Marie called out from the kitchen.

"I forgot to feed the fish!" Jesse yelled, pounding up the stairs.

The fish were only the first of what Jesse promised would be a menagerie, soon to include one of the puppies recently born to Pickle, itself a chocolate Lab and coonhound mix that belonged to Jesse's friend Ethan. Jesse had already acquired a red plaid dog bed from the bus driver, whose own dog was "too spoiled—he'll only sleep on the couch." After that—another dog, "so they can be friends," and then a cat and a goat.

Jesse took care of the fish all by himself except when it was time to empty the aquarium—which was too heavy. He did clean the aquarium, and rinse off the rocks, and every day he fed the fish and checked the temperature in the winter to make sure it was warm enough.

Jesse loved the fish. There were seven of them, and they all had names. He was allowed to keep the aquarium light on at night, and he especially liked to watch them then, from his bed. He liked the way they glided around in the water, smoothly curving in and out of the castle, hiding behind the wavy green plants. He even liked to watch the silver chain of bubbles rising from the aerator. He pushed into his room, feeling a little guilty even if he didn't forget, because he *almost* forgot.

"You guys hungry?" He carefully removed the top from the aquarium, set it aside, then got the little box of food from the bookcase below. He meticulously tapped the food into a plastic teaspoon. He'd been told many times how important it was to feed them just enough but not *too* much. He distributed the multicolored flakes evenly, across the surface of the water, and then knelt down. He liked to watch the fish eat, rising up and nipping the food from the surface and then diving back down with it. Sometimes he talked to them, and he did now. "Hey, don't fight about it, there's lots of food." Then he frowned. One of the striped ones—half hidden by the plant—wasn't moving at all, even to eat. He stood up and looked down from the top. The striped fish looked sick. He was on his side, his belly was bloated, and his tail seemed too white and kind of slimy. He was definitely not moving. And his fancy tail looked all raggedy, too. And then! Jesse saw one of the gouramis come over and take a little nibble out of the tail!

"Hey!" Instinctively, Jesse plunged his hands into the tank and cupped them under the dead fish and lifted it out. The water drained away and he cradled it in one hand and stroked its side with his fingertip a few times. "You're all right," he said, then cupped it in both hands again, lowering them slowly into the water until they were just under the surface. Then he drew his hands aside and watched.

As the fish swam away.

ABOUT THE AUTHOR

JOHN CASE is the pseudonym of an award-winning investigative reporter and the author of two nonfiction books about the U.S. intelligence community. A resident of Washington, D.C., he is the proprietor of a company that specializes in international investigations for law firms and labor unions.